THE SKY'S
THE LIMIT

STAR TREK
THE NEXT GENERATION®

THE SKY'S THE LIMIT

EDITED BY

Marco Palmieri

Based upon **STAR TREK**®
and **STAR TREK:
THE NEXT GENERATION**

Created by Gene Roddenbery

POCKET BOOKS
New York Toronto London Sydney Farpoint

Pocket Books
A Division of Simon & Schuster, Inc.
1230 Avenue of the Americas
New York, NY 10020

First Pocket Books trade paperback edition October 2007

POCKET and colophon are registered trademarks of Simon & Schuster, Inc.

For information about special discounts for bulk purchases, please contact Simon & Schuster Special Sales at 1-800-456-6798 or business@simonandschuster.com.

Cover Art by Stephan Martiniere
Interior Design by Mary Austin Speaker

Manufactured in the United States of America

10 9 8 7 6 5 4 3 2 1

ISBN-13: 978-0-7434-9255-3
ISBN-10:   0-7434-9255-2

"Let's see what's out there."

—Jean-Luc Picard

Contents

CONTENTS

MEET WITH TRIUMPH AND DISASTER

Michael Schuster & Steve Mollmann

Historian's note:
This tale is set in late 2363 (Old Calendar), sometime before
"Encounter at Farpoint," the pilot episode of
Star Trek: The Next Generation.

MICHAEL SCHUSTER & STEVE MOLLMANN

Michael Schuster lives in Austria on the other side of the pond and believes himself to be only the second nonnative speaker of English to write a *Star Trek* story after Jesco von Puttkamer. His love for science fiction in general and *Star Trek* in particular began somewhere around his twelfth birthday. While he always wanted to be one of the authors of such adventures, he never really believed he would eventually become one. The fact that this did indeed happen is generally attributed to his collaboration with Steve Mollmann, which is unlikely to end anytime soon. At the time of publication, the two will have been on the same continent four times.

Steve Mollmann lives in Colerain Township, which is a suburb of Cincinnati, Ohio, best known for possessing a large garbage dump, but he loves it all the same. He has been a *Star Trek* fan since before he can remember, for which he blames his mother, but he has to admit it's probably led to some good things. He is a graduate of Miami University in Oxford, Ohio, and like all twenty-somethings, he has no idea what he is going to do with his life. With Michael Schuster, he has previously penned an entry in the *Star Trek: Corps of Engineers—What's Past* arc of eBooks, titled *The Future Begins*.

Visit them both on the web at www.exploringtheuniverse.net.

THE FIRST TIME CAPTAIN THOMAS HALLOWAY SAW THE *U.S.S. Enterprise,* the starship was nothing more than a simulation displayed on a designer's terminal. Even back then, he had been impressed by her size, although he had no illusions that a computer model ever would be able to do the real thing justice.

The third time he saw the *Enterprise,* she had gone through every preliminary test imaginable, and the first struts of her spaceframe were about to be welded together on the Martian surface, to be lifted into orbit later on.

The seventh time he saw the *Enterprise,* construction had progressed far enough to enable people to work inside her without having to depend on space suits. That had been the day the life-support systems had been switched on, only weeks after Thomas had been chosen as the right man to supervise the construction efforts. It was also five years before the ship would leave the orbital dock under its own power, using only maneuvering thrusters.

And *that* had been eight years before the commissioning ceremony that was just minutes away.

It was quite a turnout; Thomas had the feeling that nobody would notice if he suddenly disappeared. This was an event that had drawn hundreds from all over the Federation to this place: the orbital docks of Utopia Planitia Fleet Yards, Mars. It was a celebration of Starfleet's desire to explore the unknown, an affirmation of one of the basic ideals of the Federation: the constant and never-ending quest for more knowledge.

What more fitting embodiment of this ideal was there than the *Galaxy*-class ship itself? So grand and impressive—swanlike and almost alive. It dwarfed everything else in orbit, with the exception of the spacedock cradling it. "Traveling cities" they had been called by some of their designers, and Thomas was tempted to agree with this assessment. Their purpose was to trawl the regions beyond known space, always on the lookout for interesting and curious new discoveries, be they alive or not.

On the other side of a crowd of dignitaries, Thomas caught sight of a familiar figure. "Orfil!" Thomas shouted and waved at his erstwhile colleague. "Try to come over here, will you?"

A throng of wildly gesticulating Guidons almost prevented Commander Orfil Quinteros from crossing the distance of only a few meters, but eventually he succeeded and shook Thomas's hand. Orfil had worked with Thomas for almost ten years, serving as his right-hand man on the construction team (not to mention best friend), but he had been gone for two months now, undergoing command training in preparation for his transfer to Starbase 74.

"When did you arrive?" Thomas asked.

"Late last night. HQ booked me a flight on a civilian shuttle bound for Pluto, and from there I took the ferry to Titan. I hardly got any sleep." Orfil had relatives in Christopher's Landing, and he was likely to pay them a visit whenever he had enough time. "Where's the boss?"

"Out and about, I suspect. I haven't actually seen him yet, but I don't think he'll pass on the opportunity to celebrate. Do you?"

"Nah." Having worked for many years under Admiral Theoderich Patterson, they both knew exactly what he liked, and playing host for such a celebration as today's was one of the things right at the top of that list. The admiral had started as a lowly engineer at Utopia Planitia and, having managed to stay there his entire career, now ran the place. "Most likely, he's already mingling."

"Most likely," Thomas agreed.

Without warning, Orfil slapped him on the shoulder hard

enough that Thomas's knees almost buckled. "So, what news of Solveig and the kids?"

"They're doing fine. Rupa's enjoying elementary school only slightly less than she did kindergarten, but that was to be expected. Matti . . . well, let's just say he's in a difficult phase right now."

"Ah, puberty." The two men exchanged knowing grins. "Say, why isn't Solveig here? Or did I just fail to spot her? The kids wouldn't have had much fun here, but I'm sure that your wife at least would want to celebrate your triumph with you."

What was being celebrated today was not just *his* triumph, but also the culmination of two decades' work, if one included in the count the general design and planning efforts for the entire *Galaxy* class. Twenty years ago, the project had begun, and now the third ship of that class was about to be commissioned. It would not have been such a special occasion if this had been any other ship—certainly, nobody had made such a fuss about the commissioning of *Yamato,* for example—but since this was the first starship in two decades to bear the prestigious name *Enterprise,* things were different.

Very different.

The people present at this celebration of the past and the future were mostly important figures connected with the Fleet, while others, though few in number, represented the UFP government. It was too much Starfleet top brass, too much pomp and circumstance for Solveig to enjoy herself, and they had talked about it extensively weeks ago, eventually coming to the agreement that they would celebrate on their own, with their relatives and closest friends. It was something Thomas was looking forward to, even as he stood here waiting for the actual start of festivities.

"Solveig . . . well, you know how she feels about the Fleet, don't you?"

"Oh, *yes,*" said Orfil emphatically. A few times he had been a guest of the Halloways, eating dinner with them and spending an eventful evening at their house in Central Burroughs. Orfil had experienced Solveig in action often enough to know what she thought of Starfleet, Federation politics, and just about everything else that crossed her mind.

Movement at the other end of the observation center that doubled as the locale for tonight's event caught Thomas's attention—somebody was mounting the stage. It was Admiral Patterson, about to make the first speech of many that would be delivered tonight. Beyond the transparent wall behind the admiral, the rusty orb of Mars shimmered in the sun . . . as did the star of today's ceremony.

She hung scarcely a hundred meters away, keeping close company with the station ostensibly in order to give the attendees the best possible view of her, though all they saw was the underside of the saucer section, the neck, and the front part of the secondary hull with its ringed navigational deflector.

Still, thought Thomas, *she's a sight to behold.*

The audience quieted as Patterson took the podium. "Good evening, dear guests. It is a great honor and an even greater pleasure for me to be able to welcome you all here today. Many of you have had to travel long distances to be present on this very special occasion, and for that I thank you. It is not every day that we celebrate the commissioning of a new starship, much less that of a ship with such a prestigious and famous name as that of the *U.S.S. Enterprise,* a name that goes back centuries, used long before there was a Starfleet on Earth, long before even there were any spacegoing craft on that planet at all. Now has come the time to make that name part of the Federation's fleet once again, to lead the way in expanding our knowledge and understanding of the universe and—most important—ourselves.

"We celebrate this event not only because we can, but also because we feel that we have an obligation to do so. The previous starship called *Enterprise* was destroyed with all hands nineteen years ago, and I ask you all to join me now in a minute's silent remembrance of those who lost their lives that day."

Thomas still remembered where he had been when he had heard the news. It was such an extraordinary occurrence, the destruction of the *Enterprise*-C, that one could not help but memorize every little detail about it. Such a thing did not happen, especially not with people aboard. Many had died in that Romulan attack over Narendra III, but if any good could come from such a tragedy, it was that the ship's loss had gone a long way to strengthen deteriorating relations between the Federation and the Klingon Empire.

"Thank you," Patterson said and gripped the sides of the podium, leaning slightly forward. "Let us never forget the brave souls who gave their lives for our safety throughout Federation history. It is only because of their sacrifice that we have come so far: from belonging to separate, disparate planets to being part of a vast interstellar whole that is so much more than the sum of its parts. Rather than being satisfied with the status quo, we want to know more, about ourselves, about others, about the place we live in. Who better to talk about this ship's mission"—he made a sweeping gesture toward the majestic form beyond the windows—"than our next speaker. My dear friends and supporters of Starfleet's cause, I am proud to introduce the Respectable Lady Svaath Magodin, Secretary of Science and Space Exploration of the United Federation of Planets!"

Applause followed, and a reptilian Xindi ascended the stage. Magodin was slightly smaller than average for her species, and if you didn't know her, you'd think that she was not very remarkable at all. Months previous, Thomas had made the mistake of assuming her to be just that, and he'd quickly discovered his error: she was distinguished by virtue of the way she interacted with others. She did not beat about the bush; if there was something she wanted, she said so. She reminded him of nothing so much as a Vulcan matriarch.

"Thank you, Admiral. I am glad to be here today," she said. Her voice was at odds with what you would expect from her appearance, as it always reminded Thomas of a little elf. Somehow it did not seem to belong to a woman from New Xindus. "Admiral Patterson has already mentioned the reason for this gathering," she continued, addressing the throng of guests, "but I feel it bears repeating. It is about the pursuit of knowledge, both in the reaches of deep space as well as within ourselves. This ship is a symbol of our desire and a tool with which to fulfill it. It acknowledges the immensity of the universe and how little of our own galaxy we truly know . . . and also how much yet remains to be explored. There have been setbacks—caused by war, by politics, by bureaucracy—but now it is high time to concentrate once more on Starfleet's foremost purpose.

"This vessel is one with a mission, a mission that has the potential to last longer than that of any previous ship. The *Galaxy* class is built to be almost completely self-sustaining, with an operational life of, at minimum, a hundred years. We intend to build more of them and send them out there, to find wonders we cannot imagine.

"The *Enterprise* is a special ship, as Admiral Patterson has already stated. We expect a great many things of her and her crew. She could be away from us for a long time, twenty years or even more. Let us wish her all the best, and with her all those brave men and women who take her into the unknown."

For Thomas, it was painful to listen to the science secretary. The speech itself was not the problem; what it meant for him was. Hearing first Patterson and now Magodin talk about the ship's mission was enough justification for him to continue on his intended course. After all, there was no point in having second thoughts this late in the game, and if he chose not to act now, he would forever regret it. He knew that much, at least.

Magodin continued with her passionate plea for further exploration of the universe, and while he could not find anything wrong with it, he also felt that it was meant for somebody else. Thomas Bhupender Halloway was not the ideal recipient.

Presently he felt Orfil staring at him, and when he looked to his left, his friend was peering back at him full of worry. "What is it?" Thomas whispered. Standing in the middle of a crowd of a thousand people was not conducive to private conversations, so he had to keep it short and quiet.

"Is something wrong?" asked Orfil.

"No. Should it be?"

"You tell me."

"Nothing's wrong. Now be quiet and listen!"

"We'll talk later," Orfil said, and it sounded not unlike a threat. It was just as well that they would have to have that talk much later, since there was to be a tour of the *Enterprise*'s most important interior features that Thomas himself would lead right after the speeches had concluded.

That tour would be the last official item on tonight's agenda, but it would be final in other ways as well. It didn't bother Thomas in the least; in fact, the only thing that did was the difficulty of describing adequately how he felt.

After the conclusion of Magodin's lengthy speech and another by the Bolian representative to the Federation Council, it was time for the attendees to enjoy food and drink while sitting at the tables in the back of the observation hall—a time for a quiet conversation and a bite of something tasty, though not for Thomas, sadly.

Instead, he was touring the *Enterprise* with a group of dignitaries in tow, trying without much success to give himself the air of a man satisfied with himself and with life in general. He was presently standing in the center of the bridge, accompanied only by Secretary Magodin and three Starfleet admirals: Patterson, Gregory Quinn, and Norah Satie. Satie's participation here was almost mandatory, considering her position as chief of Starfleet Operations, and even if he had wanted to do so, Thomas would not have been able to deny her this experience.

If people were in a generous mood, they might consider Gregory Quinn to be the uniformed equivalent of Svaath Magodin. He was in charge of Starfleet's Exploratory Division, supervising the various nonmilitary endeavors, and so would be the one to whom the captains of the *Galaxy*-class explorers would be reporting. Quinn was an elderly man, easily over a hundred years old, though Thomas didn't know his exact age. He had decades of experience, and he exuded a special kind of confidence that, unfortunately, did nothing to help Thomas at this time.

They all stood on the bridge, in front of the main viewer, listening to whatever informative morsels Thomas could dredge from his memory. He left out the technical details, since he knew nobody except himself and Patterson would be interested to find out about the interlaced microfoam duranium filament shell that, mounted on a tritanium truss frame network, formed the exterior layer of the bridge module. After all, he was a reasonable man, and so he knew better than to bore his listeners.

He answered a couple of perfunctory questions and realized that his audience had probably heard enough. "Now, Madam Secretary, Admirals, I suggest we continue our tour of the *Enterprise* and take a look at the main shuttlebay."

"Ah, yes," Patterson said, nodding knowingly, "we really need to go there next. It's impressive, even for people like me who've seen their fair share of shuttlebays in their life. Madam Secretary, you'll like it!"

"I have no doubt," Magodin said with a smile.

Eager to leave the bridge and filled with a feeling of unease that

was not likely to leave him soon, Thomas led the way to the aft tur-
boshaft entrance. Although the five of them would just fit into one
elevator cab, it wouldn't be a comfortable journey, so Admiral Patterson took the lead, guiding Magodin and Quinn into the waiting
cab. At that, Thomas winced inwardly, since it meant that he would
have to travel with Satie. She was a person who had earned his
respect and admiration, and that made what he had to do even
more difficult.

Perhaps it would be a good idea to postpone it. Tomorrow was
no worse a day for it than today, after all.

What followed was—thankfully—a very short trip, interrupted
only by Satie's remark about the almost ostentatious use of interior
space that bordered, in her opinion at least, on wastefulness.
Thomas had no choice but to counter her claim and assure her that
it only appeared that way. In reality, the *Enterprise*'s corridors,
quarters, and laboratories were not significantly wider, longer, or
generally bigger than on any other ship in the fleet, not even on
those built in the previous century. Perhaps, he suggested, the
Enterprise's size was misleading? People might be tempted to
assume that simply because the ship itself was bigger than others,
its rooms might be bigger than those of other ships as well.

Eventually, the doors opened onto the largest single inhabitable
space on a *Galaxy*-class vessel, the main shuttlebay on Deck 4,
where the other three members of their little group were already
waiting.

Ahead of them, the *Enterprise*'s entire fleet of shuttles had been
positioned meticulously on either side of the shuttle maintenance
bay, at an angle that had their bow pointing toward the large doors
at the far end. There were more small craft present than would be
necessary once the ship's first mission had begun, but Thomas
knew that they had been put there to make an impression on the
guests. It had been Patterson's idea from the beginning to make this
visit a part of their tour.

Thomas addressed the group. "Admirals, Madam Secretary, let
us have a view of Mars so rare that you will be sure to treasure it
forever. If you would follow me . . ."

They did so, and moments later they had arrived at the bay door,
ready for the experience that awaited them. Thomas pressed a button on a console near the left wall. Immediately the door began to

open, and he experienced a short pang of irrational fear as the entire shuttlebay was seemingly exposed to raw space, with only an invisible force field between them and the cold darkness that waited out there.

The view certainly was awe-inspiring, since the ship had been angled away from Mars—a maneuver that now gave them the opportunity of a lifetime to look down on the dusty-brown planet from the aft-facing shuttlebay without any noticeable barrier obstructing their view. They were able to see not only the work pods of various types flitting about between the ships and space-borne installations that belonged to Utopia Planitia Orbital but also the sloping drive section of the *Enterprise* herself. Fortunately, the neck of the ship prevented them from having a good view of the—

"Captain Halloway, wasn't there a dreadful accident earlier this year? Something to do with a torpedo launcher, I believe," said Satie, her face and voice seeming innocent but her intent betrayed by the fact that Satie was the chief of Starfleet Operations and had to know these things. As it was, however, he knew that she was perfectly aware of what had happened, and she was asking about it only to hear him explain—once again—how everything went down, and how it was not really his fault but was still his fault because he had been the man in charge.

There was no point in avoiding the topic, as it would certainly have come up—no doubt ably assisted by the good admiral—in a later discussion, and so Thomas had no choice but to go over all this again, after going over it so many times before.

"You're right, Admiral Satie," he said, wishing for the force field holding in the atmosphere to fail right then. "There was an accident that involved the aft photon torpedo launcher, which we are unable to see from our vantage point up here. It exploded, killing twelve unfortunate engineers who were performing tests on it. It took us a long time to find out what caused that explosion. Early on we suspected it had something to do with that thermal expansion problem we thought we'd solved years earlier, but then we discovered the real reason. It was a fault in the system that ignited the torpedo before it left the launcher housing. We had done many tests on it in the years since we spotted that other error, but that one escaped our attention entirely. The general assumption is that it wasn't a constant glitch; more likely, it occurred only occasionally.

Sadly, it took the lives of twelve people during a firing exercise whose only goal was to test the systems and clear up some space debris at the same time."

Thomas became silent, breathed in, and waited for the reactions of the others. Satie was a rock, as usual, with no indication of her feelings showing on her face. Patterson's expression was pained, but then he already knew about this, had been at least as shocked as Thomas, and had contacted four victims' families himself. Magodin's face was unavoidably expressionless, her scaly skin being far less malleable than that of, say, a human.

Admiral Quinn's reaction consisted of a quiet cough to clear his throat before he said, "I remember hearing about that. Tragic incident, really tragic. But wasn't there another one after that?"

Stemming the tide of rising desperation was impossible, but Thomas attempted it nonetheless. Many a night he had lain awake in his family's house in Central Burroughs, thinking about the children who had lost a parent, the people who had lost a loved one, all because of a stupid, unnecessary accident that should not have occurred at all. The entire launcher should have been swapped with another one back when they had had those troubles with it.

Yet even that would not have prevented the other tragedy in the starboard nacelle control room. Three engineers had died there in a plasma explosion. At first, it had seemed that they had only disappeared without a trace, but it was later discovered that their disappearance had coincided with a plasma surge, and while there were still a lot of unanswered questions, the final report's conclusion was that they had died in the surge.

"Yes, Admiral, there was. It was equally tragic, and it shouldn't have occurred, either." Thomas outlined what they knew about it, which was not much.

It had happened less than a month after that other incident, and the weeks following those disasters had been the worst in Thomas's life. They had been full of self-doubt, of insecurity, of general depression and despair at the thought of getting back to work. He had taken two months off to give himself time to come to terms with everything, and without Solveig, he would never have succeeded. In fact, he'd probably have given up early on, having been brought down by the shame of not being able to deal with this situation the way other commanding officers had done in the past.

He had finally come to the limits of his own capabilities, and he had no desire to go any farther. When he had at last been able to return to duty, it had been only because of the decision he had made . . . the one he had yet to tell anyone about.

"Are you enjoying the view?" he asked, deliberately changing the subject of their conversation to something infinitely more pleasant.

"Very much," said Magodin, and Thomas had the feeling that she was being absolutely honest.

"I'm glad to hear that." Thomas mustered a small smile. "Now, Admiral Patterson and I want to show you all a few more interesting locales on the *Enterprise,* so I suggest we move on. Our next stop is main engineering."

They followed him back to the turbolift, and this time he made sure not to travel with Satie. The bad feeling he'd experienced had returned, and while he knew that there would need to be a confrontation of sorts eventually, he didn't want to have it right now. Moving past Patterson, he maneuvered himself into position to enter the first cabin together with Quinn. Magodin came in after them, and then Thomas ordered the lift to take them into the heart of the drive section.

It was ridiculous, if you actually thought about it, to assume that such a quick tour of a handful of spots on the ship would suffice to provide an adequate impression of the entire construct. There simply was too much to see in a short time; thus Patterson had picked, naturally in coordination with Thomas ("the brain behind it all," as people were fond of saying), a handful of presumably interesting locations that would satisfy the curiosity of those Very Important Persons chosen to be part of the tour.

"Splendid day today," Quinn said, and Thomas had no idea whether his sentiment was genuine or not. Perhaps he was just being a bit too cynical, and Quinn really meant what he said.

"I'm glad you think so," Thomas said. "What is your impression of the ship in general?"

"Well, I'm not entirely new to the class, so I knew a little bit about it before. Still, the *Enterprise* is impressive, and there's a good chance she'll live up to her name. In fact, I might even have something for her to do already. We should soon have the opportunity to explore a great unknown galactic mass, and what better ship than the *Enterprise* to do that?"

"I have to agree. With a thousand people on board, most of them specialists in their field, this is a veritable warp-capable think tank."

"Absolutely! And you seem to me the perfect man to lead them out into the unknown, as clichéd as that phrase may be."

"Ah, well . . . I wouldn't know about that," Thomas said, even though he did.

"Nonsense! You've seen this ship through every stage of its construction—no one knows it as well as you do. Every advantage it offers is one you know how to make use of."

"Gentlemen," Magodin interrupted, "how many stops are there left on our tour?"

Maybe he was mistaken, but Thomas thought he heard something in the secretary's voice—not exactly boredom but something very similar. A wish to end this and return home, maybe, or a need to get back to work, do something else. Luckily for her, they wouldn't take much longer.

After their visit to engineering, there would be only one more stop, the stellar cartography lab. Thomas had wanted to take the tour group to the cetacean exchange, the spot where humanoid crew members were able to interact with the ship's aquatic-dwelling guidance and navigation experts. It was a place dear to him because he had had a hand in designing the entire facility. Patterson, however, had favored stellar cartography, since it offered people an impressive view of their interstellar surroundings and at the same time drove home the point of how insignificant everything was, despite their assumptions to the contrary—the perfect summary of the ship's mission of exploration.

He gave Magodin the answer she wanted, and mere moments after that, they arrived at their penultimate destination. Main engineering had been a hub of activity ever since there had been people on board, and today was no different. Noncommissioned crew members were mingling with officers of various ranks, and Thomas spotted one of the two chief engineers, Sarah MacDougal, who oversaw the operation and maintenance of the ship's systems.

Determined to let others experience a share of his joy, he guided

Quinn and Magodin over to the master systems display table in the center of the room, where Sarah was ostensibly busy checking figures and values.

Thomas called her name. "May I introduce you to Admiral Gregory Quinn and Science Secretary Svaath Magodin?"

Though clearly not pleased by the interruption—and Thomas had not assumed anything other to be the case, for he knew Sarah all too well—she put down her padd and shook the hands of the two dignitaries. "Welcome aboard the *Enterprise,* Madam Secretary, Admiral," she said, and it was clear that she preferred to be anywhere but here in this very moment. Thomas was not a cruel man, so he knew better than to torture her longer than necessary.

It was just as well, because Patterson and Satie had just arrived. They were apparently involved in a discussion that interested them both greatly, but as soon as Satie spotted Thomas, she stopped talking and instead waved him over to her.

"Captain, may I have a minute with you?"

"Certainly, Admiral," Thomas said, knowing now with certainty what was to come. "Let's step over to the chief engineer's office. Sarah, you don't mind, do you?"

The blond officer just shook her head, pretending to be busy with that padd in her hand. Involuntarily, Thomas smiled. Sarah was a very strange person, sometimes. One thing she didn't like at all was being forced to interrupt her work for seemingly insignificant tasks. Kowtowing to VIPs was apparently just such a task.

"Now, if you would step in here, Admiral," he said, gently guiding Satie into the alcove to the left. It wasn't the best place to have a private conversation, but it would suffice. Besides, everybody on the ship—and, indeed, in the entire Fleet, quite probably—would know about it in the morning, so privacy was not his foremost concern.

Having moved into the CE's office as far as was possible, Satie crossed her arms over her chest and looked sternly at Thomas, who was reminded of the headmistress from his boyhood school in Pune. And just as with that headmistress, he decided to get it all out now, as quickly as possible before she could cut into him. The chance was that it would be less painful that way. "Admiral, there's something you need to know."

"Yes. That much is obvious. There's an air of unease about you, of unhappiness and discomfort, that is difficult to overlook." Satie was smaller than Thomas, yet her presence was such that he almost felt he had to look up to her. "I spotted it weeks, perhaps even months, ago, and it troubled me then. It's worrying me now. What is on your mind, Captain?"

"Many things, I'm afraid. But the most important one, the one that you need to know about, is my realization that this is not for me."

Satie didn't follow him fully, and he could not blame her. "Please be more specific. If there *is* a problem, we need to address this in detail."

"I agree. I realized that whatever my title is, I'm still an engineer at heart. Even if I am placed in the center seat on a starship's bridge, I don't have the abilities to take that ship out to explore. This isn't what I want to do." Immediately after he had said it, he knew that he had phrased it wrong.

"My dear captain, this is not a weekend golf club for centenarians! Starfleet's an organization that depends on its members doing what they are expected to do even if—and that is the important part included in the oath you once swore—it means going against your own petty desires. People depend on you, and you depend on them."

"I know, Admiral. Believe me, I know. My word choice was unfortunate. What I wanted to say is that I know where my talents lie. Space exploration isn't what I do best; in fact, it's far from my area of expertise. There are many who can make the transition from one track to another, even one so huge as this, easily and without negative repercussions, but I fear I'm not one of them. The simple truth, Admiral, is that I'm an engineer, and I want to do engineering things. I know that I can serve the Fleet best that way. Not by exploring, not by commanding."

Satie seemed to need time to ponder, and so Thomas fell silent. He had absolutely no idea how this night would end as there was no way to predict Satie's reaction. Thomas didn't know her that well, after all. They had talked occasionally, usually about the ship's construction pace, sometimes about potential crew choices, but they didn't know much about each other. At least Thomas didn't know much about the admiral. In all likelihood, the reverse was not true.

Finally, she replied. "It is always good to know what you are capable of, what you like and what you would rather not do. Yet as

I have said, sometimes the saying is true about life handing you lemons. We can't always get what we want."

"There's another reason why I can't be the captain you need," Thomas said, deliberately neglecting to address Satie's remark directly. She would have to understand his point eventually.

"Is there."

"Yes. It's my family. Everybody I talk to keeps saying the same thing: the *Enterprise* could be out there for at least a decade, perhaps even two! I don't want to be separated from them for so long."

Satie just stared at him. "But you can take them with you, can't you? The ship's supposed to be big enough. And you should know, you practically built it."

"I do know, and passenger capacity is not an issue. Rather, it is my wife who doesn't want to leave the Sol system behind. She wants to raise our children here, on Mars or maybe somewhere else. We've talked about moving to Luna, maybe."

"Can you not persuade her? If she loves you, she'll be open to your point of view," said Satie, still trying to keep him from making an apparent mistake in her eyes. It was likely that the good admiral had a wrong image of him, that she thought him capable of accomplishing greater things than he himself knew to be the case.

"But that's just it," said Thomas. "I'm not sure my point of view is any different from hers. Sure, our personal reasons might be different—she's neither in Starfleet nor a scientist who could find work on the ship, and so she would essentially be a passenger on a twenty-year cruise with no chance of doing what she is trained to do—but the end result is the same. Neither of us thinks that we should be aboard the *Enterprise* when she begins her mission."

"I see." Satie scratched the side of her nose. "Isn't there anything I can do to make you stay on?"

"No, Admiral, I'm afraid there isn't."

"You're not going to threaten resignation, are you?"

Thomas shook his head. "I've no intention of going that far . . . at least not yet. I love Starfleet, and I love my work. I will do the job I'm assigned to do. But I feel as though it would be a mistake to assign me the job of commanding the *Enterprise* on a long-term mission of exploration. For myself and for Starfleet."

"Well . . . that leaves me with no other choice, then." Satie looked down at her hand, which held a padd Thomas hadn't noticed before.

"I was hoping I wouldn't need this, but at least my preparations weren't in vain. On this padd here I have the personnel file of someone Admiral Quinn has persuaded me is the ideal man to follow in your footsteps as the captain of the *Enterprise.* He is a true explorer, a man born to bring light into the darkness, as it were. Your ship will be in good hands."

That was a surprise, to say the least. Thomas took a while to form a response, as he hadn't expected to win so easily—although "win" was perhaps not the best word for what had just happened. "You aren't angry?"

"No. I am disappointed, which is an entirely different thing. I understand your reasons, I assure you. They're perfectly valid, and nobody will hold your decision against you. I thought you were the perfect man to command this ship, but there are others who can do almost as good a job. Here, take this," she said, holding out the padd, "and have a look at the man's file. I think you'll agree with me that he's a good choice. A single man, he has no commitments, is extensively experienced with long-term deep-space missions, and what's more, he's ready to get back out there. At ease, Captain Halloway, you're off the hook!" With that last comment, her expression had changed considerably, and now she was almost smiling. It certainly made for a very reassuring sight, and Thomas allowed his abdominal muscles, which had involuntarily contracted earlier on during their conversation, to relax.

Taking the padd, he quickly grabbed her outstretched hand and shook it, to seal the deal as well as to thank Satie for being so understanding. She really was a marvelous person, that was certain, and Thomas was grateful to know her. Somebody else in her position might not have let him follow his true path so easily—or, possibly, at all.

A week later, Thomas had packed up all his possessions strewn about in his quarters on UP Orbital, put them in a standard shuttlepod, and was about to leave many things behind for a very long time—some things forever.

"*Shuttlepod* Ankh, *you are go for launch.*"

"Thank you, Orbital. Good-bye!"

With that, he guided the pod through the force field and was immediately in space, a speck among giants, with the station hovering behind him, the *Enterprise* ahead, and two other large starships a bit farther off, partially built and enclosed in assembly frames. He would remain connected to Utopia Planitia. The work there was where his heart lay, and it would take something earth-shattering to change that.

However, Thomas could not help but feel slightly wistful at the sight of the *Enterprise,* so full of opportunity and unrealized potential. He hadn't said no to Satie as easily as it perhaps had seemed to her. There was a part of him that wondered what could have been, what unique wonders he would be seeing if only he had stayed on, what adventures he and his crew might have lived through.

Now he had to say good-bye to the ship and to her crew. It was a pity that he would not get to know the people whose reports and files he had browsed through on occasion, at a time when he had still thought that he'd remain their captain even despite Solveig's decision to stay behind. They were Starfleet's finest—the best and brightest representatives of at least a dozen species—but more than that, they'd seemed like people he could work well with, even become good friends with, and Thomas was unexpectedly struck now by the same sense of loss that he'd felt at the prospect of being separated from Solveig and the children. The difference, he reminded himself, was that he could feel assured that the thousand potential friends he left behind would be well cared for by their next captain . . . but leaving his family without a husband and father was simply too painful a thought to endure.

Thomas increased the speed of his shuttlepod and guided it away from the immediate vicinity of UP Orbital, away from the region of heavy traffic at the center of which sat the space station that had been his second home for years, and toward his first home, the house in Central Burroughs. Of course, he'd easily have been able to use the transporter, seeing as there was a special network of satellites linking the dockyards with ground-based transporters spread all over the surface of the planet. Nevertheless, he had opted for the slow approach, since that gave him the opportunity to look back at what could have been, and what would still be, but without him.

With the crater-covered surface of Mars coming ever closer, he turned his attention away from the *Enterprise* and toward the rest of his life, all the while hoping fervently that Jean-Luc Picard would be worthy of her.

ACTS OF COMPASSION

Dayton Ward & Kevin Dilmore

Historian's note:
This tale is set after the events of the episode "11001001,"
during the first season of Star Trek: The Next Generation.

DAYTON WARD & KEVIN DILMORE

Dayton Ward is a software developer, having become a slave to Corporate America after spending eleven years in the U.S. Marine Corps. When asked, he'll tell you that he joined the military soon after high school because he'd grown tired of people telling him what to do all the time. If you get the chance, be sure to ask him how well that worked out. In addition to the numerous credits he shares with friend and cowriter Kevin Dilmore, he is the author of the *Star Trek* novel *In the Name of Honor* and the science fiction novels *The Last World War* and *The Genesis Protocol* as well as short stories in the first three *Star Trek: Strange New Worlds* anthologies, the Yard Dog Press anthology *Houston, We've Got Bubbas*, DownInTheCellar.com, *Kansas City Voices* magazine, and the *Star Trek: New Frontier* anthology *No Limits*. Though he lives in Kansas City with his wife and daughter, Dayton is a Florida native and still maintains a torrid long-distance romance with his beloved Tampa Bay Buccaneers. Visit him at www.daytonward.com.

For more than eight years, Kevin Dilmore was a contributing writer to *Star Trek Communicator,* penning news stories and personality profiles for the bimonthly publication of the Official *Star Trek* Fan Club. On the storytelling side of things, his story "The Road to Edos" was published as part of the *Star Trek: New Frontier* anthology *No Limits*. With Dayton Ward, his work includes stories for the anthology *Star Trek: Tales of the Dominion War*, the *Star Trek: The Next Generation* novels *A Time to Sow* and *A Time to Harvest,* the *Star Trek: Vanguard* novel *Summon the Thunder,* the *Star Trek: Enterprise* novel *Age of the Empress,* and ten installments of the original eBook series *Star Trek: S.C.E.* and *Star Trek: Corps of Engineers.* A graduate of the University of Kansas, Kevin lives in Prairie Village, Kansas, with his wife, Michelle, and their three daughters, and works as a senior writer for Hallmark Cards in Kansas City, Missouri.

"YOU HAVE THE BRIDGE," ORDERED WILLIAM RIKER AS HE rose from the captain's chair and nodded to the officer assigned to oversee the evening duty shift.

"Thank you, Commander," replied Doctor Beverly Crusher, who stood between the forward conn and ops position while bridge personnel transitioned their duties to the officers relieving them. As Riker moved out of the command well, Crusher took her place in the center seat. "Computer, begin night watch," she said, and the bridge's overhead lighting dimmed in response to her command.

Standing at the tactical console situated above and behind the captain's chair, Lieutenant Natasha Yar forced her expression to remain neutral, focusing her attention on her workstation.

Here we go.

"Have fun," Riker said over his shoulder as he ascended the ramp leading to the turbolift at the rear of the bridge. Looking toward Yar, he offered one of his trademark smiles that conspired with the smooth lines of his face to give him more the appearance of a mischievous adolescent than second-in-command of the Federation's flagship. "That means you, too, Lieutenant."

He's really enjoying this, Yar thought as she watched him step into the turbolift. "I'll wait until I conduct my next aikido class to have fun, sir," she said, offering a respectful nod and a smile of her own. "See you there?"

"Wouldn't miss it for anything," Riker replied before the doors closed, his expression conveying that he looked forward to any revenge she might plot in response to this new bit of chaos he had tossed into what should have been an uneventful duty shift.

Putting aside thoughts of good-natured retaliation, Yar began the watch as she always did, moving between the tactical console and the aft engineering station to execute a series of diagnostics against the ship's weapons and defensive systems. It took little time for her to ease into her routine, dividing her attention between the workstations. While the process normally was little more than an exercise, on this occasion she paid strict attention to the results of the different scans and comparisons. Given the unexpected adventure that had accompanied the upgrades applied to the *Enterprise*'s main computer during its recent layover at Starbase 74, Yar wanted to be sure everything was operating as expected.

Who knows what else those Bynar computer techs left behind?

"You don't usually take the night shift, do you, Lieutenant?" Crusher asked from almost directly behind her.

Startled and somewhat annoyed that she had not detected the doctor's approach, Yar replied, "Not usually, but I like to rotate my people's duty assignments to keep things fresh, and I got caught up in my own master plan."

Crusher smiled, crossing her arms as she leaned against the tactical console. "It's all right, Lieutenant. Commander Riker told me you had your doubts about me taking Mister Data's place tonight." Shrugging, she added, "Even though he doesn't sleep, I figure he'd like to spend his off hours doing something else once in a while."

I should have known he'd say something to her.

"My apologies, Doctor," Yar said, trying to smile and knowing it appeared more like a pained grimace. "Don't misunderstand me. I wish there was more crew interest in expanding their skills beyond their primary specialties. But when it comes to the bridge, I suppose I'm just not comfortable with it being overseen by someone who's not in the operational chain of command."

Crusher had come aboard the *Enterprise* shortly after Yar herself, and in the months since then Yar had learned to appreciate and respect not only the chief medical officer's expertise but also her passion for her chosen profession. Despite that confidence, upon learning that the doctor would be taking charge of the night shift, she had taken her concerns to Riker. The doubts had lingered despite her own review of Crusher's service record and the commander's reassurances that she possessed both the qualifications and the experience to serve in that capacity.

To her surprise, Crusher nodded at the admission. "You're not the first to raise the issue." She smiled. "One of the reasons I volunteer to stand watch only during the night shift is that it tends to rattle fewer people the first time I do it on a new ship. Besides, I like the peace and quiet."

As if in response to her statement, the tactical station emitted an abrupt litany of high-pitched beeps clamoring for Yar's attention. Keying a string of instructions, she reviewed the console's display and frowned.

"It's an encoded message," she said after a moment.

"For the captain?" Crusher asked.

Yar shook her head. "Actually, it's for *you*, Doctor," she said, "and it's coming in on a Cardassian frequency."

Crusher's eyes went wide. "Cardassian?"

Hostilities between the Federation and the Cardassian Union had existed for decades, and Yar's daily Starfleet security briefings were rife with reports of continued engagements even as diplomatic cadres from both sides continued to labor toward some form of lasting truce between the two governments. The *Enterprise*'s current mission of exploration precluded it from being deployed against Cardassian forces, though everyone aboard knew the specter of war would continue to loom until that final peace accord was reached.

Therefore, Yar decided, the receipt of a Cardassian communiqué warranted some measure of concern.

"I'll be damned," Crusher said, standing before one of the aft science stations as she reviewed the message, and when she turned from the console, Yar saw surprise and disbelief darkening the doctor's features. "So much for peace and quiet."

"Thank you all for coming," Jean-Luc Picard said as he entered the observation lounge, raising a hand and indicating for everyone to keep their seats as he moved toward the head of the long, curved conference table. Crusher had no doubt that the captain had come from his ready room, having already studied and formed his initial thoughts on the hasty report she had delivered to him following Lieutenant Yar's startling revelation. "I apologize for the late hour, but as we all know, duty knows no set schedule. I trust you all have had an opportunity to review Doctor Crusher's report?"

"I leave you on the bridge for ten minutes," Riker said, his voice low as he regarded Crusher from across the table with a small smile. It was a brief moment of humor, which vanished the instant the captain took his seat. Crusher had come to appreciate Riker's command style, which seemed more easygoing compared to Picard's more reserved approach, but the first officer had never—in the time she had known him, at least—allowed his penchant for jocularity to interfere with his duties to any degree. "The Cardassians, sir? Are they up to something again?"

"No, Commander," replied Lieutenant Commander Data, the ship's second officer, from where he sat to Riker's left. An android, Data was the one member of the crew who did not require sleep and had come to the bridge at Crusher's request to sort through the latest intelligence briefings in preparation for the meeting—a task he had been able to accomplish with far greater speed than anyone else among the crew. "Starfleet has reported no increase of Cardassian activity in this sector. This message to Doctor Crusher is most unusual."

"This request for assistance doesn't appear to have come through official channels, Number One," Picard said. "The source of the message is an acquaintance of the doctor's."

"His name is Ialona Daret," Crusher said, "a Cardassian physician who's been given the responsibility of caring for three critically injured Starfleet personnel captured in Cardassian territory."

"Have we been able to confirm that they were not in Federation space?" asked Lieutenant Worf from where he sat to Yar's right. Nearly too large for his chair, the muscled Klingon appeared ready to burst through the seams of the red and black Starfleet uniform stretched across his imposing physique.

"Yes," Data replied. "According to our information, they were Starfleet intelligence officers on a covert mission across the border when their ship struck a gravitic mine and was disabled. Their distress message indicated that they landed on a small moon and were attempting to effect repairs when they were discovered by a Cardassian patrol ship."

"Their original complement was five," Crusher added, "but two of them died when they hit the mine. As for the survivors, their conditions have declined beyond his ability to care for them, but Daret has convinced his ship captain to attempt transferring them to Starfleet custody."

"Hard to believe the Cardassians would just surrender such valuable assets," Riker said, leaning forward and resting his forearms on the table.

Crusher nodded. "Daret's message also said that the officers have been interrogated several times despite their injuries, but the captain has ordered those sessions terminated. He seems to feel that offering this olive branch while our governments negotiate a peace treaty is best for everyone."

"Captain," Worf said, his expression one of skepticism, "how do we know we can trust these Cardassians? How can we be sure that this physician is not lying, or being coerced?"

Riker turned to Crusher. "You were contacted directly, Doctor. How well do you know this Daret? Can you vouch for him?"

Crusher replied, "Seven years ago, when I was serving aboard the hospital ship *Sanctuary,* we treated casualties from a Cardassian attack of the Federation depot on Fradon II. Daret was among several Cardassian wounded, and I tended his injuries myself. As more wounded came onboard, Daret himself got out of bed and began assisting us. I watched him fight the pain of a collapsed lung to help both Cardassian and Federation patients. His efforts saved several lives we might otherwise have lost."

Yar asked, "When was the last time you were in contact with him?"

"We spent several evenings talking aboard the *Sanctuary* before he and the rest of our Cardassian patients and prisoners were transferred to Starfleet custody. I've not heard from him since then." Crusher shrugged. "To be honest, I wasn't even sure he was still alive."

"Well," Picard said, "however he's done it, he's aware of your posting to the *Enterprise* and our current proximity to Cardassian space."

"Maybe that's why he bypassed protocol," Riker said. "Whatever the reason, he trusts you to see this through. We're certainly close enough to divert the *Enterprise* into Cardassian space in short order, Captain."

"I'm afraid that's not possible," Picard replied. "This offer comes with strict stipulations, one of which is that the *Enterprise* herself cannot enter Cardassian territory. Doctor Crusher and one assistant will be allowed to travel by shuttlecraft to a rendezvous point across the border, where they will accept transfer of the patients and bring them back here. Further, no weapons are allowed aboard the shuttle."

Yar leaned forward in her seat, her firm expression familiar to Crusher as the security chief displayed it whenever a situation did not sit well with her so far as the crew's safety was concerned. "Captain, do they really expect we'll send Doctor Crusher unprotected behind enemy lines?"

"That may be their expectation, Lieutenant," Picard replied, "but I have no intention of accommodating that demand. That's why *you* will accompany the doctor as her assistant. The *Enterprise* will maintain station just on the Federation side of the border, and I'll have no reservations about entering Cardassian space if we suspect anything untoward taking place."

Yar offered a confident nod. "Understood, sir."

Despite the succinct response, Crusher still noted the slightest hesitation as the lieutenant answered. Yar's earlier admission of her discomfort at variances in command structure was open and honest, one that may even have been difficult for her to express. Crusher knew that for this mission to succeed, the two of them would have to maintain that level of honesty, at least until the doctor could earn a greater measure of trust from Yar in the field.

"How soon can you be under way?" Picard asked.

"My staff is already preparing the list of items I want to take with me," Crusher replied, "and a shuttle's being prepared for medical transport. At last report, it would be ready within three hours, and we can leave directly after that."

Picard nodded in approval. "Excellent. Despite the unorthodox nature of this mission, I don't need to remind you that the diplomatic ramifications of your efforts may well prove as vital as the humanitarian aid you'll be providing. Good luck to both of you. Dismissed."

As the room began to clear, Crusher caught Picard's eye and walked toward him at his small nod. His gaze met hers, and their years of close friendship allowed her to read the concern and responsibility for her welfare she knew he carried.

"This Cardassian doctor and his captain are making an uncharacteristically bold step toward the Federation with this offer," he said. "Starfleet Command will be watching what happens with a keen eye. Despite what I said earlier, your first duty is to your patients, and your own safety. Leave diplomacy to the diplomats."

Yar nodded. "You can count on us, sir." Something about the way she said it even offered Crusher a renewed sense of confidence.

Her answer seemed to appease Picard as well. "I have full confidence in you, Lieutenant. Make it so."

The captain turned and left the observation lounge, leaving Crusher and Yar alone to regard each other with a mix of emotions. "Well," Yar said, offering a sly grin, "you've certainly found a way to get rid of the boredom of gamma shift. Any other surprises I should know about?"

I hope not, Crusher thought.

Shuttlecraft cockpit seats, Crusher decided, were the one method of torture condoned by Starfleet.

Crusher craned her neck, stiff from her attempts to doze in her seat in the *Jefferies*'s cockpit, and looked back along the slim corridor formed by the sides of the vessel's freshly installed emergency stasis units. Scrambling to treat any unforeseen complication within the small craft likely would prove difficult if not deadly to the people she was attempting to bring home alive. While the stasis units—which resembled coffins—would not facilitate healing by any means, they would provide safe transportation for her patients back to the *Enterprise* or a Starfleet medical facility, if necessary.

After nearly eight hours cooped up in the cramped confines of the *Jefferies*, the doctor had for the ninth or tenth time seriously considered commandeering one of the three units for herself, if only to get some unfettered rest. With every cubic centimeter of available space now repurposed for the care and transport of her patients, creature comforts within the shuttle's cabin—let alone space to stretch—were slim to none.

In the back, Crusher saw Yar kneeling next to the shuttlecraft's emergency transporter pad. To maximize space while making the shuttle as utilitarian as possible to medical needs, *Enterprise* engineers had cross-purposed the device to function as a replicator, capable of creating any equipment or synthesizing any pharmaceuticals or implants Crusher might deem necessary for treatment. At the moment, Yar was using it to conjure two cups of coffee.

"Coffee on demand has to be the greatest invention since warp drive," the lieutenant said as she moved forward, handing one of the cups to Crusher before taking her own seat in the cockpit. "I don't know how people survived these long trips before replicators."

Crusher smiled, appreciating Yar's light attitude. It went a long way toward diffusing her own growing apprehension as they neared the rendezvous point. During their trip, the longest stretch of one-on-one time she had ever spent with the security chief, her appreciation for Yar's straightforward yet relaxed style had grown. Tasha Yar was a natural leader, at ease with her responsibilities. Crusher could understand what Picard had seen in her when recruiting her for duty aboard the *Enterprise.*

Taking a moment to review the array of controls and status monitors on the helm console, Yar said, "You've reviewed Daret's latest report?"

"I have," Crusher replied, holding up for emphasis the padd that had been resting in her lap. "Ensign Weglash, the Benzite, has suffered extensive damage to his lungs, and that's apart from his being deprived of his breathing apparatus for who knows how long." Most Benzites living and working in regular Class-M environments depended on moisture and infused mineral salts provided by the vaporizers they wore to assist their breathing. She was thankful she had taken the time to replicate a quantity of the liquid and brought it along.

Yar nodded. "What about the others?"

Tapping a control on the padd, Crusher said, "The Vulcan woman, Lieutenant T'Lan, has suffered severe intracranial trauma on top of other general injuries. Commander Gregory Spires, the

leader of the mission, lost three limbs in the crash. And all are coping with severe burns on various parts of their bodies."

"What are their chances, Doctor?"

Looking up from her padd, Crusher saw the expression of worry
on the lieutenant's face. It was not surprising to encounter such
concern, despite never having served alongside these officers. That
was just one of the special bonds shared by anyone who wore a
Starfleet uniform.

"It's hard to say without examining them myself," Crusher
replied, "but thanks to Ialona, they're a damn sight better off. I've
no doubt he saved their lives." Noticing the skeptical expression
clouding Yar's features, she asked, "Something bothering you,
Tasha?"

"Force of habit, Doctor," Yar replied, reaching up to brush a lock
of blond hair from her eyes. "I guess I'm looking for more than
we're seeing."

"Because Daret is Cardassian?"

Yar nodded. "Honestly? Yes. This whole notion seems off, somehow. The Cardassians are smart enough to know they've captured
spies. I don't see how just handing them over pays off for them."

"I'm not second-guessing your judgment," Crusher said, "but
consider something. As long as there have been battles, physicians
have treated wounded soldiers despite the color of their uniforms
or the color of their blood. Daret is a healer first and a Cardassian
second. I witnessed that firsthand on the *Sanctuary*. Whatever he's
after, it's because he's a doctor, not a soldier or politician."

"Well, I certainly can't argue with the faith you've shown in him
to this point," Yar replied. "But he's really not the one I'm worried
about. You can be sure his captain will be playing at something.
He's the one I'll be watching."

"Jean-Luc did say I'd be in good hands," Crusher said just as an
alert signal sounded from the shuttlecraft's control console. "What's
that?"

"Sensors are picking up the approach of a Cardassian vessel,"
Yar replied, her fingers moving across the helm. "It's coming in on
the specified vector." Reaching across the console, she keyed the
communications system. "Federation shuttlecraft *Jefferies* to approaching Cardassian vessel. Respond, please."

A moment later, the helm's central viewer activated, coalescing into the image of a Cardassian officer, cloaked in shadow and backlit by a diffused light source. His black hair was streaked with gray similar in hue to his ridged, rippled skin. Cobalt blue eyes peered from beneath a pronounced cranial ridge. *"I am Gul Edal of the Cardassian warship* Kovmar. *Prepare to receive landing instructions."*

Clearing her throat, Crusher said, "This is Doctor Beverly Crusher. Is Ialona Daret aboard?"

"Indeed he is, Doctor," Edal replied, *"and he sends his regards. However, he is occupied in our infirmary with your patients. You will see him shortly. Follow your landing instructions without deviation.* Kovmar *out."* With that, the transmission ended.

"Warm welcome," Yar said, her attention focused on the helm. Crusher watched her enter a string of commands, and a moment later the *Jefferies* dropped out of warp.

"Could just be that renowned Cardassian efficiency," Crusher offered.

Yar shrugged. "Efficient at being inhospitable, maybe. Like I said, he's the one I'll be watching."

As an orphan living amid the turmoil gripping the failed Federation colony on Turkana IV, Tasha Yar had seen more than her share of carnage and death. As such, she considered herself at least somewhat hardened to the callous brutality that could be inflicted by supposedly intelligent beings upon one another, either in battle or in the simple withholding of urgently needed medical assistance.

That strength, forged and honed within an environment of incessant chaos and cruelty, was shaken by the scene unfolding in what passed for the *Kovmar*'s infirmary.

"You can wait outside," said Doctor Ialona Daret, the elderly Cardassian waving with one hand to the pair of security guards who had escorted Crusher and Yar from the ship's hangar bay.

One of the guards—the higher-ranking of the pair if Yar's interpretation of their uniform insignia was correct—shook his head. "Gul Edal's orders are for us to remain with the humans at all times, Doctor." Yar noted the derision in the soldier's voice as he addressed the physician.

Daret pointed to a far corner of the room. "You can remain with them just as easily from over there and out of my way." To Yar's surprise, the guards appeared relieved at the prospect of maintaining some distance from Daret and his patients.

Not that she could blame them.

It was the smell that caught her attention as she and Doctor Crusher were escorted into the room. A sharp sting assailed her nostrils from what she guessed was disinfectant, trying yet failing to cloak the stench of festering wounds and expelled body waste. Breathing through her mouth, Yar found it easy to ignore the fetid smells as she focused instead on the sight of the wounded Starfleet officers.

"It's good to see you again, Beverly," Daret said as he gripped Crusher's hand in his own. "I only wish it was for better reasons. I would have met you when you came aboard, but I did not want to leave them any longer than absolutely necessary."

"Have their conditions changed since your last report?" Crusher asked, opening the trauma kit and extracting a medical tricorder and diagnostic scanner.

Daret shook his head. "No, thankfully. They're stabilized, but as you can see, my resources here are limited."

"His lung damage is even worse than I thought," Crusher said, studying her tricorder's display as she waved a diagnostic scanner over Weglash. "Third-degree burns along the primary bronchi." She nodded toward the obviously makeshift breathing mask suspended over the ensign's face. "That doesn't look like standard Cardassian medical equipment."

"It's not," Daret replied. "His original breather was damaged, but I was able to synthesize an approximation of the gas mixture, combining it with an inhalant to help with the damage to his lungs."

"What about these?" Yar asked, pointing to the status monitors mounted above each patient's bed. They appeared rudimentary compared to those in the *Enterprise*'s sickbay, though the equipment's relative capability did not seem to be an issue as none of it was activated.

"They were useless," Daret said, his voice laced with guilt as he indicated the monitors with a wave of his hand. "The ship's medical database is out of date when it comes to many non-Cardassian physiologies." He shook his head, his expression turning to disgust. "All these years at war with the Federation and despite the efforts of numerous physicians who've been forced to treat prisoners, our government has allowed almost none of the knowledge acquired in those instances to be retained."

"I suppose that's one indication of how serious the Cardassians are about any peace treaty," Crusher said. Eyeing Daret, she offered a small, grim smile. "Present company excepted, of course." Completing her initial examination of Weglash, she turned from the patient bed and moved to Commander Spires, continuing her rapid triage. "Tasha, help replace Weglash's respirator and start the new vapor mixture."

Opening the case she had carried with her from the shuttlecraft, Yar searched through its assortment of medical supplies until she identified the vapor device and the fist-sized pressure cylinder Crusher had requested. She affixed one to the other and handed the assembly to Daret, already feeling overwhelmed and out of place as the two doctors quickly fell into an efficient rhythm. According to Crusher, it had been several years since their last correspondence, but their actions made it seem as though the physicians worked together every day.

The sound of the infirmary doors opening caught her attention, and Yar turned to see another Cardassian entering the room. Like most of his kind, he was tall and brawny, with large, muscled arms and legs evident even beneath the hard segmented plates of his brown uniform.

"Glinn Malir," Daret said, looking up from where he stood next to where Crusher now was examining Lieutenant T'Lan. "A pleasant surprise, seeing you here." Yar recognized the new arrival's name as that of the *Kovmar*'s second-in-command, and she noted the slight yet still perceptible trace of sarcasm lacing the Cardassian physician's greeting.

Malir nodded, remaining near the door with his hands clasped behind his back. His eyes moved, taking in everything in the room, then narrowing as they focused on Yar. "It's my understanding," he said, "that officers in Starfleet's medical and science branches are designated with blue as one of their uniform colors, whereas gold is usually worn by their engineers and security personnel." The words sounded almost playful, though his expression remained neutral, and Yar felt a slight chill as his eyes regarded her with wanton interest. "You do not strike me as an engineer."

"What the hell happened to her?" Crusher's voice was loud and sharp, cutting off Yar's attempted reply. "Some of these injuries are more recent than the crash." She leveled a harsh glare at Malir. "What did you do to her?"

With a casual air that Yar found irritating, the first officer shrugged. "She sustained some damage while resisting the efforts of security personnel charged with restraining her. It is an unfortunate consequence."

"Why was she being restrained by security at all?" Yar asked, already knowing the answer. "You interrogated her, didn't you?"

"She was *questioned*," Malir countered, malice now creeping into his voice. "Standard procedure when dealing with spies and other enemy combatants."

"Even though she required medical attention for her injuries sustained in the crash?" Crusher asked. She looked to Daret. "Is this true?"

Daret nodded. "Unlike the others, her injuries were not life threatening. Gul Edal ordered the interrogation ended when he learned of it." He cast his eyes downward. "But by then it was too late."

"You're damned right it was," Crusher snapped. "She's sustained a cerebral hemorrhage and there's blood in the surrounding cerebrospinal fluid." She leveled another withering stare at Malir. "One of her molar teeth is missing. You didn't waste any time with that bit of idiocy, did you?"

Yar knew of the Cardassian Union's practice of collecting for the purposes of identification the first molar of all citizens prior to their entering adolescence. The distasteful measure was also exacted on non-Cardassians when taken into custody.

"Again, standard procedure, Doctor," Malir replied, and Yar heard the first hint of annoyance. "We each have our respective duties to perform. I suggest you see to yours, rather than worrying about mine."

Shaking her head in disgust, Crusher turned to Daret. "Ialona, we need to start prepping for surgery right now."

"That is," Yar said, glowering at Malir, "unless you plan to *question* her again."

"Tasha," Crusher said, and Yar heard the warning in the single spoken word.

For the first time, Malir frowned. It was clear that he was unaccustomed to being addressed in this manner. His eyes narrowed, boring into her, and Yar was certain she saw anger and determination there. He was dangerous, she decided, particularly if provoked.

Easy, her inner voice cautioned, though her body tensed as Malir stepped forward.

"As it is obvious that you are neither a doctor nor an engineer, perhaps I should question *you,* to determine your true identity and reason for being here."

"No, thank you," Yar said, feeling her pulse quickening. "I like all my teeth where they are."

Malir was fast—very fast. He lunged forward, raising his right arm. She registered the movement, but by then instinct had taken over and she stepped into the attack, her left hand blocking his arm before it could complete its downswing. Knowing the Cardassian had the advantage in weight and strength, Yar wasted no time following the hasty defensive movement with something more aggressive.

"Tasha!"

She heard Crusher's cry but ignored it. Gripping Malir's arm at the wrist, Yar shifted her weight and pivoted to her left, carrying his body across her hip and dropping him to the metal deck plating. She heard the Cardassian's forceful exhalation as he slammed into the deck, the impact echoing in the crowded infirmary. She twisted his wrist, eliciting a sharp cry of surprise and pain.

"Do not move!"

She looked up to see the security guards moving toward her. One of them had drawn his disruptor pistol and was pulling it up to aim at her, giving Yar only a moment to consider the notion that she should have taken Malir's own sidearm when she had the chance.

Commander Riker would never let me live that down.

"Stop."

Though the single word was spoken with relative calm and restraint, there was no mistaking the commanding presence behind it. Coming from directly behind her, it made Yar flinch—and had a similar effect on the guards, both of whom halted their advance. The Cardassian who had brandished his weapon promptly lowered it and both guards turned their attention to the new arrival. Yar did likewise and immediately recognized the speaker's wizened countenance.

Gul Edal.

"Glinn Malir," the *Kovmar*'s commanding officer said, the infirmary lighting playing off the gray in his otherwise dark, backswept hair as he stepped farther into the room and allowed the doors to close behind him. "I trust there is an explanation for this disruption?" The gul's voice was low and raspy, whether a sign of age or some unidentified health issue, Yar could not surmise. He moved slowly but retained the confidence of an experienced, even comfortable commander.

Yar stepped to her right as Malir pulled himself to his feet, making no attempt to straighten or brush his uniform. Fury burned behind his dark eyes, not merely at having his attack thwarted but also, she suspected, that his attempt at retaliation had been interrupted by the superior officer's appearance.

"Gul Edal," Malir began but stopped when Edal raised a hand and shook his head.

"Wait outside, please," the gul said before nodding to the pair of security guards and adding, "You join him." He moved past Malir to where Crusher and Daret still stood, their faces bearing matched expressions of surprise.

Emitting a grunt too low for Edal to hear but audible to Yar, Malir tugged on his heavy tunic. "We will finish this later," he hissed, glowering at her as he passed her on his way to the doors with the guards following behind him. Not until they closed did Yar allow herself to exhale in relief.

I should have gone into stellar cartography.

"Doctor Crusher," Edal said, his hands at his sides as he addressed her, "it is a pleasure to make your acquaintance, though I do regret the dire circumstances that have prompted our meeting." Nodding to Lieutenant T'Lan, he asked, "Have you had sufficient time to examine your patients?"

Yar saw the uncertainty in Crusher's eyes as she reached up to brush a lock of dark red hair from her eyes. "All three will need emergency surgery for the most serious injuries. I can perform that here and stabilize them for transport, but they need better care facilities than you're able to provide. The *Enterprise* sickbay will do, but a starbase would be better."

"Then we shall endeavor to get you on your way with all due haste," Edal replied. Turning to Yar, he added, "I apologize for my second's behavior, Lieutenant. Rest assured it will not happen again."

Yar was not so foolish as to be taken in by the gul's apparent civility. Still, she was forced to admit, there was something in the Cardassian's eyes—weariness, perhaps even guilt—that implored her to believe him.

Oldest trick in the book, she mused. *Even if he's on the level, Malir's probably the type who gets in trouble for disobeying orders.*

Watching Edal leave the infirmary, Yar pushed aside her thoughts of unease. Doctor Crusher might need her help as she prepared for surgery, and she would not benefit from a distracted assistant.

"Have you taken leave of your senses?" Edal asked, barely waiting until he and Malir had stepped out of earshot of the guards positioned outside the infirmary doors. He was mindful to keep his voice low so that it would not carry down the narrow corridor. As with most common areas of *Galor*-class warships, this passageway of the *Kovmar* lacked sound-suppression paneling, requiring one to stand in close proximity to a companion in order to talk at a reasonable volume. Conduits for ventilation, plumbing, and power distribution were visible overhead and below the deck's metal grating, contributing enough background noise to mask the Cardassian officers' conversation.

Though Malir had taken a moment to compose himself, Edal still saw the harnessed fury burning in his second-in-command's eyes. "She was insolent, and in front of subordinates. They both were. I cannot allow that sort of challenge to my authority."

"I witnessed the exchange," Edal replied. "It was an excellent demonstration of articulating your position."

Bristling, Malir released a sharp exhalation. "She's definitely not a nurse."

"Of course she's not," Edal replied, unable to help the small laugh that escaped his lips. "She is the *Enterprise*'s chief of security. I'm surprised you did not consult the intelligence briefings once the humans identified themselves prior to coming aboard. I had no doubt Captain Picard would send someone capable of protecting Doctor Crusher." He had expected nothing less from the Federation flagship's commander. Jean-Luc Picard, a well-respected officer by all accounts, was renowned in Cardassian intelligence circles for his military prowess as well as diplomatic accomplishments. For him to allow his chief medical officer to venture into enemy territory spoke volumes about the trust he placed in her, as well as the esteem in which Crusher herself held Ialona Daret.

I only hope such faith is not wasted.

"All the more reason to keep them both under watch," Malir said. "A security chief makes for a capable spy."

"They're not here to spy," Edal said, "and if they were, there is nothing here for them to learn. We are but a single ship, tasked with no mission of great import. Besides, are our governments not at this moment negotiating for peace? Allowing the humans here to treat their comrades, particularly at this critical time, cannot help but be viewed as a cooperative venture illustrating how our peoples can work together."

Malir shook his head. "It seems like such a waste, much like those endless peace talks. We can defeat the Federation. All we require is for our leaders to stop wavering in their support of the military and provide us what we need to secure victory."

Again, Edal smiled, though he felt no humor. Much of the same passion and ambition that once had driven him was visible in Malir's eyes. That fire was long extinguished, snuffed out by years of unremitting conflict with numerous peoples who disagreed—sometimes vehemently—with the notion of living under Cardassian rule. While he once had shared beliefs similar to those harbored by his younger counterpart, age and experience had made Edal weary of war, teaching him that reality rarely conformed to such stark perceptions.

"We have been at odds with the Federation since I was a child, Malir," he said. "After all that time and despite our best efforts, we have achieved little more than a stalemate, and at what cost? Worlds stripped of resources in order to support the war, entire populations dying for simple lack of food and medicines. Our civilization wavers on the brink of collapse. No, my friend, peace is the better course."

Grunting more in acknowledgment than approval, Malir said, "If our leaders decide as much, then I'll obey. Until then, are we not better served by maintaining our vigilance, seizing every advantage and allowing no quarter until an accord is reached?" He nodded toward the infirmary doors. "They may possess valuable information about their ship and its orders, something we can exploit."

"I granted them safe passage," Edal said, checking himself as he realized his voice was loud enough to be heard by the guards still posted before the infirmary entrance. "I gave my word to Daret," he continued in a softer tone. "The humans will be allowed to treat their patients and leave in peace."

"And what of Central Command?" Stepping closer, Malir's next words were little more than a hissed whisper. "You have no authorization for this action. How do you think they'll react when they learn of this? What of the crew? Many will see this as treason."

"I will see to Central Command," Edal snapped. "As for the crew, they will follow my orders. Your concern is seeing that they do so." He knew that his decision to let the human prisoners receive Starfleet aid was an unpopular, even risky proposition, which was the reason he had acted without first seeking clearance from his superiors.

"Malir," he said after a moment, "we have a duty to act in the best interests of the Cardassian people. Bringing the humans here is consistent with that duty, even if *you* don't realize it at this moment."

Though he may not have been satisfied with that answer, Malir offered a formal nod. "Very well, Gul Edal. I only hope you've not made a grave mistake."

"Should that prove the case, then I will endure the consequences," Edal said, tiring of the conversation and deciding that he had indulged his subordinate long enough. "Return to your station." To his credit, Malir said nothing else, instead turning and walking away and leaving Edal to stand alone in the corridor.

Closing his eyes, the gul found himself listening as he frequently did to the steady thrum of the *Kovmar*'s engines, feeling their power reverberate through every surface of the ship. It always comforted Edal to hear the vessel's steady pulse of life, and he now allowed that gentle rhythm to ease his momentary irritation.

When he opened his eyes, he saw the security guards regarding him. Their expressions were unreadable, though he sensed in them the same doubt Malir had voiced. Was their uncertainty but a representation of the crew's? *Had* he made a mistake? If so, what cost would that blunder exact?

Such questions would demand answers, Edal knew, one way or another.

"Doctor!"

Crusher turned away from Weglash, who after nearly three hours had just begun to show positive response to the correctly synthesized vapors he now was breathing, toward the new call of alarm. She saw one of Daret's assistants turning T'Lan's head to one side as foamy vomit sputtered from the Vulcan's mouth.

"She's seizing," Crusher said, rushing to T'Lan's side and using her fingers to clear the quivering woman's airway. Eyeing the portable diagnostic scanner positioned at the head of her bed, she shook her head. "The swelling in her brain isn't subsiding. Damn!"

"I thought your drugs were working," said Daret from where he stood next to Commander Spires, who remained unconscious and who, despite the loss of both legs as well as his right arm, was currently the most stable of the three patients.

"The cortical regenerator isn't stabilizing her like I'd hoped," Crusher said as she grabbed a hypospray and pressed it to T'Lan's neck. Within moments, the Vulcan's spasms subsided, but Crusher knew it was a temporary respite. Until she could arrest the swelling of T'Lan's brain tissue, she did not dare risk merely tossing the woman into a stasis unit. "As much as I hate the idea, Ialona, we're going to have to drain the excess fluid physically. I'll have to bore into her skull." The very idea turned her stomach. Such procedures had long ago fallen out of everyday use, thanks to modern technological advances, but when those seemingly miraculous methods failed, even obsolete practices still proved useful.

Crossing the infirmary floor, Daret said, "I'm more accustomed to such a procedure than you are. Let me help."

Crusher nodded. "Absolutely. I'll need your help pinpointing where to drill." Handing him a medical tricorder, she added, "You can guide me through the subarachnoid space with this."

Sudden movement at the infirmary door caught Crusher's eye, and she turned to see Gul Edal enter at a brisk pace. "How are things progressing, Doctor?" he asked, maintaining a respectful distance from the operating table. Crusher could not help but notice the tinge of anxiety in his voice.

"This isn't a good time," she snapped, returning her attention to T'Lan. "We may lose her if we don't act quickly."

"My concern, Doctor," Edal said, "is that each of you may be at greater risk than you realize. I suggest you do what you can to get everyone aboard your shuttle and out of here as quickly as possible."

Crusher sensed the warning underlying the Cardassian's words, but there was nothing to be done about that now. "I can't move her until she's stabilized."

Edal shook his head. "Doctor, I don't think you appreciate the gravity of the situation. If you choose to remain here, I don't know that I can guarantee your safety."

"It's not a wager I'd make."

The new voice came from behind Edal, and Crusher recognized it as belonging to Malir. Looking past the gul, she saw his second-in-command flanked by a pair of guards—each of them holding weapons to Edal's back.

Edal turned to face Malir. "And what is *this?*"

"Consider it my refusal to stand by and watch you subvert Central Command's authority," Malir replied. "I'm taking command of the *Kovmar* and placing you and everyone in this room under arrest."

"On what grounds?" Edal asked.

"Dereliction of duty with respect to the treatment of spies and prisoners of war," the glinn answered. "You've had ample opportunity to take the correct course of action, but instead you've chosen to follow this other path. That cannot be allowed to go unchallenged."

"The crew will never support this," Edal warned.

Malir smiled. "I think you'll find that a sufficient number of the crew are behind me. After all, they have no desire to be executed as traitors, as their commander will be."

Crusher exchanged looks with Yar, and she noted the way the lieutenant's body seemed to tense in anticipation. She mouthed a silent *no* to her, hoping to keep Yar out of the deteriorating situation. Beneath Crusher's hands, Lieutenant T'Lan still demanded her attention.

We don't have time *for this idiocy!*

Then everything went to hell as Edal made the choice for everyone in the room.

With no warning, he lunged for Malir's disruptor. Malir was faster, swinging his sidearm toward the gul and firing. The weapon's discharge howled in the infirmary's confines as the violet energy bolt struck Edal in the midsection, and he fell backward to the deck with a heavy thud.

"No!" Crusher shouted as Daret rushed to the fallen Cardassian's side. "Not in here!" By then it was too late, as Yar took advantage of one guard's distraction. Lashing out with her right foot, she kicked the guard in his throat, forcing him back as he coughed and sputtered. The lieutenant followed that vicious strike with an elbow to the side of his head, dropping him to the deck where he released his grip on his disruptor. Yar wasted no time, scooping up the weapon and firing toward the already retreating Malir.

Finding himself in the middle of a firefight, the other guard was confused, and he hesitated. Crusher saw the look in his eyes as he backpedaled away from the melee, the muzzle of his weapon swinging dangerously close to where Commander Spires lay defenseless even as he came abreast of her and seized her forearm in a tight grip. Without thinking, Crusher thumbed the exoscalpel in her hand to its highest setting and aimed it at the guard's weapon hand.

The guard shrieked in pain, dropping his disruptor and releasing his hold on Crusher to clutch his wounded hand. He staggered away from the doctor and Crusher again heard weapons fire as Yar targeted the guard with her own disruptor, the energy pulse striking the Cardassian in the chest and pushing him into a freestanding surgical tray. Instruments and other equipment scattered as he fell unconscious to the deck.

More shots echoed in the infirmary and Crusher glimpsed Malir crouching near the door. When Yar swung her weapon in his direction and loosed another barrage, the glinn pushed the control to open the door and scrambled outside in search of cover.

"Seal the room!" Daret yelled from where he knelt next to Edal. "That large orange button near the door. It will initiate a containment field around the entire infirmary!"

Yar slammed the large oval button with the heel of her hand, and an adjacent indicator illuminated at the same time a low-resonance hum flared into existence. "Quarantine procedures are now in effect," said the monotone voice of the *Kovmar*'s onboard computer. "Entry to infirmary restricted to medical personnel only."

"That won't hold Malir for long," Daret said, "but it will give us some time." He rolled Edal onto his back, and for the first time Crusher could see the ghastly wound in the gul's left side.

"Doctor," she heard Edal say in a weak voice. "You . . . alert . . . crew."

Grunting something Crusher did not understand, Daret rushed to a control panel and smacked it with his fist. "This is Doctor Daret to all hands. Glinn Malir has just tried to murder Gul Edal. He intends to take over the ship. All personnel to duty stations. Malir must be apprehended at once!" Deactivating the communications panel, Daret shook his head. "Enough of that."

"What will they do?" Crusher asked.

"It depends on how many of the crew Malir has convinced to follow him," Daret replied. "I have no idea what to expect." He shook his head. "This is my fault. I should never have brought you into this."

"Too late for that now," Crusher said. Still hovering over T'Lan, her attention split between her own patient and the one Daret now served, she nodded toward Edal. "How is he?"

"He's dying," Daret replied. "The disruptor ruptured his mulana. The organ's destroyed. I can keep him alive only a short time without a replacement or a bypass of some sort, and I don't have that type of equipment here."

Crusher considered the diagnosis. For Yar's benefit, she said, "It functions like a liver in humans. We might have something that can help." She recalled how she had overseen the packing of the cargo containers they had brought with them, instructing her staff to include a number of items as a contingency. "Tasha, on the shuttle is what's called a portable dynamic organ stimulator. You'll have to get it. Transport over and bring it back."

"Understood," Yar replied, nodding.

"Wait," Daret said. "Assuming internal security hasn't already blocked your ability to communicate with your shuttle, they will the moment they detect any signal. You may have time for one transport before they react—but that will be all."

Shaking her head, Crusher exhaled in growing irritation. *It's always something.* "Take him with you," she said. "Treat him aboard the shuttle." Looking to Yar, the doctor was not surprised to see the startled expression on the young lieutenant's face.

"Me?" Yar asked. "I've received only basic medic training." She glanced to Edal's unconscious form. "I can't do this."

"It's a simple process," the doctor countered. "Ialona, go with her. I can talk you through it if necessary, but you need to go *now.*"

Yar seemed to relax, if only slightly, perhaps buoyed by Crusher's crisp, decisive manner. Drawing a deep breath, she offered a single taut nod. "Let's do this," she said, reaching up to tap her combadge. "Yar to shuttlecraft *Jefferies.* Activate emergency transporter and lock on." Kneeling beside Edal, she looked to Crusher, who turned toward her and offered an encouraging smile.

There was a brief pause before the feminine voice of the shuttle's onboard computer replied, "Acknowledged. Transporter standing by."

Yar waited for Daret to indicate that he had deactivated the quarantine fields surrounding the infirmary before nodding to Crusher one last time. "Three to beam to the *Jefferies,*" she said, gripping her purloined disruptor pistol in her right hand. "Energize."

"Good luck," Crusher offered as the transporter beam enveloped Yar, Daret, and Edal and the three of them disappeared, leaving the doctor alone in the infirmary with Daret's assistants. As one of the nurses reactivated the quarantine procedures, Crusher exhaled in resignation. She was getting too old for this sort of excitement.

"Okay," she said, "let's get on with this."

A shower of transporter energy swept away the Cardassian infirmary, replacing it with the shuttlecraft's cramped interior. The tingle on her skin was still palpable as Yar confirmed that both Daret and the wounded Edal had made the trip with her.

She eyed the shuttle's open door. "Keep a watch out. I'll get the gear," she said, moving toward the bulky cargo container at the rear of the shuttle's passenger compartment.

Kneeling beside Edal, Daret waved a portable scanner over the unconscious Cardassian's chest. "There's not much time," he said. "We must hurry."

"There should be a portable sterile field generator in there, as well," Crusher said, her voice distant and washed out as it was filtered through Yar's combadge. *"Once Ialona's ready, place it on either side of Edal's torso. The field should cover his entire upper body."*

"I've got it," Yar said after a moment, gripping the generator by its molded carrying handle and extracting it from the container. Handing the device to Daret, she asked, "Do you know how to work this?"

The Cardassian nodded. "Doctor Crusher taught me how to use them on the *Sanctuary*."

It took Yar an additional minute to locate the organ stimulator, even with Crusher guiding her. "Found it, Doctor," she said, feeling momentary relief at the small victory but knowing the larger battle still lay ahead. "What do we do now?"

"First," Crusher said, *"you'll need to . . ."*

Yar flinched as the rest of the doctor's instruction disintegrated into a burst of static erupting from her combadge, the chaotic hiss and pops echoing within the shuttle's cramped interior. "They're jamming our signals."

"They know we're here," Daret replied as he set up the stimulator and activated its start-up diagnostic protocols. "We'll need to be ready."

Nodding, Yar reached for the Cardassian disruptor she had set aside while hunting through the cargo container. Daret's simple statement had spoken volumes; there likely would be no way to know if whoever found them was loyal to Edal or Malir until someone shot at someone else. Though the weight of the weapon in her hand was of some comfort, Yar would have preferred the familiar heft of a Starfleet phaser. A sudden surge of isolation and fear reached out to grip her, a sensation that had been a fact of everyday life on Turkana IV but that also had revisited her on infrequent occasions throughout her adult life, despite her best efforts to bury them beneath training and experience. Clenching her jaw, she felt her muscles tense as she fought back the impulses.

You're not a child. You're supposed to be ready for this kind of thing.

Behind her, Daret had succeeded in activating the organ stimulator and the sterile field generator. She watched as the doctor wielded a laser scalpel over the wounded Edal's stomach. Before her eyes, the Cardassian's thick gray skin parted beneath the scalpel's beam to reveal dense, fibrous muscle tissue. With a dexterity similar to what Yar had earlier seen Crusher exhibit, Daret proceeded with the impromptu surgery, cutting with one hand while the other controlled the removal of excess blood from the incision site as he worked to facilitate connecting Edal to the stimulator and initiating the process of bypassing the gul's damaged mulana.

"How long?" she asked.

Without looking up, Daret replied, "Just a few moments, assuming he's not too weak to withstand the stress of the bypass. Regardless, he will require more extensive care if he's to make a complete recovery."

Yar began to ask something else but forgot all of that when she detected movement in her peripheral vision, outside the shuttle. Then harsh violet energy struck the *Jefferies*'s hull just to the left of the open hatch, rocking the small craft.

"Stay down!" she shouted from where she crouched near the hatch, searching among cargo crates, Cardassian shuttlecraft, and other assorted detritus for the source of the attack. She caught sight of a dark shadow near an open door leading out of the hangar bay and fired more from instinct than training. Instinct was rewarded as her weapon belched energy and the disruptor bolt struck the Cardassian in the chest, driving him to the deck.

More shadows loomed in the corridor beyond the doorway, and Yar fired again, not at the Cardassians this time but instead at the control panel set into the bulkhead near the door. The panel exploded in a shower of sparks and—as she hoped—the hatch promptly closed, blocking any more Cardassians from entering the bay.

Right. As though there's no other way in here.

"Close the hatch!" Daret called out, still engrossed in his treatment of Edal.

"No," Yar replied. "I don't want to give them a chance to surround us." She had no illusions that the Cardassians would let something as simple as a locked hatch keep them from getting into the hangar. They had only minutes before the soldiers regrouped at another point of entry.

Unless she did something to prevent that.

"Computer," she said, rising from her crouch, "once I close the hatch, you're to open it only on my voice authorization or Doctor Daret's. Acknowledge."

"Acknowledged," the shuttle's computer voice replied. "Standing by."

Daret looked up from his field surgery, his eyes wide. "What are you doing?"

"Stay here," she replied. "I'm sealing you in." Bounding down the shuttle's rear ramp to the hangar's metal deck, she turned and gave him a final look. "If you need assistance, the shuttle's onboard computer can help you." Before the doctor could respond or protest, Yar hit the control set into a recessed cavity next to the hatch and the ramp began to rise. "I'll be right back," she called out as the shuttle sealed itself, then turned and headed across the hangar bay in search of the other entry points she was certain to find.

Assuming they don't just depressurize the whole bay. Though the thought rang in her ears, she doubted Glinn Malir would stoop to such a tactic. If the Cardassian had wanted her or Crusher dead, Yar was sure he would have taken care of it before now. No, she decided, Edal's would-be successor had loftier aspirations in mind, and the capture of two supposedly important Starfleet officers would likely play into achieving those goals.

Good luck with that.

She located a second hatch along the same bulkhead as the one she already had disabled. The door was locked, and she used her disruptor to destroy its control panel. Recalling what she knew of *Galor*-class warships, Yar figured similar hatches would likely be found on the opposite side of the bay. Using the haphazard arrangement of cargo containers and shuttlecraft for cover, she maneuvered around the chamber's perimeter to where she believed she would find the next hatch.

As she moved past stacks of cargo, she felt the hair stand up on the back of her neck just before the shadows to her right shifted.

Without thinking, she turned in that direction, her weapon arm coming up but far too late to be of any use. The Cardassian's own muscled arm was slashing down at her and Yar ducked to her left to avoid the knife slicing toward her, feeling the sensation of displaced air as the jagged blade passed through the space just occupied by her head.

There was no time to look for a shot, as Yar heard and felt Malir lumbering after her. Using her free hand to push away from a nearby crate, she threw herself around a corner, bobbing and weaving around the clutter as she fought to gain some maneuvering room.

"There is nowhere to run, human," Malir called out, his voice low and menacing. "We have unfinished business."

It was not the first time Yar had heard such taunts leveled at her. As with the words themselves, the contempt they harbored was also not new, nor was it to be taken lightly. Like the gangs that had chased her throughout much of her childhood, she had no doubt Malir would carry out his implied threats.

Dodging around another cargo container, Yar abruptly found herself in an open section of the hangar deck, with nothing in front of her to provide cover. Then there was no time to consider the tactics of the situation before she heard Malir's heavy footsteps behind her and she turned, once more bringing her disruptor to bear. The Cardassian was too close, his left hand sweeping beneath her arm and slamming into her wrist, ruining her aim and sending the weapon flying from her hand. Backpedaling, Yar brought her hands up and assumed a defensive stance as Malir regarded her with raw hatred.

"I know you've locked Edal in your shuttle," Malir said, stepping to his left and holding the knife in his right hand low and near his side. "Give him to me, and I'll spare your life along with those of your comrades."

"I'm having a hard time believing that," Yar replied, her attention on the knife and Malir's hips, watching for any hints as to which direction he might move when he elected to attack again. Then he lunged forward and she jumped back, realizing as she stumbled that she had stepped on some kind of thick cabling running across the hangar deck. Yar tried to correct her momentary loss of balance, but it was too late. She staggered over the cabling and landed hard on the deck, feeling the wind forced from her lungs at the same instant Malir made his move, reaching for her with his free hand while bringing the blade around toward her.

With no time to regain her feet, Yar instead kicked out with her right leg, sweeping around and catching Malir behind his left knee-cap with sufficient force to drive his leg from beneath him. He stumbled, dropping to his left knee with a distressed grunt. Yar rolled to her side, coming up on one knee and driving the heel of her hand into the Cardassian's nose. She was rewarded with what sounded like cartilage breaking from the force of the strike as Malir howled and reached for his face, his weapon hand slashing more from rage and pain than in any real attempt to hit a target.

He tried to get up but Yar was faster, pulling herself to her feet and loosing another kick, this one to the side of his head. It was enough to drive him to the deck and make him release his grip on the knife, the weapon clattering to the deck. She retrieved the blade just as Malir growled in unrestrained fury and lurched to his feet, outstretched hands grasping for her throat.

Without thinking, Yar stepped into his attack and sank the blade into the soft flesh just above the neckline of his chest armor. Malir's reaction was immediate, his eyes widening in shock and renewed agony, reaching for the knife even as Yar pulled it free. He coughed and spat, blood appearing around the edges of his mouth as his hands moved to the wound in his neck. Staggering backward a few steps, he crashed to the floor of the hangar bay, his muscled body going limp as he lost consciousness.

Panting and feeling the ache of stressed muscles as she fought to bring her breathing back under control, Yar could only stand with her hands on her knees, gripping the huge ugly knife that still dripped with the blood of her adversary. The urge to kill the now helpless Malir was all but overpowering. For the briefest of moments, as she looked upon him and noted his chest rising and falling in a weak rhythm, she saw not a Cardassian soldier but rather one of the countless thugs and tormentors who had pursued her throughout her tortured youth. She had fought several such enemies on Tur-kana IV, and her memories were haunted by those few instances where she had been forced to kill in defense of her own life.

No, she reminded herself. *This isn't that place, and you're not that frightened girl anymore.* While it would be so easy to finish Malir, and though she might even be able to rationalize that act after a fashion, Tasha Yar knew that there was at least one person who would never approve, one whose opinion and judgment mattered more to her than those of anyone else in her entire life. Were she to obey every primal instinct currently screaming for vengeance, she was certain she would never again be able to look Jean-Luc Picard in the eye. What would he expect from her, here and now?

Yar sighed as she loosened her grip on Malir's knife, the clatter it made against the deck echoing across the *Kovmar*'s hangar bay.

For the first time in uncounted hours, Crusher allowed the tension to flee her tired muscles, slumping in her seat and making no attempt to keep her worn body from rocking along with the maneuvering of the *Jefferies* as Yar piloted the craft out of the *Kovmar*'s landing bay and into open space.

"I hope this isn't the last time we meet, Beverly," said the image of Ialona Daret as displayed on the helm's central viewer. *"And when we do, let us both hope it is to celebrate peace between our people."*

"I'm looking forward to that, Ialona," Crusher said, offering a weary smile. "Thank you again, for everything."

On the viewer, Daret nodded. *"And to you, and Lieutenant Yar. Thanks to you both, Gul Edal will likely make a full recovery, as will Glinn Malir."*

Crusher nodded at the prognosis. Though bedridden and weakened from his ordeal, the *Kovmar*'s commander had already dispatched his own thanks to Crusher and Yar. Although brief, Malir's failed mutiny attempt had resulted in several dozen injuries and claimed three lives on board the Cardassian ship. Crusher and Yar both had assisted Daret in the treatment of the wounded.

"Until that time comes, then," Daret said, nodding, *"safe journey, my friends."*

"And to you, Ialona," Crusher replied before the communication ended. A moment later, the stars before them stretched to multicolored streaks and Crusher felt a shift in the deck beneath her feet as Yar accelerated the *Jefferies* to warp speed.

Turning in her seat, the doctor studied the portable monitor that relayed to her the status of the three stasis units, each bearing its precious cargo. Crusher, with Daret's help, had succeeded in stabilizing all three patients for transport until they could receive extensive treatment at a Starfleet medical facility. Commander Spires would receive bionic transplants for the limbs he had lost, but it appeared that Ensign Weglash's lungs would heal on their own and not require replacement. T'Lan would likely have the hardest road to recovery, though Crusher was thankful that extensive brain damage had been avoided.

For the moment at least, there was nothing else Crusher could do except close her eyes and rest.

Who'd have thought this damned chair could feel so comfortable?

From her left, she heard Yar say, "Still with me, Doctor?"

"Barely, but yes," Crusher replied, not bothering to open her eyes. "And, you know you can call me Beverly, right?"

"Well, Beverly," Yar said, and this time the doctor heard the humor in her voice, "the *Enterprise* has been allowed into Cardassian space, thanks to our new friends back there, so we'll have a much shorter trip this time. Our rendezvous point is less than two hours away, if that helps any."

"Actually, it does," Crusher said. "Thanks."

There was a pause before Yar said, "It's good to hear that Gul Edal will be okay."

"All thanks to you," the doctor replied, opening her tired eyes and straightening her posture in her chair. Looking to Yar, she added, "Getting him to the shuttle and the organ stimulator made all the difference. How does it feel, saving your first patient?"

Yar tried but failed to hide a satisfied smile. Nodding, she said, "I'll definitely be stepping up the field medicine training for my people, that's for sure." Her smile turned mischievous as she added, "I'm thinking I might also add something about the tactical applications of exoscalpels and other medical equipment. That was some fast thinking on your part, I have to say. In fact, I was amazed at how well you handled yourself during the whole incident." She paused a moment, and her expression faltered as she added, "I have to admit I had my doubts when things started to go bad. I wasn't sure how you'd react."

"Well, I had my own doubts," Crusher replied, "but not anymore. Jean-Luc was right about you."

It took physical effort for Crusher not to smile at Yar's shocked expression. "The captain's talked to you about me?"

The doctor nodded. "A few times, most recently just before we left," she said. "I wasn't sure you were up for something requiring this kind of finesse, but he told me not to worry. He's never doubted you, not once." Leaning closer, she added, "And not for nothing, but impressing Jean-Luc Picard is no easy feat."

Yar was silent as she seemed to let the affirmation sink in. "Thank you, Beverly."

Closing her eyes again for a moment, Crusher wondered if their little adventure would do anything to further Federation-Cardassian ties as both sides lobbied for peace. The cynic in her said it was unlikely, but the healer and romantic in her wanted to believe that such acts of bravery and compassion might be just enough to make two societies look differently at one another and act for the greater good. After all, it had been more than sufficient for two individuals to alter their own perceptions.

Reaching out, Crusher tapped Yar on the forearm. "By the way, I'm still owed a shift on the bridge. Think you can handle it?"

Yar actually laughed at that. "Absolutely. I do have one request, however."

"What's that?" Crusher asked, her brow knitting in momentary confusion.

"Please, no more personal messages when you're on duty."

REDSHIFT

Richard C. White

Historian's note:
This tale is set during the second season of
Star Trek: The Next Generation.

RICHARD C. WHITE

Richard C. White's first *Star Trek* story, "Echoes of Coventry," was released in May 2006 as a part of the *Starfleet Corps of Engineers* series.

Other works include the novel *Gauntlet: Dark Legacy #1—Paths of Evil,* which was released by ibooks, inc., and became one of their bestselling tie-in titles for 2004. In addition, Rich contributed to the *Ultimate Hulk* anthology (Byron Preiss/Marvel Comics) in 1998, co-writing *Assault on Avengers Mansion* with Steve Roman. Additionally, he has a short story, "The Price of Conviction," coming out in the 2008 *Dr. Who* anthology, *The Quality of Leadership.*

After graduating from the University of Central Missouri in 1982 with a degree in medieval history, Rich spent fifteen years in the army as an analyst, a linguist, and a cryptanalyst, which helped him land the *Corps of Engineers* job writing about Bart Faulwell, who is also an analyst, a linguist, and a cryptanalyst. He now works as a tech writer in the wilds of corporate America.

He greatly appreciates the support of his very patient wife, Joni, and daughter, Katie. His four cats are reasonably supportive, as long as this writing stuff doesn't get in the way of their feeding times.

"LOOK, DOCTOR PULASKI, I'M NOT TRYING TO BE UNCOOPERA-tive, but you're not giving me much choice. You're asking an awful lot of the system."

Katherine Pulaski took a deep breath to regain her composure and stared at the curly-haired man standing across the transporter console from her. "Once again, Chief, it's not that difficult. I realize that I've been on the *Enterprise* only a couple of months, but these are changes I want to implement. As chief medical officer, I have that privilege."

She watched as Chief O'Brien ran a hand through his hair. His recalcitrance was infuriating, but instead of giving in to impatience, she shifted to her best bedside manner. "I want to conduct an exercise with my emergency medical response team and I can't accomplish that without your cooperation. The team is scattered throughout the ship. I need you to lock onto them, wherever they are, and beam them into sickbay."

"I understand your request, Doctor. It won't be easy, but that's not what's worrying me."

Pulaski pushed on as if Chief O'Brien hadn't said a word. "Once you have transported them to sickbay, start your timer. When it reaches five minutes, lock onto them again and transport them to the various parts of shuttlebay 2 to deal with a simulated emergency. It's vital they arrive at their designated positions. I'll be down there to grade their reactions and time."

Chief O'Brien ran his hand through his hair one more time and tried to step in front of the tsunami. "And I still stand by my objection, Doctor. A site-to-site transport takes a lot of energy out of the ship's reserves. Two of them back to back is just begging for trouble, especially one that requires so many separate sets of coordinates. You realize the danger they're going to be in if anything goes wrong? I might not be able to recover their signal in time."

Pulaski patted him on the arm. "That's why I wanted you on the job. It'll be up to you to make certain nothing goes wrong."

"Oh, no. No, you're not laying that on me. I think Lieutenant La Forge should be consulted before we go any farther."

"Chief, I realize my dislike for these contraptions is well-known, but I do understand how they work. I have run series of simulations, and the energy requirements of this exercise fall within an acceptable range of *Enterprise*'s resources. There is no reason to bother Lieutenant La Forge. If it makes you feel better, I hereby assume full responsibility as chief medical officer for the entire exercise. If anything goes wrong, which it won't, you won't be blamed."

She heard him mutter, "Famous last words," but she turned and left before he had a chance to raise another objection.

Reaching shuttlebay 2, she went to a pre-positioned monitor screen and signaled O'Brien to begin the exercise. She glanced at her display and noted the decrease in ship's power as the transporter chief worked his magic. Another section of the monitor showed O'Brien gnawing his lower lip as he made adjustments on the console as he tracked down the last member of the EMR team. She admired his technique, keeping part of the team in stasis while he locked onto the others before transporting the entire team into sickbay at once.

The team materialized in various positions and states of dress. Pulaski hadn't told them what time the exercise would kick off, simply that it wouldn't be during their regular duty hours. She was pleased to see how they reacted to their sudden appearance in sickbay. She focused the monitor to follow them once they realized what had happened. The monitor didn't have an audio channel set up, but she could watch as they gathered their equipment and changed into proper uniforms.

Outstanding. Only two weeks of training and they're already starting to work like a team. If everything goes well, I may invite Captain Picard to watch their next exercise. I think he'll be impressed.

Checking the chronometer, she was even more pleased to see them assembling near the doorway to sickbay in less than three minutes. *Fantastic, shaved thirty seconds off their best time. I have to put something in Technician Johannson's file for her work as the team leader.*

Watching the monitor, she saw Chief O'Brien begin preparations for the second stage of the exercise. She glanced at the sensors she'd set up around the shuttlebay. They would determine how accurately O'Brien could position her people. She knew he was a wizard with the transporter, but she was grading him along with her team. At exactly five minutes, he engaged the transporter again and the EMR team disappeared into a flickering haze of lights. Pulaski smiled, visualizing the successful conclusion, when the alarm on her monitor went off and the shuttlebay's lights began flickering.

What the hell? She saw Chief O'Brien on the monitor, his hands flying over the controls of the transporter as the lights flickered in the transporter room also.

She turned and rushed out of the bay. *I need to get to the transporter room. He'll try to divert them to his location to save power.* Rushing down the corridor, she headed toward what she hoped was a working turbolift. It took a couple of tries, but after some agonizing moments, she was able to reach the main transporter room's deck.

Crap, this can't be happening. There should have been plenty of power. What went wrong?

She leaped out of the turbolift as soon as it stopped and rushed down the hallway. The lights began to stabilize as she entered the room. Lieutenant Wallace had joined O'Brien and the two were manipulating the transporter controls as fast as they could. O'Brien gave the transporter console one last tap with his left hand, and a familiar whine filled the room. Sparkling lights coalesced into her team and they slumped to the floor, stunned from being held in transit for so long.

Finally able to take action, Pulaski rushed to the dais and gave them a quick going-over, relief and frustration warring for control. *Disoriented and weak, but nothing life threatening. When I find out what happened, someone's going to get a piece of my mind.*

She turned to thank O'Brien for his work, but the words died unsaid when she spotted the ship's first officer, Will Riker. He stood by the door, his face set in a familiar scowl. Nearby, Geordi La Forge talked to a nervous Chief O'Brien. The ship's newly promoted chief engineer was upset, but he was following Riker's lead at the moment.

"Doctor Pulaski, if you would be so good as to accompany us. I believe you have an appointment in the conference lounge . . . right now."

Damn. Oh, well. Can't say I didn't earn this one. "Very well, Commander. I'll be happy to join you as soon as someone arrives to take over here."

Just then, a med team came rushing in. *How's that for irony?* She took a few seconds to ensure no one on her team was seriously injured and then followed La Forge and a smiling Riker out of the transporter room back toward the turbolift. *The least he could do is not look so bloody happy that I'm in trouble again.*

Pulaski looked around the room and spotted Captain Picard sitting in his usual place at the head of the conference table. From the look on his face, she anticipated this would go as most of her conversations with the captain had gone—badly. Taking her seat, she noticed that Riker and La Forge sat on either side of Picard. *If I didn't know better, I'd think this was a court-martial.*

The captain leaned forward, resting his elbows on the table and bringing his fingers together in an inverted V. "Doctor Pulaski, do you have any idea what your stunt today has cost the *Enterprise*?"

"With all due respect, Captain, I would hardly call training medical personnel to respond to an emergency a *stunt*."

"May I point out to the good doctor the problems your *exercise* caused? Problems, I'd like to add, that could have been avoided with a simple call down to engineering to ensure that power would be available. In fact, did not Chief O'Brien suggest contacting Lieutenant La Forge before you began the exercise?"

Pulaski paused before responding. "I believe he might have

made such a suggestion. However, the simulations I prepared showed that the drain of two site-to-site transports would be well within the *Enterprise*'s capabilities."

The young chief engineer leaned forward, adjusting the VISOR that covered his eyes. "And it would have, if today had been a normal day. But we took several power couplings off-line for standard maintenance. If I had known, I could have put that maintenance off until your exercise was complete. But, since you didn't inform anyone of your plans, we couldn't support you."

Pulaski leaned forward preparing to speak, but Riker cut her off. "I know what you're going to say, and you're right. You have the right and obligation to train your people as you see fit. In fact, from what Chief O'Brien told Lieutenant La Forge, there's merit in your plans. That isn't the issue. What is the issue is that one of the *Enterprise*'s senior officers failed to coordinate her training with the rest of the staff."

Riker leaned forward, tapping a finger on the table as he began reciting. "It was only because of Chief O'Brien's skill and Lieutenant La Forge's team restoring power when they did that we didn't lose your team today. Still, several scientific experiments on board have been compromised and may have to be scrapped. In addition, ship's sensors were damaged by the power fluctuation. We'll be without our long-range sensors for at least another three hours. Also, there was a spike in the warp core temperature that will force us to put in at a repair facility as soon as this mission is over."

As Riker paused for a breath, Captain Picard took over. "Doctor Pulaski, this is not the first time you've disregarded ship's protocol since you came on board. I've been inclined to overlook some of your indiscretions due to your unfamiliarity with the *Enterprise*. However, while you make a fine replacement for Doctor Crusher as a chief medical officer, you do not appear to be making any effort to fit into shipboard routine and insist on doing things your own way. Well, that stops as of today. I *cannot* overlook this behavior any longer, especially when doing so puts members of my crew in jeopardy. Do I make myself clear, Doctor?"

Pulaski's mental claws flexed, but she could tell that this was neither the time nor the place to have this conversation. Forcing herself to remain calm, she held her tongue and nodded.

"Thank you. Doctor, Mister La Forge, that will be all. Number

One, I'd like to talk to you about—" Picard looked up when a sudden chirp interrupted him. He keyed a small switch on his table. "This is Picard."

Data's familiar voice filled the room. *"Captain, could you and Commander Riker please come to the bridge? There is something here I believe you would be interested in seeing."*

"Can't he just patch the feed through to here?"

"Actually, Doctor, we are having problems with the sensors and are unable to provide a visual of the phenomenon at this time." The android's matter-of-fact reply did nothing to tone down the accusatory look Riker shot her. *"However, in this instance, it would make little difference. That is why I have requested Captain Picard's presence."*

"On my way, Data. Come on, Number One, let's go see this phenomenon, whatever it is."

"Right behind you, sir."

As the two senior officers left, Geordi looked over at Pulaski. "You were really trying to do two site-to-site transfers involving eleven separate sets of coordinates?" A big smile crossed his face. "I have to give you credit, Doctor. When you do something, you go all out, don't you?"

Pulaski stopped and stared at Geordi. He sounded almost envious. Giving him a confused look, she sat back down. "That was the idea. The scenario said a shuttlecraft had been on an emergency approach to the *Enterprise* and crashed into the shuttlebay before the inertial dampeners could halt its forward progress. There would be multiple casualties, debris, and hazardous material, so they couldn't transport in as a group. I was testing Chief O'Brien as much as I was testing my team."

"I get it. A worst-case scenario forces your team to improvise even before they arrive. I like it."

She frowned, letting her confusion show. "I'm not getting something here. A few minutes ago, you were ready to hang me by my ankles over the warp core. Now you're showing an inordinate amount of interest in my exercise. Did I miss something?"

La Forge laughed and adjusted his VISOR. "No, not really, Doc. It's true I was pretty hot when I found you in the transporter room, but I've been thinking your exercise has some potential." He leaned forward in his chair. "So, how did you go about choosing your response team?"

"First thing, I called for volunteers. An emergency medical response team isn't a place for someone who's not gung-ho enough to volunteer. After that, I went through their files, trying to find people with a wide variety of experiences and interests besides being a medical technician. We're going to be putting them in high-stress situations where there may not be time to get further instructions. They have to be able to think on their feet and have the courage to act on their instincts."

"I see, so you were looking for energetic, independent thinkers, coolheaded, yet with a passion to get right to the heart of the matter without being distracted."

"By George, I think he's got it."

Geordi grinned at her. "I've been trying to think of a way to get my damage control teams into position faster, and I think you may have hit upon something. Your demonstration today gave me some ideas, even if it didn't go as well as it could have."

"Oh, really, Lieutenant? Do tell."

Geordi shook his head. "Uh-uh. Nope. I've got a germ of an idea, but I want a chance to test it first. I've played poker with Commander Riker enough to know not to show my cards too early."

"I can't say I've ever had the privilege."

"They're still getting used to you. If we hadn't taken our trip to Victorian London a few weeks ago, I'd still be trying to figure you out too. You're a hard lady to get to know."

Pulaski blinked, shocked at his outlandish notion, when the communicator chirped again. Geordi reached over and tapped it. "La Forge here."

Captain Picard's voice came over the system. *"Lieutenant La Forge, is Doctor Pulaski still there with you?"*

"Yes she is, Captain."

"Excellent. I need the two of you to come up to the bridge."

"Right away, sir. La Forge out." He looked over at Pulaski. "Let's not keep the man waiting."

Pulaski nodded. "No, I think being punctual might be a pleasant change."

* * *

Pulaski and La Forge stepped onto the bridge just as Data was finishing his report. "We cannot be sure of the craft's exact location because of the sensor anomalies. All we can state with certainty is that it appears to be matching our speed and running a course parallel to ours."

Riker gave Pulaski a dour look as he phrased his next question. "Would the sensor anomalies have anything to do with the power fluctuations we had earlier today?"

"Possibly, but unlikely, Commander. It appears the craft has a means of disguising itself from our sensors."

Pulaski moved forward to get a better look at the viewscreen. The ship, if you could call it that, seemed archaic compared to the sweeping lines of the *Enterprise*-D. *Whoever's out there is either very brave or very stupid.*

She turned to face the android occupying the helm. "So, Data, do you have any ideas on how that machine out there flies?" Out of habit, she mispronounced his name, shortening the first *a*.

The android didn't let it slip by, either. "Data."

"Excuse me?"

"My name. It is Data."

"Oh, yes, my mistake. Well, do you have an answer?"

"Not at this time. There are a number of possible propulsion systems that might explain how they are able to maneuver through space. However, most of those are more advanced systems, some even beyond Federation technology." He pointed to the screen. "They appear to be several generations behind our current technological level."

She sighed before continuing. "Data, if you're not sure, you can say so."

"I thought I just did, Doctor."

The *Enterprise*'s tactical officer broke in. "I agree with Commander Data, Doctor. The sensors are not the source of the problem. We have been attempting to hail the craft ever since we began visual observations. There has been no response."

Picard turned in his seat and faced the large Klingon warrior standing behind him. "How would you rate the level of the threat from our visitor, Mister Worf?"

The question seemed to fluster Worf. "I . . . cannot rate our opponent, sir. When it failed to respond to our hails, I attempted to achieve weapons lock on the ship. . . . Our weapon systems do not register the vessel."

"A weapons lock? Do you believe that was the wisest course of action, Mister Worf?"

"Sir, it was strictly a precautionary measure. It may not have been the most diplomatic way to get their attention, but the safety of the ship is utmost in my mind."

"Very well, Mister Worf. But you say the ship's weapons do not see the other ship?"

"No, sir, they do not. I have run several diagnostics to verify the readings. Our systems are functional; they simply tell me there is nothing out there."

Pulaski turned to face the large Klingon. "Don't be overreliant on your sensors, Mister Worf." She snuck a glance at Data. "No matter how smart they are, they're still just machines. I don't believe the ship out there is a ghost any more than I believe I can walk through this railing. It's more likely they've discovered a cloaking method without the huge power drain that the Romulans suffer. We'll just have to trust our own senses instead of letting machines think for us."

"I believe we should take the doctor up on her suggestion," Picard said as he rose from his chair. "I want all staff personnel to report to the observation lounge in fifteen minutes with whatever data we can discover about our uninvited guest. I'll be in my ready room until then. You have the bridge, Number One."

Pulaski waited on Deck 12 for the turbolift to arrive. She didn't know any more about the situation than when she'd left the bridge. Without any knowledge of the inhabitants of the strange ship, there was little the medical staff could do. At least it had given her time to check in with Doctor Selar and reassure herself the EMR team was all right. In fact, she'd overheard Technicians Johannson and Tarses discussing ways to pre-position their equipment for the next exercise.

Returning to the observation lounge, she took her usual seat. *I hope the captain's not counting on me to pull a rabbit out of my hat. Maybe one of the others found something to give me a clue where to start researching.*

As usual, the first to report was Data. "With the sensors still off-line, we have been forced to rely on visual observation. The ship appears to be a semispheroid shape, approximately three hundred meters in diameter. The lower quarter tapers down to a flat bottom, which suggests it is able to land, although whether or not it is capable of surviving entering an atmosphere is unknown. Given its size and shape, we estimate there are probably no more than one hundred crew members, assuming they are humanoid-sized."

Lieutenant La Forge stepped in seamlessly, as if Data and he had practiced before the meeting. "There is no apparent means of propulsion and nothing to indicate where its engineering section might be. I've checked with Chief O'Brien, and he's unable to get a transporter lock on the other ship, either. We have no idea how it flies or what it uses for fuel. Based on the external makeup of the ship, though, it appears to be several generations behind current Federation technology."

"Very good, Mister Data, Mister La Forge. Counselor, do you have anything for us?"

Deanna Troi turned to face the captain before she spoke in a clear, measured voice. "I have been unable to sense much from the other ship. The distance could be too great, or perhaps their minds are too different from ours. I do sense feelings of curiosity and envy from time to time, but I can't be sure."

A smile spread across Riker's face at the idea of meeting new alien life. "Curiosity is a good thing. We're certainly curious about them."

"Indeed, Number One."

"Perhaps we could take one of the shuttles and attempt to reach them, since our sensors and communications seem ineffective. Their technology can mask them from our sensors, but they don't seem to be able to fool our eyes."

The large Klingon squirmed in his seat. Pulaski could tell he wasn't happy with Riker's suggestion, but it wasn't his way to tell a senior officer he was wrong. She started to say something to give Worf a chance, but Picard beat her to it.

"Mister Worf, I believe you have some feelings on this subject?"

"Captain, I believe it would be unwise to approach this ship without more data. The curiosity the counselor senses could be that of a warrior sizing up an unknown enemy. To send a shuttlecraft over without the *Enterprise* able to defend it makes me . . . uncomfortable."

"I'll certainly take your concerns into consideration, Mister Worf. Mister Crusher, anything?"

"The ship seems to be matching the *Enterprise*'s heading and speed, sir. We have been keeping it under observation from several points on the ship and have pooled our observations. It appears to be maintaining a distance of five hundred kilometers. I conducted a small experiment by adjusting our speed at random as well as making minor course corrections. Their ship may not look like much, but it's nimble. They were able to match us, maneuver for maneuver, without difficulty."

Pulaski decided to go ahead with her report since everyone else was finished. "The medical staff is standing by in case we're needed, Captain. However, with no further information, we're reduced to waiting like everyone else."

Picard frowned at her, but nodded. "It seems we all are stymied by a lack of information about our visitors. Mister Crusher, when we return to the bridge, move us to within one hundred fifty kilometers of the other ship. Number One, prepare a shuttlecraft to investigate but ensure its crew understands they are to take no provocative acts. Mister Worf, continue attempts to make contact with them before the shuttle is launched. Everyone else continue your observations of this ship and try to get me some answers. Meeting adjourned."

Various conversations broke out as the bridge officers began filtering out of the room. Will looked over at Geordi and Troi. "Anyone up for poker after we get off shift?"

"Thought you'd never ask," La Forge said. "I need to make up for the last game. I never thought you had that third queen."

Riker grinned as the door slid shut. "I know . . ."

Pulaski stood in the back of the room, staring at the door. *This is just not my day. My exercise was spoiled by routine maintenance, and now I'm actually angry because Kyle Riker's kid didn't invite me to a game of cards. I think I'm going to prescribe some time in Ten-Forward for myself. A little unwinding is just what the doctor ordered.*

Pulaski felt the energy of the room wash over her as she entered the maelstrom known as Ten-Forward. The lounge was a favorite hangout for the *Enterprise* crew and the enigmatic El-Aurian known as Guinan ensured the place ran smoothly. Before Pulaski could pull up a chair at the bar, Guinan placed a smoldering blue drink in front of her.

Pulaski looked at the wavy glass with suspicion. "Okay, I give up. Am I supposed to drink this or use a fire extinguisher on it?"

"Give it a try. It's the perfect thing for a day that's been less than perfect."

Deciding Guinan had been right more often than not, Pulaski took a sip and a smile crossed her face. It had just enough kick to get her attention but not enough to detract from the taste. She raised her glass in a salute to Guinan and decided to walk around the room.

The noise and random conversations helped her relax and gave her a protective cocoon to think about all that had happened. She stopped in front of a viewport and admired the changing starfield outside the ship, focusing on a spectacular nebula off in the distance. *I have to admit, I may have sold our young lieutenant short. Mister La Forge may not have as much experience as some of the chief engineers I've worked with, but his hunches are pretty darn good.*

"Impressive, isn't it?"

Pulaski turned to see Guinan standing there with a fresh drink. She started to wave it off, but Guinan slipped the glass into her hand before she knew what had happened. She gave Guinan a smile and nodded. "I wonder how long ago that star exploded. It's strange, seeing something so beautiful and realizing it may have happened thousands of years ago."

"The past has a funny way of finding us when we least expect it. The question is, do we learn from it, or do we make the same mistakes again and again?"

Pulaski gave her a puzzled look as Guinan excused herself and disappeared into another section of Ten-Forward. She looked at the nebula again, making out the bright spot at the center. It was hard to imagine that death could produce such a majestic sight.

She started to place her drink down when she noted Wesley Crusher standing behind her, nervously shifting his weight from one foot to the other. "Is there something you wanted, Mister Crusher?"

"No, nothing really. We never had a chance to sit and talk, so I thought I'd come over. I mean, we don't know each other and . . ."

"Mister Crusher, I don't mean to be blunt, but why would we get to know each other? It's not like we run in the same social circles on this ship. In fact, I expect to be the chief medical officer of the *Enterprise* long after you leave for the academy. If you could do me a favor and take the tin man with you, I'd appreciate it."

Wesley's face clouded over at her last remark. "What have you got against Data? This is the second time today you've had to get in a dig on him."

"I don't have anything against it. It's obviously a capable machine since the captain allows it on the bridge, but it's just a machine. It does what it's programmed to do and nothing else. It may be able to perform thousands of calculations a second, but it can't get a hunch, make a leap in logic, just 'know' something's right. It'd never cut it as a doctor, that's for sure. You'll never see a sickbay turned over to a machine."

"I think you're selling Data short. There's more to him than meets the eye."

Pulaski eyed the young man with amusement. "You'd have to prove that to me."

Wesley pushed on. "I just thought I should get to know you, since you're my mother's replacement. I've spent a lot of time down in starship sickbays. Most of the people I knew growing up were the doctors and nurses."

Pulaski lowered herself into a seat and took another sip of her drink. Looking up, she gave him a wan smile. "Ah, yes, the joys of being a child of Starfleet. Here today, gone on a glorious new adventure tomorrow. But you raise an interesting question. Why didn't you go into the medical field?"

Wesley eased into the chair next to her. "Couple of reasons, actually. I've heard so much about my dad, I wanted to follow in his footsteps and be on the bridge. Besides, it's tough enough being Beverly Crusher's son. Everyone sees Mom in me and expects me to act like her. It'd be even worse if I were a doctor. You understand how it is."

"I do?"

Wesley gave her a funny look. "You had to have noticed. Mom was popular with the whole crew. She's got to be a hard act to follow. I admire your self-confidence, Doctor Pulaski. I don't think I'd want that kind of shadow hanging over me."

Pulaski set the glass down and tried to keep her voice even. "Mister Crusher, if other people on this ship are comparing me to your mother, they're making a mistake. I am not Beverly Crusher. I never will be her and I don't have any desire to become her. If members of this crew can't accept me because they 'see your mother's shadow,' then that's their loss."

Wesley leaned back in his chair, caught off guard by the vehemence of her statement. A mixture of sadness and surprise was etched on his face. "I'm sorry, Doctor Pulaski, I didn't mean—"

"To make her feel uncomfortable or unwanted?" Guinan's voice broke in, gently separating the two and drawing their attention to her. She placed a hand on Wesley's shoulder. "The best of intentions don't always pardon hasty words. I know you meant to give Doctor Pulaski a compliment, Wes, but you've really got to work on your delivery."

She inclined her head toward Pulaski before continuing. "She's content to blaze her own trails and to be recognized for her own work. Isn't that the real reason you didn't consider medicine? You're afraid others wouldn't push you as hard or hold you to the same standards because they're friends or colleagues of hers. You want to make a mark all your own. Just like Doctor Pulaski."

Pulaski watched Wesley's face flush as he realized Guinan was closer to the truth than he wanted to admit. She felt Guinan's eyes on her and turned to face the bartender. "Also, some people should learn to accept a compliment without looking for a fight." Before Pulaski could reply, Guinan took Wesley's arm in hers. "Come with me. I have a new concoction to test and you look like the perfect volunteer."

Pulaski watched the two disappear into the swirling crowd. She picked up her drink and stared out at the nebula, her thoughts troubled.

Later, as she entered sickbay, she suddenly lurched to one side. *I'm going to have to have a talk with Guinan. Two of those shouldn't affect me this much.* The blaring of a klaxon told her there was more to her unsteadiness than mere alcohol. The flashing red light in the corridor confirmed her suspicions. Something was going on and she needed information.

She reached the companel just as it started beeping at her. "Sickbay, Pulaski here."

She was surprised to hear Mister Worf's voice. *"Doctor Pulaski, the alien ship shifted directions before we could react and rammed into the ship near engineering. There are casualties being reported on Decks 32 and 33."*

"Rammed the ship?"

"I cannot explain how it happened. It was inside the ship's deflector shields before we had an opportunity to raise them. Whatever technology they are using to cloak themselves seems to give them an advantage over our eyes also."

Now that's a nasty thought. "Understood, Mister Worf. Deploying medical teams to Decks 32 and 33." Motioning to Doctor Martin, she signaled for him to head to the auxiliary sickbay in the stardrive section. If engineering was the target of the mystery ship, having a med team in close proximity made good sense.

Flipping the switch on the communicator, she gave a command opening a channel to all her off-duty personnel. "Med teams 1 and 2, report to sickbay. Med teams 3 and 4, report to auxiliary. Med team 5, stand by." Turning to the current staff, she smiled and tried to keep her voice calm. "You heard Mister Worf's report. They'll try to keep us informed. Taylor, Prender, I want you two to go through supplies. Replicate anything we're short on. Nurse Temple, call up a complete list of all the current engineering personnel. Cross-reference with the medical database and make a note of any allergies, special needs, or specific treatments. Peterson, monitor the communications channels. If you hear anything that might require us to react, let me know stat."

She acknowledged the chorus of responses and turned to keep an eye on the communicator, waiting for Martin to call. *Well, that'll keep them busy. They may think I'm nuts ordering all these checks, but as long as they're busy, they won't have time to get nervous.*

I hate the waiting. At least on the bridge, you have an idea of what's happening. Here, we just sit.

As the minutes ticked by, the two off-duty med teams filtered into the room. Pulaski spotted Nurse Ogawa coming in just as Martin checked in over the comm.

"So far, Katherine, most of the injuries have been minor, a few sprained wrists or bumps on the head from when the two ships collided."

Pulaski felt herself relax at the report. "I'd say we got off pretty well if that's the worst of it."

Doctor Martin's voice took on an excited tone. *"Well, I can't swear to that. I just saw a bunch of security guys running toward engineering. Not sure what's going on, but I'm going to see if there's anything we can do to help."*

"Is someone there to watch sickbay if you're out?"

"The other med teams are here now. If anything's going on, the quicker I can treat them, the better."

"Point taken, Doctor. Make sure you don't take any unnecessary chances."

"No worry there. Mrs. Martin didn't raise dumb children, Doctor. That's why security has more rigorous fitness standards than mere doctors."

Pulaski shook her head. *Martin, one of these days your desire to be on the front lines is going to get you killed. No one can question your self-confidence, though, can they?*

That thought brought her earlier conversation with Wesley back into focus. Was it really confidence that drove her, or was it sheer stubbornness? What kept her from accepting help when it was offered?

Her introspection was interrupted when she felt a shudder run through the ship. "Martin, what the hell was that?"

Martin didn't reply at first, but Pulaski could hear someone talking to him in the background. When he came back on, his voice was rushed. *"There's been some kind of explosion in engineering. Not sure what caused it yet, but it was powerful. You may need to send more people up here. I'll let you know when damage control gives me the word."*

Pulaski motioned med team 2 over and ordered them to report to auxiliary. She turned back to the communicator when the sounds of a disturbance drew her attention. "Martin, what's going on down there?" The sounds of fighting could be heard in the background.

"The aliens breached the hull in engineering and there's a fight going on . . . Watch out, Tim! Holy— I never even saw—"

"Martin? Martin? Answer me, Martin." Pulaski smashed down

the communicator button. "Pulaski to bridge. Captain, what the hell's going on?"

Captain Picard's voice sounded unruffled on the communicator in contrast to the chaos in engineering. *"The unknown ship has attached itself to the* Enterprise, *Doctor, and is attacking engineering. We're dispatching security, but our intruder control system was damaged in the explosion. We're assessing the situation."*

"I've lost contact with Doctor Martin and one of my med teams down there."

A familiar, but somewhat frantic voice broke into the conversation. *"Captain, La Forge here. The aliens have taken over main engineering and are spreading out. I can't explain what I'm seeing, but they're able to strike before we can put up a defense. Our weapons don't seem to do any damage to them, either."*

Pulaski frowned, cut in. "Lieutanant, this is Doctor Pulaski. Do they seem immune to the phasers?"

"No, Doctor. It's more like the beams pass right through them. They're solid beings, though. I've seen them carrying boxes of equipment back to their ship."

"Scavengers." Picard's reaction was more comment than question.

"Looks like it, sir. I haven't seen them use any weapons, but they're stronger than they look. I don't think anyone's been seriously injured, but I can't swear to it. I managed to hide, but I don't know how long I have before they notice me."

"Where are you located, Mister La Forge?"

"I'm on a catwalk above Deck 33, looking down into main engineering. They're concentrating on going through our stores."

"Stay put, Mister La Forge. Security is en route to your area and is sealing off the rest of the ship."

"Understood, Captain. La Forge out."

Pulaski motioned for Nurse Ogawa to join her. "I'm going with team 2 to the auxiliary sickbay. I'm not certain what's going on, but we need to beef up the medical staff aft. You're in charge here."

"But what if something goes wrong, Doctor? We can't afford to lose both Doctor Martin and you."

Pulaski bit back a sharp retort, recognizing the concern on Nurse Ogawa's face. "It's not an optimal solution, but there are casualties in engineering. The quicker medical support gets there, the better off they'll be. Contact Doctor Selar and have her report to main sickbay as quickly as possible. If the intruders break through the security perimeter, have her lock down all the sickbays to prevent them from getting in." She patted Ogawa on the shoulder and then turned and told med team 2 to follow her.

The turbolift trip from Deck 12 to Deck 34 seemed to take longer than usual, but Pulaski chalked that up to nerves. As the doors to the turbolift opened, they were met by a small contingent of security personnel.

"Doctor Pulaski, what are you doing here?"

"I'm taking a med team down to sickbay and getting ready to deal with the casualties, Ensign Carson. May we have an escort?"

The red-haired ensign blushed and motioned for two members of her squad to follow the doctor aft. Pulaski and her team made their way into sickbay, while the security team took positions on either side of the door.

Pulaski began assessing the situation. "All right, folks. I want a status report and I want it yesterday. What's been going on since Doctor Martin left? Who was in charge? Status of casualties? Come on, people, I don't have all day."

The barrage of questions shook the personnel in sickbay out of their shock. The recent arrivals began assessing the patients while the original teams hurried over to Pulaski and began filling her in on the current situation.

"The intruders are being reported from Decks 32 to 35. From what security told us, there's no apparent pattern to their attack. It's like they're just wandering about aimlessly."

"That's not too hard to figure out," she replied, trying to remember the name of the medical technician in front of her. "I would guess they've never been on a *Galaxy*-class vessel before. They have no idea where anything important is kept. Since they're looting engineering, it's reasonable to assume they're doing the same everywhere they can reach."

"But that doesn't make any sense. We could make whatever they needed with our replicators, as long as we have raw materials. There's no reason to attack us to get supplies."

"Look, you know that and I know that, but I don't believe they know that. We haven't been able to communicate with them for whatever reason. They don't know what we can or can't do. Worrying about how to deal with them is the captain's job. Our job is to deal with the injured. When security takes control of engineering, we'll be right behind them to render aid to both sides."

A sudden shout in the corridor drew Pulaski's attention. Before she could move, the familiar sound of a phaser being discharged rang out, followed by the sound of a body striking the wall hard. The door to the sickbay opened and shut on its own. Then, before the disbelieving eyes of the medical staff, one of the intruders walked through the closed door as if it weren't there.

The intruder appeared reptilian to Pulaski and her staff. Its dark purple eyes stared at the various people in the room, its lack of pupils making its already inhuman features even more pronounced. With an air of extreme confidence, it seemed to dismiss them as unworthy opponents as it walked through the room.

One of the orderlies dove at the intruder as it passed, but to everyone's surprise, he passed straight through the alien's body and slammed headfirst into the wall. Another technician rushed toward the alien only to fly backward, landing awkwardly on the floor. He grimaced in pain and wrapped his arms around his chest.

Pulaski grabbed her medical tricorder and headed toward him. *Probably has a couple of broken ribs from the way he's holding his side.* Then, to her surprise, the alien raised its arms and made a shoving motion at the air, before turning toward the supply room.

That doesn't make sense. How could it hit Rizuto before it raised its arms? It's like seeing a replay . . . Of course!

As she watched, the door to the supply room opened and closed before the alien arrived, which confirmed her suspicions. As he reached the door, he seemed to disappear right through the solid structure. Pulaski headed toward one of the smaller supply cabinets.

Grabbing an aerosol anesthetic, she rushed toward the supply room, wedging a pin into the dispenser as she ran. Just as she felt her left hand beginning to go numb from the spray, she opened the door and tossed the dispenser inside. Hitting the override, she locked the door and waited.

The sudden commotion inside the room told her she'd gotten the intruder's attention. The door shook under the assault of the alien trapped inside. She barely got out of the way as the door came smashing off the wall. Before anyone could react, the creature continued to beat against the nonexistent door while a thud was heard several feet away. One of the technicians hit the fans to vent any remaining anesthetic fumes out of the area, while everyone moved away from the bizarre intruder. After a few moments, its motions grew sluggish and it stumbled forward and collapsed where the noise had been heard earlier.

The medical staff was buzzing with questions and speculation. Two of the technicians lifted the creature onto a table and began examining it. Pulaski hit her combadge and called the bridge.

"Picard here."

"Captain, we've captured one of the intruders. It broke into sickbay. Apparently, they're vulnerable to our anesthetics. I recommend we use that in engineering."

She could hear some muffled orders on the bridge, and then La Forge's voice crackled over the communications link. *"La Forge here, Captain."*

"Mister La Forge, Doctor Pulaski has determined that the intruders are vulnerable to anesthetics. Is there any way of restoring the intruder control system from your current location?"

"Negative, Captain. The breach in the hull threw the entire system off-line. We're going to have to do something else."

"Geordi, if we transported sprayers into the middle of engineering, do you think that would work?" Pulaski asked.

"Good idea, Doctor. Yes, if you could have O'Brien deposit them in some specific spots on Decks 32, 34, and 39, we could flood the engineering section with the gas."

Pulaski did a few mental calculations, then tapped her combadge again. "Whoa, whoa! How much anesthetic do you think we have on board? It'll take a while to synthesize that much."

There was a pause, then Geordi's voice came back on-line. *"Okay, how about enough for Decks 32 and 34? If we can secure those areas, we can cut off any stragglers from their ship."*

An unfamiliar voice broke in on the channel, cutting off Pulaski's reply. *"Lieutenant La Forge, what about the aerators we were going to drop off on Lennix IV? They're meant to spread liquid fertilizer over a couple of hectares. It wouldn't take much to convert those things for the doc."*

The relief in Geordi's voice was obvious. *"Great idea, Duff. Can you get those to the transporter room?"*

"Consider it done. I'll meet the doc there."

Captain Picard came back on line, his voice conveying a confidence that Pulaski certainly didn't feel. *"Mister La Forge, Doctor Pulaski, sounds like you have your work cut out for you. Keep me informed with your progress."*

"Captain, before you go, there's something else you need to know."

"Yes, Doctor?"

"The aliens, they're not where we see them. It's like we're seeing them in time delay. When we captured the intruder, we heard his body hit the floor several meters from where he was at the time. Advise security to set their phasers on the widest beam possible."

"Time delay?"

"I think we're seeing afterimages, like with a distant star. We don't see where it is, just where it was. Same with the intruders, although I can't tell you why yet. Maybe our examination will turn up something."

"Mister Worf will pass that on to security. Good luck with your mission, Doctor."

With your shield or upon it, eh, Captain? Fine. Pulaski pointed to a couple of the technicians in the sickbay. "You two, start working on synthesizing more anesthezine. Blake, contact main sickbay and have Ogawa get started making some up there. Bring it to transporter room 2 as soon as you're done. I'm going to go ahead and see what I can do to help with those aerators."

Pulaski stood by one of the portable monitors that had been brought to transporter room 2. They'd jury-rigged a visual feed from engineering, and La Forge was helping them decide where to send the aerator for his section.

Chief O'Brien flipped a switch on the transporter console, activating the voice communicator. "Lieutenant La Forge, we're ready to begin transport. I'd advise finding an emergency oxygen mask unless you want to wake up with a heck of a headache."

"Understood, Chief. Good luck."

"Thanks, sir. Energizing in thirty seconds."

As the countdown commenced, Pulaski shook her head as the engineers congratulated themselves on the conversion of the aerators into gas bombs. The lieutenant in charge grinned like a kid who'd just made his first model spaceship. He didn't seem like the kind of engineer Geordi would trust with a major task, but she had to admit that what he lacked in decorum, he made up for in skill. He'd stripped and reassembled the aerator faster than anything she'd ever seen.

Chief O'Brien's voice cut into her reverie. "Energizing."

Pulaski held her breath as the first aerator was surrounded by a nimbus of flashing light and then disappeared from sight. Turning to the monitor, she could see it appear near the breach. The top of the machine began spinning slowly, then gained speed with each revolution.

The aliens didn't seem to notice anything at first, but it wasn't long before their movements became disoriented and then they began slumping against the bulkheads and engineering stations in a vain attempt to remain upright.

Geordi's voice crackled over the communicator, muffled by the mask he had pressed over his mouth and nose. *"Doctor Pulaski, it appears to be working. I can't see any of the intruders awake from my position."*

Pulaski nodded as she watched the second aerator wind down to a halt on Deck 34. "Keep an eye out, Geordi. We're still trying to see if it's having the same effectiveness on Deck 34. I'll contact the captain to let him know."

Pulaski started as Picard's voice broke in on their conversation. *"No need, Doctor. I've just heard Mister La Forge's report. Good job, both of you. We'll need to get security in there before it starts wearing off."*

Nice of you to let me know you're listening in, Captain. "Affirmative, Captain. We'll be going in right behind to tend to the wounded."

Before Captain Picard could respond, another shudder rippled through the *Enterprise. "Mister La Forge, what is going on down there?"*

"Captain, we've had a rupture in one of the plasma conduits. It was probably weakened in the earlier explosion. A section of the bulkhead has blown out into the engineering compartment. Some

of our people and the aliens are trapped beneath the rubble and we've got a plasma fire going. We need help now."

Pulaski gritted her teeth as Captain Picard ordered Lieutenant Worf to alert damage control and get them to engineering.

"Captain, we need to get my EMR team in there now," she said, when the captain came back on-line.

"I agree. How long before you can get them assembled?"

"Too long, Captain. We need to use the technique from earlier today. I'm certain it'll work this time."

Riker's voice cut in, his earlier annoyance noticeable. *"I'm inclined to disagree, Doctor. With the rupture of a plasma conduit, your energy supply is even more unstable than it was earlier."*

Geordi broke into the conversation with a note of triumph in his voice. *"Actually, no, it's not."*

Picard's voice cut in, overriding both Pulaski's and Riker's questions. *"Explain yourself, Mister La Forge."*

"I took the liberty of establishing an independent power backup for an emergency like this. It should be more than sufficient for what the doctor has in mind."

Pulaski caught herself standing there with her mouth open. "When did you do that?"

"Right after our meeting. I told you I had something I wanted to try. I just didn't think it would be this soon."

Pulaski shook her head in bemusement. *Could today get any stranger?* "Captain?"

"All right, Doctor. Initiate your plan."

She knew it killed Jean-Luc to give that command, but now was not the time to rub it in, so she merely tapped her communicator. "EMR Team, Alpha One. Engineering."

Before she finished that short phrase, she saw Chief O'Brien beginning to initiate the point-to-point transport. She moved next to the terminal where he was working. "When you get them to sickbay, let me know. I want you to transport me into engineering with them."

Miles looked at her in surprise. "You, Doctor?"

"Yes, Chief. I am the most experienced medical officer on this ship. If the damage is as bad as Mister La Forge said, I'll be needed."

The young engineering lieutenant stepped over next to her. "Better set this transport for two, Chief. I'm going with her."

"Excuse me, Lieutenant . . ."

"Lieutenant Duffy. Look, Doc, they're going to need help to get that fire out. Especially if most of the on-duty engineers are unconscious."

Pulaski looked at the young man's earnest face and nodded. "Make that a transport for two, Chief."

Miles looked up at the ceiling as if hoping for divine assistance and then released a deep sigh. "Aye, ma'am. Adjusting transport for two additional personnel."

As the familiar whine of the transporter faded, Pulaski unclenched her teeth and glanced down to ensure she was still in one piece. Convinced she'd beaten the cosmic craps table yet again, she assessed the damage in engineering. The plasma fire cast strange shadows as the flames jetted from one of the bulkheads. She hadn't spent much time in engineering when it was intact, but clearly it had seen better days.

The EMR team split up into two groups. Technician Johannson led her team toward the collapsed bulkhead with the arriving security personnel. They began triage and helped extricate the wounded from the debris. Technician Peters took the remaining members and began searching for any injured away from the blast. Pulaski spotted Geordi coming down a ladder to the main floor and went over to join him.

"Well, you certainly know how to throw a party here, Lieutenant."

Geordi gave her a quick grin before turning serious. "We've got to get this fire under control. We're losing power to the warp core."

Lieutenant Duffy stepped forward. "Just point me in the right direction and I'll take care of it for you."

"Kieran, good to see you. Grab the first people you find and stabilize that power. You've got to give me time to get that fire under control."

"You've got it, boss. Drinks are on you in Ten-Forward tonight."

"You've got it, Duffy. Now get moving."

As Lieutenant Duffy sprinted toward a bank of controls, Geordi moved toward the jet of purplish flame that gouted into the room. Pulaski tapped her communicator and linked into the main sickbay.

"Sickbay, this is Pulaski. We'll begin moving the injured into auxiliary sickbay in a few minutes. I need medical team 5 to join us there. We'll keep main sickbay as a reserve for now. There may be more casualties than we know about, so stand by."

"Understood, Doctor. Dispatching team 5."

Pulaski gave silent thanks to the Starfleet personnel officer who ensured the *Enterprise* had an outstanding medical staff. She hurried toward Technician Johannson's team to lend a hand when she saw Mister Worf and other security personnel enter and begin securing the invaders. She smiled, knowing how disappointed Worf was going to be with all his foes unconscious.

A piece of debris shifted on the other side of the fire. Pulaski peered through the flames and saw movement behind the collapsed bulkhead. Shading her eyes, she barely made out the shape of four people trapped there.

Tapping her combadge, she contacted the transporter room. "Chief O'Brien, this is Pulaski."

"What can I do for you, Doctor?"

"We've got four people trapped under debris behind the plasma jet. Can you get a lock on them and get them out of there?"

A few tense seconds went by before O'Brien's voice returned. *"Negative, Doctor. Too much interference. Can't get a good fix on them."*

She paused. "All right, Chief. Can you get a reading on me?"

"Aye. It's faint, but I have you."

"Good. I need you to transport me about eleven meters from my current location due aft. There's a gap between the collapsed bulkhead and the far wall. I'll be able to reach them from there."

"Are you crazy, Doctor? I'm having enough trouble holding your signal. If I try to move you farther into the interference, I could materialize you inside the bulkhead."

"Chief, that was not a request, that was an order."

Will Riker's voice broke in, surprising her. She hadn't realized the bridge was still monitoring her transmissions. *"Doctor Pulaski, I have to side with the chief on this one. It's too risky."*

"With all due respect, Commander, you're not the doctor here. Energize as soon as you're ready, Chief O'Brien."

She waited with held breath, wondering if the transporter chief would side with her or the first officer when she heard a familiar whine and the universe became fuzzy. When it came back into focus, she found herself about eight centimeters away from the far wall. Ignoring the blistering hot air, she turned around and examined the situation as she pulled out her medical tricorder.

No way to dig them out without the rest of the wall collapsing. All I can do is make them comfortable and treat what I can reach. Come on, Geordi, your turn to be a miracle worker.

She knelt down and began examining the first casualty. The young technician seemed to be stable, but Pulaski recognized shock when she saw it. "Don't worry, we'll get you out of here."

She weakly smiled up at Pulaski. "Thanks, Doctor. I think my left leg is broken."

"The tricorder agrees with you. Are you hurt anywhere else?"

"Bruises, bumps, nothing serious, I think. Bill is hurt a lot worse than me."

"I'm going to give you a shot and then I'll check him out next. Try to relax. The damage control teams will be here in a moment."

The lieutenant sighed as the painkiller hit her system. "Thanks for coming after us, Doc."

"What? Your old doctor didn't make house calls?"

The engineer gave a lopsided smile before drifting off to sleep. As Pulaski concentrated on the other casualties, she glanced up from time to time and could see Lieutenant Duffy over at the console making frantic gestures to a young female engineer who'd joined him. Together, they manipulated the controls almost as one person, while Geordi's damage control team fought the plasma fire.

She administered a painkiller to the last of the four when she noticed a sudden drop in the temperature. A cheer rose and she looked up in time to see the plasma jet flicker and die. Geordi didn't waste time celebrating, though.

"Good work, people, but we have to get that warp core under control. Dennings, stay with this team and ensure that rupture is fixed. Schmidt, al-Fahedi, take your teams and check out the hull breach. Take some security guys with you."

Pulaski wiped her brow and stood up. "Mister La Forge, I need a team over here. You've got some people trapped in this mess."

Geordi wheeled around. "Baker, get the antigrav manipulators. Thomas, Phillips, don't just stand there. Give the doctor a hand."

Pulaski did her best to stay out of the way as engineers and medical staff converged on her position and extricated the four personnel from the rubble. It was only when one of the engineers offered her a hand to step over the remaining debris that her knees began to shake. She was grateful to have someone else to lean on for a second.

Geordi pointed a couple of engineers toward the rear of the compartment and came over to where Pulaski leaned against a bulkhead. "That was pretty gutsy, Doctor. You've won a lot of fans today."

Pulaski smiled, trying to hide how shaky she was. "Just doing my job, Mister La Forge. Thanks for believing in my technique."

"Just doing *my* job, Doctor."

Once everything was under control, Captain Picard recalled all the senior staff for an after-action review. Pulaski reclined in her familiar chair and noted that the *Enterprise*'s senior staff seemed a lot more relaxed than the last time. Everyone, that is, except Commander Riker, who looked like he'd rather be anywhere else but in the room.

Captain Picard put his cup of tea down on the table and turned to Lieutenant La Forge. "How are repairs coming down in engineering?"

Geordi frowned as he considered the question. "We suffered less damage than I thought. The intruders were surprisingly efficient. We'll have to hit a drydock to make complete repairs, but we've established a temporary patch and we have a localized force field backing that up. I don't anticipate any problems unless we're forced to do some fancy maneuvering."

Captain Picard favored him with a small smile. "We'll try to avoid that, Mister La Forge. Doctor Pulaski, status report."

She glanced at her padd and then looked up at the captain. "All things considered, we were very lucky. Fourteen crewmembers seriously injured, most in the explosion in engineering. Fifty-two suffered minor injuries, most during the attack, and there were four reports of allergic reactions to the aerosol used to subdue the attackers. Eleven of the aliens were also injured, none seriously as far as we can tell. Doctor Martin and his medical team were found by security shortly after the fire was contained in engineering. All were treated for concussions and various bruises and returned to duty."

"Speaking of that, Doctor Pulaski, how are you and Mister Data coming along with our uninvited guests?"

Data started to answer and then paused, as though seeking Pulaski's permission. She gave a small motion for him to proceed. Fatigue was setting in now that the crisis was over, and letting Data do the report suited her fine.

The android nodded, then turned to Captain Picard. "We have completed the preliminary examination of this new race, Captain. As best we can tell, they live outside of our time continuum, which is why we have had so much trouble communicating with them."

"I don't understand, Data. They live 'outside our time continuum'?" Counselor Troi's question echoed on many of the faces around the table.

"Our research suggests that something or someone has altered their bodies as well as the materials of their ship. Based on our calculations, their atomic structures vibrate exactly two-point-three-four seconds faster than the universal standards of time. They're literally out of sync with the rest of the universe."

Picard leaned forward in his chair. "How could such a thing be possible?"

"I believe I can answer that, Captain."

Picard turned to his hulking security chief. "Please do so, Mister Worf."

"We have inspected the intruders' ship. Going through their logs, we've determined the beings are known as the Cizinec. We learned that a temporal anomaly struck their planetary system. The survivors found their world altered by the time wave. Unable to communicate or interact with other beings in this sector, they turned to salvage or raiding to survive."

"It is true we have had difficulty communicating directly with them, Captain," Data continued, building on Worf's information. "Indeed, this is what confused not only our sensors but our own eyes. We were seeing where they were two seconds ago. This rendered both our phaser fire and physical attacks ineffective. Thanks to Doctor Pulaski's observations, I have been able to alter the sensors to compensate. It is similar to the technique used to track the movement of stars through space by watching the blueshift and redshift, which, as you know, is how astronomers see in what direction and how fast a star is moving through space."

Picard held up a hand to cut off Data's lesson in astronomy. "Very good, Mister Data. Do you believe we'll be able to establish communications with them?"

"We are setting up terminals in the brig in hopes of establishing a way to take the time difference into account. I am certain by the time we reach Starbase 28, I will be able to converse with them, at least digitally."

Jean-Luc smiled at the crew. "With any luck, we'll be able to aid the Cizinec and put an end to their raiding. Mister La Forge, have their ship brought aboard and store it in one of the shuttlebays. Well done, everyone. Dismissed."

As one, the officers rose and headed toward the door, except for Commander Riker, who rose only when Pulaski reached his seat on her way out. "Doctor, could I speak to you for a moment?"

Pulaski tensed, but she sensed Riker didn't want a fight. "Of course, Commander."

Will waited for the room to clear and then spoke. "I'd like to congratulate you on your actions today. I've recommended you to the captain for a commendation both for your personal bravery and for the actions of your emergency team."

Pulaski bit back her usual caustic response. *No sense in making this any harder than it already is.* "I'm flattered, Commander, but it's not necessary. If anything, it should go to Lieutenant La Forge for having the foresight to prepare those reserve batteries."

Riker swallowed and then pushed on with what was obviously a prepared speech. "Ah, I also wanted you to know there's a poker game at my room this evening. We'd love to have you join us."

That, Pulaski hadn't been expecting. She took a breath to compose herself and then replied, "Thank you again, Commander, but I'll have to take a rain check. I promised to meet Lieutenant La Forge in Ten-Forward. We'll be discussing creating an elite damage control team similar to my medical teams, and then I'm going to get some much-needed rest."

"Another time, then?"

"I'll check my calendar."

Before Riker could reply, she turned and slipped out of the conference room. She headed toward the turbolift, her smile growing with every step she took.

AMONG THE CLOUDS

Scott Pearson

Historian's note:
This tale is set during the latter half
of Star Trek: The Next Generation*'s third season.*

SCOTT PEARSON

Scott Pearson was first published in 1987 with "The Mailbox," a short story about an elderly farming couple. Over the last twenty years he has published a smattering of humor, poetry, nonfiction, and short stories, most recently his first mystery story, "Out of the Jacuzzi, Into the Sauna," in the anthology *Resort to Murder*. A *Star Trek* fan for thirty-five years, Scott has had two previous *Trek* stories published, "Full Circle" in *Strange New Worlds VII* and "Terra Tonight" in *Strange New Worlds 9*. He's grateful to Marco Palmieri for the chance to join this anthology with his first solicited sale. Scott also tips his hat to Carl Sagan and Edwin Salpeter, who imagined animal life in Jovian clouds way back in 1976, providing inspiration for some of the creatures herein. Scott makes his living as an editor for Zenith Press, a military history publisher in St. Paul, Minnesota, and X-comm, a regional history publisher in Duluth. He lives in St. Paul with his wife, Sandra, and daughter, Ella. Please visit him on the web at www.yeahsure.net. "Among the Clouds" is in memory of Scott's cousin, Kevin Zegan, who loved science fiction.

"GEORDI, BEHIND YOU!" WORF'S URGENT SHOUT SEEMED TO echo inside the helmet of La Forge's environmental suit. It was not something you expected to hear while aboard an orbital elevator stopped in the lower stratosphere of a Jovian planet.

La Forge adjusted his precarious position atop the elevator's drive unit, several pairs of powered rollers on both sides of the support tether. The relatively thin ribbon stretched hundreds of kilometers up into space and down into Askaria's mostly hydrogen atmosphere. Extending from the drive unit on one side of the tether was an oval passenger platform with twenty seats, while an aerodynamic stabilizer and counterweight extended from the other side.

Billowing ammonia ice clouds, red with sulfur compounds, prevailed at this altitude, but La Forge had no trouble seeing the danger. Just a dozen meters away, a swarm of hundreds of scarflike creatures, some more than three meters long, undulated toward the away team. Railings around the platform and lap belts on the seats were the lift's only safety features. Worf and Deanna Troi remained belted in, but La Forge, placing a communication relay, was perched a few meters above the railings, his safety line bonded to the tether by phased molecular adhesion.

If they had not had a couple hundred kilometers of bone-crushingly dense atmosphere below them, La Forge would have found it difficult to be concerned about the approaching life-forms. Joyfully fluttering along the strong winds, they looked like brightly colored Argelian silks. He wondered what they used for blood; up here a hundred below Celsius was a warm day.

"Thanks for the warning," La Forge said, bracing for the swarm of flutters (as he found himself calling them). The leading edge soon reached him, but he barely noticed. The creatures, floating up here at about half of Earth's atmospheric pressure at sea level, were paper-thin. But they accumulated on him and writhed with surprising strength as they tried to free themselves. Dozens stuck to the faceplate of his EV suit, and soon he couldn't see. He slipped, banging his helmet on the tether, and felt his safety line tug at its harness.

Troi, unlike Worf, had a calming influence. *"Are you all right up there?"*

"Yeah, I think so." La Forge pushed his estimate of the size of the swarm up into the thousands. "How about you?"

"Most of them are flying over our heads."

La Forge felt himself being pushed sideways by the sheer number of flutters impacting him. The wind had shifted a bit, and he felt the platform twist slightly. "I'm starting to get a little worried. Are they almost—" He stopped talking as his stomach lurched. He couldn't see what was happening.

"Geordi!"

The fear in Troi's voice told him what he feared was true—he was in free fall. All the flutters pressing against him must have hit the tab that deactivated his safety line's adhesion plate. He flailed his arms, trying to grab something, anything, the tether, the railings. Then the flutters cleared off his faceplate.

He was almost below the level of the platform, falling backward. Worf and Troi, up and out of their seats, leaned against the railing, their arms outstretched as they tried to grab him on his way down. They missed as the wind carried him away. Ignoring the panic welling up in him, La Forge rolled into an orbital skydiving pose and attempted to steer back to the lift.

"I'll lower the platform," Worf said.

"I'm trying to reach the tether." La Forge adjusted his outstretched arms and legs. His VISOR allowed him to see temperature variations in the atmosphere and predict winds and sheers, but four-hundred-kilometers-per-hour gusts minimized that advantage. The upper anchor for the tether, far above them, orbited in the direction of the wind; being on the platform was like drifting down a fast river in a boat, but now he was overboard in the river itself.

Above him he could hear the platform descending, but not as fast as he was. Even under these circumstances, the engineer in him was making calculations: *The acceleration of gravity on Askaria is about twenty-two meters per second squared. At this altitude I'll be at terminal velocity, almost eight hundred kilometers per hour, in under ten seconds.* The EV suit could protect him at that speed, but not at the crushing pressures he would eventually plummet to. He directed himself toward the tether, even though he was falling too fast to grab it. Reaching down to his waist, he drew out more slack in his safety line. If he could reattach it to the tether, the harness mechanism would automatically reduce his rate of descent. He'd probably break a few ribs when he hit the end, but it beat the alternative.

He raced toward the tether and reached out with the safety line, activating the phased adhesion plate. But moving his arms forward altered his course. The fingers of his left hand brushed the tether, but the safety line was in his right hand. The tether shot by in a blur. Before he could try to turn around for another pass, he was caught in an eddy, roughly spun around, and thrown in a different direction. With a concentrated effort of arms and legs, he came out of the nauseating tumble, completely disoriented, tired in just seconds from fighting the wind.

"On your right." He'd never heard Worf's voice sound so gentle.

Spinning to his right he saw the tether. Bending backward to raise his head, he caught a last glimpse of Troi and Worf, standing at the edge of the descending platform looking down at him. At this distance he couldn't see their faces. Then they disappeared into an ammonia ice cloud.

As La Forge continued to fall, he found that it wasn't his whole life that flashed before his eyes—just the last few days. The events leading to his perilous descent into the deeps of Askaria had begun on the bridge, while he'd been overseeing some system diagnostics.

* * *

"Captain, I've picked up a distress call," Lieutenant Worf said.

At the aft engineering station, La Forge paused the diagnostic program he was running and faced forward.

Worf didn't look up as he continued to work his controls at tactical. "Now I've lost it. It's light speed, sir—radio frequency. We will need to drop from warp to pick it up again."

Captain Picard exchanged a surprised look with Commander Riker, who scratched thoughtfully at his beard. Picard said, "Mister Crusher, take us out of warp. Get the heading from Lieutenant Worf."

"Aye, sir." Crusher dropped the *Enterprise* to sublight and came about. He transferred the coordinates Worf had sent him into the helm. "We should be able to pick it up soon. I'll plot a triangulation course."

La Forge turned back to his panel and started tapping in commands. "Captain, I'm maximizing the sensors for the radio frequency spectrum."

"Good." Picard leaned forward. "Let's see if we can help."

Lieutenant Commander Data looked over his shoulder from the ops station. "Captain, it is likely we are too late to answer a light speed distress call. And, as I learned with Sarjenka, even an RF broadcast brings the Prime Directive into play."

"Quite right," Picard said.

Ostensibly, Data didn't have emotions, but La Forge still thought he could see a hint of sadness on his friend's pale face. La Forge gave Data a sympathetic look. The engineer had no regrets about his part in violating the letter of the noninterference policy to save the Dreman civilization by tectonically stabilizing their planet. After hearing the little girl whom Data had been communicating with via low-level RF signals, Picard had chosen a course of action La Forge felt was true to the spirit of the law. But that had also required erasing Sarjenka's memories of Data, almost as if the Sarjenka Data had befriended had died anyway.

"But we were able to save the Dremans nevertheless," Picard added. "Let's reserve judgment until we have more information."

As Data nodded hopefully and turned back to his station, Worf spoke up. "I've picked up the signal, Captain. It's a recorded loop. The translation is coming up."

"Let's hear it." Because there was no video component, Picard glanced upward at the speakers in the ceiling.

"We come from Narsosia, the second planet of seven around a white-yellow star." The computer rendered the voice as forceful, but La Forge thought it sounded sad as well. *"Our clouds, infused with centuries of pollution, are opaque to infrared, causing global temperatures to soar. All of Narsosia is dying. A handful of our population is traveling to the fifth planet, Askaria, a gas giant with several moons that we hope are habitable. While many of us believe in the possibility of sentient alien life, we have no evidence of it. Still, in our desperation, we have invested our failing resources in constructing this distress beacon. Please help us if you can."*

After the playback stopped, there was a moment of quiet on the bridge. Troi looked stricken but didn't indicate she had sensed anything with her empathic abilities. La Forge shook his head. As Data had explained, this catastrophe had probably already happened, and they were hearing the voice of someone long dead, like a ghost. But La Forge didn't want to believe that.

Softly, Riker broke the silence. "Have we located the source yet?"

"I believe I have, sir," Data said with a glance at Worf. Worf gave a respectful nod as the ever-polite Data continued. "I have cross-referenced the points of triangulation with scans of nearby space. There is an uncharted system within the possible broadcast cone that matches the description in the message." Data turned to face the screen as he brought up a tactical schematic of the region. "The system is only four days away at warp." He turned back to face Picard. "Unfortunately, that indicates an RF travel time of nearly fifty years for the distress call."

"Captain," La Forge said. "Environmental disasters like this can take hundreds of years to develop. Terraforming technology, like we used at Browder IV, could reverse the effects of even an advanced greenhouse effect."

Picard turned to look up at his chief engineer. "That may be, but fifty years is only a minimum age for the message. We have no way of knowing how long it's been broadcasting."

Troi added, "Or how long the Narsosians waited before sending it."

"But they were still fighting their fate," said Worf with a warrior's glint in his eye. "Even if driven to ask for help."

La Forge nodded his head. "That's right, and I'm not ready to give up hope. As far as the Prime Directive goes, simple baristatic filters might be closer to their tech level and—"

"Relax, Geordi," Picard said, holding up a hand in surrender. "No one has given up. Mister Crusher, set a course for Narsosia, best possible speed."

"Aye, sir." He looked over his shoulder with a grin. "It's been plotted and laid in since Data located the system."

"Then, by all means, engage."

La Forge had been falling for just over thirty kilometers. *It's only taken four minutes,* he thought. *Since I'm moving at a body-bruising average speed of 475 kilometers per hour, I'm actually decelerating as I fall. Increasing atmospheric pressure is decreasing terminal velocity.* The heads-up display in his helmet indicated he was now at one and a half Earth atmospheres, the equivalent of about fifteen meters underwater. The HUD also showed that the temperature had risen to fifty below Celsius. The clouds had changed to ammonium hydrosulfide, the colors subdued tans. Lightning frequently lit up the sky, forking through the clouds around him. He contemplated just putting his legs together, his arms forward, and diving to his death below. *No, I won't give up.* There could be a shuttle heading for him right now, almost close enough for its transporter to cut through the ionized atmosphere. He had been determined to help any survivors on Askaria, and now he had to hope he would be a survivor himself.

La Forge entered the bridge and came to a halt as he looked at the viewscreen. *Enterprise* was still one day out from Narsosia, but he'd been summoned from engineering to see the ship they were approaching—the source of the distress call. Comparable to human technology of the late twenty-first century, it was definitely built for atmospheric flight: about one hundred meters long, thin from top to bottom, and its V-shaped body tapering out gracefully into wings. As the silver craft tumbled slowly along, he saw booster engines in its tail and, on either side of the main engine intake, what appeared to be chemical rocket engines on the underside of the wings, which seemed out of place on the sleek craft.

"Mister Worf," Picard said, "why don't you bring Commander La Forge up to speed."

La Forge stood beside Worf to look at the sensor readouts as Worf filled him in.

"Aye, sir." Worf glanced down at La Forge. "There are no life signs. The interior is at ambient temperature and at low pressure." He looked back at his readings. "The main engines have few moving parts, relying on supersonic atmospheric speeds to compress the intake air for combustion with fuel—"

"It's a scramjet," La Forge interrupted. "They've jury-rigged a suborbital craft with chemical rockets to take it into space as a last-chance lifeboat. But they're out of the ecliptic plane. They must have gone off course. And to be this far out of the system . . ." He trailed off as he realized the implication.

Data turned to face him. "At this ship's maximum speed, it would have taken approximately six hundred years to reach this distance."

"So we *are* too late," said La Forge, his shoulders slumping.

Data tilted his head. "There is still the chance that other ships made it to the moons of Askaria according to their plans."

"Perhaps we can get some answers on that ship," Picard said. "Worf, stabilize it with a tractor beam." He turned toward Riker. "Take an away team over there and see what you can find."

"Aye, sir." Riker stood up and headed toward the lift. "Data and Worf, you're with me." He paused by La Forge. "Want to tag along?"

La Forge nodded. If it turned out the entire population of Narsosia had perished, the least they could do would be to save this ship and whatever records might be aboard her. It could be all that remained of Narsosian civilization. "Yes, I do. Thanks."

"See if you want to thank me after you suit up." Riker clapped him on the shoulder. "I hate those things."

La Forge had fallen another twenty kilometers, plunging into the next layer of Askarian clouds, bluish with water ice. His HUD showed three Earth atmospheres pressure, as if he were twenty meters underwater. *It took over six minutes to fall just that much farther,* he thought. *Since I'm falling at "only" 185 kilometers per hour now.* The attempted joke didn't bring a smile to his face.

His EV suit was still compensating for the increased pressure, but it was at the edge of its capabilities. *After all, it's a soft suit, designed for low-pressure conditions. On the other hand, the temperature's up to freezing, so I'm saving heating power.* But extra power or not, it was time to admit he was going to be crushed in the deep atmosphere. Like a submarine sinking under the ocean.

Five minutes passed. He felt mentally and physically numb. And then—

A submarine. Like I'm sinking underwater. He shook his head, at least as much as he could inside his helmet. *Why didn't I think of this before? This is a simple buoyancy problem.*

La Forge reached down to an emergency supply pouch strapped to his left leg. Leaving the skydiving position, his descent increased. He rolled over, back down, which made it a bit easier. He glanced at the HUD—four Earth atmospheres and increasing. He was now 60 kilometers below the altitude he'd fallen from, traveling at 113 kilometers an hour. Carefully opening the pouch so everything wouldn't fly out, he withdrew a one-person survival shelter. It was compact, about the size of a tricorder. He played out his safety line again, looped it through a carry strap on the shelter, and attached the adhesion plate to one of the straps of its harness. Then he slipped his left hand through the strap and pulled the shelter's activation tab with his right. A chemical reaction caused support ribs to stiffen, forcing the shelter to unfold. He reached behind his back, fumbled around, and found the auxiliary oxygen line. Pulling it out as far as he could, he inserted it into a valve on the side of the unfolding shelter and flicked the release on the end of the line.

As the compressed oxygen in the tank on his back expanded into the shelter, his rate of descent decreased. Soon he was dangling from the swollen hemispherical shelter, a bubble of oxygen inflated to about a meter and a half across. He detached the oxygen line and stowed it as he checked the HUD. *Three and a half Earth atmospheres . . . and decreasing. I'm actually rising.* Grunting with the pain of being battered by the wind during his fifteen-minute plunge, he tightened up the safety line to get some support from that and reached up to grab the carry strap with his right hand as well.

Then a red light came on, warning that his oxygen tank was low.

* * *

It was like arriving late at a play, the room dark, the show sold out. La Forge, Riker, Data, and Worf stood at the back of a large passenger compartment in the scramjet, playing their palm beacons across the rows and rows of seats, each one occupied. It was as if the Narsosians were waiting for the curtain to rise—but they were all dead. The away team moved up a center aisle for a closer look.

The Narsosians were, on average, tall by human standards. Nearly without exception both males and females were more than two meters tall. They wore undecorated jumpsuits and boots in a variety of colors. Most looked quite peaceful; many held hands. The Narsosians had dull red downy hair that appeared to cover most of their skin, head, hands, and faces alike. Their noses were very small, their ears almost nonexistent. Their teeth were large, the males' noticeably broader.

Data lowered his tricorder. *"There are five hundred and three Narsosian corpses aboard this ship."* Data also wore an EV suit; although the environment was not a problem for the android, anti-contamination regulations required he suit up too.

La Forge frowned. "How did they all die so . . . neatly?"

Riker looked back and forth at the partially mummified bodies by twisting at the waist in his EV suit. *"Maybe they were medicated. They knew they were going to die."*

"Asphyxiation is not an honorable death," Worf said. *"Better to choose your own time."*

As Worf and Data headed off in different directions in the passenger compartment, La Forge took out his tricorder to trace the distress call. It was coming from a compartment beneath the passengers. With a glance around, he noticed a gangway leading below.

"Commander, I'm going below to check on the beacon."

Riker gave him a wave. *"Keep in touch."*

La Forge nodded and headed down the stairs. He used a palm beacon; at near absolute zero there was little thermal variation for his VISOR to pick up. As he stepped onto the deck at the bottom, he turned slowly back and forth, waving the tricorder. The signal beacon was up ahead. He tramped forward, the low pressure keeping sounds to a minimum as his boots met the deckplates.

This compartment was full of machinery, and La Forge wished

he had the time to stop and investigate every piece, but he had to keep the larger rescue mission in mind. With that thought, he reached a smaller compartment that had to be the location of the signal beacon. Shining his light through the open hatch, he illuminated a sole Narsosian body.

He drew back a bit, startled. *Why was this Narsosian down here alone?* Stepping into the compartment, he knelt beside the body, which appeared female. Her mummified features, softened by the reddish down on her skin, still seemed to show a determined expression. She sat right beside the signal beacon. *She must have been making sure it was still functioning. Or she wanted to be here if someone found them—whether dead or alive, she's the first Narsosian to meet an alien.*

La Forge suddenly had no doubt he was right, that he'd had an insight into this person's last thoughts. It was difficult to believe those thoughts had occurred six hundred years before. With a sad sigh, he scanned the signal beacon. It was powered by a radioisotope thermoelectric generator, still running at 23 percent capacity. It had served its purpose, if belatedly, so after identifying a power switch he tapped it off.

Standing, he took a last look at the Narsosian and then headed back to the gangway. Reaching the passenger level, he spotted the rest of the away team huddled around a computer terminal. Data was tapping away at the keys and occasionally referring to his tricorder.

"I have found only text journals, no audio or video recordings," Data said. *"Using universal translator data from their recorded distress call, I have been able to infer the correlation between their spoken and written language. I am going to upload the data into my internal processors, and then I will be able to read the journals directly."* Only a second passed, and Data blinked. *"Transfer complete."*

"Sometimes I wish I could learn that fast," La Forge said.

"Not me," said Riker. *"I like the challenge of the process. That's half the fun."*

Data looked back and forth at La Forge and Riker. *"I do not have 'fun,' but I agree that the organic learning process is usually preferable. Under the circumstances, however, the approach I chose seemed the expedient one."*

Riker grinned, then returned to a subdued expression. *"Right, as usual, Data. Please, continue."*

With a nod, Data went back to studying the monitor of the Narsosian computer. La Forge leaned in and saw that the text was scrolling by in a blur that only an android or a Scalosian could follow.

"Interesting," Data said. *"The Narsosians, for various political and cultural reasons, never developed a space program before they needed to evacuate the planet. But they did have a high-speed transit system of suborbital scramjets. Then, early in the evacuation, they used carbon nanotube technology to build orbital elevators connected to space stations circling Narsosia."*

"Wait a minute," said La Forge. "With this level of technology, they should've been able to stop the pollution causing the greenhouse effect and maybe even reverse it."

Data looked up from the monitor. *"You are correct. If they had heeded the early warnings, they might have been able to avert the catastrophe. However, within their system of privatized industry, it was more profitable to maintain the status quo. By the time the severity of the situation could counteract the profit motive, it was too late."*

"Much like Earth's history," Riker said. *"It took World War III and the Vulcans to get humanity onto a different track."* He glanced down at the monitor, although he could not read the text. *"But why weren't the space stations mentioned in the distress call?"*

Data referred back to the monitor, beginning the high-speed scroll again. *"Because they failed. It was never within the Narsosians' capabilities to evacuate the entire population. There was hope that those who remained behind would somehow find a way to save the planet, but ensuring the survival of their species was the priority. The selection process was transparent and equitable, but those left behind were not satisfied. Civil unrest led to civil war. The descent into anarchy doomed any final attempts at solving the environmental problems."* Data paused, his expression changing subtly, and La Forge could see his dismay. *"By the time this scramjet left, six hundred and twelve years ago, all the stations were under attack. Some were falling from orbit. The scramjet was forced to take evasive action to avoid debris from the stations. Given their limited maneuvering abilities, they were never able to get back on course.*" Data turned off the monitor. "*As Commander Riker surmised, they committed suicide instead of suffering slow deaths by asphyxiation. One waited until the last to ensure the others all died peacefully, then released the atmosphere to help preserve the bodies, as was their custom. She made the last entries to this journal after her crewmates were dead.*"

"I found her," La Forge said. "She was sitting by the beacon. Waiting for us."

After a moment of silence, Riker looked at his away team. "*Let's hope the other scramjets had better luck.*" He opened a channel to the ship. "Enterprise, *this is Riker. Bring us back home.*"

"*Warning: oxygen supply is below recommended refill level.*" The bland computer recording sounded again inside his EV helmet, but La Forge could do nothing about it. He couldn't even recall how to disable the alert so he wouldn't have to listen to it again.

Drifting along peacefully among the clouds at two Earth atmospheres of pressure, the temperature about fifteen below Celsius, La Forge had a beautiful view. The clouds around him were water ice, a hint of blue to them. A kilometer above was the layer of tan ammonium-hydrosulfide clouds, lightning playing back and forth through them. He'd stabilized at an altitude about forty kilometers below where he'd fallen from the lift.

He knew it would be risky to pilot a shuttle through that weather, but not impossible. Of course, this was a big planet, and with long-range sensors almost useless in the ionized atmosphere, *Enterprise*'s shuttles could miss him even if every last one of them was flying around down here. But he had to try to hold on—literally. Though his shoulders ached and his fingers were numb, he still clutched the carry strap of the inflated shelter with both hands. At this point, he might not have been able to let go if he tried.

Of course, if he did, he would just end up dangling from the safety line like a child's toy tied to a balloon. That image brought a smirk to his face, which rapidly faded. Whether from exertion or oxygen deprivation, or both, he was getting sleepy. He would have to double his efforts, but he could feel his eyelids drooping behind his VISOR.

"*Warning: oxygen supply is below recommended refill level.*"

He jerked his head up, having come close to falling asleep. *One way or another, this will be decided soon,* he thought. It was not reassuring.

"They were wrong about the moons," said La Forge, shaking his head. He stood by the engineering station at the back of the bridge.

"Only the largest one is tectonically stable enough for colonization," agreed Data. "And even that one does not have a breathable atmosphere. There are no life signs."

As *Enterprise* neared Askaria, the recovered scramjet in tow by tractor beam, La Forge's hopes for survivors had already fallen considerably. They had entered the system on a course that took them past Narsosia first, easing into standard orbit near the only remaining space station, comparable in size to Earth Spacedock. The surface of the planet was invisible beneath a thick cover of clouds.

Data had reported the findings of his sensor scans to a bridge crew subdued in the face of an obviously dead world. "Captain, the atmosphere has a carbon dioxide level of approximately six thousand five hundred parts per million by volume, far above breathable levels for the Narsosians. The combined effect of all greenhouse gases present has driven the average surface temperature to one hundred twenty-five point three degrees Celsius. The atmosphere also has an elevated sulfur dioxide content, causing highly acidic rainfall with a pH of one point two. Ozone levels are severely depleted. There are numerous surface structures that could withstand these conditions, but there are no life signs above the level of various unicellular extremophiles. There are no artificial energy readings on the surface.

"There are also no energy readings aboard the station. Its hull has been compromised in at least thirty-three locations. There is evidence of the use of explosives throughout the structure. The pattern of Narsosian remains located in the station seems to indicate several factions fortified within their own sections. A carbon nanotube tether appears to have been purposefully severed from the base of the station."

"An attempt to stop further incursions by hostiles," Worf said.

Troi had looked up at Worf, her eyes shining with tears. "They were not 'hostiles,' they were desperate people, living in horrible conditions."

Worf looked down with a scowl. "I am not judging *why* they became hostile." He looked back at the screen. The station had slowly rotated, exposing a hole in the hull large enough to pilot an *Oberth*-class starship through. "But they *were* hostile."

Worf's comments at Narsosia still haunted La Forge's thoughts as he watched another uninhabitable Askarian moon slide by the forward screen. *How could they have survived all these centuries?* wondered La Forge. *Everything was stacked against them.*

"Captain, I have found something," Data said.

Picard sat up straighter. "Good news this time, I hope."

"Inconclusive for now; Askaria's intense electromagnetic field is interfering with sensors. But I have found scramjets in equatorial orbit around Askaria. I have detected one hundred and five total, although several of them appear to be open to vacuum."

"The one we boarded had five hundred people on it," said Riker. "There could have been fifty thousand Narsosians aboard those ships."

Wesley Crusher looked back from the conn. "Could they have survived all this time?"

"We can only hope so for now," said Picard. "Take us in closer. We'll see if we can cut through the interference at close range."

"Aye, sir."

"I've isolated the nearest scramjet on screen, sir," Worf said. All eyes focused on the silver ship standing out from the immense tan background of Askaria.

Troi squinted at the image. "What's that cable on the ship extending away from the planet?"

La Forge recognized its purpose immediately. "It's a counter-weight." He walked closer to the screen, pointing. "See, look below the craft, there's a planar ribbon tether descending into the atmosphere."

"An orbital elevator?" said Riker.

Data turned around. "Technically, such an elevator must be tethered to a planet's surface. On a gas giant such as Askaria, that would not be possible."

"No," La Forge said. "But you could just sink something deep into the atmosphere where the pressure would help anchor it. Kind of like the ocean platform on Argo."

"Are there any life signs?" said Picard.

"Scans are still indeterminate." Data continued adjusting the sensors as he spoke. "In addition to the strong EM field, the atmosphere is highly ionized, inhibiting sensors, transporters, and long-range communications below the troposphere."

La Forge moved back to the engineering station. "I'll route extra power to the sensor grid. Data, with that boost you might be able to tweak the scanning frequencies and punch through that field."

"That is a reasonable possibility," Data said. "Shall we proceed, Captain?"

"Make it so." While his crew wrestled with their technology, Picard turned toward Troi. "Are you sensing anything, Counselor?"

Troi closed her eyes for a moment to focus. "No, Captain." She opened her eyes, staring at the screen. "Not exactly. But . . . all I can say is that while I'm not directly feeling any consciousness out there, I'm also not getting the void in my empathic sense like I did at Narsosia."

As La Forge worked on the sensors, he realized he was smiling. *There must be Narsosians still alive down there somewhere,* he thought.

"With Geordi's assistance, I have partially compensated for the EM field," Data said. "I am getting more detailed scans of the orbiting scramjets. Some of them contain sophisticated manufacturing facilities, which appear to be in working order. Others have living quarters but no life signs. There are strong signs of plant growth on some ships, apparently viable gardens. There are no shuttlecraft. Outside of spacewalks, the only means of leaving the scramjets would appear to be the orbital elevators. I have detected sixty-seven more tethers among the other scramjets."

"Captain," Worf said loudly, "I am detecting life signs on the largest moon."

"I thought there was nothing down there," said Riker.

"The moon orbits within the planet's EM field," Worf explained. "So I rescanned it with the boosted sensor frequencies. There are at least eight scramjets on the surface. Two appear to have crashed, but the rest were soft landed."

"Confirmed," added Data as he personally scanned the moon again. He looked back at Picard. "And to clarify, the life signs are emanating from underground. I believe they have built a pressurized environment within natural caverns."

"This is remarkable," Picard said. He glanced back at La Forge. "I guess your optimism has won the day, Geordi."

"Thank you, sir."

"They may be prewarp, but they sent an interstellar distress call and successfully settled another world in their system," said Picard. "I don't see any significant Prime Directive issues here. Worf, can we hail them?"

"Possibly, sir. But I'm not detecting broadcast signals of any kind from the moon."

La Forge said, "Maybe they don't have the technology anymore. Or what they do have doesn't have the strength to make it through the rock and the EM field."

"If there's a chance they wouldn't be able to signal back," said Troi, "I recommend not trying to signal them. A voice out of nowhere that can't hear them could be quite disturbing to a race without any alien contact experience."

Picard nodded, then turned to Riker. "Take an away team to the moon."

"Aye, sir." Riker stood up.

"But remember," Picard added, "as Deanna pointed out, this is also a first contact mission. Take a shuttlecraft down but approach on foot—no beaming in. I'm sure the Askarians gave up on anyone coming to their aid centuries ago. We don't want to overwhelm them."

"Of course, sir. Any chance to wear an EV suit." He glanced around the bridge. "Same as before, Data, La Forge, and Worf, you're with me." He smiled down at Troi. "And, Counselor, perhaps you'd like to lend your expertise to a first contact?"

"I thought you'd never ask," she said as she stood.

"But, Captain," La Forge said, "what about Askaria?"

Picard stood up to make better eye contact with the away team. "Right now the life signs on the moon are our priority."

"I understand that, sir, but . . ." La Forge hesitated. Somehow this whole mission had become quite personal, and he wasn't sure why. But he did know that if he didn't continue pursuing it, he'd regret it later. "Captain, I'd like to take an away team into the Askarian atmosphere. All the people from the orbiting scramjets must be down there."

"I appreciate you volunteering, Geordi, but there's no reason why Askaria can't wait until after we contact the Narsosians on the moon. They may even have information about the other possible survivors."

"I understand that too, sir." La Forge looked around the bridge at his crewmates and friends. He wasn't as self-conscious as he thought he'd be, arguing with the captain in front of everyone. "I know you could say they've survived over six hundred years, they can get by for another day. But when I think of the Narsosian I found, her body by the beacon . . . I just don't want any of them waiting anymore."

Picard exchanged a look with Riker. Then he nodded his head with a smile. "How can I stand in the way of such enthusiasm? Lieutenant Commander La Forge, you will take an away team into the clouds of Askaria."

"Thank you, Captain."

Picard turned toward the screen, watching the orbiting scramjets. "We don't know how they're living down there. I'm reluctant to have you fly in." He looked back at La Forge. "Your team will beam over to one of the scramjets and use its elevator. Knock on their front door, if you will."

"Aye, sir."

"Take Mister Worf and Counselor Troi with you." Picard looked at Riker. "I'm confident you can handle the first contact, Will. Just get another security officer to accompany you and Data."

"Aye, sir."

"Everyone dismissed. It's time we introduced ourselves."

"Warning: oxygen supply is critical. Refill now."

La Forge took a deep breath, knowing it might be his last. He looked around the sky as best he could, hoping to see a shuttle appear. Nothing.

And then movement. A shape appeared from the clouds, rushing toward him. His spirits soared, and he felt as though he'd gotten a shot of tri-ox.

"Over here!" he yelled, then laughed at himself. Yelling wouldn't help over a comm signal, and he was the only thing here, easy to spot hanging from the inflated shelter. Besides, odds were they'd picked him up with sensors, not just stumbled upon him in this vast atmosphere. He looked forward to the teasing Riker would

give him when he heard about it. Maybe it was Riker himself piloting the shuttle.

But then the shape dissolved into several shapes. Dozens of
shapes. There was no shuttle.

A group of flying creatures banked away from him, then swerved
back again. They looked like manta rays, broad and flat, their wings
at least three meters wide. They were tan on the underside and
blue on the top, camouflaged to blend with the clouds. The mantas
dove beneath him and raced away as more animals burst from the
same cloud bank, clearly in pursuit.

These creatures were long and slender, squidlike, with more
than half of their eight-meter length made up of tentacles streaming
behind them. They were pinkish in color, indicating they probably
spent more time higher up in the reddish clouds. There was a dark
hump on their back by the tentacles. Along the tops and sides of
their bodies were clusters of small appendages, grouped around a
central protrusion; on every squid several of these protrusions
extruded a yellowish, ropelike substance into the air.

Confused, La Forge kicked his legs, burning precious oxygen to
get a better look at the squids—six of them had appeared from the
cloud—as they pursued the mantas. His eyes followed the ropes
upward. High above he saw the ropes attached to what looked like
large billowing parachutes made of the same substance as the
ropes. As he stared at the parachutes, one of them tilted, seemed to
hang in the sky. Following its ropes downward, he saw that one of
the squids had fanned out its tentacles, forcing itself into a wide,
high arc as the small appendages on one side of its body reeled in
rope to the protrusion, which now looked more like a mouth
devouring the yellowish substance.

Finally he understood that the squids were actually flying on
silken sails that they wove and controlled, directing them to different atmospheric layers and winds as needed. The squid that now
pirouetted toward him was apparently coming for a closer look,
maybe to see if he'd be tastier than a manta.

Shifting his weight to his left arm and the safety line, La Forge
lowered his stiff right arm to reach for his phaser. His feet swung to
his left, and he started spinning around. In his oxygen-deprived
state he felt dizzy already, and now as he spun he felt helpless. He
forgot about the phaser and stretched back up to grab on again with

his right hand to stabilize himself. But he found that he couldn't raise his arm high enough; he was just too sore and tired.

Maybe it's time to give up, he thought. *And be eaten by a bunch of flying squid. All the times I thought I might die in Starfleet, it was never anything as ridiculous as that.*

La Forge watched the squid as it circled him, and it watched back with a dark blue eye the size of a large melon. The hump on its back near the base of the tentacles was moving. *Is that its mouth?* La Forge wondered. *Is that a flying squid licking its lips before a nice snack?*

The squid zipped by and headed back in the direction it had come from, apparently having caught a different wind. It was only as the squid faded back into the clouds that La Forge, no longer focused on the idea of being eaten, realized that the hump on the squid's back was actually a humanoid in an environmental suit, its body below the waist grasped firmly within the tentacles.

"How long will this elevator ride take?" said Troi.

They had beamed into the lower level of the closest pressurized scramjet with an orbital elevator. The away team, carrying their helmets, looked around what La Forge thought of as the "lobby." The lobby was empty except for the tether's anchoring structure in the middle of the room, an airlock near the anchor, and a control console at the bottom of the gangway. Thanks to Data's earlier work, he could translate the Narsosian labels on the controls. He had already figured out the elevator wasn't pressurized.

"The elevator's at the bottom, but there's a high-speed setting for when it's unoccupied. It'll zip up here in about an hour. The ride down, however . . ." La Forge shrugged. "That'll take several hours."

Troi frowned. "I should have brought something to read."

Worf bared his teeth as he continued to take tricorder scans. "There will be enough time to tell the story of *Aktuh and Melota.*"

"Klingon opera?" Troi said. "You're not going to sing, are you?"

"No. Not alone."

La Forge held up his hands. "Don't look at me. Just listening to Klingon makes my throat hurt." Leaving Troi and Worf to sort out the entertainment for the ride down, La Forge walked across the compartment to the anchor. The tether actually passed through the anchor and on up through the scramjet; it continued to stretch outward from the planet to counterbalance the elevator. Reaching into a supply pouch on his right leg, he pulled out a communications relay, stretched up to affix it to the tether, and activated it.

He tapped the test button on the side. "La Forge to *Enterprise*."

"*Enterprise, Picard here.*"

"Captain, I'm just testing the comm relay." By placing the comm relays as they descended, the away team would be able to conduct a signal up the tether itself and out of the ionized Askarian atmosphere, maintaining contact with the ship. They would have to stop and remove the relays on the way back up. "Any word from Commander Riker?"

"*Their shuttle's nearing the moon. Close-range scans show the grounded scramjets are the entrances to the caverns below. They're still figuring out which is the easiest to approach on foot.*"

"Thanks, Captain. We'll check in at the next relay."

"*Very well. Picard out.*"

La Forge turned to face Worf and Troi. "We've got some time to kill. Let's check out the upper level."

With a nod, Worf led the way. As they got to the top of the gangway, Troi said, "What happened here?"

They glanced around the large main compartment. On the other scramjet, this had been the passenger compartment; here, except for the tether running through another structural anchor at the center of the compartment, the entire space was devoted to a hydroponic garden. Full-spectrum lights illuminated the space like high noon on a planet. Instead of a peaceful atmosphere, however, the garden had the feel of a natural disaster. Racks of hydroponic containers were lying on their sides, their nutrient solutions spilled and evaporated, leaving dried remains of various roots. Other plants survived, but as La Forge inspected them he could see that the fruits or vegetables had been carelessly torn away, perhaps leaving the plants unable to produce in the future.

"It looks like a raid," Worf said. "The rightful owners would not have done this."

"It could have been some sort of emergency during the harvest," said La Forge. "A fluctuation in the scramjet's orbit, maybe."

Worf said nothing, but his expression was skeptical. He continued taking tricorder scans as he walked down the rows of hydroponic racks.

Troi stepped closer to La Forge. "I agree with Worf." She looked around the room again. "Something's not right here."

La Forge sighed. "Maybe the start of the same kind of unrest they had on their homeworld."

"I recommend we take additional security personnel with us," Worf piped up from across the compartment.

"We can't show up like an invasion force," La Forge said. "Look, there's nothing here that couldn't have been an accident or even an adolescent prank."

Worf grudgingly acknowledged that, which caused La Forge to wonder what sort of mayhem teenage Klingons caused. *Probably a lot worse than this.* They continued exploring the scramjet but found no conclusive evidence. Finally La Forge said, "It's almost time. Let's get our helmets on and run through a suit check."

They headed down the gangway to where they'd left their helmets. Just as they finished the safety protocols, the elevator control console emitted a loud tone and a light came on inside the airlock.

"Well," said La Forge with a smile, "I guess our ride is here." Troi rolled her eyes as Worf grimaced. "What? That was exactly like something Commander Riker would have said."

"But he would have made it work," said Worf. Troi laughed, tried to cover her mouth, but only hit her faceplate with her gloved hand.

La Forge shook his head as he opened the airlock, leading them inside. A red-striped hatch on the floor was clearly off limits, so they stood back from it. The entrance hatch sealed behind them and, after a quick cycling of air, the red-striped floor hatch opened, revealing a ladder. Leaning forward, La Forge peeked down the ladder to an oval platform with a short railing around it and seats with lap belts.

"Guys, the elevator is a bit . . . minimalist," La Forge said.

La Forge stared at the cloud where the squid had vanished, his oxygen-starved brain still trying to process the image of the humanoid. *That was a Narsosian* riding *one of those flying squids,* he thought. *They were hunting the mantas.* He didn't know what he had expected if he found the Narsosians, but he hadn't let his imag-ination run this far.

Then a movement in the cloud focused his fading attention. But it was no squid. A bulbous shape appeared out of the mist. a dark-ness behind it hinting of a larger shape still hidden. *What is that?* The shape continued to expand. It reminded La Forge of an ancient dirigible, an airship, but he knew it was another Askarian life-form. Its skin was mottled tan with streaks of bioluminescence. Clusters of bright red stalks sprouted from it in random spots. *Sensory organs, maybe,* La Forge thought. And still it emerged, its shape continuing to expand. It looked a couple hundred meters long and fifty meters across. Dangling below it was a patchwork of nets and ropes, suspending an array of platforms and shelters. Dozens of Narsosians in EV suits moved about on the platforms and in the rigging.

As La Forge watched, a group of them walked to one side of the airship and pulled some ropes, adjusting rudders that hung below the platforms. Slowly, the airship turned toward him, its body undulating strangely as the creature followed its riders' wishes, guided by the rudders. As it drew closer, several of the stalk clus-ters vibrated and angled toward him.

Okay, so now I'm going to be eaten by a giant balloon.

Instead, as the airship floated past him, a Narsosian reached out with a hooked rod and snagged his safety line, pulling him into the rigging. A group of them grabbed him. They fumbled around with his safety line until they succeeded in deactivating and re-tracting it, and he was carried along a series of platforms, his feet dragging behind him. He was pulled up an angled platform that led to a dead end, the skin of the airship. The Narsosians pushed him against the creature. Its body yielded a bit, like an inflated cushion.

"What are you doing?" La Forge gasped, though he doubted they could hear him. He felt that inhaling to ask his question had finally exhausted his air supply to the last molecule.

Then the creature's skin suddenly parted like a mouth and he was sucked inside.

The first six hours of the descent went smoothly, once La Forge and Troi got used to plummeting toward a giant planet at a couple hundred kilometers per hour on an open platform while listening to the plot of a Klingon opera. They sank through the thermosphere, mesosphere, and stratosphere. At the beginning of the transition from stratosphere to troposphere, La Forge slowed the elevator.

"Time to place a comm relay," he explained as he brought the platform to a complete stop.

"Good, I could use a break," said Troi.

Worf scowled as he paused in his recitation. *"From what?"*

Troi looked from Worf to La Forge, blinking her dark eyes innocently. *"From the rapid descent, of course."*

"We're still under less than one atmosphere of pressure," La Forge said, smiling. "Besides, your suit's compensating for the pressure increase."

"Thanks for clearing that up for me, Geordi." She squinted at him. *"I'm sensing someone owes me a chocolate sundae."*

With a chuckle, La Forge got out of his seat and reached to disconnect his safety line.

"What are you doing?" Troi said.

"I have to take my line with me." He moved over to the drive unit, reached as high as he could, and reattached his safety. "If I keep it above me, it can break my fall. *If* I fall. And it's less likely to get tangled with you two."

Worf got out of his seat to give La Forge a boost as the engineer clambered up the drive mechanism. Once La Forge was high enough to reach above the rollers, he dug into the supply pouch on his right leg for another relay, placed it on the tether, and activated it.

"La Forge to *Enterprise*."

"Riker here. I win."

"What's that, Commander?"

"I've already found 'my' Narsosians. There are a couple thousand survivors. And I brought back a pair of negotiators to the ship."

La Forge's brow furrowed as he climbed back down. "I don't understand. What is there to negotiate?"

"Well, they're very . . . independent." Riker's smile came through his voice. *"They're negotiating the terms of their rescue."*

"Terms of rescue?" As La Forge got back down to the passenger platform, he deactivated the adhesion plate of his safety line and took in some slack before reattaching the line beside his seat. "That's just crazy."

"*Not necessarily,*" said Troi. "*Most people don't really like having to ask for help.*"

"*And they have survived all this time without anyone's help,*" said Worf.

"Okay," La Forge said. "So I guess we know not to expect an enthusiastic welcome."

"*That's not all. The delegation is quite concerned about the 'clouders,' as they call the people you're looking for. When the Narsosians first got here and found just one moon they could colonize, they were forced to choose the few who would settle the moon, leaving the rest to make a go of it in orbit.*"

Troi said, "*The same nightmare they'd gone through when deciding who would leave the homeworld.*"

"*Exactly. They avoided violence this time, but it was a terrible situation. They were able to stay in contact at first, while the clouders still lived in the scramjets. But as the clouders devised ways to enter, and then live in, the atmosphere, they became more withdrawn and resentful. Even though they could still make contact from the scramjets, they stopped doing so. There's been no contact between the two groups in over four hundred years.*"

"So they can't give us any idea of what to expect down there," La Forge said.

"*No, they can't. Sorry, Geordi.*"

"Then I guess we better just go find out for ourselves. La Forge out." He looked at his away team. "Everybody buckled up? Let's get going."

Half an hour later, La Forge eased the lift to a halt again. They would have to stop more frequently to place the relays as they got deeper into the atmosphere. After scrambling atop the drive unit and attaching another comm relay, La Forge was startled by Worf shouting.

"*Geordi, behind you!*"

Taking a huge gasp of air brought La Forge rushing back to the present. His surroundings spiraled into focus. He lay on his back, helmet off, still gulping more than breathing. Several Narsosians stood around him, peering down. From his vantage on the floor, the tall

Narsosians seemed to stretch to the ceiling. Their clothes looked like they were woven of squid silk and dyed with random splashes of color. As his brain was replenished with oxygen and his thinking cleared, he realized that the ceiling really was just a few centimeters above their heads. And the ceiling was . . . undulating.

La Forge reached up to his VISOR to make sure it was properly attached to its contacts on his temples. Just as he confirmed it was working properly, he finally recalled the airship sucking him into a dark, cramped space, then being "spit out" again, through a biological airlock, into this place. The realization jolted him to action, and he rolled quickly onto his hands and knees then sprang to his feet. The Narsosians stepped back, giving him room as he spread out his arms for balance. The floor yielded a bit under his feet, making it difficult to stand still. He glanced around at the dome-shaped space, its wavering walls, the bioluminescent stripes that lit it. It was about the size of the observation lounge back on the *Enterprise* and was clearly inside the airship.

"It's all right," said a female Narsosian as she stepped forward. She made calming gestures with her hands and spoke in exaggerated soothing tones. "I know you can't understand me, but you're safe now . . ."

La Forge forced himself to relax. He got a better stance as he remembered trying out a trampoline on the holodeck once; the inside of the airship had much the same feel. "I can understand you." Surprised at the translator's effects, the Narsosians whispered nervously among themselves. La Forge tapped his VISOR. "Like this helps me see, we have a specialized computer for translation. We translated your language from the distress call."

The woman looked suspicious. "We sent no distress call."

La Forge shook his head gently. "Not you personally. I meant the old distress call, when your ancestors left Narsosia. We recovered the scramjet the beacon was on."

Now they all looked suspicious. A couple of the males chomped their wide teeth together a couple times.

"We detected the signal a few days ago. My ship, the *Enterprise,* is in orbit around Askaria. We came here as fast as we could." He took a careful step forward, noticing something that had been missing from the mummified Narsosians. The downy hair that covered their skin could subtly shift colors. A quiet wave of blue seemed to wash over them, and although La Forge had no idea what that might mean, he pushed on. "Our ships are faster than light. Space travel is much easier now. Like most things."

The woman took another step toward him. "I'm Ontra. I lead on this float." Her down had turned a pale white.

"I'm Lieutenant Commander Geordi La Forge." La Forge smiled. *Now I'm getting somewhere.*

"What do you want with us?"

Or maybe I'm not getting anywhere. "We want nothing from you," he said, thinking about what Riker had told him about the delegation from the moon. "But I do want to thank you for rescuing me. I thought I was going to be doing the rescuing."

Ontra frowned. "Do we look like we need rescuing?"

La Forge wasn't sure how to answer that, and he wished he had Troi here. *But I don't. I'll have to handle this myself.* "I'm sorry, I didn't mean—"

"Our ancestors fought their way here and into orbit, losing dozens of ships along the way and to the depths. More fell as they built the elevators. We've lived here for generations, maintaining our technology, domesticating the floats and the flyers." She gestured around the room. "We bred the floats to have these large oxygen chambers and allow us inside. We are Askarians now. There are forty thousand of us, living on over four hundred floats. What could you do for us?"

"If you want, we could relocate you and the Narsosians on the moon to—"

"The grounders!" Ontra's down flushed a soft orange. "They were given up on long ago."

"Just listen a second!" Realizing how loud he'd spoken, La Forge forced himself to take a breath. "If everything's so great, why did we find a wrecked garden in orbit? Why are all the scramjets abandoned? Why hasn't your population grown in six centuries? You can't tell me you don't need help."

Ontra opened her mouth as if to yell back, then hesitated. Her down faded to white again, and when she spoke it was just above a whisper. "We've tried to live honestly, not like on Narsosia. But our resources are dwindling. "

"Ontra," said one of the men as he walked up beside her. He was well over two meters tall, and his head rubbed the ceiling. "Please, don't talk this way."

She smiled at him, and when she put a hand on his shoulder, his down turned light tan. "Ruro, we all know it's true." Ontra turned back to La Forge. "There have been raids on the scramjets. The technology, nurseries, and gardens we used to share are now being plundered."

"That's what I'm trying to tell you," La Forge said sympathetically. "We're from the United Federation of Planets, which has a hundred and fifty members on thousands of worlds. We will freely share our resources with you. There won't be any more raids. If you take me back to the elevator, you could speak directly with my captain. My crewmates might even still be there."

Ontra turned away from him. The rest of the Askarians came forward and formed a circle with her. They whispered among themselves, too quietly for the translator to pick up. When they broke out of the circle, their down had turned light blue again, which La Forge hoped was a good sign.

Ontra said, "You recovered a ship?"

"Yes. It's in orbit."

"Thank you. Families were split up among the ships. There may still be descendants who wish to perform burial rites." She looked away for a moment, then back. "I'll take you to the lift. I just hope your crewmates are safe."

La Forge couldn't let go of Ontra, no matter how tightly the squid's tentacles held him. When Ontra had said she'd take him to the elevator, he'd assumed they'd take the airship. But the airships, as their Askarian name said, just floated. They could be steered a little bit, like when they had rescued La Forge, but that was all. To go someplace fast or against the wind, you needed to take a flyer.

Ontra had gathered together five of her people, including Ruro. After suiting up, getting their comm systems to work together, and refilling La Forge's oxygen tank, they'd crawled into the pink tentacles of six waiting flyers, with La Forge riding behind Ontra. The flyers had quickly spun their sails high into the air to catch the right wind. There was a lot of tacking and circling to avoid wind shears and lightning storms, and La Forge had finally done the VISOR equivalent of just closing his eyes.

"*I can see the lift,*" Ontra said. "*There are two people on it, in suits like yours.*"

La Forge reactivated his VISOR. Although it made his stomach lurch, he loosened his grip around Ontra's waist so that he could lean over to look around her. He could see Troi and Worf on the platform, but there was something about the way they stood, almost back to back, that bothered him.

Then Ruro said, "*Raiders!*"

La Forge caught a glimpse of two other squids with riders circling down on the far side of the elevator, closing on the away team. That's why they had taken a defensive posture.

"*Take them,*" Ontra said icily, and she urged her flyer forward. They raced in with their superior numbers, but the raiders didn't retreat.

The air quickly turned into a confusion of circling squids and crisscrossing sails. The colors of the clouds blended together, and La Forge could barely keep track of whether he was looking down into the yawning depths or up into open sky. The squids' sail lines would tangle, break, and be respun, sometimes they were even shared, momentarily entwined sails pulling flyers off in unexpected directions. He wasn't sure how this was supposed to capture the raiders but assumed it would involve more of the squid silk. Once, Ontra's flyer was forced to sever all its lines, doing so as it pulled into a tight spin and launched itself high above the elevator. As it reached the peak of its trajectory, it erupted with silk, spinning a full sail in record time as it began to dive back into the fight.

In the middle of this aerial ballet, La Forge caught another glimpse of Troi and Worf on the elevator. He switched back to the standard Starfleet frequency. "La Forge to Troi."

"*Geordi, I don't believe it, we thought we lost you! We scrambled a shuttle, but lightning drove it back.*" She was yelling, but La Forge didn't mind. "*Where are you?*"

"I'm on one of these crazy flying squids. The two that came after you first are the raiders—"

Worf's deep voice broke in. "*Which side does that belong to?*"

A shadow suddenly covered the platform as a float descended from the clouds. The two raider flyers quickly retreated behind it. The crew in the float's rigging held primitive weapons, which La Forge realized were crossbows.

He switched his comm frequency. "Ontra, we've got to pull back."

But the air was already full of projectiles, simple but deadly, especially in this environment. An arrow plunged into one of Ontra's people. A fog of oxygen rushed out of the breach in her suit as subzero hydrogen rushed in. She was dead in moments, and her terrified flyer turned and sailed away. Ruro retaliated, moving against the airship itself, rocketing forward as his squid severed all its sail lines. Slamming into the skin of the airship at speed, the squid sank its clawed tentacles deep, letting its momentum carry it forward, tearing three deep gashes several meters long.

The entire airship flinched as it vented freezing gas from the wounds. Ruro and his squid were blasted free, and the flyer quickly spun a new sail as it fell. The float rolled forward, listing steeply as it lost buoyancy, pitching four of its crew out of the rigging. As they tumbled downward, Worf and Troi grabbed one to the elevator, and they collapsed in a heap on the floor of the platform. The others continued falling toward the deeps.

Their two riders rushed after them, the squids shooting silken ropes down to catch them. Two were snared by the sticky lines, but the last disappeared into the clouds below.

La Forge watched the depths for a few seconds, but no other rider dared pursue. He looked back up at the wounded airship, which had started to slowly sink. "Ontra," he said.

She did not respond but turned away from the float. Through his grip around her waist he felt her go limp.

He resisted the urge to physically shake her. "The float is sinking!"

"Yes. A hundred more will slowly fall to their deaths."

"We can save them. Spray silk between the float and the elevator."

After a pause she said, "That could work." She straightened up. "Everyone, follow my lead." They swooped in close, her flyer letting loose a long silken spray that spread from the tether to the float. Her remaining team, Ruro included, came in close behind, adding their silk to the first line. As they circled around, La Forge saw the raiders join in.

Looking back at the wounded airship, La Forge saw that the strain put on its skin by the silk lines was opening the wounds farther. "Let me off," he said.

"What do you mean?" said Ontra.

"Drop me on top of the float."

After adding another strand between tether and float, Ontra guided her flyer in close, pulling up at the end to give La Forge a short drop. He landed on both feet, the surface of the airship sinking beneath him, then rebounding. Stumbling, he fell on his back and slid across the rounded surface, gaining speed until he grabbed one of the stalk clusters.

"Geordi, you will not fall again," Worf growled, having adjusted his comm frequency to match the Narsosians'.

"You can't order me not to fall. I outrank you." He scrambled to his feet and moved closer to the center of the float, struggling to keep his balance on top of the shuddering animal.

"I *can order you,*" Troi said. *"I can pull medical rank by questioning your sanity."*

"Well, all right, if it's doctor's orders . . ." La Forge stopped and looked around, trying to see the flyers. "Ontra, Ruro, aim for my feet. These anchor points won't open the wounds more."

They followed his directions, and soon all the flyers were spraying lines wherever he pointed. The strain on the float was now pulling the wounds closed, and the float started excreting a slimy film over them to stop the leaks. The silk stretched, then held, and the float's descent halted.

"We did it!" La Forge walked to the tether, attached his safety line, and slid down to the platform where Troi hugged him as much as could be done in an EV suit, while Worf clapped him on the back. Their reunion was cut short as armed guards from the airship arrived to escort them away.

In the wounded float's oxygen chamber, its leader, Fushol, yelled, "There has never been an attack on a float!"

"Your people fired first," Ontra said, her quiet voice as full of anger as Fushol's shouting. "I lost a great hunter and friend today."

"And we lost a technician, and our float is seriously wounded." Fushol stomped in a circle around Ontra, Ruro, La Forge, Worf, and Troi. He stopped near Ruro. "A flyer skirmish is one thing, but to endanger an entire float? That goes against everything."

Ruro started to respond, but Ontra stopped him with a glance. She stepped between him and Fushol. "Yes, a flyer skirmish is one thing, but firing on flyers from a float is something else entirely. As is raiding a communal garden."

The two stared at each other nose to nose, silent and fuming, rapid waves of color washing across their down.

"Both of you have legitimate complaints," Troi said. "If you let me mediate—"

"You?" Fushol turned and glared at Troi. "Your crewmate flew with those who tried to sink us."

"It was that same crewmate who saved you from sinking."

"You know nothing about our laws," said Ontra. "How could you mediate?"

La Forge said, "Listen, everyone—" But Ontra and Fushol were back to arguing. "Ontra, please." The float leaders moved off to the side of the chamber, ignoring La Forge. He looked at Worf.

Worf simply nodded and then bellowed, "Be quiet!"

The command was so loud it startled the float, which flinched around them. Everyone stumbled and looked at Worf, who shrugged and gestured to La Forge.

"Okay, now that I have your attention. For you to keep arguing when—"

"This is between us," Ontra and Fushol said in unison. Then everyone went quiet as a shudder moved through the float.

Troi said, "The float didn't do that."

"Data to La Forge."

This can't be good, La Forge thought. "La Forge here. What's going on?"

"The scramjet is losing orbit. If the float's wounds have not sealed completely, it could still be losing buoyancy and adding more mass to the tether. I will put a tractor beam on the scramjet to stabilize it."

"Belay that." Even as La Forge said it, the airship began to list noticeably. "They want us to mind our own business."

Troi looked nervous but said nothing. Worf gave La Forge a wicked smile. As La Forge turned to Ontra and Fushol, the airship suddenly dropped a full meter, sending them staggering, guards and captives alike.

Data's tone was as concerned as the android could sound. *"Geordi?"*

"Stand by, Data," La Forge said, as he struggled to keep on his feet. He staggered back toward Fushol and Ontra. "We can help as much or as little as you want. We can reunite you with the grounders or keep you separate. We can introduce you to the whole Federation or leave you here alone."

The airship dropped again, at least two meters, throwing them all to the floor. Before they could get to their feet, it tilted about thirty degrees, tumbling everyone into the wall. The bioluminescent glow in the room dimmed considerably.

"Geordi, I suggest we activate the tractor beam."

"Go ahead, Data."

"Activating tractor now." Slowly, as the float was pulled to its previous altitude, the floor leveled off.

La Forge got up and then held his hands out to Ontra and Fushol. "It's your decision."

They exchanged looks and, while keeping an eye on each other, allowed La Forge to help them to their feet. With a tilt of his head, Fushol led Ontra aside to again talk between themselves. Troi and Worf joined La Forge to wait for the outcome. Over the next several minutes, the dim light pulsing through the walls of the float increased to its regular level. Fushol's voice raised a couple times, but Ontra calmed him down. La Forge watched them as closely as he could without being too obvious. The riot of colors across their down eventually quieted, and they both became a soft shade of blue. After a couple more minutes of hushed talking, they returned to face La Forge.

Ontra said, "We'll call a meeting of all the float leaders. Together we'll recommend choosing representatives to talk with you and the grounders."

"I'm happy to hear that." La Forge turned to Worf. "Could you help Fushol contact the other leaders? Some atmospheric probes might speed the process."

"Aye, sir. I'll work with Data on those probes." Worf gestured for Fushol to follow him. Fushol looked at Worf as if for the first time. The tall Askarian glowered down at the Klingon. Worf glared back until Fushol appeared almost to laugh, and then he followed Worf to a quiet side of the chamber.

"Ontra," La Forge said, "would you consider letting Counselor Troi help the meeting stay on track?"

"On your word, Geordi, I'll present her to the leaders." She gave

Troi an appraising look. "I'll get you some background on our laws and customs. I'll see what Fushol has here. If need be, I can send Ruro back to my float for more records." The leader headed off.

Troi smiled at La Forge. "You're quite pleased with yourself."

La Forge nodded. "Yes, I am. Listen, about the tractor beam business . . . I'm sorry if I scared you."

She shrugged. "I knew what you were up to, of course. Unlike some diplomats I've met, I knew you wouldn't force the Askarians to agree with you before you activated the tractor beam. But the situation was a bit unpredictable."

"Are you talking about their decision or the decaying orbit?"

"Yes." They both laughed at that.

"Well, I'm an engineer, not a diplomat. I like to use technology, not people."

Troi gave him another big smile and a pat on the shoulder, then followed after Ontra.

La Forge contacted *Enterprise*. "La Forge to Riker."

"Riker here."

"It'll take a while, but we're going to have several more delegates for your negotiations."

"Congratulations, that's great news."

"And my delegates will be representing a lot more people than yours, so . . ." La Forge smiled. "I win."

THINKING OF YOU

Greg Cox

Historian's note:
This tale unfolds concurrently with the episode
"New Ground," during the fifth season of
Star Trek: The Next Generation.

GREG COX

Greg Cox is the *New York Times* bestselling author of numerous *Star Trek* novels and short stories, including *The Q Continuum, The Eugenics Wars, To Reign in Hell, Assignment: Eternity,* and *The Black Shore.* He recently contributed a novel to *Star Trek Mirror Universe: Glass Empires.* He has also written the official movie novelizations of *Ghost Rider, Daredevil, Underworld,* and *Underworld: Evolution,* as well as the novelizations of two recent DC Comics mini-series, *Infinite Crisis* and *52.* Over the years, he has written books and stories based on such popular series as *Alias, Batman, Buffy, Fantastic Four, Farscape, Iron Man, Roswell, Star Trek, Underworld, Xena,* and *X-Men.*

He lives in Oxford, Pennsylvania.

Personal log, Lieutenant Reginald Barclay, Stardate 45376.3

As a favor to the Betazoid ambassador, Captain Picard has dispatched Ensign Ro and me to rendezvous with Ambassador Troi's private yacht, the Cataria, *in order to provide technical assistance while she conducts delicate trade negotiations between Betazed and the Tadigeans. The* Cataria *has been newly fitted with a holodeck expressly for this meeting . . .*

"LOOK SHARP," RO LAREN SAID AS THE *CATARIA* CAME INTO view. The Bajoran ensign piloted their shuttlecraft while Barclay rode shotgun beside her. Lwaxana Troi's personal vessel soon filled the cockpit's front windows. Over fifty meters long, the sleek, warp-capable yacht dwarfed the smaller shuttle. "Time for our command performance." Her dark hair met in a widow's peak above the ridges of her nose. "How exactly does Counselor Troi's mother rate our services, anyway? Since when does Starfleet loan out its officers to Betazed's trade commission?"

"The ambassador is a c-close personal friend of the captain's," Barclay stammered, attempting a professional tone to mask the apprehension he felt as they drew nearer to their destination. He had been dreading this rendezvous the whole way here. "Besides, it's always in the Federation's interest to promote closer relations between different worlds, especially in cases like this. The Tadigeans are notoriously xenophobic; increased trade with Betazed might encourage them to overcome their mistrust of strangers."

"I suppose," she said, sounding dubious. New to the *Enterprise,* Ro had a prickly edge that made her hard to get to know. Their voyage to this sector had been full of uncomfortable silences, at least as far as Barclay was concerned. For all he knew, Ro liked it that way. "Anyway, here we are."

Already? He swallowed hard and wiped his sweaty palms upon his trousers. *If only I could have gotten out of this mission,* he thought glumly. He had tried to talk Geordi into delegating someone else, but the *Enterprise*'s engineering chief had insisted that Barclay was the right man for the job. *Especially since I couldn't admit to him the* real *reason I wanted out of this assignment . . .*

The shuttle docked with the *Cataria,* and Barclay thanked the fates that at least they weren't beaming over to the other ship. One of these days, he knew, he would have to do something about his transporter phobia, but right now that was the least of his worries.

He reached beneath his seat and brought out a visored cap, in the same black-and-gold shades as his Starfleet uniform. A mild jolt rocked the shuttle as its landing gear touched down on the roof of the *Cataria.* He hastily clamped the cap onto his head.

Ro gave him a quizzical look. "That's not exactly regulation."

"M-my head was cold," he said unconvincingly. "It's a well-known scientific fact that human beings lose thirty-five percent of their body heat from their heads."

Ro shrugged. "If you say so."

The silvery Bajoran earring dangling from her left ear reminded Barclay that Ro wasn't much of a stickler for the rules either. It occurred to him that they were both sort of misfits aboard the *Enterprise.* He wasn't sure she'd appreciate that observation, however, so he kept it to himself.

"Powering down," she reported.

Ro killed the shuttle's engines. An access panel in the floor connected with one of *Cataria*'s airlocks. There was no way to put off boarding the yacht any longer. Barclay felt like a condemned man going to face a firing squad.

Let's get this over with, he thought as he reluctantly rose from his seat. If nothing else, he figured they could count on a warm welcome from Ambassador Troi.

"You? You're the best Starfleet can send me?"

Lwaxana Troi, daughter of the Fifth House, Holder of the Sacred Chalice of Rixx, Heir to the Holy Rings of Betazed, and roving ambassador extraordinary and plenipotentiary, glared scornfully at her two visitors. A low-cut burgundy gown, woven from the finest Vulcan damask, clothed her imposing figure. Gold-pressed latinum glittered upon her ears, hands, and throat. Curly auburn hair piled atop her head like an ominous storm cloud. She had the indignant expression and body language of someone who had been expecting Thalian chocolate mousse only to be served a plateful of wriggling *gagh* instead. "Where are Captain Picard and my daughter?"

"I'm afraid that the captain and Counselor Troi are busy with other matters," Barclay said vaguely. For security reasons, he could not divulge that the *Enterprise* and the rest of its crew were currently engaged in a top secret test of the new soliton wave technology. Barclay fervently wished that he was taking part in that test as well, and not just because the soliton wave experiment, if successful, promised to revolutionize interstellar travel. "They send their apologies."

"'Other matters'?" His explanation failed to mollify the miffed ambassador. "I can't possibly imagine what could be more important than the vital talks to be conducted aboard this very ship, but I suppose I'll just have to make do with whatever feeble assistance Jean-Luc deigns to bestow upon me." She eyed Barclay with obvious disdain. "And where are your manners, Lieutenant? Don't you know that you should doff your hat in the presence of a lady? Let alone a daughter of the Fifth House."

Barclay's heart sank. "With your p-permission, I'd rather keep it on." Despite the yacht's cozy environmental settings, which were actually several degrees warmer than the *Enterprise*'s, a chill ran down his spine. "Humanoids lose thirty-five percent of their body hea—"

Lwaxana couldn't care less. "Take off that ridiculous cap at once."

Barclay hesitated, frozen like plasma caught in a stasis beam.

His eyes darted from side to side as he desperately looked for some way out of this situation. But there was no escape. He was trapped.

This is just what I was afraid of!

He fought to keep his hands from shaking as he reached up and removed the cap from his scalp. His mousy brown hair, mussed from its recent captivity, was in complete disarray. He nervously attempted to slick it back into place, while trying unsuccessfully to avoid the ambassador's eyes. Her large black orbs, so very like Counselor Troi's, seemed to bore into his skull. He tried, and failed, to clear his mind of any incriminating thoughts. How do you *not* think about something?

"Telepaths?" she blurted, immediately picking up on the source of his discomfort. "You're afraid of telepaths?"

Barclay felt exposed, in more ways than one. Now everyone would know how much mind readers spooked him. Especially powerful and indiscreet ones like Lwaxana Troi. *She can see right through me.* Mortified, he fingered the lining of his cap. Specialized circuitry, which Barclay had cobbled together from pieces of a discarded neurocortical monitor, generated the psychic equivalent of white noise. In theory, the jury-rigged cap could protect his thoughts from prying minds. But only if he was actually wearing it.

"A little," he admitted.

Lwaxana acted as though she couldn't believe what she was hearing—and sensing. "Telephobia? In this day and age?" Her hand went to her chest as she struck a horrified pose. "I am shocked, shocked to encounter such a barbaric attitude—and in the mind of a Starfleet officer, no less." She peered down her nose at Barclay. "And I can't say I approve of your fantasies concerning my daughter, either. 'The Goddess of Empathy,' indeed!"

Barclay's face turned a bright shade of red. Having his atoms ripped apart by a transporter beam suddenly seemed preferable to having Deanna's mother rifle through his brain. Why couldn't the ambassador just be an empath like her daughter? Dealing with Counselor Troi was one thing; she could sense only his emotions, not what he was thinking. Besides, he knew that Deanna would never pass judgment on him. Her mother was another story altogether.

"Well, maybe there would be less telephobia in the galaxy," Ro challenged Lwaxana, speaking up for the first time, "if certain telepaths had more respect for other people's privacy."

Lwaxana's jaw dropped. Taken aback by Ro's blunt rejoinder, the ambassador was rendered momentarily speechless. Barclay was caught by surprise as well. He hadn't expected Ro to come to his defense. *I didn't even think she liked me.*

Unable to refute Ro's argument, Lwaxana blustered instead. "I'm not sure I approve of your tone, Ensign." She treated the younger woman to her most withering look, but Ro neither budged nor flinched. She held her ground until Lwaxana finally threw up her arms in defeat. "Oh, go ahead and wear your absurd headgear if it makes you feel more comfortable," she snapped at Barclay. "Needless to say, I fully intend to speak my mind to Jean-Luc about both of you once the present crisis is resolved."

"Then perhaps we should get down to business," Ro suggested.

Barclay agreed one hundred percent. He relaxed a little as he gratefully fitted the cap back onto his head. The built-in psychic baffler generated a mild buzz at the back of his mind, like a tune you can't get out of your head, but the odd sensation wasn't enough to keep him from reviewing the details of their mission:

The Tadigeans were a reclusive species who lived in a remote corner of the Alpha Quadrant, far from the beaten path. Tadigea had never formally joined the Federation, but, in recent years, had cautiously begun to do business with other planets in the quadrant. Although seldom seen, the Tadigeans were reputed to be mildly telepathic, which gave Betazed a definite edge when it came to forming a mutually advantageous relationship with the other planet. One of the most gifted telepaths Betazed had ever produced, Lwaxana no doubt hoped to find common ground with the Tadigean trade representatives.

Just what I need, Barclay moaned silently. *More telepaths.*

The ambassador's diplomatic efforts had been complicated by the fact that the xenophobic Tadigeans hated leaving their own planet almost as much as they hated allowing aliens onto their native soil. The newly installed holodeck on the *Cataria* was intended to simulate the Tadigeans' natural environment, to make them as comfortable as possible during the negotiations. The yacht itself was positioned at a neutral spot in deep space, equidistant from both Betazed and Tadigea. The location also had the advantage of being safely remote, so that the delicate negotiations could be conducted in relative secrecy.

"Unfortunately," Lwaxana lamented, "this wretched contraption still isn't working properly." She gestured impatiently at the king-sized holodeck surrounding them. Glowing yellow gridlines divided the stark black walls of the inactive holochamber, which now took up the better part of the *Cataria*. "It's been behaving erratically . . . and the Tadigean delegates are arriving in a matter of days."

A Betazoid aide, who had been lurking in Lwaxana's shadow all this time, stepped forward. "I'm sure our own technicians would have figured out the problem in plenty of time," he insisted. He glared resentfully at Barclay and Ro. "There was no need to call in Starfleet."

"That's what you told me a week ago," Lwaxana chided the man. "You'll forgive me if I didn't want to risk the success of these talks on your flimsy promises." She gestured unenthusiastically at the aide, not even bothering to look in his direction. "Permit me to introduce Flev Ubaan, my temporary attaché." She put extra stress on the word *temporary.* "He's been responsible for managing, if that's quite the right term, the particulars of this venture."

"If you'd just permitted me a larger staff," Ubaan protested. He was a portly man, at least a head shorter than Barclay, wearing a conservative gray suit. An elaborately waxed mustache compensated for his receding hairline. He held out a blinking datapadd. "It was all in my original prospectus." You didn't have to be a telepath to realize that he saw Lwaxana's appeal to Starfleet as a personal rebuke. Barclay hoped that the attaché's bruised ego wouldn't complicate matters. "I needed a full holodeck installation and support team."

"We've already been over this," Lwaxana said impatiently. "These negotiations are politically sensitive, especially on Tadigea. The fewer people who know about them, the better." A heavy sigh hinted at the dreadful hardships she had endured in the line of duty. "Why, I'm even having to get by without the services of my precious Mister Homm, who is recovering from a bout of Carellian laryngitis." Barclay recalled the ambassador's looming attendant from her past visits to the *Enterprise*. "Poor dear. He scarcely has any voice left at all."

How could you tell? Barclay wondered. "I'm, um, very familiar with holotechnology," he volunteered. "I'll do my b-best to debug this chamber in time for your meeting."

Lwaxana's eyes flashed like a phaser set on kill. "You had better."

The Arabian desert stretched endlessly before them. Crescent-shaped dunes of shifting sand rolled on for kilometers beneath the pitiless sun. Heat waves shimmered above the wind-scoured bones of a lost bedouin. Craggy rock formations jutted from the desert floor. On the horizon, plodding camels carried a merchant caravan toward a far-off oasis, or was the splash of greenery merely a mirage? Dust devils danced in the breeze, while a scorching wind pelted Barclay's face with grit. A camel brayed in the distance.

"'The desert is an ocean in which no oar is dipped,'" Barclay whispered softly to himself. The intense heat, which had to be at least fifty degrees Celsius, instantly dried up his sinuses. The visor on his cap helped shield his eyes from the glare. He could readily imagine joining the caravan for a trek across the boundless sands. Exotic Middle Eastern bazaars called out to him.

"Come again?" Ro asked.

Her puzzled remark brought him back to reality. "Er, nothing." He scanned the arid landscape with his tricorder. "The simulation appears to be functioning," he reported. "I'm not detecting any unusual fluctuations in the polarized interference patterns."

"We already checked for that," Ubaan said sullenly. The truculent attaché was constantly looking over Barclay's shoulder and second-guessing him, which did nothing to ease Barclay's mind. "And where did this oppressively hot simulation come from, anyway? This isn't the Tadigean program."

"This is one of my personal favorites from the *Enterprise,*" Barclay explained. "I wanted to determine if the problem was with the holodeck or the Tadigean simulation itself, so I'm running a program that I know has no glitches." He consulted the readout on his tricorder. "Just to t-test the hardware, you know?"

Ubaan rolled his eyes. "Sounds like a waste of time to me."

Barclay could practically feel the other man breathing down his neck. Hoping to put a little distance between himself and Ubaan, he strode across the desert toward the horizon—only to bump face-first into an invisible barrier. "Ouch!" He stumbled backward, clutching his nose. Caught by surprise, it took him a moment to realize that he had collided with one of the holodeck's actual walls.

That's not supposed to happen, he thought. In theory, the holodeck should have employed a force field treadmill, and constantly scrolling scenery, to create the illusion of unlimited space. Barclay knew that this particular program was capable of simulating vast distances; he had once ridden a camel all the way to Aqaba from this site. *Looks like the problem's with the holodeck itself.*

"Are you all right, Lieutenant?" Ro inquired from atop a nearby sand dune. Not an engineer herself, she was along to pilot the shuttle and provide an extra pair of hands as needed. Barclay would have preferred one of his colleagues from engineering, but Geordi had needed the rest of his staff for the soliton wave test. Barclay couldn't help feeling somewhat expendable. *Me and Ro both, I guess.*

He checked to make sure his nose wasn't broken. "I think so, but it looks like we've got a lot of work ahead of us." He decided to run a diagnostic on the chamber's omnidirectional holo diodes next. "Computer, end program."

Nothing happened. The harsh desert sun continued to beat down upon the three humanoids. Ubaan snickered. "Now you see what we've been dealing with for the last few weeks."

Barclay got the distinct impression that Ubaan would like nothing better than for the Starfleet engineer to fail, Lwaxana's negotiations be damned. Knowing that the petulant attaché was rooting against him didn't help Barclay's confidence any. Sweat soaked through the collar of his uniform. "We're here only at the ambassador's request," he pointed out for the umpteenth time. "It's nothing p-personal."

"Tell that to your captain after you've disappointed Ambassador Troi," Ubaan said. "The Tadigeans will be here in two days. Time is running out."

Between the ticking clock and the attaché's hostile attitude, Barclay was definitely feeling the pressure. His gaze drifted to the colorful caravan up ahead. Only a few years ago, he would have sought escape from the stress by immersing himself in some captivating holodeck scenario, but, with Counselor Troi's help, he had managed to get his holodiction under control. The temptation was always there, however, and at times like this it could be hard to resist.

The program's already running, he thought. *It would be a shame to let it go to waste.*

Perhaps there was a way to send Ro and Ubaan on some meaningless errand, so that he could have the holodeck to himself for a while? A thrilling camel race across the burning sands was just what he needed right now. Or perhaps a stealthy visit to the harem of some fabulously wealthy Arab sheikh . . .

No, he told himself firmly. He had made too much progress over the last few years to backslide now. *The captain and Geordi trusted me with this mission. I'm not going to let them down.*

"Computer, end program," he tried again. When the holodeck failed to respond once more, he gave up on voice commands and used his tricorder to locate the manual controls instead. He touched a button on the invisible wall and a keyboard materialized in the air before him. His fingers tapped against the control panel, shutting down the program. The inhospitable desert vanished like a mirage, replaced by the usual checkerboard grid pattern. The blazing sun and torrid temperature evaporated into the holodeck's memory banks.

"That's more like it, " Ro commented. "These devices are overrated, anyway. Just a way for spoiled, complacent people to avoid confronting reality." She sniffed disdainfully, further crinkling the distinctive ridges on her nose. "There aren't enough real problems in the galaxy that we need to waste our time fighting holographic monsters and villains? Why not put all that energy toward a cause worth fighting for?"

Like the plight of the Bajoran people? Barclay guessed that Ro was thinking of the generations of persecution her people had been subjected to by the Cardassians. Still, holotechnology had its uses; numerous studies had proved that it helped starship crews cope psychologically with the rigors of interstellar travel. Only rarely did an individual become overly dependent on the escapist fantasies it provided.

Like me.

"You've never used a holodeck?" he asked her incredulously. "Not even for harmless recreation?"

"Well, maybe once in a while." She blushed slightly. "Strictly as a means of exercise, of course. To maintain physical fitness."

Barclay was relieved to hear that Ro wasn't completely averse to the occasional holographic diversion; it made her somewhat less intimidating. But before he could ask her what her favorite programs were, a doorway whooshed open and Lwaxana Troi burst into the holodeck. "Is it working?" she asked anxiously. She looked flustered and out of breath. "Please tell me you have it working by now!"

"N-not quite," Barclay admitted, reluctant to disclose that he hadn't even isolated the problem yet. Perhaps the matter conversion and holographic imagery subsystems were not integrated properly? "But we're making progress. There's still time—"

"Not anymore!" Lwaxana shook her head. "The Tadigean delegates have just arrived, forty-eight hours early, and they want to start the negotiations right away!"

Under the circumstances, there was no choice but to fire up the Tadigean program and hope for the best. Barclay held his breath as the holodeck transformed itself into a dank, humid, moonlit swamp, complete with bugs, moss, mud, and rotting vegetation, all of which the holodeck did an impressive, if uncomfortable, job of simulating. A sour miasma, redolent of decaying leaves and mildew, hung over the scene. A leafy canopy filtered the luminous glow of the planet's twin moons. Moss hung from drooping tree branches. Mosquitoes swarmed over the stagnant water. Algae coated the surface of the pools. Fungi sprouted atop rotting logs. A carnivorous plant captured a slow-moving spider. Snakes slithered through the tall grass and shrubs.

Lwaxana eyed the murky setting with distaste. "Next time," she vowed, "I'm insisting on a species that comes from a tropical beach planet."

Something splashed in the shadows. Ro muttered beneath her breath.

"What was that, Ensign?" Lwaxana asked.

Ro patted her hip. "Just missing my phaser."

"I had no choice but to confiscate it," Ubaan reminded her. He had removed the phaser from the holochamber a few minutes earlier. "Our agreement with the Tadigeans was quite explicit on this point. No weapons of any kind are allowed at the meeting."

"So you said," Ro said, not sounding very happy about it.

Barclay wondered why Ro felt she needed a phaser at trade negotiations. She seemed a little fuzzy on the concept of peaceful diplomacy. Personally, he was worried more about the stability of their holographic environment. Lwaxana had insisted that he and Ro be on hand to deal with any technical glitches that might arise during the meeting. He crossed his fingers and hoped that their services would not be necessary.

Like I've ever been that lucky.

They were convened beneath a tented pavilion located upon a solid patch of land, surrounded by a densely forested network of shallow ponds and tributaries. A lighted brazier burned ceremonial incense. A polished metal gong hung from a carved wooden frame. A waterproof carpet, boasting intricate geometric designs, protected their shoes from the mushy soil. Plush velvet cushions awaited the delegates' posteriors; by all reports, the Tadigeans weren't big on chairs.

Barclay didn't notice any obvious flaws in the program. The flames flickered convincingly. Incense tickled his nose. *So far, so good.*

"Very well," Lwaxana declared. She was even more ornately dressed than before. Her floor-length purple silk gown was trimmed with shimmering golden lace. A collar of Joranian ostrich feathers fanned out behind her head. A silver tiara, studded with polished Spican flame gems, crowned her auburn curls. The seductive scent of Deltan perfume competed with the incense. She hefted the Sacred Chalice of Rixx, a large clay pot that looked considerably less impressive than its title. Barclay thought he glimpsed a bit of mold along its brim. "Let's meet our guests."

Ubaan banged on the gong with a mallet. A resounding clang echoed across the swamp, hurting Barclay's ears. All eyes turned toward the gleaming steel archway opposite the pavilion. The door slid open and the delegates hopped in.

The Tadigeans were a nocturnal race of amphibious bipeds. In other words, they were big, talking frogs. Bulging throats, slimy skin, bug eyes, wide mouths, webbed fingers . . . the whole nine yards. Mucus coated their skin in lieu of clothing; most of the Tadigeans wore only a scaly belt bearing various tools and insignia. Larger and more massive than Barclay and the others, they were about the size of a gorilla or *mugato*. Their smooth skin was mostly dark green but displayed a lighter shade of chartreuse upon their bellies. A pair of bright orange sacs bulged above and behind their blood-red eyes. They smelled like onions. Barclay mentally flashed on a dog-eared copy of *The Wind in the Willows* that he had read to pieces as a child. Mister Toad had come calling on the *Cataria*, along with four of his associates. The archway vanished as the holodeck doors sealed behind them.

"Welcome, honored guests," Lwaxana said grandly. She held aloft the Sacred Chalice. "In the name of my illustrious ancestors, and in the spirit of universal friendship, I ask you to accept our humble hospitality."

Barclay winced as Ubaan banged the gong again.

"Thank you, Madam Ambassador," the lead Tadigean croaked. A translucent crystal pendant dangling from a chain around his neck distinguished him from his companions. A set of bony "horns" crested his skull. Along with the other Tadigeans, he gazed about the simulated swamp in wonderment. "This is astounding. When you said you could approximate our environment, I had no idea you would go to such lengths." A long pink tongue snatched a holographic firefly out of the air. Barclay hoped the program had gotten the taste right. "If I did not know better, I would swear I was back on Tadigea!"

Judging from their reaction, Barclay guessed that their visitors were unfamiliar with holodeck technology. *They must not get out much.*

Lwaxana handed off the chalice to Ubaan. She held out her hand to her froggy counterpart. "Ambassador Ghebh, I presume?"

"I am Ghebh," he confirmed brusquely. His horizontal pupils narrowed as he spotted Barclay and Ro standing off to the side. His vocal sac swelled aggressively. "What is Starfleet doing here?"

"Independent observers," Lwaxana said smoothly. "Nothing to be concerned with."

Ghebh obviously disagreed. "That was not part of the agreement!" His fellow Tadigeans croaked quietly between themselves.

"We'd be h-happy to leave," Barclay volunteered. He stepped toward the archway a little too eagerly.

"Stay where you are, Lieutenant," Lwaxana ordered. She gestured at the verdant marsh around them. "Starfleet's assistance is required to duplicate your environment, in order to ensure your comfort during these talks. Surely you won't hold that against us?"

Ghebh contemplated the uniformed officers. Barclay fidgeted nervously, uncomfortable at being the center of attention. Ro seemed to take the awkward situation in stride. "How many Starfleet 'observers' are aboard this vessel?"

"Only these two," Lwaxana assured him. "Believe me, they're of no importance. Just pretend they're not even here. Heaven knows that's what I do." She indicated the cushions upon the carpet. "Please, let us begin our negotiations."

The Tadigean ambassador hastily conferred with his associates. "Our plans are unchanged. There will be no negotiations." The other amphibians took up defensive positions in front of their leader. "You are our prisoner."

"What?" Lwaxana said indignantly. "This is outrageous. You must be joking."

Instead of responding, Ghebh grimaced in concentration. A clear membrane slid upward over his eyes. The crystal pendant upon his chest began to emit an unearthly blue light. He chanted hoarsely in a language unrecognized by Barclay's universal translator. Perhaps there was a telepathic component to the chant that the translator couldn't pick up on?

"Ughh!" Ubaan grunted and clutched his head. Veins bulged alarmingly upon his temples. His eyes rolled upward until only the whites were visible. He toppled forward onto the carpet.

The man's collapse startled Barclay. "Mister Ubaan? Flev?" The stricken attaché lay unconscious on the carpet. His limbs twitched spasmodically. Barclay shared an anxious look with Ro, who appeared equally baffled by this unexpected turn of events. *I don't understand,* he thought. *What's happening?*

Lwaxana Troi seemed to be affected as well. She teetered unsteadily upon her feet but somehow managed to remain conscious. "My thoughts!" she groaned. Her eyes glazed over. "Get out of my brain, you toad . . ." Her voice faltered. "It hurts . . ."

They're targeting the telepaths, Barclay realized. Both Betazoids were obviously being subjected to some kind of psychic assault. Lwaxana's mental defenses were apparently more formidable than her aide's, yet she was clearly weakening. He guessed that she couldn't hold out much longer.

Unless . . .

Jumping forward, he removed his cap and pressed it down onto Lwaxana's head. The desperate move yielded immediate results. Lwaxana stood up straight, regaining her balance. She shook her head to clear her thoughts. Her eyes came back into focus. "My head," she gasped. "I can think again!"

How about that? Barclay thought. *It actually worked!* Just as he'd hoped, the psychic baffler in the cap was shielding Lwaxana from Ghebh's attack. *Now, if we can just get her away from these frogs in one piece . . .*

The nictitating membrane over Ghebh's eyes retracted, but his crystal pendant continued to glow intensely. He glowered at Barclay and Ro. "Subdue the Starfleet mammals!" he commanded his subordinates. "Bring me the ambassador!"

Four large, menacing bullfrogs stomped toward Lwaxana. Sharp claws slid from their webbed fingers. One of the Tadigeans glanced in Barclay's direction. A bright orange fluid sprayed from the parotid glands behind his eyes. Barclay jumped backward and the spray fell short of its target. Only a few stray drops hit the back of his hand. His skin went numb wherever the drops touched.

Some sort of natural neurotoxin?

"Watch out!" he shouted. "They spit poison from their eyes."

"Is that all?" Ro replied sarcastically. She reached instinctively for her phaser but came away empty-handed. "Oh, hell." Forced to improvise, she kicked over the smoking brazier, spilling burning embers on the carpet. A cascade of sparks set the holographic tent ablaze. Brilliant yellow flames climbed the silk walls of the pavilion. The sudden flare of heat and light repelled the nocturnal swamp dwellers. Ro took advantage of their confusion to rip the metal gong from its moorings. She glanced back impatiently at Barclay and Lwaxana. "What are you waiting for? Run!"

She hurled the gong like a discus, straight at the crystal pendant on Ghebh's chest. Barclay held his breath, waiting to see if she succeeded in shattering the crystal, which was evidently some sort of psychic amplifier. But instead the spinning missile slammed into the head of one of the other Tadigeans, who sprang between Ro and Ghebh at just the wrong moment. The beaned bullfrog tumbled backward into his companions, resulting in a tangle of webbed feet and hands. An irate Ghebh shouted at his fellow amphibians, "Pull yourself together, you incompetent tadpoles. They're going to get away!"

Not a bad idea, Barclay thought. He tugged on Lwaxana's arm. "Come with me, Madam Ambassador! We have to get you to safety."

"But . . . what about Flev?" She dug in her heels, reluctant to leave the unconscious attaché within the burning pavilion. "He'll be burned alive!"

"No, he won't," Barclay promised, lowering his voice. In theory, the holodeck's safety protocols would protect Ubaan from the holographic inferno. "It's just a simulation, remember?" He pulled harder on her arm, eager to get her away from the hostile Tadigeans, who were bound to regroup any minute now. "Please, we have to go!"

Lwaxana nodded, seeing sense at last. "Just one moment!" Before he could stop her, she reached into the fire and rescued the Sacred Chalice, which she clutched to her bountiful chest. As Barclay had predicted, her hands came away unburned. "All right, Lieutenant." She kicked off her high heels. "*Now* we can make a strategic retreat."

Abandoning the narrow spit of land, they splashed into the shallow water and ran from the blazing tent into the densely forested swamp. Ankle-deep mud sucked at their heels, slowing their progress. The cool water came as a shock after the sultry heat. He tried not to think about what sort of aquatic life-forms might be swimming beneath the surface of the brackish water. A slimy layer of pond scum clung to his uniform.

Ugh!

"Keep going!" Ro shouted from behind them. They could hear her splashing through the water after them. "Don't slow down!"

The enraged croaks of the Tadigeans echoed across the swamp. Barclay could hear them leaping through the underbrush in hot pursuit. "You cannot escape us, Ambassador!" Ghebh bellowed loudly. "Surrender and we will spare the Starfleet officers."

Spare? Barclay didn't like the sound of that. These frogs were obviously playing for keeps. "Don't w-worry about us, Madam Ambassador," he said, swallowing hard. "Don't even think about turning yourself over to those terrorists."

"Thank you, Lieutenant Barclay," Lwaxana said. Her dark eyes regarded him with new respect. "I appreciate your dedication to duty." She panted as she dragged her soaked gown through the waist-deep water while simultaneously trying to keep the Sacred Chalice dry. The effort was obviously exhausting her. "And, please, call me Lwaxana."

Younger and fitter than either Barclay or the ambassador, Ro soon caught up with them. "Those slimy bastards aren't giving up," she said tersely. "They're on our trail like a pack of Cardassian riding hounds." She shook her head in disgust. "*This* is why I wanted to keep my phaser!"

"Your point is well taken, Ensign," Lwaxana conceded. "Not that you seemed to need a phaser back there at the meeting site. You certainly turned the tables on our foes—in quite a resourceful manner."

Ro shrugged. "You grow up in refugee camps, you learn to think fast."

"I want you to know that I've always had a great degree of sympathy for your people." Lwaxana swatted a mosquito away from her face. "Betazed has been in the forefront of the Federation's efforts to negotiate an end to the Cardassian occupation."

"Glad to hear it," Ro said, only half listening. Right now, there were more urgent issues to deal with. She kept glancing back over her shoulder. Barclay and Lwaxana were slowing her down. "Get a move on."

Easier said than done, Barclay thought. Lwaxana was sounding increasingly out of breath, and, to be honest, he could use a break himself. His legs were already tired from slogging through the mud and clotted vegetation. A stitch in his side throbbed with every step. Protruding roots threatened to trip him. Looking around for a safe place to rest, he spied a hummock of solid earth that was partially veiled by a thick curtain of hanging moss. "Over there," he suggested, leading the way. He pulled back the moss so that Ro and Lwaxana could pass beneath it, then let it fall back into place behind him. They found themselves amid a cluster of gnarled willows and cypresses. Fallen leaves and needles littered the forest floor. "We can rest here, at least for a m-moment."

"Thank goodness!" Lwaxana exclaimed. She settled down onto

a fallen tree trunk and patted the fungus-covered wood beside her. He gladly joined her on the log.

Ro remained on her feet, standing guard. "What now, Lieutenant?" she asked him in a low voice.

As the highest-ranking officer present, Barclay found himself in charge. He gulped and tried to take stock of the situation. They were alone, outnumbered, and unarmed. The one thing they had going for them was that the Tadigeans seemed to be taking the swamp simulation at face value. *They don't realize we're trapped in a finite space,* Barclay thought. Right now, the holographic environment was their best defense. The phony swamp offered infinitely more opportunities to run and hide than an empty holochamber would. *As long as the program keeps running, we have a chance.*

But what about the rest of the *Cataria*'s crew? Barclay tapped the combadge on his chest. "Lieutenant Barclay to the bridge. We have an emergency situation in the holodeck. Please respond." He waited expectantly, but no one answered his page. "Requesting immediate assistance. Please respond."

"It's no use, Lieutenant," Lwaxana said, shaking her head. "The entire crew is Betazoid. They've doubtless been incapacitated by the same telepathic onslaught that felled poor Flev." She massaged her temples, as though some lingering soreness persisted. "You should have felt the psychic energy emanating from that infernal crystal. It was all I could do to keep from collapsing like Flev." She adjusted the cap atop her head. "Thank providence for this convenient helmet."

Ro scratched her head. "I don't get it. Why weren't Barclay and I affected?"

"Because you're not telepaths," Lwaxana explained indulgently. "No offense, Ensign, but you and the lieutenant lack the sensitivity to succumb to such an insidious attack. One of the few advantages of being thought-blind, I suppose."

Barclay decided to accept the remark in the spirit in which it was intended. "Did you have any idea that the Tadigeans might resort to violence?"

"Not at all!" Lwaxana insisted vehemently. "I am utterly perplexed by this unfortunate turn of events. Nothing in my preliminary negotiations with the Tadigean government led me to expect anything other than a civilized diplomatic conference. I can't imagine what's come over them!"

"You're discussing trade agreements, right?" Ro paced restlessly, too keyed up to sit down. "Maybe they figured they'd gain the upper hand by taking you hostage first. Use your safety as a bargaining chip to negotiate a better deal for themselves." She looked at Barclay. "Unfortunately, that strategy doesn't extend to us."

Barclay's reply caught in his throat as, to his surprise, Lwaxana stood up and began peeling off her clothes. "Ambassador . . . ?"

"Just shedding a few layers," she explained, as her sodden garments landed in a heap at her feet. Jangling bracelets and earrings soon joined the ruined finery. "These soaking rags were weighing me down dreadfully." She blithely stepped away from the discarded clothing, wearing only a lacy silk chemise that barely covered her buxom figure. The protective cap upon her head clashed somewhat with her intimate apparel. "And I told you before, call me Lwaxana."

"Yes, Ambass . . . Lwaxana." Barclay's face was nearly infrared. He chivalrously turned his back on the disrobed diplomat. That her unexpected striptease made perfect sense from a strictly pragmatic point of view didn't make him any less uncomfortable. This was Counselor Troi's mother, for heaven's sake!

Lwaxana chuckled softly behind him. "No need to be embarrassed, Lieutenant. Why, on Betazed, nudity is considered formal attire in some circumstances." She sighed nostalgically. "You should have seen me at my wedding. I assure you I was absolutely stunning."

I'll take your word for it, Barclay thought. He reluctantly turned around to face Lwaxana, while trying to look everywhere but. Ro smirked at his discomfort. He was suddenly very glad that Lwaxana's borrowed cap kept her from reading anyone's mind. The very thought of Betazoid weddings provoked some *very* vivid pictures in his brain, which he would just as soon keep to himself. *This is awkward enough.*

"That's better." Lwaxana started to slip out of the chemise, then reconsidered, perhaps as a concession to Terran modesty. She smiled at the two Starfleet officers. "Do feel free to get out of those wet clothes yourselves."

Not in a million years, Barclay thought. He didn't even like changing clothes in front of other men. "I think it b-best that I remain in uniform."

"I'm good, too," Ro declared.

Barclay thanked the Bajoran Prophets for Ro's restraint. He was almost relieved when the unmistakable sounds of pursuit penetrated their hiding place, interrupting the awkward moment. They heard the bellicose frogs getting closer.

"Just our luck," Ro grumbled. She wadded up Lwaxana's discarded clothing and hid it in a knotty thicket of grass and shrubs. The golden jewelry sank to the bottom of a nearby puddle. "We're playing on their turf."

Barclay knew what she meant. The wooded swamp was the Tadigeans' natural environment. An idea occurred to him: perhaps he could adjust the parameters of the program to give them more of an advantage? Maybe even switch to another scenario entirely?

"Computer, an archway, please." Barclay didn't want to shut down the Tadigean simulation right away, for fear of ending up exposed in a vacant chamber, but a holographic archway would allow him to access the controls to the holodeck from the safety of the secluded arbor. He could then superimpose another environment onto the imaginary swamp. He knew just the program, too.

Unfortunately, no such arch appeared. "Computer?"

"Let me guess," Ro said dryly. "The voice commands are still down."

So it appears, Barclay thought. "I guess I'm going to have to find the manual controls again."

"Do you know where they are?" Ro asked. The constantly shifting scenery made it all but impossible to know where they really were in the holodeck. "I don't have a clue where the exit is."

He consulted his tricorder. "I *think* I can locate them." He looked up from the visual display. Through the gauzy veil of moss, he glimpsed a chorus of hostile Tadigeans bounding toward them. His mouth dried up. He wrung his hands. "If only I had more time!"

"That's good enough for me." Ro yanked aside a clump of needle grass, exposing the open end of the hollow tree trunk. "You hide here while I lure them away."

Before Barclay could object, she raced out of the hidden arbor into the murky sloughs beyond. She splashed loudly through the water, making as much of a ruckus as possible. "Come on, you goggled-eyed bug eaters!" she shouted. "Try and catch me."

The Tadigeans took the bait, or at least most of them did. "That's the ugly female!" a nameless bullfrog croaked. His throat swelled enormously as he broadcast the news to the other searchers. He sprang through the overgrown shrubs and saplings, covering several meters in a single leap. A few more bounds like that and he would eat up Ro's lead in no time. "After her!"

Barclay hoped Ro knew what she was doing. In the meantime, he had no choice but to try to take full advantage of her diversionary tactic. At first, it seemed like the entire hunting party was going to head off in pursuit of the fleeing ensign, but a lambent blue glow testified that Ghebh himself was still in the vicinity. "Keep searching for the others," the Tadigean ambassador ordered. "Look everywhere!"

The glow from the crystal pendant intensified as Ghebh approached the arbor, flanked by two of his soldiers. Snakes and marsh rats fled from their noisy approach. Stealth was not on the frogs' agenda.

"The log," Barclay whispered urgently to Lwaxana, but the canny ambassador was already way ahead of him. Getting down on her hands and knees, she scurried inside the hollow tree trunk. Barclay waited until she was fully hidden, then squeezed in after her. It was a tight fit, especially with Lwaxana already taking up much of the empty cavity, but he just managed to pull his feet in after him. *You can do this,* he told himself. *It's just like a Jefferies tube.*

Inside the log, the rotting wood was slick and clammy to the touch. The damp air reeked of decay. Small insects and other invertebrates wriggled beneath him. Claustrophobia threatened, but he took a deep breath and the sense of panic receded (mostly). Darkness added to his anxiety; he could barely see a thing. The heat was suffocating.

On second thought, I think I prefer the crawl spaces on the Enterprise.

Moments later, webbed feet slapped against the soggy ground outside. A sinister blue glow shone through minute cracks and knotholes in the log's crumbling epidermis. Barclay could hear Ghebh and his soldiers only centimeters away.

He froze in place, afraid to move a muscle. His heart was beating so loudly he couldn't believe that the nearby Tadigeans couldn't hear it as well. Lwaxana's muffled breathing echoed thunderously in his ears. Water trickled beneath his collar and down his spine. His mouth felt as dry as Ceti Alpha V. Cramped limbs began to ache in protest. Perspiration dripped into his eyes, stinging them. Unable to rub his eyes, he tried to blink the sweat away.

"This is taking too long," Ghebh grumbled. "We should have been long gone by now. At this rate, the real delegation will be here before we've fled with Ambassador Troi." He croaked in disgust. "Traitorous scum. I'll send that pompous female back to Betazed in pieces before I'll let those greedy cloacae in the Trade Commission open our sacred borders to outsiders."

Suddenly, everything made sense, sort of. *These aren't the actual delegates,* Barclay realized. *They're imposters out to sabotage the talks.*

No wonder they showed up two days early!

"We'll find them, Povz," another frog promised the Tadigean posing as Ghebh. "You can rely on us."

"Well, be quick about it," Povz snapped. "Even with the Eye of Dread, I can't shut down all these Betazoids' minds forever. My brain is killing me!"

To Barclay's horror, the bogus ambassador sat down on the log. The soggy timber sagged beneath Povz's weight and Barclay found himself literally supporting his enemy. He couldn't imagine how this situation could possibly get any worse.

Then a bug crawled onto his face.

A holographic wood louse, at least a centimeter long, skittered down his forehead toward his right eye, which he shut just in time. Seven pairs of scratchy little feet danced across his eyelid as he tried heroically not to squirm or brush it away. *Don't move,* he thought. *Don't even flinch.* Finally, after what felt like forever, the louse crawled off his eye and down the side of his nose. *It's not real,* he reminded himself. *It's only a miniature force-field construct.*

But that didn't stop the bug from tickling his nose. An overwhelming urge to sneeze came over him as the louse slowly ambled below his nostrils. He sniffed quietly, holding back the sneeze, until the disgusting insect scuttled onto his lips. A sudden solution to his predicament came to mind, but he wasn't sure he could go through with it.

It's not real . . .

He opened his mouth and gobbled up the bug. He didn't dare crunch down on its brittle shell, for fear of being heard, so he had to swallow it whole. His gorge rose as he felt the wriggling insect slide down his throat. He clamped his jaws shut to keep from vomiting.

Just pretend you're Worf, he thought. The louse was so disgusting that it just had to be some sort of Klingon delicacy. *Or maybe a Ferengi one.*

"At least it feels like home," Povz muttered, shifting his weight atop Barclay's back. *Was the treacherous amphibian planning to sit here all night?* "Once we have the ambassador, we must force the Betazoids to tell us how they managed to create such a magnificent environment aboard a starship. By the Toadstone, I swear this swamp seems larger than the ambassador's yacht can possibly contain!"

"Perhaps some sort of tesseract technology?" another Tadigean speculated. "Extending the ship's interior into subspace?"

"It's all witchcraft to me," Povz groused, shifting his weight. Barclay's back strained beneath the burden. His cramped arms and legs felt numb. Barclay suppressed a sigh of relief as Povz lurched to his feet at last. "Spawn it all!" he swore. "Do I have to capture those mammals myself? Let's see what's keeping those lekking idiots."

Webbed footsteps receded into the distance, taking the ominous sapphire glow with them. Barclay found himself back in the dark. He cautiously rearranged his limbs inside the log.

"Did you hear them?" Lwaxana muttered, deeper inside the rotted-out hollow. "'Pompous female,' indeed! Some people have no sense of occasion or proper decorum." Indignation echoed in her voice. "I should have known that wasn't the real ambassador!"

"Sssh!" Barclay hushed her. He counted slowly to one hundred, then counted again. He strained his ears but could not hear any frogs hopping close by. "All r-right," he whispered to Lwaxana. "Stay where you are while I make sure it's safe."

He backed out of the log, then cautiously stood up and looked around. He shook his arms to restore the circulation to his fingers. His legs throbbed as the blood rushed back into them. His eyes anxiously scanned the moonlit swamp.

"It looks clear," he reported. "Let's g-go."

Lwaxana crawled out of the log. "About time," she said. "I haven't endured such tight accommodations since that First Federation reception." Crushed insect carcasses and bits of bark clung to her hair, skin, and slime-caked shift. She cradled the Sacred Chalice against her bosom. "I'll never complain about the size of the staterooms on the *Enterprise* again!"

Barclay made a doomed attempt to brush the moldy detritus from his own uniform but quickly abandoned the effort. *If we get out of this alive,* he thought, *I'm going to need history's longest sonic shower.* He could still taste the wood louse on his tongue. *Plus a couple gallons of quantum-level mouthwash.*

But first he had to find that control panel. Unhitching his tricorder from his waist, he double-checked the readings on the display panel. According to the sensors, the controls were only twenty meters away, although how that translated to distances within the holographic swamp was anybody's guess. "This way," he instructed Lwaxana.

They waded against a sluggish current. Mud invaded Barclay's boots, squishing between his toes. Occasionally something swam past him beneath the surface of the water, brushing against his leg. Barclay shuddered every time. Did they have leeches on Tadigea? Or some variety of alien piranhas?

He was afraid to ask.

A muffled roar reached his ears, like water cascading over a cliff. "What's that noise?" he asked Lwaxana. They seemed be heading toward it.

"The Forever Falls," she said. "It has great symbolic meaning to the Tadigeans, embodying abundance and generosity. Ubaan suggested that we include it in the simulation." She brushed a damp strand of hair away from her eyes. "It seemed like a bright idea at the time."

"That was very c-clever of him," Barclay said. He just hoped that the falls weren't between them and the control panel. Simulated or not, he had no desire to go over Niagara in a barrel—or whatever the Tadigean equivalent was.

The roar of the falls grew steadily louder as they trekked through the marsh. As before, the muddy quagmire made for rough going. Barclay wondered how much longer the pampered ambassador would be able to maintain their pace. To her credit, though, Lwaxana did not complain. If anything, her spirits seemed more indefatigable than his own. "So how long have you known my daughter, Lieutenant? Perhaps you can explain to me what exactly she sees in Commander Riker?"

They made a sharp turn, putting the falls on their right. *Maybe we won't have to cross them after all,* he thought hopefully. He caught a glimpse of the falls through a stand of leafy cypresses and paused to take a closer look.

The Forever Falls tumbled over the edge of a crescent-shaped cliff that looked to be approximately thirty meters across. Water from the swamp, fed by some source farther upstream, spilled down the sides of the cliff to a rocky pool at least eighty meters below. Churning mist and foam obscured the bottom of the falls. Barclay experienced a touch of vertigo just looking over the precipice.

That's a long way down.

He was backing away from the falls when a booming voice rang out over the din of the falling water. "Ambassador Troi! Starfleet!" Povz shouted, his words electronically amplified by his personal comm unit. "We have your companion. Show yourself if you value her life."

Povz and his accomplices were standing at the opposite end of the crescent, only a few meters from the edge of the falls. To his dismay, Barclay saw Ro being held captive by two of the duplicitous amphibians. She squirmed and twisted in their grasp but could not seem to break free. Povz looked out over the falls, his crystal pendant still glowing brightly against his slimy chest. Had he chosen the top of the falls for its high visibility, Barclay wondered, or did the would-be kidnapper just have a flair for the dramatic?

"Do you hear me, mammals? Surrender at once!"

Barclay hesitated, uncertain what to do next. He felt torn between his loyalty to Ro and his duty to protect the ambassador. He shared a distraught look with Lwaxana. "Don't worry about me," she urged. "They won't hurt me. I'm too valuable to them as a hostage."

She started to step out from behind the cover of the trees.

"Don't do it!" Ro shouted. "Not over my dead body!"

Going into action, she jabbed her heel into one of her captor's ankles, then butted her head into the other frog's jaw. As they reacted in pain, she tore herself free from their webbed fingers and, without hesitation, ran for the edge of the cliff. Milky orange poison sprayed at her heels.

"Remember Ubaan, Barclay!" She threw herself over the brink. *"Don't let me dowwwwwwn . . . !"*

Her final cry stretched out endlessly as she plummeted toward the rocks below. Her plunging body disappeared into the turbulent white water and mist. Lwaxana gasped, clasping her hand over her mouth. Her face was ashen beneath her smeared makeup. "That poor, brave girl!"

"She'll be okay," Barclay reminded her hurriedly. "The holodeck's safety protocols will protect her from any serious injury. Like with Ubaan." The Tadigeans obviously assumed that the unconscious attaché had burned to death in the fire, or else they would have used him as a hostage by now. "Trust me, it looked worse than it was."

Lwaxana clutched her heart as the color came back into her face. "Thank the fates." She leaned against a lichen-infested tree trunk as she recovered from the shock. "That was far too realistic for my peace of mind. You're quite sure that she survived?"

"P-pretty much." In truth, he was slightly less confident than he would have liked. This holodeck had been acting up, after all; who was to say if the safety protocols were one hundred percent reliable? Certainly it wouldn't be the first time that a faulty holodeck program put someone in genuine danger; Geordi liked to joke that the *Enterprise*'s holodecks tried to kill them at least once a year. At the moment, that quip didn't seem very funny.

Ro had taken a calculated risk. The odds were in her favor, but still . . .

"I found them!" A camouflaged frog dropped from the treetops, splashing down in their path. His extended claws glinted in the moonlight. Barclay gagged on the pungent odor emanating from his slimy secretions. "Over here!"

"Finally!" Povz's voice croaked from the Tadigean's comm. "Hold them there, Jhirm! Don't let them get away!"

The looming amphibian blocked them with his bulk. "They're not going anywhere."

"W-we'll see about that," Barclay said, feigning confidence. He shoved Lwaxana behind the widest cypress and stepped between her and their foe. Inspiration struck and he snapped off a low-hanging tree branch, which he brandished before him like a sword. Hours spent playing D'Artagnan in a holographic re-creation of *The Three Musketeers* emboldened him. "En garde!"

Watch out for those poison tears. He fixed his gaze on the parotid glands behind Jhirm's eyes. The fleshy sacs pulsed, giving Barclay a split-second warning. He dived beneath the water just as the neurotoxin sprayed from the corners of the amphibian's eyes. Barclay held his breath, loath to swallow any of the fetid water, then scrambled to his feet to the right of his batrachian adversary. The point of the broken branch stabbed Jhirm right in his poison gland. The Tadigean yelped in pain.

"I shall speak with my sword, sir!" Barclay crowed, doing his best to stay in character. For better or for worse, he felt considerably more courageous facing the enemy as D'Artagnan than as himself. He wiped the slimy water from his eyes. "One for all, and all for Starfleet!"

"Hot-blooded filth!" Real tears, not poison, leaked from his eyes. "Are all primates insane, or are you more brain damaged than most?"

He slashed at Barclay with his claws, but the embattled lieutenant deftly parried the attack with his makeshift rapier. The claws scarred the fresh bark, but the sturdy limb held together. Bending a knee, Barclay ducked beneath Jhirm's attacks and thrust.

The pointed branch passed through the frog's flesh and bones without leaving a scratch.

Huh?

Encountering no resistance, Barclay stumbled forward, almost falling face-first into the pond scum. He withdrew the branch, which still looked solid enough, and waved it back and forth through the startled Tadigean's torso. The wooden sword was suddenly intangible.

Another holodeck glitch, Barclay realized. *Just when I didn't need it.*

This never happened to D'Artagnan . . .

Fortunately, Jhirm was momentarily transfixed by the sight of the insubstantial weapon passing harmlessly through his flesh. "How in the Heavenly Hatchery—?"

"Excuse me, Mister Jhirm," a female voice called out. "If I could have your attention . . . ?"

The baffled amphibian spun around to find Lwaxana standing a meter or so behind him. She pulled back on a leafy cypress branch with both hands, so that it was as taut as a coiled spring. "Stay right where you are, please." She released the branch, which snapped forward into Jhirm's face, hitting him with the force of a reverse tractor beam. The impact flung him backward into the unyielding mass of a solid tree trunk. A groan escaped his blubbery lips as he slid limply into the water. Bubbles rose from his submerged gills.

"So much for that annoying toad," Lwaxana said, wiping her hands against each other. She smirked at Barclay. "I hope you don't mind that I rescued myself."

He couldn't helping feeling a little upstaged. *Well, sure.* Her *branch stays solid.* He tossed aside his own useless weapon, even as the engineer in him considered the possible implications of this latest malfunction. The three-dimensional image of the branch had remained intact, but the replicated matter had evaporated. Maybe the visual and tactile systems really were interfering with each other in some way?

"N-not at all," he lied. "But we can't stay here." Povz and the other Tadigeans were already on their way. He hastily consulted his tricorder; according to the readings, the control panel was not far away. "Just a little bit farther, I promise."

"You don't need to coddle me, Lieutenant. I'll have you know that I once walked the Pilgrimage of a Thousand Steps barefoot, wearing nothing but a large floral hat. Of course, I was much younger then . . ." She reclaimed the Sacred Chalice from the soggy ground at her feet. "Lead on, Mister Barclay."

Keeping one step (or hop) ahead of their pursuers, they continued their trek through the seemingly endless swamp. *We have to come across the wall with the control panel eventually,* Barclay thought, following the sensor readings, which led them to a natural levee along the shore of a slowly moving stream. Tall grass and skunk cabbage carpeted the slope. A bed of pink carnivorous plants, resembling a Vegan weeping flytrap, snapped at unwary insects. According to the tricorder, the concealed panel was right above the voracious flytraps.

Naturally, Barclay thought. *Why not a nest of Denebian slime devils, too?*

The hungry plants nipped at his ankles as he approached the apparent location of the control panel. Their high-pitched screeches hurt Barclay's ears. His finger stabbed the empty air—and the panel materialized before his eyes. *Eureka!* Now he just had to figure out how to fix the defective holodeck before Povz and his venomous colleagues caught up with them. What could be simpler?

Barclay opened the panel to expose a complicated array of isolinear chips. He ran his hand through his thinning brown hair, daunted by the challenge before him. The weepers biting his ankles didn't make it any easier to concentrate on the problem at hand. *Boy,* he thought, *could I use some of that Cytherian superintelligence now.*

Almost a year ago, an alien species had artificially enhanced his intellect for their own purposes. For a brief interval, his IQ had exceeded 1200, but that augmented intelligence had completely faded away over time.

Or had it?

Was any of that incredible genius still lurking somewhere in his brain cells? Sending his mind back to those heady days aboard the *Enterprise,* when he had effortlessly thrown together a revolutionary new warp propulsion system, Barclay tried to call up what it had felt like to have all that sheer intellectual power at his command. His brow furrowed in concentration as he sought to squeeze just one more burst of inspiration from his straining gray matter. Maybe if he just pretended he was still a supergenius?

Let's start with trying to reactivate the voice controls, he decided. He began rearranging the isolinear chips in hopes of bypassing the bug in the system. Diagnostic lights flashed green, giving his confidence a much-needed boost. *Yes! Now we're getting somewhere.* He began to transfer the verbal recognition codes to one of the auxiliary subprocessors. *This should do the trick.*

He realigned the final chip—and the entire program crashed.

The sheltering swamp, with its many secluded nooks and crannies, vanished before their eyes, instantly replaced by the wide-open space of the dormant holodeck. Barclay and Lwaxana found themselves abruptly exposed to view, as were Povz and his murderous cohorts.

The stunned Tadigeans looked about the empty chamber in confusion. "What the spawn?" Their bewilderment, however, did not stop them from immediately spotting their unarmed prey. "Get them!" Povz croaked harshly. "Don't let them trick us again!"

Their backs up against the grid-marked wall, Barclay and Lwax-ana had nowhere to hide. *Another program,* Barclay thought franti-cally. *We need another program, pronto!* He opened his mouth, hoping that the voice controls were truly functioning once more, only to feel the spray from a Tadigean's eyes splatter against his face.

Oh, no! he despaired. *I was too slow . . . !*

The neurotoxin took effect instantly. His entire body went numb, freezing him in place. He tried to speak, but his tongue and vocal cords were paralyzed. He could barely breathe, let alone summon a new holographic environment. Out of the corner of his eye, he watched helplessly as Povz's minions surrounded Lwaxana. They hadn't poisoned her, at least not yet. Perhaps they judged the middle-aged matron not much of a threat on her own?

"Keep your warty hands off me," she said imperiously, declin-ing to cower before her foes. "As an ambassador in full standing for the people of Betazed, I demand that you abide by the conventions of the Treaty of Pullayup."

Barclay was impressed by Lwaxana's indomitable attitude but doubted that Tadigean terrorists were likely to respect any legalis-tic niceties. *But she can still talk,* he realized. *She can instruct the holodeck herself, if she just knows what to say.*

A last-ditch ploy presented itself. It meant overcoming his tele-phobia, but right now he had more tangible dangers to grapple with. Straining against the immobilizing effect of the neurotoxin, he turned his eyeballs enough that he could stare fixedly at the gold-and-black cap atop Lwaxana's head. He poured everything he had into his eyes, urgently trying to communicate with the ambas-sador.

Read my mind, he entreated her. *You have to read my mind!*

It took her a moment, but she got the message. She threw the insulated cap across the room. Her face contorted in pain as the telepathic assault besieged her once more. Still, she fought back against the agony and looked deeply into Barclay's eyes. Her searching brain found a single command shouting inside his skull:

"Activate program: 'Lawrence of Arabia.'"

In a heartbeat, the vacant chamber was replaced by kilometers of arid desert beneath a blistering sun. Shifting sand dunes rolled on for as far as the eye could see. Heat waves shimmered above bleached bones and weathered sandstone formations. A hot wind blew grit in Barclay's eyes. The desert was an ocean in which no oar was dipped . . .

"Gaakk!" Povz croaked. The sudden change, from murky swamp to blazing wasteland, came as quite a shock, especially if you were, say, a nocturnal amphibian. Blinded by the glare, the flabbergasted aliens threw their webbed hands over their eyes. They reeled about in distress, bumping into one another at random. The merciless heat sapped their strength. Dried slime slaked off their quivering flesh. All but Povz collapsed into the hot sands, gasping like fish out of water. A mouthwatering smell reminded Barclay of a delicacy he'd once sampled on New Caribe. He had a sudden craving for frog legs.

Povz wobbled onto rubbery limbs. The sapphire glow from his pendant flickered and faded. "Uh-oh . . . ."

That was all Lwaxana needed. She charged forward, trampling over the bodies of the debilitated henchfrogs, and swung the Sacred Chalice of Rixx against the Eye of Dread. The fragile crystal shattered into dozens of broken shards and splinters. Povz's eyes bulged from their orbits as a burst of psionic feedback fried his brain. He tumbled backward down a sloping sand dune. His limbs twitched, as though part of some primitive galvanic experiment.

"Be thankful that you can't read my thoughts right now, you revolting toad." Lwaxana lowered the uncracked chalice. She posed with arms akimbo atop a mountain of sand. "That will teach you for trifling with a daughter of the Fifth House."

"Barclay! Ambassador!" An archway appeared in the desert and Ensign Ro came rushing into the holodeck. She held her phaser before her. A Starfleet medkit was clutched beneath her arm. A black eye and split lip suggested that she had not been taken captive by the terrorists without a fight, but she had obviously survived her death-defying plunge off the waterfall. The holodeck's safety protocols must have indeed kicked in at the last minute, transporting her to safety before she hit the bottom. Skidding to a halt at the sight of the defeated Tadigeans, she slowly lowered her phaser. "Nice."

"Please see to Lieutenant Barclay, Ensign," Lwaxana instructed her calmly. "Otherwise, I believe I have matters well in hand."

Personal log, Lieutenant Reginald Barclay, Stardate 45376.5

By the time the real *Tadigean delegates arrived, precisely when they were supposed to, Flev Ubaan and I had succeeded in reconciling the matter conversion and holographic imagery subsystems so that they were no longer incompatible. Along with the rest of the* Cataria's *crew, Ubaan recovered from the terrorists' psionic ambush with only a slight headache . . . and a somewhat improved attitude toward Starfleet "interference."*

Povz and his accomplices have been turned over to the Tadigean authorities. Seems they belonged to a rival faction that was bitterly opposed to opening up trade with Betazed and other foreign powers. From what I hear, the negotiations themselves are proceeding smoothly. According to Lwaxana— I mean Ambassador Troi—the Tadigeans are so impressed by the way we handled the terrorists that they're even talking about joining the Federation at last.

As Ensign Ro and I prepare to return to the Enterprise, *I like to think that Captain Picard and Commander La Forge will be pleased with the results of our assignment . . .*

"I think you both should know," Lwaxana Troi said as she bid them farewell, "that I intend to give Jean-Luc a positively glowing report of your performance here."

"Thank you, Ambassador," Barclay said. For a second, he wished that he hadn't left his protective cap behind in the holodeck, but the feeling quickly passed. He didn't find telepaths quite so intimidating anymore. As it turned out, they actually came in handy sometimes. "We're glad to be of assistance."

Lwaxana smiled warmly. "Are you quite sure you have to leave so soon? Our holodeck is working perfectly, thanks to your expert attentions. Perhaps you'd like to enjoy its restored capabilities before you embark on your journey home?"

For once, Barclay wasn't even tempted.

"No, thanks!"

TURNCOATS

Susan Shwartz

Historian's note:
This tale is set immediately after the events
of the episode "Face of the Enemy," during the
sixth season of Star Trek: The Next Generation.

SUSAN SHWARTZ

Susan Shwartz has co-authored five *Star Trek* novels with Josepha Sherman and specializes in Romulans. She has also written novels such as *Hostile Takeover, Second Chances, Grail of Hearts, Shards of Empire,* and *Cross and Crescent,* which take readers from interplanetary finance and first contact to retellings of *Lord Jim* and a radical Grail quest, then to events leading up to and away from the First Crusade. She is also the editor of seven anthologies.

Published in ten languages, she has been nominated five times for the Nebula Award, twice for the Hugo, and once each for the World Fantasy and the Edgar. She has a B.A. from Mount Holyoke College and an M.A. and Ph.D. from Harvard University, and has studied at Dartmouth, Oxford, and civilian seminars at the U.S. Army War College. She has also lectured at such places as Harvard, Princeton, Smith, SUNY-Binghamton, West Point, the Air Force Academy, and the U.S. Naval War College. For the past twenty years, she has worked in marketing communications on Wall Street.

She lives in Forest Hills, New York, loves opera, has notable art and shoe collections, and admits to being a third-generation Red Sox fan.

ENTERPRISE SPED TOWARD THE DRAKEN SYSTEM AT WARP 9, leaving the warbird *Khazara* far behind. The threat of battle was over. Stefan DeSeve had accomplished the mission Ambassador Spock had set him. Now, he fought the shakes. He always shook after a mission and always fought not to let it show. Romulans had always found the shakes vastly amusing. Their amusement usually carried unpleasant consequences—another reason he had defected back to the Federation, years after fleeing it in the first place.

Live and learn. In a manner of speaking.

"You will come with me," declared the huge security officer who wore his barbaric Klingon metal sash over his Starfleet uniform. At least, Worf was an adversary DeSeve could understand. Far more frightening was the enemy whom the *Enterprise*'s bridge crew had seen on board the Romulan ship and recognized as their Betazoid ship's counselor. Even Captain Picard's austere features had lit.

That was the face of the enemy DeSeve feared.

Only DeSeve's stammer, a consequence of spending half his life protecting himself in the Romulan Star Empire, stopped him before he cried out in alarm.

Quiet, he commanded himself, harsh as any centurion.

He was already a traitor. Did he want to look like a bigger fool than he already was? That hardly seemed possible, given the charges against him. He stiffened his knees to hold himself upright. At least, he could try to manage not to humiliate himself before that Klingon.

If the woman were really Tal Shiar and not this Deanna Troi, once she got into sickbay she would make certain the three Romulan defectors would die before they emerged from stasis. Then, how would she move against *Enterprise*?

DeSeve didn't know. But he feared it.

The most terrifying thing about the Tal Shiar was that you never knew what they could do or where. You might assume the worst, but then you always learned how much more terrible their "worst" could be. Many loyal Romulans had disappeared from the fleet DeSeve had thought he knew, the work of Tal Shiar political officers. Even after twenty years of service, DeSeve knew they had him under constant scrutiny. That, even more than the empire's discipline, kept him in constant fear.

It had been worth returning to the Federation to face treason charges to rid himself of that fear, but now he had failed at that too, it seemed.

DeSeve balled his big, ineffectual fists together behind his back. The game was over. He had lost twice.

Compared with that, Lieutenant Worf's too obvious restraint in not turning his broad back on a traitor made DeSeve stifle a laugh. Bad idea even to smile. Worf would probably shove him into the turbolift and, safely out of Captain Picard's sight, smash his face against the paneling, then sling him over his shoulder and haul him into sickbay, claiming he had tried to escape. If that scenario played out, DeSeve might be just in time to see Major Rakal snap this ship's medical officer's spine.

But Doctor Crusher had been kind to him. If he could try to help her, it was worth getting his face bashed into the turbolift.

"What if the woman you beamed on board really is Major Rakal, not your ship's counselor?" At least, he could try to warn the Klingon.

"The words of a traitor hold no truth. You will be silent." Lieutenant Worf's bass voice practically made the gleaming bulkheads rattle.

Like most Klingons, Worf had no love for Romulans. But was he aware that in escorting DeSeve to his quarters, he was trying to protect Vice-Proconsul M'ret and his aides against a human traitor while a deadlier enemy might rove free? The irony would have been ridiculous if it weren't so terrifying. Hysteria threatened again, but the control that Starfleet and Grand Fleet military discipline had taught him kept DeSeve from disgracing himself even more—assuming he could.

"His" door slid aside. Worf jerked his chin at him to enter and be quick about it. The cabin they had assigned to him would have been considered luxurious for a warbird's commander. Harmonious tones on paneling, flooring, and chairs. Separate areas for work and sleeping.

DeSeve heard the locks engage and Worf's deep voice instruct the guards posted outside to take every precaution to prevent "the traitor" from sneaking out to assassinate valuable Romulan defectors. As if an aging traitor had the strength. Or the will.

DeSeve sank onto the nearest of his cabin's chairs and shook with silent, incongruous laughter. After that spasm subsided, he finally gave in to the shakes, but still managed to choke back the dry sobs that security scanners could pick up. He wouldn't give this ship's crew the satisfaction any more than he'd provided it for the Romulans.

Romulans, as he had told Captain Picard, were a moral people with an admirable clarity of purpose. He simply hadn't counted on living every moment of his life among them in a state of abject fear.

No, that wasn't true. It wasn't simple at all. He had grown tired of the kind of clarity of purpose that had turned a moral people into predators under the lash and mind games of the Tal Shiar.

Romulus had left him with few illusions, least of all the pleasant fantasy that aiding Ambassador Spock in his "cowboy diplomacy" (whatever that meant, it had extracted a bleak smile from the captain) would spare him a court-martial for treason. He had earned the dishonorable discharge and, probably, life imprisonment that were the only possible verdicts. More ruthless than the empire, the Federation did not execute traitors.

At least, for now, he could make use of the luxury of a replicator that could produce more than field rations.

"Romulan ale," he ordered.

Was he imagining it, or did the computer, as it requested he provide the formula for a drink banned in the Federation, sound disgusted? He shrugged. If his hands didn't shake so badly, he could probably *make* the replicator produce Romulan ale. Assuming security didn't just shoot him because it decided he was trying to destroy the ship.

Trading what he knew of Federation engineering for Romulan training, DeSeve had been competent enough to win himself service as an aging subcenturion in engineering on board various warbirds of no particular reputation. Once the political officers had mined him for what intelligence he could provide, he quickly learned that engineers were as closely watched on board as aristocrats with a political agenda. Romulans might accept a defector, might let him learn some of their technology, but they trusted him even less than they trusted the other—the *real*—engineers who monitored the quantum singularities that powered their ships and spent their watches under armed guard.

No, DeSeve would not tamper with the replicator. But he was cold and thirsty. Cups had been passed around on the bridge, even to him. But that had been some time ago.

"T-t-tea. Earl Grey. Hot," DeSeve ordered, imitating Captain Picard. The replicator instantly produced a steaming cup. After all these years away, he found it savory, even invigorating. If only Picard's drink could give him Picard's valor, integrity, and professionalism. Ambassador Spock respected Picard. DeSeve was merely a weapon to his hand.

Confined now to quarters, DeSeve found it hard to believe he had actually sat on the bridge at the captain's side in the very chair that his ship's counselor had occupied. He had given advice that Picard actually listened to. For a while, he had even succumbed to the cherishable illusion that it was all real, all his to keep. But it was an expedient. DeSeve knew all about expedients. The instant *Enterprise* fled the Kaleb sector, his use was over, and he was back under arrest.

He set down his cup, half emptied, but his hand shook again, and it rolled from his grip onto the table. Quickly, he restored the table's sheen with the sleeve of his heavy brown tunic. It was the least conspicuous garment he could find after Commander Riker ordered him to get rid of his Romulan uniform. Staggering a little, he headed toward the bunk.

Why would you *need a bunk like that?* Romulans would have found the wide, cushioned bunk another reason to taunt him. Especially the female underofficers. He had been lonely there; he was even lonelier here among those who had once been his own.

DeSeve let himself fall onto the soft, smooth covers. The shakes subsided, and he lay still, listening to the "song" of the ship's engines and systems. For the first time in years, a ship's system was tuned to a pitch that did not set his teeth and nerves on edge. He knew that warbirds were deliberately pitched to stimulate production of the Romulans' analog for adrenaline. He would keep the lights on, he decided, even if he did let the ship's song lull him all the way back to the Draken sector, even if only debriefing, trial, and disgrace awaited him.

He was locked in, safe. For a little while, he could forget.

The door signal thrust DeSeve back into consciousness. He thrust his hand under the pillow for the disruptor his shipmates had finally decided he was entitled to call his own. For a moment of pure panic, he had forgotten he had surrendered it at Research Station 25. He had never been given an Honor Blade.

Unarmed, then.

Rising, he raked his fingers through the Romulan military crop he had retained—why? As a mark of what he had been? "C-c-come," he said.

The door slid aside. Standing in it was Deanna Troi, restored to her rightful appearance. That meant nothing: Tal Shiar would have no compunctions about changing their appearance if it accomplished the destruction of *Enterprise*.

The woman was a head shorter than he and very pale. Her delicate ears were round now, not pointed, and her brow was smooth. Long dark ringlets cascaded halfway down her back over the blue dress she wore instead of a military crop, armored uniform, and spiked harness. Her clothing was almost a gown, with a low neck and soft panels that floated about her as she entered his cabin.

She fixed him with deep, deep dark eyes, then ran one hand over her forehead.

"Beverly calls it 'phantom ridge syndrome,'" she explained with a smile. "It feels good to look like myself again. To act like myself again. You must have found it very difficult to spend twenty years among Romulans."

He stood, feeling like a Krocton dweller hulking over one of the Noble Born.

"Are you still afraid I am truly Major Rakal, not Deanna Troi?" she asked.

He had forgotten that the *real* Troi was half-Betazoid. An empath. In that case, even his silence would be futile. An officer of the Tal Shiar might deduce that, but what was the point of pretense when she, even unarmed as she seemed, held all the weapons? He shook his head, confused.

"Not as easy to believe me a Romulan agent now that we're face-to-face, is it?" she asked. "Imagine how I felt waking up on board a warbird and seeing myself in the mirror!" She smiled. "This may take some time. Meanwhile . . ."

DeSeve felt an awkward flush rise from the too-high collar of his tunic, drawing sweat from his face.

Painfully taught Romulan courtesies took over. He bowed and gestured her to the other chair. "What may I offer you?" he asked.

Aside from his soul on a plate and all the information on the empire that he could spill. False to one master, false to all, as the saying went. He foresaw he was going to become very tired of answering questions. Life imprisonment wasn't the worst thing he faced; it was being talked to death, urged to disclose what he felt.

Counselor Troi cocked her head at the empty teacup and smiled. "Hot chocolate, please. Whipped cream. And chocolate shavings."

Her smile grew even wider as she contemplated the immense mug he handed her. "Romulan food . . ." She shuddered. "Especially the *viinerine.* Just one smell was more than enough."

She settled herself comfortably among the cushions and dipped her face toward the chocolate, inhaling with deep pleasure.

DeSeve found himself laughing helplessly. She had disarmed him. It was impossible to see in this small, curved woman curled up in a chair too big for her as she savored the aroma of hot chocolate the arrogant Tal Shiar officer who had been beamed, however hastily, onto *Enterprise.* She, or perhaps the chocolate, had finally convinced him. A mild intoxicant to Romulans, chocolate was a minor vice of aristocrats rich enough to smuggle it in. He remembered liking it before he had defected.

"That's better, isn't it? Now that you have decided that I am not Major Rakal. The dissidents killed her and made me take her place." Her dark eyes turned somber. "You may feel that the empire can do with fewer Tal Shiar operatives, but the loss of life . . ."

Khazara had destroyed the Korvallan freighter that had been supposed to receive M'ret and his aides. She hadn't forgotten those eighteen lives. Probably, she would never forget. After all, she was an empath. She might even regret *him*. Those deep, forgiving eyes . . .

He couldn't stand it.

"What's the point?" he snapped. "We all know the price of treason. In some ways, the Federation's tougher than the Romulans. The Federation doesn't execute traitors, so I get to spend the rest of my life in New Zealand talking about my feelings and listening to lectures on rehab."

She shook her head, giving him priority over the chocolate. "You have knowledge that could be very valuable to Starfleet intelligence."

"As it was to Romulus."

She inclined her head. "You are in an awkward situation," she agreed, then shook her head at her own understatement. "But even Commander Riker agrees you helped save the ship when *Khazara* was cloaked and stalking us. And the Vice-Proconsul is deeply grateful. I was in sickbay with him, and I believe he never forgets those who help him. So you have a possibility of clemency. And even if you didn't, you still have an obligation to yourself to grow and change. To achieve true rehabilitation."

"I almost think I'd rather be ejected from an airlock," he heard himself admit. He felt the unfamiliar stretch of muscles around his mouth in a wry grin.

"From what I understand, you had some close escapes. We should talk further. I shall set up a schedule of appointments and—"

"Picard to Ensign DeSeve. Please be ready in five minutes to be escorted to my ready room," Picard's voice interrupted from a speaker hidden in the bulkhead, rather than from DeSeve's workstation. *Ensign.* He would have a right to that title until he was dishonorably discharged.

Setting aside her chocolate, Counselor Troi rose and smiled as if the captain could see her. "No need for the guards, Captain. I'll bring him up with me."

Once again, DeSeve found himself smiling as he stood aside for her to precede him out the door.

In Captain Picard's ready room, twin rows of light glowed above the textured russet bulkheads. Starlight, refracted into streaks of rainbow fire, shone through the ports. The captain sat at his desk, with Lieutenant Worf standing at his back at full attention and full glare.

"Mister DeSeve," said Picard, "my other guests wanted the opportunity to meet you."

Other guests? The captain was acting as if DeSeve was not under arrest.

Seated by Picard's desk was a tall Romulan, whose sharp, distinguished features were familiar to any subject of the empire. DeSeve had last seen him lying on *Enterprise*'s bridge in stasis. Behind him, half hidden in the shadows, stood two younger men. All wore quasi-military gray suits seamed in darker fabrics that looked like black velvet.

As Counselor Troi entered the room, DeSeve at her heels, Vice-Proconsul M'ret rose. He favored her with a sharp, admiring smile and an inclination of the head. Then he stepped forward, his shrewd, well-informed gaze on DeSeve himself. For an instant, DeSeve saw the desolation in his eyes, a mirror of the losses he himself felt. Of a home. An allegiance. His honor. All for reasons he had thought good. All gone.

DeSeve straightened to attention. Just in time, he stopped himself from bringing his fist up in salute. Instead, he bowed. Less deeply than appropriate, but who here besides the Romulans would know to rebuke him? A deeper bow might antagonize Captain Picard and definitely would annoy the Klingon. The courtesies of a culture he had abandoned were simply not worth the risk.

To DeSeve's shock, the aristocrat gave him a nod of approval before reaching out to shake his hand in the human style.

"Noble Born," DeSeve murmured.

If you believed some rumors, M'ret was of the Imperial line. If you believed others, he was part Vulcan.

"Just M'ret," the Romulan corrected him.

A tilt of his head summoned his aides forward. They bowed in disciplined unison, masking the loss they shared with their chief. None of the three wore body armor under their costly suits. They had left that behind, with—he noticed—the Honor Blades they would not dishonor by taking into exile.

He could not resist glancing over at Worf, who looked predictably outraged. Almost, but not quite, he growled. M'ret, who had been watching a tank of gleaming fish with some wistfulness, favored the Klingon with another sharp, quick smile, finding such consolation as he could in Worf's discomfort.

"*Captain,*" came Commander Riker's voice from the bridge. "*Incoming message from Draken IV. Admiral William Ross.*"

"Put him through, please, Number One." Picard rose punctiliously.

DeSeve started to back away. Surely three sought-after Romulan defectors had to be of more importance to an admiral than one aging Starfleet traitor. He blinked, forcing his eyes back into focus. Surreptitiously, he touched a bulkhead. Something about the vibrations in bulkhead and deck troubled him. He dismissed it as nerves, of a piece with his stammer. Twenty years of fear and only disgrace to look forward to could do that to a man. He forced himself not to flinch.

But the way the ship was tuned had started to sound *wrong.*

Worf growled. Odd that the Klingon sensed what Romulans with their Vulcanoid hearing apparently did not. But Worf knew this ship. He heard it too. M'ret's two aides, hearing only Klingon anger, bristled.

"Gentlemen," M'ret murmured. They subsided without looking at Worf, awaiting further orders.

The blue seal of the Federation formed on Picard's desktop monitor, angled now so that the captain and all his guests could see it, and bright enough to make DeSeve's eyes water. By the time they cleared, Admiral Ross's image had replaced it.

"*Captain*"—he acknowledged Picard, gesturing for him to seat himself once again—"*I understand you had some difficulty making pickup.*"

"We encountered *d'Deridex*-class imperial warbird *Khazara,* Toreth commanding, sir. You should be in receipt of Counselor Troi's report by now."

The admiral nodded. Even from his limited field of vision, he surveyed the ready room. The tired, pained look on his face at the sight of DeSeve only intensified his resemblance to the man from whom DeSeve flinched every day in the mirror, from burly height to graying hair to the jowls of early middle age. If only DeSeve's loyalty had matched his waywardness of mind, he might have been someone like Ross.

"My thanks, Counselor. And my regrets for your kidnapping. An investigation is in progress to prevent additional such incidents."

"Thank you, sir."

Picard returned to business. "Admiral, may I present our guests?"

"I think I am fairly well acquainted with them, by reputation at least," Ross answered. Now, that was an answer that could cut several ways.

Intelligence, DeSeve thought. This admiral had to have deep connections with it, or Starfleet would not have selected him to receive M'ret.

"Mister Vice-Proconsul. Gentlemen." Ross inclined his head.

A formal nod from M'ret. Stiffer bows, accompanied by old-fashioned heel clicks, from his aides.

"I am somewhat premature in welcoming you and your aides to Federation space, but there has been a change in plans."

Picard paused as if listening to something. Then he stiffened, clearly prepared to take *Enterprise* to Red Alert.

"Nothing like that, Captain. We sent out patrol ships and enabled our tachyon detection grids the instant your first transmission arrived. Vice-Proconsul, we had planned for you and your aides . . ."

"N'veran and Revaik." M'ret supplied their names crisply, as if Admiral Ross had been courteous enough to ask. They were of old families; they deserved the dignity of an introduction, even to an admiral. After all, who knew what Ross's parentage might be?

Stop thinking Romulan, DeSeve rebuked himself. *Birth doesn't matter, only integrity.*

". . . to be debriefed here. In fact, that's why I came out to take charge of this operation. However, Vulcan has convinced us of the logic"—Ross almost concealed his grimace—*"of debriefing Romulans on Vulcan."*

Some things didn't change. Vulcan was at least as politically obsessed as Romulus. Spock, although officially under his homeworld's censure, retained a number of highly efficient and influential contacts there.

"In fact, Vulcan is most insistent that we make early contact. They even sent out a legate who insists that if you do not make all deliberate speed, he will take his own ship out to meet you."

DeSeve could see Picard brace himself for a display of logic that would be called arrogant from any lesser being than a Vulcan.

"A legate?" Picard mused. "Not an ambassador?"

The admiral rose, gesturing to someone offscreen to take his place.

"I requested this mission." The man who faced them now was deeper voiced and taller than the admiral. He seemed energetic by nature, restrained only by his heavy robes of office.

"As the most logical choice of envoy and host." His voice became more solemn. *"I name thee guest friends."* The words sounded like something out of the most solemn of Romulan observances, the ones where redbloods, to use a term that was in official disfavor but wide use, were permitted to listen only in the back rows, if at all.

The legate raised his hand, his fingers parted. *"I am Ruanek, legate of Vulcan. I come to serve."* Then, astonishingly, he grinned.

"You!" M'ret seemed to unbend. "So you wound up on Vulcan after all! Spock never told me. Nor did *she."*

"Plausible deniability," said the legate-who-was-no-Vulcan. *"How is your lady?"*

"Disappointed at my choices. But she will survive. That is her great genius. To combine survival with honor." M'ret turned to Picard. "I have known Ambassador Spock since I was an eaglet. He doesn't make mistakes, not that I know of, but he is highly adept at compelling others to make them."

Ruanek and Picard shook their heads, almost identical gestures. Picard narrowed his eyes, as if concentrating on the same vibrations that made DeSeve swallow with increasing dizziness.

"Well, Captain?" the legate asked. *"Shall I rendezvous with the* Enterprise? *We have not traveled together since 2344. But I am disappointed. I was given to understand that you visited the homeworld, but it seems you still have not received the medal you won in our last encounter."* His eyes glinted with mischief.

"I prefer peace and quiet to ceremony." Picard smiled. Then his face changed. "It is indeed agreeable to see you."

Ruanek bowed. His face twisted with an emotion DeSeve identified as sorrow before he got it under control *"I had heard that you had helped Ambassador Sarek complete his last mission. So the rumors were true after all,"* he murmured.

Picard nodded once. "The need was sufficient." For an instant, his voice resumed that ceremonial tone. "I see no logic . . . there is no reason for you to take a small craft out into what could be disputed space. We should reach you in twenty-three hours forty-five minutes . . ."

The "legate" laughed. *"Captain, it would very much please me if you would honor my house with your presence along with my other guest friends,"* he said. *"I have a case of Chateau Picard 2360 Burgundy in what I believe to be appropriate storage, a thing that is difficult to achieve on Vulcan. I am reliably informed that it is just becoming drinkable. I would be honored to return hospitality I thought never to be able to repay."*

Again, Picard's face went almost Vulcan. "A life for a life. It is I who can never repay you."

M'ret raised an eyebrow. Deanna Troi's eyes grew moist. They were the only ones who seemed to understand.

"Legate, if your people have finished your highly illogical and highly classified reminiscences," Ross cut in, *"I have a station on alert to run. Captain, if you will . . ."*

His words ended in a shriek as *Enterprise* lurched, then lurched again, trying to reach equilibrium. High warp caught the ship and seemed to make it twist. Now the vibrations of its song howled upward until the three Romulans winced as it reached pitches only they could hear.

Beyond the windows, the starfield flared, spun, and flickered back into the normal rainbows of warp speed. Admiral Ross's image re-formed, grainy, then blacked out again. The screen flickered from black to a kind of fluorescent purple, kindling to a white that hurt the eyes.

DeSeve fell forward, one hand catching the table. He thought he could see his bones. He looked away and for an instant saw what seemed to be a room full of skeletons.

"Red Alert!" Picard shouted. "Number One, come about!"

Again, *Enterprise* lurched, struggling to obey the helm.

"Engineering," Picard spoke more quietly. "Report."

Commander Riker answered first, shouting from the bridge. *"We've dropped out of warp. Impulse engines and structural integrity are intact, Captain. Life support operational. Ship's systems are on emergency power. Radiation levels are rising, though."*

Worf, struggling with the impossibility of both guarding his captain in the ready room and returning to his duty station on the bridge, strode away to check his tactical console after a sharp nod from Picard. His voice boomed over the comm. *"Khazara's disruptor beam had almost no power."*

"It was linked to the transporter," came Data's lighter tones, also from the bridge. *"We know very little about Romulan technology."*

"We should not instantly assume we are under attack," Picard said. "Do you detect any ships?"

"None, sir," replied Riker. *"No imbalances, and no signs from the gravitic sensors. Data, get down to engineering to tune the tachyon detection grid."*

"Negative, Will. Another radiation burst like that could wipe Data's positronic circuits. Data, how are you feeling? Concisely, Data," Picard added quickly.

"Unimpaired, sir. Thus far."

"Mister La Forge." Only the way Picard drew out the engineer's name indicated his impatience, "Come in, Mister La Forge."

"We've got casualties. Two dead. Mister La Forge is down, sir," came a female voice, between bursts of static. *"A discharge took out two men. Geordi went to the controls, said he hadn't seen energy spikes that bad since Galorndon Core. Another one hit, and he put both hands on his VISOR, ripped it off, and collapsed."*

"Sickbay," Picard continued. "Beverly . . ."

"Initiating precautionary radiation protocols shipwide. En route to engineering, Captain. On foot," came a voice DeSeve recognized. His fears for Doctor Crusher's safety seemed far in the past. They were all in danger now.

Data appeared in the ready room. "With respect, Captain . . ." Android he might be, but he knew when to fall silent. Quickly, he joined Worf in passing out radiation sprays. M'ret's aides interposed themselves between the android and their leader.

"Sirs, these sprays are not species-specific," Data said. "I can assure you they will do no . . ."

"We have had Romulans on board before," Worf added. "One survived. Are you afraid?" The sneer in his voice would have kindled a small nova, much less Romulans' volatile tempers.

"Enough," M'ret snapped. Grasping a hypospray, he set it against his arm, then raised an eyebrow at his aides. They too injected themselves, then pressed their backs against the viewports, taking themselves out of the action. At least DeSeve no longer saw their bones through their flesh.

"Engineering," Picard called again. "I am coming down there, and I will expect a full report. Beverly, we've got to get Geordi functioning again."

Not to mention the ship.

"Data, are you still all right?"

"At the moment, I remain operational, sir. But the entire ship is being subjected to increasing levels of radiation," Data observed.

"Back to the bridge with you," Picard said. "If you feel anything . . ."

"If my systems deteriorate sufficiently to render me unreliable, I will report myself unfit for duty, Captain."

"You'll shut yourself down! You're one of the best resources we have."

"Aye, sir," Data's imperturbable voice replied. Eerie shadows flickered over the gold of his face and hands as he nodded.

"Number One, you have the bridge. The rest of you, with me."

"With respect, Captain," said Commander Riker as the group strode onto the bridge. The first officer was clearly reluctant to risk his captain in the presence of three Romulans and a traitor.

"Commander, if they've come this far, they probably want to live too. Objection noted, Number One. You can note it in your log."

Picard hurled himself into the turbolift, followed by the Romulans, the traitor, his security chief, and the ship's counselor. The lift took off at speed.

"Suggestions?" Picard spoke into his combadge.

Voices barraged him from all over the ship. Picard seemed untroubled by the ship's vibrations as he listened to his crew, processing different voices over the comm with ease.

"*Think,*" M'ret hissed at him urgently. His hand grasped

DeSeve's arm and pressed with almost enough strength to break it. Almost. DeSeve had long practice at not flinching. "If they can't use the android, you're the only one here who knows enough about both systems to be of any help!"

"What are you talking about?" Worf demanded.

"Your captain called for ideas. Do you have any?" M'ret replied as if he were questioning an antagonist on the Senate's floor. That too was a form of blood sport.

DeSeve had heard Romulans furious, amused, and even—shortly before their execution—afraid. He had never heard desperation from one of them before.

They probably want to live, too, Picard had said.

M'ret had discarded his honor on Romulus to perform a mission in which loss of life was the smallest risk he faced. The imprisonment he had been threatened with, even death itself, would have been far easier. He had to want to live not just to succeed, but also to justify his loss.

M'ret was not alone in wanting to live. In wanting to repair his name.

They both knew the empire. They both wanted the impossible.

DeSeve struggled not to add spacesickness to treason and let the greater strength of the Romulans, used to help him for once, brace him until the turbolift shuddered to a halt.

This close to the warp drive, DeSeve felt it beat like an imperiled heart when the turbolift, shaking and speeding by turns, finally released them into engineering. He lurched out onto the deck and steadied himself against a blank console.

Blue light spasmed across the vast bay from the engines, splashing the high bulkheads in uneven patterns. Deck, consoles, rails, and bulkheads vibrated, subsided, then shook. Lights high above flared red while the computer's voice reported constant rises in ambient radiation.

Engineering was not a safe place to be and was about to become less safe.

But even the sight of the great tower of the jeopardized warp drive struck DeSeve as an oddly welcome change from a warbird's engineering deck. Every Romulan engineering deck DeSeve had served on had been cramped, confined, and tense. Armed guards prowled,

SUSAN SHWARTZ

gazing over engineers' shoulders as they tended the mysterious sealed violence of the captive singularity that made the warbird fly.

Picard raced past DeSeve to where Doctor Crusher leaned over Lieutenant Commander La Forge. The chief engineer sat, hands over his face, hunched over on a spare container. His dark skin was almost ashen, especially where his fingertips pressed against his temples.

"Starboard nacelle shut down!" came a call. "We got it!"

The flickering lights and shrill deranged vibrations subsided, but only somewhat.

"Well done," Picard said. "Mister La Forge . . . Geordi . . ." He laid a hand on the engineer's shoulder while silently consulting the physician. She nodded once.

Picard shut his eyes in relief, then made himself look at the covered bodies on the deck and the surviving crew who fought to bring *Enterprise* back under control.

La Forge sighed. "Wish I'd been able to get the other one before I blacked out. Any chance you can shut down portside before the warp core blows?" he called to the engineering crew. One woman broke away from the struggle and leaned over the rail.

"Negative, sir. Conduits are fused. Sorry."

"Don't be sorry. Back to work!" La Forge called.

He pushed himself to his feet. "No, let me up," he told Doctor Crusher as she tried to restrain him. "The VISOR connections took a hit when the warp core malfunctioned. I should be all right now."

As all right as any of them could be, DeSeve thought.

La Forge put the VISOR on over wide, blind eyes and flinched.

"You're not all right," said Crusher. Her hand went to her combadge to order transport to sickbay, but the engineer pushed it away.

"If I don't get back to work, none of us are going to be all right. I can see—" He waved concerned hands away and turned toward the captain. "Sort of. There's lots of distortion. If the painkiller holds out . . . You'd better give me a spare, just in case . . ."

Taking the hypo she held out, La Forge flung himself toward one of the few displays that still looked marginally operational. His shaking hands fugued on the keyboards, sending up a pattern of shifting lights. As they steadied, so did the rhythms of the ship.

"Got the starboard nacelle on auxiliary power," La Forge reported. "Enough to compensate. Ambient radiation's within acceptable limits. For now."

– 174 –

Picard nodded at the chief medical officer's questions about radiation safety protocols on the bridge, his attention focused on his engineer.

"Engines are just drinking the power. Consumption levels are off the scale, Captain. You can feel the drain. Once it's gone, I estimate warp core breach in 20.6 minutes."

"Eject it," Picard ordered.

If *Khazara* were pursuing them, they would be a sitting target, then, swiftly afterward, protons and debris. If *Enterprise*'s crew abandoned ship, *Khazara* would take them prisoner. Including the three Romulans for whose sake *Enterprise* had been jeopardized in the first place. Assuming any survival pods survived the warp core breach, which was not an assumption that was safe to make.

La Forge shook his head. "Negative, sir. The fail safes are frozen. We're working on them, but . . ." He shook his head again, then winced as if his VISOR hurt him. "Sorry, sir."

There wasn't enough time. That was the problem with engineering. There was too much time until you had an emergency, and then you had no time at all.

Picard straightened. "Mister Worf," he ordered. "You will accompany our guests to a shuttlecraft and escort them to Draken IV, assuming you are not met en route by Admiral Ross or Legate Ruanek. Presumably, they are aware of our predicament. They've probably sent at least one ship out already. Once you establish communications, tell them to keep out of range."

"Respectfully, Captain, we refuse," M'ret said. "We will not leave you. We will fight to stay. And you have a greater priority than forcing us to leave."

"This disruption of ship's systems does not make sense," said Picard, instantly turning back to his main priority. "*Enterprise* took a direct disruptor hit. At the time, Lieutenant Worf reported that it had almost no impact. It was intended to serve as camouflage for the transporter beam that brought over our . . . stubborn guests. And, as Commander Riker pointed out, there are no ships in the area from which we can assume a second strike."

"There may be something else," Deanna Troi spoke unexpectedly. "Initially, N'vek refused to tamper with the cloak. I had to threaten to reveal what he'd done in bringing me aboard to Commander Toreth before he would agree to talk to a sympathizer in engineering. If I had seen the engineer, I would have known for certain . . ."

"Whether his sympathies extended as far as preserving *Enterprise*?" Picard guessed.

Troi nodded. "He must have been hedging his bets. Avoiding betrayal while retaining a weapon that would ensure regaining the commander's favor."

"A highly prudent strategy," M'ret commented. "The man saw our plans on the verge of exposure. He wasn't an active member of the movement, only a sympathizer, and sympathy is cheap. So he resorted to damage control—in this case, a way of getting the cargo—us—off *Khazara,* destroying *Enterprise,* a ship that the empire can hardly be said to favor, and protect both his ship and his commander, who is a woman of unquestioned integrity. I would call that highly logical."

"We can debate logic later, Vice-Proconsul," said Picard.

If we live hung unsaid in the controlled clamor that was the engineering deck confronted with an emergency that could destroy the ship.

"I am not an engineer," Troi added, "but let's look at it this way. What could a Romulan engineer have used that would disable *Enterprise* long enough for *Khazara* to get away? Assuming Commander Toreth preferred flight to destroying us, and believe me, Toreth wanted little more than to destroy us. Except, perhaps, to interrogate me, then eject me from an airlock."

Using the stealth he had developed as a survival skill throughout his years in the empire, DeSeve edged unobtrusively over toward the chief engineer and the screens he studied. The engineer was reviewing the failure analysis as if he could force solutions from it. Failure, now, that was a subject DeSeve understood with all his heart.

"Suggestions?" This time Picard's question was directed toward him as well as the Romulans.

M'ret glanced at his aides, then down at the deck, as if abashed.

"Engineering is not a study for the Noble Born," DeSeve heard himself say. He flushed to find himself the center of attention, which always had been the worst place to be in the Romulan Star Empire. "They not only prefer to keep their hands clean, the Senate considers it unsafe for them to study this particular discipline."

"Twelve minutes," came the computer warning as it ticked down toward warp core breach. Radiation levels were rising, too, but not fast enough to render the ship's crew unconscious before the warp drive blew.

"The Senate fears what warring factions could do with expert knowledge of quantum singularities," M'ret agreed. "My own clan had trouble enough even with an early cloaking device."

"Where precisely did the disruptor beam hit?" DeSeve asked. Then, remembering his status, he added, "Please, sir."

La Forge pointed at a ship schematic. "The blast hit here, in this power transmission nexus, like a ganglion transmitting nerve impulses to the rest of the body." His hand went again to his VISOR. That was where he had taken his worst hit, barring some burns to his hands and face. It had left him shocky, still practically out on his feet but forcing himself to keep alert.

"Apparently, when you combine disruptor fire with Romulan transporter technology, you get an unexpected—and very dangerous—synergy. It begins small, in power couplings, then spreads . . . just as it's doing now . . ."

"And we wouldn't know this because ordinarily, shields are up, and you can't transport when shields are up."

Picard brought his fist down quietly on a console. In the flickering blue light, he looked very pale.

"Can the fail safes be operated mechanically?"

"My people have been trying, sir," Geordi said. "Someone's got . . . The only way I can see to work them is to get in there and do it by hand."

"There's more than that," DeSeve spoke up again. "The last ship I served on, before I was sent back . . . the ship was decommissioned. They were experimenting with a kind of grenade. It doesn't blow at once: it radiates. The idea is to render a ship incapable so it can be captured."

"You think Khazara's engineer might have known about them?"

DeSeve shrugged. "Stories get around. Even to me. If I heard it, so did most of the fleet."

"Toreth had no love for Tal Shiar," Troi added. "Khazara would have been exactly the sort of ship a disaffected engineer, who felt himself being watched, would try to serve on."

DeSeve edged in closer toward the screen. "Can't see . . . the thing is probably cloaked," he muttered.

"Oh, there's something there, all right," La Forge backed him. "I don't like that at all. Whatever it is, it's getting stronger too."

Computer's warning confirmed that. At this rate, they would need a backup injection soon, and there were only so many of those a body could take before breaking down—assuming the warp core didn't blow first.

The solution hit DeSeve like disruptor fire. He straightened to face the captain as a proper officer would.

"You'd have to go up and check," he said. "I would assume the weapon is cloaked. At that close range, even if I couldn't see it, I could pick it up as the source of the emissions."

"Then I'd better be on my way," La Forge said, somewhat too casually. "That Jefferies tube is a long hike at the best of times."

Picard's face went completely expressionless as he prepared to watch one of his most trusted officers go to certain death. A Romulan officer wouldn't have thought twice, DeSeve thought. Then he saw the expression on the Vice-Proconsul's face.

But La Forge admitted to only limited experience with Romulan technology. The Romulans, whose physiology might allow them to endure hard radiation for longer, hadn't the training. And Picard would not trust them, assuming the Klingon did not physically restrain him. He had already violated a direct order once.

That left only him. He was a traitor, yes, but he was a traitor who had traded Federation engineering technology for twenty years of experience in the Romulan Fleet.

The ruthless morality that had first attracted and then alienated DeSeve on Romulus suddenly fused with the ethics he had failed to learn in Starfleet. "Sir, he can barely walk, and he doesn't know what he's looking for. I do."

Somewhere during the emergency, he realized, he had lost his stammer.

Picard was listening as he always listened, not dismissing any expedient that might help his ship.

"You . . . ," growled the Klingon. "I will not allow you to destroy this ship."

"If I wanted to, all I'd have to do is stand here and wait for the warp core to blow," DeSeve said quietly. "I know as much about these systems as anyone on board. Besides," he said, "if they blow, we all die. If it doesn't, you all have futures I'm sure you'd rather keep on working toward."

What is the best I can expect? Life imprisonment with counselors talking at me? Clemency, maybe even a pardon? A life spent with my back turned to whispers? Not a chance.

A spray hit DeSeve's arm as Doctor Crusher made the rounds, reinjecting everyone in engineering against the growing levels of radiation.

DeSeve kept his eyes fixed on Picard. Better than anyone else, the captain knew how quickly time was running out. It would take DeSeve five minutes to reach where the grenade was. If he didn't start out now, they might as well abandon ship and hope for the best.

Khazara might not be out there. But Picard would not bet so many lives on it.

"We would offer to return to the empire if it would save you," Proconsul M'ret said. "But it won't. Send someone with him, if you must. But let him try."

"I will assist him," Worf announced.

If only the Klingon could. Klingon physiology could take more damage than the relatively frail human model. DeSeve fought against an incongruous laugh.

"I'm coming too!" La Forge declared. He straightened from the console and nearly keeled over. He was going nowhere.

"Let the man make good on his crimes," M'ret urged Picard. "He is a tool to your hand. And he will serve."

How had the Vice-Proconsul known that, more than anything in his life, DeSeve wanted to finish the mission with which Spock had entrusted him, the mission that had brought him back home. He wanted to give these decent people and this magnificent ship a chance at life. And he had spent enough time in the empire to know that there truly was only one punishment for treason.

Maybe that was all M'ret knew. Maybe he was simply allowing a man for whom he had—in some strange way—assumed a debt of gratitude a chance at Final Honor. It was more than any other Romulan had ever granted him.

DeSeve saw when Picard's face changed that M'ret had gained his point, and he, his last wish.

Doctor Crusher injected him again. This time it burned. "It may give you a fighting chance," she said.

Keep morale up. Yes, Doctor.

He made himself smile at her. It probably would not suffice to save him from fatal radiation burns, but it would give him time.

Maybe even enough.

"Salute!" ordered M'ret, and his aides brought their fists to their chests. So did he.

Last of all, Picard faced him. What was he going to say? Good luck? Godspeed?

The captain's face was ashen. "Thank you." He reached out to clasp DeSeve's hand and did not flinch from the sweat and tremors that gripped it.

That was more than DeSeve ever expected or deserved.

DeSeve walked past the mingled frustration and respect on Lieutenant Worf's ridged face.

"You'd better suit up!" ordered La Forge.

Could he spare the time? Engineers swarmed him and thrust him into the protective suit as if they valued him. Making what haste he could in unfamiliar gear, DeSeve lumbered away.

The Jefferies tube that led toward the nacelle, the grenade, and the fail safes was a maelstrom of small explosions, white shading past a livid purple off the spectrum, and the whoops of alarms. In here, the vibrations of the endangered ship seemed to take possession of him and shake him through and through.

Time until the warp core breach was running out, but he knew his personal time would run out even faster unless he made haste. He bent double, a tall man in a small space, and crawled faster than he had even in the grueling Romulan basic training they had insisted he undergo. He had entertained them mightily, but, in the end, he had passed their tests. He would pass this one too.

The protective gear got in his way, wedging him for precious seconds. He thought he heard something tear. No time to check, to make any repairs. He wrestled free and moved forward again, trying for as much speed as he could, as if this were a Romulan live-fire exercise.

As much as the explosions and shrieks of deranged systems, the radiation was a palpable thing. It was a light-filled mist in the air, a burning sensation on his skin, and it grew harder to bear the closer he got. *Enterprise* lurched hard, hurling him against the side of the tube and wedging him in firmly against panels that had buckled. As time ticked down to warp core breach, it would become harder and harder to control. He struggled away from the panels and felt his suit tear, slipped on one hand and went down. Frantically tearing free, he righted himself and clambered even faster through the tube. This was his one chance to redeem a life that had been one long dishonor.

A red light blinked on his heads-up display. That last fight to extricate himself had torn his suit, all right. Torn the back and one glove.

He looked down. His injured hand had left a smear of blood on the metal. There would be more. He pushed himself to move faster, before the rising levels of radiation stopped him. By now, the first stigmata of radiation poisoning were forming, spreading and growing darker on his skin. Was that sweat he felt, or blood as capillaries weakened and then broke?

By the time DeSeve reached the nexus where the cloaked Romulan weapon was probably lodged, his hand had begun to ooze blood within the torn glove. He braced himself up on his knees and groped ahead. Now he could feel the small, deadly object. Cloaked, all right, and he could not manipulate its triggers in the heavy gloves that had failed to protect him.

Well, it wasn't as if he had ever expected to make it out of here alive, he told himself and ignored the spike of fear that followed. He was used to fear. He could live with it—just a little longer.

He ripped off both gloves, the torn, useless one and the one that still afforded him protection. The heads-up display pointed to almost exponential radiation hikes, but he needed both hands to manipulate the weapon. First, though, he had to see it.

Blood dripped from both hands. It splashed and spread out over an invisible, roughly spherical object. The thing was burning hot. No time to cry out or find the med-delivery system in his useless gear. He caught up the gloves again and grabbed at the object. They began to smolder. He smelled smoke along with his own blood and sweat. But they would last long enough. Long enough for him to find the tiny, secret switches that were Romulan engineers' protection against intrusive political officers.

His helmet had clouded with sweat or worse. Half crazed from the pain, he ripped it off. Stories he remembered from his brief, unlucky Starfleet career came back to him. Hadn't they whispered that Spock once lost a battle with radiation yet lived to fight another day? Could DeSeve dare do less—not just for Spock, but for this captain, this crew, these Romulans? So now he was comparing himself with one of Starfleet's greatest heroes and the very person who'd used him to help Romulans betray their own empire? He laughed and fought not to cough. Blood was trickling down his chin anyhow. It was almost purple in the weird light. Red blood, not green.

Red.

By now, he could scarcely see. But he could hear the warning as time ticked down toward a warp core breach. Behind him, in engineering, they were trying to talk to him, urge him on, ask him questions. He ignored all of them but did not turn off the signal: no need to make them fear he had turned traitor once again. Let them busy themselves with lesser worries.

It was getting darker fast now. Odd: the shriek of the ship in torment seemed softer. His hearing was failing, along with the rest of him. He realized he had one last chance to use his waning strength to force the power coupling closed.

La Forge had been right. They were all but fused. DeSeve abandoned his charred gloves over the deactivated grenade even though the ship's true engineers would be able to see it now that it was uncloaked and deactivated. Only the couplings remained. He struck them hard with joined, bleeding fists. Pain radiated through him as his bones snapped, but at last he felt the switches give.

The deadly pyrotechnics in the Jefferies tube subsided. Even if he could not see them, or truly hear the screams of the ship's engines, he felt the shaking of the tube around him diminish, then steady until he crouched, panting in the stillness and the dark.

He expected at any second to begin convulsing, to roll about and batter himself unconscious in the Jefferies tube. He guessed he just didn't have that much strength left. He dropped, panting. He was beyond pain now. For a moment, he savored the triumph and the silence.

"DeSeve, Ensign DeSeve! Come in, man. Report!"

"Radiation levels are dropping . . ."

". . . Power drain ceasing . . ."

"*He did it!*" a feral hiss in a most aristocratic accent. It was almost funny.

"*Stefan!*" Picard's voice again, pain filled. "*Are you there? Can you answer me?*"

He wanted to reply, but his mouth was filled with blood. By the time Picard called his name again, he was beyond hearing, beyond reply, beyond life itself.

The cup of tea on Picard's desk had cooled a long time ago. The lights were dim, compared with the skidding rainbows of stars at warp speed he could see through the viewscreen in his quarters.

"*Captain's log. Repairs on* Enterprise's *engines are proceeding satisfactorily, even after Lieutenant Commander La Forge was apprehended in an unauthorized attempt to leave sickbay in order to get back on the job. Doctor Crusher has declined to bring charges. Similarly, I have declined to arrest Lieutenant Worf for disobeying my direct order to remove Ambassador Spock's . . . associates from danger, although I have accepted his personal apology.*

"*Mister La Forge, now restored to duty and Doctor Crusher's good graces, informs me that we shall be operational within six hours. All tachyon emissions appear to have vanished.*" Picard allowed himself a thin smile at the paradox.

"*Admiral Ross has spoken to me from Draken IV. He had indeed sent out a ship, the* Nolan*, as soon as communications broke down. Once it makes rendezvous*"—he remembered how Ruanek had stammered over the word—"*Vice-Proconsul M'ret and his staff will transfer from* Enterprise *and be taken to Vulcan as quickly as possible.*"

Presumably by Starfleet, rather than Vulcan shuttle, Picard assumed. The transfer would be accomplished quickly, efficiently. Picard would take an honor guard down to transporter room 3. As much as M'ret might protest, Picard gave honor where he saw it.

It *was* unfortunate, though, that he would have no time to speak with the "Vulcan" legate, let alone take up his offer of hospitality back on Vulcan. It would have been pleasant to see how the exile whom he had saved had prospered, but the legate would have to continue to store the 2360 against the day when Picard might actually have a moment to savor the vintage.

Not that he would sit still for long on Vulcan. The planet was a treasure for archaeologists.

A treasure . . . highly emotional terminology, but accurate, came that inner voice again. It was logical that that voice had come to the fore of his thoughts: its owner, like Picard, had risked what he valued more than life on his judgment of one man. Both had been right, much to their satisfaction.

"Finally, I come to the matter of Ensign Stefan DeSeve. We took him into custody at Research Station 25 and were bringing him in to stand court-martial for treason. In the battle to extract Vice-Proconsul M'ret and his staff, Mister DeSeve's knowledge and prompt action saved the Enterprise *at the cost of his own life. I have already reported—and I will uphold it at any board of inquiry—my recommendation that all charges against Mister DeSeve be dismissed. In token thereof, I have given orders for him to be buried in space with full military honors"*—his voice grew almost harsh to prevent it from shaking—*"with the rest of my crew before the Vice-Proconsul leaves* Enterprise. *I can only add that I consider Stefan DeSeve's sacrifice to be in the highest tradition of the service."*

Picard ended his log entry. Granted, he had not actually said *which* military service he actually meant. He didn't have to. And, if he pushed Fortune even more than *Enterprise* had been doing lately, no one might ever ask. Besides, did it even matter? DeSeve, N'Vek, even Spock himself—they all served the same cause. Like many others who had died and still more who fought and waited and hoped.

For freedom.

He picked up his cup and raised it to the stars outside. It was just tea, not the Burgundy that would have to keep waiting for him on Vulcan, but it would serve.

"Absent friends," said Picard, and drained his cup.

ORDINARY DAYS

James Swallow

Historian's note:
This tale unfolds concurrently with the episode
"Journey's End," during the seventh season
of Star Trek: The Next Generation.

JAMES SWALLOW

James Swallow is proud to be the only British writer to have worked on a *Star Trek* television series, creating the original story concepts for the *Star Trek: Voyager* episodes "One" and "Memorial"; his other associations with the *Star Trek* saga include "Closure" for the anthology *Distant Shores,* scripting the video game *Star Trek Invasion,* and writing over 400 articles in thirteen different *Star Trek* magazines around the world.

Beyond the final frontier, as well as a nonfiction book (*Dark Eye: The Films of David Fincher*), James also wrote the Sundowners series of original steampunk westerns, *Jade Dragon, The Butterfly Effect,* and fiction in the worlds of *Warhammer 40,000* (*The Flight of the Eisenstein, Faith & Fire, Deus Encarmine,* and *Deus Sanguinius*), *Stargate* (*Halcyon* and *Relativity*), and *2000AD* (*Eclipse, Whiteout,* and *Blood Relative*). His other credits include scripts for video games and audio dramas in the worlds of *Battlestar Galactica, Doctor Who, Blake's 7,* and *Space: 1889.*

THE TWIN SUNRISE ON DORVAN V PAINTED THE SKY WITH A cherry-red tint that reminded Mika of her grandmother, of the dresses she used to wear. Unlike the rest of her clan, the old woman had never left the land where she had been born, married, had children, and died, and yet Mika felt like she was still with her, casting an eye over their township each time the suns came over the horizon.

Mika wondered what Grandmother would have made of the colony. As long as one didn't look too hard at the fields of *kittik* wheat, the second orange star on the horizon, or the odd birds that wheeled in the skies, it wouldn't be difficult to fool yourself into thinking you were still on Earth. But the fifth planet in the Dorvan system was so very far from the lands of Mika's ancestors, and the distance was not just a measure of simple light-years. It was a distance of the heart. At night she would see the stars, all the alien constellations, and feel it most strongly. As she walked, she gave a rueful half smile to the emerging day. It was strange for her to think of abstractions like "home" when she had spent so much of her life rootless and wandering.

But that had changed now. Marriage had a way of turning your life about, so Mika's sister Liso had said. Without noticing, Mika had grown connected, the need to wander that characterized her youth fading and a yearning for reconnection rising in its place.

She got a wary nod from Hectu, the Denobulan botanist who lived in the house just past the school; she was one of the few non-humans in the township. The portly woman was, as ever, up to her arms in Dorvan's powdery brown dirt, leafy plants in her big, thick-fingered hands. Mika didn't stop to talk. It wasn't that Hectu was bad company, but she had a tendency to make every issue into a drama, no matter how small—and with the current situation, a circumstance of *real* importance, Mika knew that she'd be listening to her fret for hours if she stopped to be polite.

The treaty announcement was all that anyone could talk about now, the shifting of ghostly and unreal borders on some computer-projected map of the galaxy, decisions made by unknown men on worlds orbiting stars so far away as to be invisible in Mika's night sky. The talk was of lines of influence, demarcations between nation-states that were as removed from the township on Dorvan V as to be almost inconceivable. The settlement had existed on the fringes of human space for centuries, but because of the consequences of a slow-burning conflict that had never even touched their lives, the colonists awakened one day to learn their world had been ceded to alien control. Cardassia or Sol, Federation or Union—the name upon the territory where the Dorvan system lay was an abstract concept, not something that had a bearing on their every-day lives. Not until now.

The girl walked on, threading her way through the open paths between the adobe buildings. Here in the township proper, the sense of tension hanging over the community was more noticeable. As today had drawn closer, the laughter and freedom of the place had become less obvious, more forced. People were worried, and worried people stayed in their homes. They ruminated and let their thoughts turn to dark places. Last night, while her husband slept soundly beside her, Mika had heard raised voices from the house two doors down, an argument over something petty inflated by fears about other, deeper concerns. She looked up into the morning, saw the faint lights of the last bright stars of dawn. The starship would be coming soon.

"Hey, Mika." The voice drew her attention and she turned as a friendly figure approached. He gave her an easy smile and she did her best to match it.

"Lakanta." She nodded back. "You're up early."

"It's going to be a long day," he noted, without even the smallest hint of irony. He was quiet for a moment, and Mika knew he was trying to frame the question. She made a little wave with her hand.

"I've asked him," she said. "He hasn't given me an answer."

A frown creased Lakanta's pleasant, open face. "It's . . . difficult for him," he noted. "I don't think the elders really understand that. They only see his connection, and—"

"His obligation," she finished. Mika looked away. "Marriage makes him family and an extension of the tribe."

"The nature of family often forces us to places we don't want to visit," he said quietly. "I do not envy him."

Mika hesitated and gave Lakanta a long look. "They asked you to come speak with me, didn't they?"

He nodded again. "Don't think ill of the elders. They see your husband as the only line of resistance against the Starfleet people. Their fears are strong."

"He's just one man," Mika retorted, more sharply than she wished. "He's not a soldier or a diplomat."

"He used to be one of them."

She snorted. "He was *never* one of them. That's why he chose to leave all that behind."

A curious expression passed over Lakanta's face, a peculiar look of knowing that seemed oddly alien. "Choices always return to us when we least expect them. The cost of them is never fully apparent at the time." He blinked, and his manner changed again. "I'll come by in a little while. Perhaps he'll listen to a friend."

Lakanta wandered away and Mika walked into her house alone.

The smell of warming oatcakes met her and she was instantly hungry. A pot of tea steamed gently on the kitchen table, and her mug waited for her, a spoon resting beside it. For a moment, the simple gesture wiped away her darker musings.

A hand snaked around her waist and Mika felt the bristles of an unshaven chin tickle her neck as her husband kissed her there. "Hey," he said.

Mika turned in his embrace and took up the thread of their little ritual. "Good morning, Mister Crusher," she told him.

"Good morning, Missus Crusher," he replied and kissed her again. "Breakfast's ready."

She slipped from his grasp, and the casual warmth in his expression faded. The question hung in the air between them.

"Wes," she began, but he turned away and went to the stove.

"I said I would think about it," he replied. "I'm doing it. I'm thinking about it."

She felt a knot of tension in her chest. A moment ago she had been ready to take his side to Lakanta and the others, defend her husband's right to his privacy, and now she found herself on the other face of the argument. Wesley had come to live with Mika's clan on Dorvan V because he had walked away from that life, and now she was asking him—they were *all* asking him—to return to it again for the good of the colony.

Finally she spoke. "I hate this. I hate that you're being asked this." Mika sighed. "You should refuse."

"I want to." Wes brought her breakfast and poured her tea. "More than anything, I want to."

"Then say no," she said in a rush. "Tell the elders to take the weight of this themselves, just as they should. You're not a councilman. It's wrong to make these demands of you, you're just a—"

"A what?" He eyed her. "An ordinary man?"

"Wesley Crusher." Mika touched his hand. "You have *never* been ordinary."

The knock at the door broke the moment. She pulled it aside and found Lakanta there, breathless from running.

"Wes," he called, looking past her. "There's word from the lodge. The Federation ship has made orbit. They're sending a delegation down by transporter to the square." He swallowed hard.

Mika saw the flicker of emotion when her husband said the next word, there and then gone. "*Enterprise*?"

Lakanta nodded.

Wesley studied the tea in his cup for a moment, then took a sip of it. He put it down and touched Mika's wrist. "I won't be long," he told her and followed the other man out into the brightening morning air.

There were five of them: old Anthwara; Sinta and Otakay, the more senior of the elders; Lakanta; and Crusher himself. Sinta's leathery face had a cast of genuine gratitude upon it as Wes walked up to them, the woman looking at him as if she thought he would save them all. *She'll be disappointed,* he thought.

Otakay looked like he was on the verge of saying something acid, as he always did, but the noise of splitting air molecules silenced him before he could speak. All of them were drawn to the spot by the fountain where five dashes of blue-white scintillation appeared in midair, elongating in moments to resolve into columns of light and then into the solidity of humanoid forms. Wes found his gaze falling on the chest of the man materializing at the head of the landing party, on the oval-and-arrowhead sigil that rested on his left breast. The deep crimson of the uniform stood out against the muted earth tones of the clothes favored by the colonists.

The transporter cycle ended and the man in the burgundy tunic scanned them with a severe and uncompromising gaze that cut through Wes as if he were just empty air.

"My name is Edward Jellico," said the officer. "I'm captain of the *U.S.S. Enterprise.*" Jellico made no move toward introducing the rest of his party, two watchful security men with holstered phasers at their belts and a slim Cygnian female in a mustard-colored uniform who kept her attention on a tricorder. The fifth and final member of the group wore a sky-blue overcoat that accented the plume of terra-cotta hair falling over her shoulders. Doctor Beverly Crusher gave her son a brittle smile of greeting but said nothing.

Wes returned the gesture woodenly. *She looks older.* The thought popped unbidden into the front of his mind, and he found he didn't know what to say to his mother. How much time had passed since that day in San Francisco, when he told her he was leaving? *Four years, five?* Their last words had been hurtful to one another, and then as he traveled, it had become so easy simply to let her slip from his mind. Wes felt the sting of guilt; she'd aged and he couldn't help but think it was his fault.

Anthwara cleared his throat, and with nods of his head the old man introduced the representatives of the colony. Jellico gave all of them an arch look in turn but ignored Wes when his name was mentioned. "I speak for this settlement," concluded Anthwara, talking with his usual air of calm deliberation. "I will hear your petition."

"Petition?" repeated Jellico. "Has there been some kind of mis-communication here? A subspace message was transmitted to you over nine solar weeks ago, from the Office of Colonial Affairs on Starbase 310. You did receive it?"

"We did," snapped Otakay, bristling, "and we chose not to concede to the authority of your 'office of affairs.'"

Jellico smiled thinly. "Is that right? You're happy to be a part of the Federation for two hundred years, but the moment it's not going your way you decide to strike out on your own?"

"This colony has been on its own since the tribe first left their birth world behind," ventured Lakanta. "It has always maintained its independence and self-sufficiency."

The captain's cold smile became a sneer. "And you can thank Starfleet for that. While you lived your lives on this backwater, it was Starfleet vessels, *Federation vessels,* that kept the Dorvan sector free from invasion and piracy—" He stopped himself. "Mister Anthwara, I'm not here to debate politics with you. The *Enterprise* is here to do a job, and I intend to see that task through to its conclusion. Teku?" Jellico gave a sideways look to the Cygnian woman—a lieutenant, Wes noticed—and in turn she offered Sinta a datapadd with a milk-pale hand.

"This is a complete transcript of the Federation-Cardassian Treaty and all communications and stipulations attending to it," said the woman, "along with a copy of the formal orders of relocation signed by the president of the United Federation of Planets."

Sinta took it and passed it to Wesley without even looking at the device. He glanced at the page of orders. It was all there, in dense boilerplate legalese.

"*Enterprise*'s cargo spaces and holodecks have been converted to serve as temporary accommodation for your people," Jellico continued. "You'll find details of individual allowances for personal items for each transportee. Any special medical requirements should be made clear to Doctor Crusher, here."

Lieutenant Teku gestured toward the *kittik* fields. "Sir, I'd suggest that area would be best as a staging point for transport groups. We can beam up ten, perhaps sixteen people at a time and the sensors will give a clear lock—"

"We're not going." The words slipped out of Wesley's mouth.

He looked up from the padd and met Jellico's hard gaze. "No one wants to leave here."

Jellico's jaw hardened. "You talk like you have a choice, son. Don't make the mistake of thinking you do."

"I'm not your damn son," Wes retorted, and he saw his mother stiffen at the words, "and I'll tell you again, one more time so there's no misunderstanding between us. None of us will leave Dorvan V."

The captain looked at Anthwara. "I thought you did the speaking for your people."

"Wesley is one of my people," replied the old man. "His words are my words."

"Wes," said Beverly, and he tensed. Just hearing her say his name pulled his emotions tight. "You . . . The colonists can't stay. This planet belongs to the Cardassians now. They already have a ship on its way to establish an outpost. If they arrive and find humans still here, they'll consider you trespassers."

Otakay gave a sour chuckle. "Trespassers? On our own land?" He glared at Jellico. "You make this pact without consulting us and expect everyone in our settlement simply to agree to it?" The elder snorted. "I imagine these Cardassians will be angry when they get here—but that will be your problem, not ours! You'll have to answer for bartering away that which was never yours to begin with!"

Teku's face creased in concern. "With respect, sir, you will not be simply deported and left to fend for yourselves. Once you arrive at Starbase 310, you will be given the opportunity to resettle on any one of a thousand worlds all across the quadrant."

Anthwara spread his hands. "This is our home, miss," he told her. "What my grandson-in-law says is what every one of us will say." The elder looked at Jellico. "I apologize for your wasted journey, Captain."

In turn, Jellico shot Wesley a poisonous glare, as if the whole turn of the proceedings were his fault. "Crusher," he began, "these people have lived here all their lives, and maybe they don't know the score. But you? You've traveled, out on the fringe worlds. You've seen Cardassians and what they're capable of." He took a step closer. "Explain the difference between us and them to your friends here. Tell them how Cardassia Prime won't beam down representatives to talk but will just wipe this township off the map with a disruptor barrage from orbit."

"If they come, we will reason with them," said Anthwara.

Jellico ignored him, fixing Wes with a hard eye. "Two days. This colony will be evacuated within two days. This isn't some negotiation. It's a fact."

"The treaty terms allow for no flexibility," said Teku. "After the assassination of Ambassador Spock and the fallout from the Klingon Civil War, the Federation cannot afford any incident that might disrupt the tenuous stability we have with the Cardassian Union. There is no alternative."

Wesley met the older man's gaze and did not flinch from it. "Go home, Jellico," he told him after a moment. "Starfleet's not wanted here."

The captain of the *Enterprise* stepped away and nodded to his subordinates. "Two days," he repeated, then tapped his combadge. "This is the captain. Bring us back."

Wes watched the look on his mother's face as she faded away into the grip of the transporter beam, her sadness and concern melting into the morning air.

He felt Lakanta's hand on his shoulder. "Thank you, my friend."

"For what?" Crusher said bitterly. "Everything he said was right. The Cardassians will come, and they'll arrive with guns first and questions later." A heavy weight settled on him, and with old regret he realized the sensation was unpleasantly familiar.

"Perhaps we should consider their offer in more detail," said Sinta. "Put it to the community, let the tribe take a vote upon it."

"Anyone who wants to go can go!" snapped Otakay. "They'll find themselves in the minority! Our forefathers were forced from their lands by the hands of men who cared nothing for their tribes and their culture. . . . Have we come so far and done so much on this world to let that happen all over again?"

"Kin," Anthwara said, "this is not an excuse to fight battles of the past. We must take the path that we know to be the true one, and keep to it. This man Jellico, he will see that we will not be swayed, and he will go on his way with his starship."

"And when the Cardassians come?" said Sinta. "What then?"

"We'll answer them with the same voice." Anthwara approached him. "Wesley. The woman, your mother?"

He nodded.

"The distance between you is great. If you wish to, none of us would think ill of you to visit her on the starship."

Wes found himself shaking his head. "That won't be necessary." He began to walk away.

"Where are you going?" Otakay demanded.

"To be with my wife," he replied and left the square behind him.

He did not see Lakanta watch him go, measuring the desolation in his manner.

In the evening, Mika went to the porch and adjusted the gain on the telescope rig as it turned gently on automatic servos, plotting the star positions and correlating them with the data matrix in the house's computer. The information would be collated and processed by the settlement's central database for the farmers, allowing them to manage the growing season with even finer control than in previous years.

She suddenly halted, her hand on the body of the device. Was there any point to doing this now? If they were going to be forced to leave Dorvan V, it mattered nothing how many readings she took and figures she gathered. Her hand slipped to the manual control pad and she shifted the telescope around. The autosensor quickly found the ship in high orbit and displayed the image of it on a monitor. Mika made out a bright white oval and a cluster of tubes and smooth forms beneath it, gleaming dully like carved animal bone.

"Never thought I'd see that again." Wesley's voice issued out of the darkness, startling her. He stepped out of the house to her side. "Come in. It's cold out here." Her husband reached toward the power switch for the monitor.

"It won't go away that easily," she said quietly. "Everyone is afraid, Wes. And they look to me because—"

"Because of your husband?" He sighed. "Go ahead and tell them there's nothing I can do to make this unhappen. I'm not Starfleet and I never was."

Mika embraced him. "But you wanted to be. Once."

"No." He shook his head.

"Don't lie to me," she replied firmly. "You know you can't. You can't hide anything from me, Wesley Crusher."

He smiled ruefully. "That's right. That's why I love you so much." The smile faded almost as soon as it had formed. "It was all so far away from me. I wanted it like that. And now . . . now it's all come back, it's found me again. That ship . . . that life . . ."

"Your mother?"

A slow nod. "Yes."

Gently, Mika tilted his face down to meet hers. "Tell me," she said. "Tell me why it hurts you so much."

And so he did.

On the transport ship from Earth to Deneb IV, he watched the other kids playing together. They were younger than him, sure, but he still felt a little jealous. They had a freedom, a kind of randomness about them that was outside his experience, and Wesley found himself wondering what it would be like to be like them. As he sat with his padd and thumbed through books he didn't want to read anymore, he realized that he was missing something. It took the duration of the trip for him to form it in his mind. Back home, his life had been a landscape of adults. The friends of his mother, his teachers, librarians, neighbors. Rarely did he meet children of his own age, and even then he found it hard to connect with them. They played elaborate games full of shifting rules, social conflict, and noise. Wesley liked to talk but they didn't want to listen. The things that earned him attention and praise from adults gathered derision and disinterest from his peers. His intelligence didn't count there; he stayed on the outside, pressed against a membrane of schoolyard laws he didn't understand. He was fifteen and he had no friends.

But all those boys and girls were gone. On the ship, no one but his mother knew who Wesley Crusher was. He came to understand that he had an opportunity to change the map of his life, to reinvent himself. On Earth, all the adults had talked around him of the great futures he would live—as a doctor following in his mother's footsteps, perhaps a mathematician or an explorer like his Starfleet father—but now he rejected them all. The pressure of being different, of such expectation, weighed on his young shoulders. He wanted to make that go away. Suddenly, the novelty of being *ordinary* seemed like the greatest challenge of them all.

At Farpoint Station he slipped his mother's watchful eye and fell in with another youth, the child of a botanist due to ship out with *Enterprise* just like the Crushers. The boy was named Eric, and he had already made friends with Jake and Annette in the Deneban marketplace. Wesley put his books aside and stood among them, fighting down his need to impress, just listening, just surfing on the edges of their new and easy comradeship. He let himself go slack, be lazy, and it was like nothing he'd ever felt before. Wesley closed the door on the precocious little genius inside him and drifted, with all the aimless indolence that only adolescents have.

Sometimes the starship went to places where things more strange and fascinating than anything his books had shown him existed. He heard secondhand about dangers and deaths, and now and then the pull of the unknown threatened to tug him back to the path he had left—but science fairs and alien worlds were a poor second to the attentions of Annette as Wesley's first fumbling attempts at romance brought him into conflict with Jake. Best friends became rivals, vying for her affections in a contest that embarrassed him now to think of it as a man. And at home, under his mother's judgmental eye, Wesley became sullen. She told him that things were expected of him, better and more important things than wasting his life on the holodeck and chasing a flighty girl whose looks concealed a dull and unchallenging nature. Perhaps, in his heart, he had known she was right, but he was a teenage boy, and everything that didn't come from his generation was something to kick against. The only one who seemed to know him was Picard.

At first, he refused to see past the uniform and the line of four gold pips on his collar. The man was authority incarnate, he was the adult world made manifest aboard *Enterprise*. Wesley expected stern lectures from him, but the opposite occurred. Picard watched him make his own mistakes, let him find his own path. When he had advice, it was on the mark and it never felt like reproach. Despite himself, Wesley Crusher found his respect growing for Jean-Luc Picard. He found common ground with the Starfleet officer; Picard had grown up in a family where much had been expected of *him* and where he too had refused to follow the road laid out by his parents. By degrees, Wes let his barriers fall, let this man rekindle the brilliance inside him. As much as he would have hated to say the words aloud, he needed a father, and Jack Crusher was more than a decade dead and gone. Picard represented what was missing from the boy's life—direction, purpose. The captain offered him the chance to apply to Starfleet Academy and for a while he rested on the cusp of that choice. Jake Kurland was, naturally, already in the program to become an acting ensign, making up in bravado what Wesley had on him in intellect. And Annette? Annette was dazzled by the cut and dash of a man in uniform. He was falling into the choice, dragged toward it by the inertia of his life, and perhaps he would have taken it, if not for an ill-considered argument in the ship's mall.

Jake had found out about Picard's offer to Wesley and he was incensed. Kurland had worked hard to prove himself capable of application to Starfleet, and the undercurrent of barely masked dislike toward Wes and his casual genius finally emerged in a furious tirade. He still remembered the other boy's words, the sting of them fresh after all these years.

"It all comes so easy to you, doesn't it? You could snap your fingers and be in Starfleet, but I have to work for it! I have to fight for it, just like I have to fight to make Annette notice me!" Jake's outburst cut Wes like a knife. *"You don't deserve it, Crusher! You don't deserve any of it! Picard's only good to you because he's in love with your mother!"*

He remembered the punch, the impact of his fist on Jake's face. Kurland spinning away, blood issuing from his nose in a dark fan. Annette screaming at him, disgust in her eyes. Eric's static expression of betrayal.

He ran and found the two of them, the captain and his mother, talking over tea in the Crushers' quarters. Picard's face, schooled and calm, and yet without a doubt Wes saw into the man he had just begun to trust and knew it was true. Jake and the others—who knew how many others?—had seen the growing bond between the doctor and the captain while Wesley the boy genius had been blind to it. His life detonated into wreckage, crashing down around him. He felt cheated.

"Wesley," Picard had spoken with a metered, paternal tone,

"your mother and I are good friends. She and I only want what is best for you, for all of us."

And every rage and frustrated fury from his life channeled into his retort, all his hurt and loss, all his betrayals and loneliness. *"Get out! You are* not *my father!"*

Mika's hands clasped around his and she swallowed hard. Her husband was stoic, betraying no emotion as his story spilled out of him. She had heard parts of it before, in moments when he had been sad or melancholy, but never the whole thing, never in such rich and poignant detail. Wesley's wife gasped, holding in her tears. She wanted to hold him, but there was more to tell, and he needed to let it out of himself.

"What happened then?" she asked.

He gave a shuddering sigh. "After that, I met *him* for the first time."

The *Enterprise*'s lifeboats were cubes no more than three meters to a side, arranged in rings on the dorsal and ventral faces of the starship hull, ready to accept passengers and eject themselves into the void if the vessel succumbed to some catastrophe. Normally, a lifeboat hatch would not open unless a command from the bridge allowed it, but Wesley's idle cunning had made short work of the control systems; he had a favorite boat, at the end of one ring, the hatch out of sight from the main corridor. He could find some quiet inside, a place to brood and to sneak synthehol or just to *get away.* Many times he had sat in there, his hand on the manual ejection lever, wondering how much pressure it would take to fire the pod into space. One jerk of the wrist, and he would be away, thrown out of the warp bubble and deposited in the interstellar void between stars. Free to drift. Free of everything.

Wesley's hand dropped away and he pulled his dark jacket close around his shoulders. Would anyone notice? He was tempted to do it just to see how sorry they would be when he was gone.

In the next second, the hatch below him was opening and he reacted with shock. If Yar's security people caught him, Wes would be in serious trouble. But the head that intruded into his hiding place was decidedly nonhuman and non-Starfleet. A face of pale, silvery skin turned to him, kind eyes beneath a thick brow that belied the intelligence of the alien's expression. The youth had a moment of recognition; he'd seen the humanoid aboard the ship some days earlier, in the company of an engineer from off-ship as part of some upgrade program. Wes recalled his mother talking about how a near accident had occurred belowdecks, where only Lieutenant La Forge's quick thinking had stopped *Enterprise* from racing away into subspace. He reverted to a default surliness. "You're not supposed to come in here," he grunted.

"I could say the same to you," the alien said mildly, and he pulled himself up into one of the vacant seats. He glanced around, running broad, long fingers over the walls. "So small and so complex," he breathed, "a very clever design. . . . But it lacks poetry, don't you think? It's so functional."

"It's a lifeboat," Wes retorted bluntly. "Doesn't matter what it looks like."

To his surprise, the alien nodded. "That's true. What lies beneath the surface is the true measure of a thing." He blinked slowly. "So, Wesley. Are you ready to go back yet?"

"Back?" Crusher leaned away. "Back *where*? What are you talking about?"

The alien frowned slightly. "Ah. Forgive me. My use of human speech is not as polished as I would like it to be. One can forget simple things when one travels as much as I do."

"How do you know who I am?"

"I'm very well informed," came the languid reply. "I make it my business to seek out people with . . . unique insights. I thought you might be one of them."

Wesley snorted. "Unique? How I am different from every other teenager who ever lived?" The words tripped off his tongue. "I'm angry at the world, nothing moves fast enough, my life is all rules and things I can't do . . ."

He got a smile. "True. But how many of your fellow adolescents have the capacity to step outside themselves and see that?"

"Seeing it doesn't make it go away," Wes replied. "I can't make something vanish just by thinking about it."

The smile drew short. "For the moment, I would suppose not."

He took a breath. "Look, if you want something from me, spit it out. Otherwise, could you go away? I like my privacy!"

"I will," replied the alien, moving back to the hatch. "I was look-ing for something in you, Wesley Crusher, but I can see it is not there."

"What the hell is that supposed to mean?"

The dark, deep eyes met his, and Wes felt a sudden sense of impossible, unknowable distance. "For all species, how we meet a challenge defines what we are and what we will become. But if we refuse it, that too is a choice, the price of which is never fully apparent at the moment in question."

"I don't understand," Wes replied.

The alien climbed down through the hatch. "No," he said, with sadness in his words, "you do not."

The youth watched the strange humanoid go and a chill passed through him. Wesley felt a peculiar sense of loss in the pit of his stomach, but when he searched inside for something to define it, it melted away, leaving nothing.

He was approaching seventeen when his mother announced that they were going home. Starfleet Medical offered her a posting in the San Francisco campus on Earth and she accepted. Things had become awkward for Beverly Crusher aboard *Enterprise* ever since the incident between Jake and Wesley, and in the aftermath as her son had become a self-made pariah among the youth community aboard ship, the doctor's relationship with Captain Picard had become stiff and professional to the point of brittleness. On his last night aboard *Enterprise,* Wes happened into an impromptu gathering taking place in one of the arboretums. Watching from a distance, he saw Jake Kurland dancing with Annette, the girl laughing as Jake made a show of his new cadet-gray bridge duty uniform.

Crusher crossed paths with Lieutenant La Forge. The engineer's easy and open manner had lessened in recent weeks, ever since the destruction of his android friend Data during a disastrous away mis-sion on Vagra II. The mechanoid's remains would be accompanying the Crushers on the ship that would take them back to Earth.

"Hey, Wesley." La Forge nodded. "I didn't think I'd see you here."

"I'm not stopping," he explained. "I'm just . . . taking a last look around."

Geordi was silent for a moment. "I'm sorry things never worked out for you and your mom here."

"I'm not," Wes replied, and found he meant it. "Out here there's no room to breathe, Lieutenant. Out here it's all about being on the edge every second of every day, and if you make one mistake it can wind up ending you . . ." He trailed off, feeling a pang of guilt at reminding La Forge of his loss. "I don't fit that," he continued. "I just want an ordinary life."

"Yeah," said Geordi. "Well, good luck."

Eric was coming over, a questioning look on his face, but Wesley was already leaving.

A week later they were orbiting Earth and *Enterprise* was just a memory.

In a store off a side street on Telegraph Hill, Wes bought a battered reproduction of an old electric guitar and found something that could, for a little while at least, take his mind off things. The Telecaster was at least a hundred years old, modeled on an original instrument from the middle of the twentieth century. He picked up the ability to read music as easily as a plant drew in sunlight, and in the residential block where he lived, Crusher would sit on the balcony in warmer days and write music in his head, composing strings that bled out all the angry and the sad inside him. He played in coffee shops; he made, if you could call it that, something of a minor name on San Francisco's scene. People who came to see him left with their emotions stirred; the slight, moody teenager played with muted brilliance. He made the Telecaster sing. There were some girls and some good times, but mostly he was drifting, drifting with the music.

He didn't see his mother much. They couldn't stay in one another's company for long before conflicts and disappointments rose up and bred the same arguments, time after time. That they loved each other was never in doubt, but things had changed so much, to the point that Wesley and Beverly saw only the roads not taken when they were together.

Wes had been back on Earth for less than a solar year before his mother told him she was returning to space. Planetbound duty had not agreed with her, and word from Picard had filtered back that *Enterprise*'s post of chief medical officer was hers to take. He should have been happy for her. Seeing things through the eyes of a man, he knew now that the offer meant so much more to Beverly than just a better posting; it also offered a rapprochement with Jean-Luc. But on some level, despite all the growing up he had done in the past two years, Wesley was still a boy in many ways. He couldn't see past a fear that she was abandoning him, and to go back to *Enterprise* with her, to be forced to see Jake and Annette and the others all over again, it was more than he could take. He packed the Telecaster and what little he had, and on the same day Beverly Crusher boarded a starship for the Kavis Alpha sector, Wes was on a tramp freighter lighting for Risa.

"You know all this part," he said ruefully. "Risa, Lya Station Alpha, Rakon, and Kappa Depot."

Mika smiled slightly. "If you'd have stayed on the main colonial circuit, you would have been discovered."

"I didn't want that," Wes admitted. "I wanted to be rootless. I was sick of expectations." Her husband's fingers tightened around her hand. "You know how that feels."

She nodded. "I do." That was what had brought them together, that first time on Kappa, some shared experience. Mika's path, if one stripped the surface from it, had followed a similar road to Wesley's. Born into the family of ranking tribal elders, she too had gone through life with a raft of demands placed upon her head, of things she was to do and to say. Dutifully, Liso had bowed to the burden, but not Mika. Mika had fled, as soon as she was able, caught starry-eyed by a freighter captain who frequented the Dorvan system, a man by the name of Okona. He had turned out to be a mistake, but her ventures had not. In wandering, Mika gained an insight into the worlds beyond theirs that none of her kindred had, and when she met Wesley, somehow she had known that it was time to return.

He smiled and stroked her cheek, reading the memory in her face. "That was the best and worst day of my life." The smile fractured.

She remembered. His guitar, his precious Telecaster, had been stolen. Mika had come across him, dejected and sorrowful that the last unbroken link he had to his past was gone. Together they searched fruitlessly for it. Instead, the two of them found like souls in each other and something deep and powerful between them. He had asked her to marry him shortly thereafter, and Mika's joy when she said yes told her that no other choice she had made in her life was as right as this one.

"I saw him again that day," Wes said distantly. "Before I met you. I'd gone back to the landing field, looking to see if someone had seen anyone with my guitar. I was on the way back . . ."

Her eyes narrowed. "The alien from the *Enterprise*? The . . . Traveler?"

He nodded. "He didn't look any different. It was like no time had passed."

"Wesley Crusher."

He turned toward the sound of the voice and the humanoid was there, on the side of the rough-hewn Kappan street, resting against a shuttered storefront. "You," Wes replied, "I know you. What are you doing here?"

"Looking for you."

He blinked. "I'm trying to find my guitar . . ." His words sounded ineffectual and weak. He was a child with a misplaced toy.

"You know that you have already lost it," said the alien. "These actions you are performing serve only to fix a frame of reference for this event, so that you might justify the loss to yourself."

Wesley's lip curled. "And here I was about to ask you to help me find it." He resumed walking along the battered thermoconcrete roadway and the tall man fell in step with him. Evening was drawing in over the port town. In a couple of hours it would be twilight, lit in cold hues by the far distant blue companion star high on the horizon. Cooking smells and the clatter of nonhuman conversation washed over them. They skirted a party of grim-faced Klingon traders and he shot another look at the alien. "Where'd you say you're from?"

"A system your species knows as Tau Alpha C."

Wes picked the location from memory with careless ease. "That's a long way from here. And I thought I was far from home."

"You are." The alien's head bobbed. "Distance isn't only a matter of abstracts like space-time, but also of emotion."

"Thanks," he replied, "that makes me feel a whole lot worse."

"I am sorry for that," continued his companion, "and I must apologize for what else I have to tell you."

A fist of ice formed in Crusher's chest. Something in the alien's manner stopped him dead. "What is it? Mom—?"

A slight shake of the head. "Your mother is not injured, you need not fear for her well-being." He sighed. "The other human, Captain Picard. His life has just ended."

Wesley's legs turned to lead and he halted in shock. "What? How?"

"The cause was a critical lack of hydration, brought about by the conditions on Lambda Paz, a moon orbiting the fifth world of the Pentarus system." Genuine sorrow was visible on the alien's face. "I regret bringing this news to you, Wesley, but I believed you would wish to know."

"What was he doing there?" he demanded. "Tell me!"

"There was a shuttle crash. The Pentaran pilot and a junior officer from the *Enterprise* died on impact. Picard survived but was unable to summon help."

Somehow, Wesley instantly knew the identity of the other Starfleet crewman. "Jake."

The alien nodded. "Ensign Kurland perished instantly. His end was mercifully swift."

He sagged against the wall of a building and tried to take it in. *Picard was gone.* For all the distance from the man, for all the cross words between them, Wesley had always felt a connection to the captain that transcended those things. He was suddenly hollow inside, the Traveler's quiet words resonating through him. Years ago, when his father died on a mission, Wesley had been only a child and the full reality of the event had not been clear to him. Now, Picard's death brought all those feelings crashing to the surface, their power undimmed by the passage of time. His vision swam with tears as he remembered Jean-Luc standing before him, his hand held out, the offer of sponsorship at the academy on the captain's lips.

"I am sorry, Wesley," repeated the alien. The pale-faced humanoid offered his hand, mirroring Picard's long-forgotten gesture. "Are you ready to go back?"

Crusher shoved away the outstretched arm and pushed off the wall. "Leave me alone," he grated, his voice thick with emotion. "Just get away from me."

* * *

"I don't know how he could have known," Wes explained. "We were light-years from Pentarus, and Starfleet didn't get to Lambda Paz until much later. Somehow, he knew it the moment it happened. . . . And it was as if, when he told me, I knew it too, almost as if I had been there."

"You can't blame yourself for Captain Picard's death, or Jake Kurland's or that pilot's." Mika shook her head. "Wes, you left that life behind years ago. All of those men knew the risks they were facing. They could have made the same choices that you did, but they didn't."

Crusher's eyes were fixed on the cup in his hand. "Jake had just been accepted into Starfleet Academy. The Pentarus mission was going to be his last assignment with the *Enterprise* before he shipped back to Earth." He gave a bitter chuckle. "He always swore to Annette that he'd command his own starship one day. Instead, he died for nothing in some alien wilderness."

Mika heard severity in Wesley's voice. "He was your friend once."

"He wasn't good enough!" spat her husband. "If he hadn't been aboard *Enterprise*, with everything that ship ran into, he would never have made the cut! Jake Kurland wasn't good enough to be an ensign! He never would have seen the signs, he wouldn't have been ready for it to all go wrong! Picard would still be alive if—" The sudden tirade faded out as fast as it had come.

"If what?" she asked him. "If *you* had been there, is that it? If Wesley Crusher had been a Starfleet ensign, he would have kept Jean-Luc Picard alive?"

"Yes," Wes growled, and he fixed Mika with an intense look. "I know this as clearly as I know how much I love you. It's my fault, Mika. I could have prevented it, if only I had made a different choice. I see it like one of Liso's weavings, the threads of time and past in different colors . . ."

She backed away a step. "Wesley, you're scaring me. I've never seen you this way."

His face fell. "Oh, no, please. Mika, no." The outburst melted away and he came to her, took her in his arms. "Mika, I love you. I'm sorry. It's just . . . Sometimes, the regret . . ."

She kissed him into silence. "If you had not been on Kappa that day, if you had been on Lambda Paz, what would have happened to me?" Mika grasped his hands. "To us? Do you regret that?"

He shook his head. "No. Meeting you was the best thing that ever happened to me. You've given me something I never had before. Focus. Purpose." Wesley cupped her hand in his. "I love you, wife. Never doubt that."

She was trying to find the right words when a discreet knock sounded at the front door.

It was late, and he was already forming a stern rebuke to give to Lakanta for interrupting them at this hour. The wooden door creaked open, and he kept one hand on it, ready to push it closed at a moment's notice.

His mother stood there on the wide stone step, her hands knotted at her waist, a fragile smile on her lips. "Hello, Wes," she began. "I hope I'm not disturbing you."

"Mom." He blinked and glanced around. There was no sign of Jellico, Lieutenant Teku, or anyone else.

"I came alone," she said by way of explanation. "I asked Geordi to transport me down."

Wesley's mouth opened, but the thoughts he had so easily marshaled moments before fled from him. He was at a loss for what to say. Another surge of old, long-buried feelings turned over inside him, threatening to break the banks of his silence.

Just then the door was taken from him and Mika pushed it all the way open. Beverly Crusher's eyes widened at the sight of the athletic, tawny-skinned girl with her bright smile and her open, elfin face. "Wesley," she said gently, "you're being rude." Mika stepped forward and took his mother's hands in hers. "Welcome to our home, Doctor Crusher. My name is Mika. I'm your son's wife."

He heard the small gasp from his mom's lips. "Hello, uh, Mika. Call me Beverly, please."

Mika inclined her head and gestured into the house. "Come in, Beverly. We have tea brewing."

Wes went to the kitchen to search for an extra cup, and it took him a few moments to find a clean one. He remembered how his mother took her tea and brought the steaming drink back into the room to find the two women sharing a smile over something. Mika was like that; she had a warmth about her that could disarm anyone.

"There's a lot I want to tell you," he said as he sat. "A lot of things . . . that I'm sorry for."

His mother clasped the cup in her long-fingered hands, and her smile wavered a little. "I'm pleased for you, Wes. You've found someone to share your life with. The only thing I was ever afraid of is that you would be lonely out here."

He glanced at his wife. "I was for a while."

She put down the cup. "I have to tell you something. I came here tonight because I wanted to see you, but I'm here against Captain Jellico's orders."

"Jellico? He's wasting his time here, Mom. Nothing's changed. Nobody will evacuate, not now, not in two days."

Beverly nodded. "He knows that. He's not even going to try to convince you otherwise. The captain is already making plans to remove everyone down here by force."

Mika's jaw dropped in shock. "He can't do that! It's illegal!"

"Apparently he has orders from Admiral Dougherty that allow him to suspend certain clauses of colonial law in this situation."

Wes nodded grimly. "We did declare ourselves outside their jurisdiction. There's nothing to stop Jellico acting first and dealing with the consequences later." He stood up. "We have to take this to Athwara and the other elders, right away."

Mika pulled a shawl over her bare shoulders and followed Wes and Beverly toward the lodge hall. Despite the seriousness of the moment, she found a peculiar elation coursing through her at meeting Wesley's mother. The other woman glanced at her. "My son has grown up. He's truly become a young man, and you've made him very happy," she noted. "I can't remember the last time I saw that look in his eyes."

Mika frowned. "He wanted you there when we were bonded," she told her, "but the *Enterprise* couldn't be reached. Starfleet wouldn't tell us why. . . . We heard there was an incident involving the Romulans. Your ship was incommunicado for weeks."

"I understand," said Beverly. "I'm sorry."

"Don't be!" Mika insisted. "You're here now, and that's all that matters. What you've done today, going against your captain's orders for us . . . I see where my husband gets his strength of character from."

Wesley's mother looked away. "Edward Jellico isn't a bad man. He's just not . . ."

"Not Jean-Luc Picard?"

She frowned. "No."

There was a commotion up ahead, and Mika saw Athwara and the other elders outside the lodge talking over one another.

"Jellico's going to take us out of here no matter what we do," Wes was saying. "I'll bet he's calibrating the *Enterprise* transporters to beam as many of us up as the ship can manage in a single go. I doubt he'll give us much warning."

"How can we stop him?" Sinta asked.

Wes glanced back at his mother. "I can try to rig a transport inhibitor to fake out the sensor lock. If we get everyone into the lodge hall, or as close to it as we can, I might be able to project a field bubble they can't beam through."

"You know how to do that?" said Otakay.

"I travel. I've picked up a few things along the way." He touched Beverly on the hand. "Mom. Thank you for what you've done, but you should go. I don't want you to get hurt."

The other woman's eyes glittered. "I've only just met my daughter-in-law. I think I'd like to stay."

Mika's heart leaped when she saw Wesley smile at his mother's words. It was like the sun coming out, all the old hurts melting away.

The lodge door banged open and Lakanta was there, his face grim. "Wes!" he shouted. "We have a big problem!"

"Great Spirit, what now?" Otakay grated.

"The sensors," he bleated, stabbing a finger at the simple grid of scanner antennae on the lodge's roof, "they've picked up *another* ship entering orbit."

"Another Federation ship?" said Athwara. "A transport for us all, perhaps."

Lakanta shook his head. "Not Federation, elder. A Cardassian *Galor*-class warship, the *Reklar*."

Beverly's hand flew to her mouth. "Oh, no. Wes, this is bad. Captain Jellico has a history with Gul Lemec, the *Reklar*'s commander."

"I'm guessing they're not well disposed toward each other?"

"Last time we crossed paths with him, it was a stalemate and we had to back down. Jellico won't let that happen this time. He won't let Starfleet—or *himself*—lose face over Dorvan V."

"This changes things," said Sinta. "Even if Wesley's idea works, what happens then? These Cardassians, this alien Lemec, they come here with weapons and hold us at gunpoint?"

"I will appeal to both commanders for calm," began Athwara. "We can resolve this through clear and honest discourse."

Wes shook his head. "Forgive me, old grandfather, but I think that what matters to us will carry no weight with Lemec or Jellico."

"Then what choices are open to us?" demanded Otakay, his color rising. "Deportation is unacceptable, we all agree on that. Occupation of our world by the Cardassians? We have all heard the stories of their death camps and their persecution of other races, like the Bajorans and the Lyshani! We will have to resist them!"

Mika gasped. "You're advocating armed revolt?"

"If it comes to that!" Otakay snapped. "I am an old man, but I have fought for my home and I will do it again if need be."

"Do you have weapons? Any defenses?" Beverly asked.

"A meteorite shield, some hand phasers and plasma shotguns," noted Sinta. "Toys compared to those of a real military."

"No one will shed blood over this!" Athwara's voice cut through the air, the old man's authority silencing them all. "It is not our way."

"It may have to be," said Wes grimly.

He felt a hand on his shoulder. "Wesley Crusher."

Wes turned to see Lakanta staring at him with a fixed, rigid gaze. A chill ran down his spine; something in his friend's manner rang a wrong note with him. The man seemed *different* somehow, as if the intelligence behind those sleepy eyes had suddenly altered. "Lakanta, we have to do something," he began, the night air around him abruptly still.

"Yes, you do," said the other man.

Crusher realized that they were surrounded by silence. No one was speaking, there were no sounds of distant chirping insects, no gentle wind through the streets. He turned to see Mika, his mother, the others, all of them statues frozen in a moment of glassy, solidified time. "What . . . ? What's happening?"

Lakanta's face hazed and shifted like slow smoke. The man he had known for years re-formed into a familiar alien aspect of pale, silvery skin. "Wesley," said the Traveler, "hello again."

"Where's Lakanta?" Wes growled. "What have you done?"

"Lakanta is still here," said the alien, tapping his chest. "He has always been an aspect of me. Just like the owner of the store on Telegraph Hill, the captain on that freighter for Risa, the Ferengi who stole your guitar." He gestured at the others. "I haven't done this, Wesley. You have. You've come to this place, to this point of choice, and something inside you knows that it will be the most vital one of your life." The Traveler glanced around, taking in the township. "What you do and say here will lead these people down a path to dissolution or destruction." He smiled slightly. "The one called Otakay, he was correct. Your choices are all ill-fated."

"I don't understand," he said. But he *did.* There was a pressure in his mind, like a strange double image. Another set of memories flashed through him, of events from the life of a very different Wesley Crusher. *A gray uniform, a girl who changed shape, incredible sights at the edge of the galaxy, a father figure, choices made, and a vision quest . . .*

The alien was nodding. "You see it now. You understand why I followed you through this life, from the moment we first met aboard the *Enterprise.* I've been the steward of you, Wesley Crusher. Waiting for you to come to this moment, to understand the greatness inside you."

"I'm not great," Wes insisted. "I'm just a man. A musician, a husband. I'm nothing special."

The Traveler chuckled. "Humans. You have such potential, and yet you shackle yourselves with doubts." He nodded to Mika. "All these events are the skein of one possible time line, the evolution of a future from a moment in your past when you dreamed of leading an 'ordinary life' . . . A life where you were not someone with a destiny, where you were just a commonplace man."

Anger flared inside him. "You played games with my life? What gives you the right?"

"I did nothing but watch," said the alien. "You did this, Wesley. You felt the burden of your gift so strongly that it threatened to break you. For one moment, more than anything, you dreamed of living a life without such a responsibility. And so you have." He held out his hand. "Are you ready to go back?"

The frustration crackled through him, and Wes felt his hands contracting into fists. The decision he had made in that divergent moment was hard and dark there in his thoughts. "Why?" he shouted. "Why should I be forced to make that choice?" Full of undirected fury, he advanced on the alien. "Why can't I choose to live a life that doesn't have such great importance?" He shot a look at Mika and his heart ached. "Why can't I live in . . . in ordinary days?"

"My friend," said the Traveler, his words heavy with an infinite, solemn sadness, "I have lived for a very long time and I have learned a single, simple truth; *there are no ordinary lives.* Everyone has a path, and each person's journey affects the motion of the universe around him or her. The smallest of events ripple out to change things on a cosmic scale. This is life." He placed a hand on Wes's shoulder. "If you cannot embrace who and what you truly are, and the potential you represent, you will never be content."

The alien's candor struck any thought of argument from him. He could see the paths clearly now, if he closed his eyes and imagined them. The path he had trodden, and then this one, branching and diverging but ultimately leading toward darkness.

A darkness with a single point of light. "Mika . . ."

"She exists where you do," said the Traveler. "You can still find her there, if you choose to."

"And all this?" he asked. "What happens to all this, to the people, to Dorvan V?"

"Time and causality will return to their original form, if you allow it. The tragedy about to unfold will not occur." For the last time, the alien offered Wesley his hand. "Are you ready to go back?"

Wes leaned close to Mika's cheek, taking in the scent of her skin, the warmth of her closeness. He kissed her gently and then stepped back from the static tableau.

"I'm ready," he said. "I've made my choice."

The Traveler smiled as the world around them became ghostly and insubstantial. "We have a long journey ahead of us. But the first step on any road is always the hardest."

"Where are we going?" Wes asked.

The alien's smile deepened. "You tell me."

'TWOULD RING THE BELLS OF HEAVEN

Amy Sisson

Historian's note:
This tale is set between "All Good Things,"
the series finale of Star Trek: The Next Generation,
and the feature film Star Trek Generations.

AMY SISSON

Amy Sisson is an academic librarian living in Houston, Texas, with her NASA husband, Paul Abell, without whom "'Twould Ring the Bells of Heaven" would not exist. Her *Trek* fiction includes "The Law of Averages" in *Star Trek: Strange New Worlds VII* and "You May Kiss the Bride" in *Star Trek: Strange New Worlds 8.* Short stories in her "Unlikely Patron Saints" series have appeared in *Strange Horizons, Lady Churchill's Rosebud Wristlet,* and *Irregular Quarterly.* She is a graduate of the Clarion West class of 2000.

In addition to library work, Amy regularly reviews books for *Voice of Youth Advocates (VOYA)* and *Magill Book Reviews.* She also writes encyclopedia articles on random subjects ranging from Pixar Studios to Qantas Airlines to the Doobie Brothers, and tends to her collection of ex-parking-lot cats, which she only recently learned (from fellow *Trek* author Jim Johnson) can be termed a "clowder."

AS THE SPACE-SUITED FIGURES PULLED DATA THROUGH THE airlock, the android struggled to move, to speak—to simply understand what was happening. But the struggle was entirely internal. His brain sent commands that were not received; he lay limp and uncomprehending while he was dragged several meters and propped against a rocky outcropping.

One of the figures stooped down, placing itself in Data's unmoving line of vision. Its mouth moved, but even if Data's auditory input had been functioning properly, he dimly realized that he would have heard nothing, because there was no atmosphere. He tried to make sense of the mouthed words, but he was distracted by the face inside the helmet. It was attractive by humanoid standards, he knew. It was familiar.

And then it was gone.

As Data once again tried in vain to reestablish control over his motor functions, the departing ship crossed the edge of his field of vision, leaving only distant stars in its wake.

Ennis Outpost director Jarod Maher looked older in person than he had over a viewscreen. His pleasant countenance was frequently creased with anxiety, and his short, sandy hair was streaked with gray.

As Maher led the visitors from the shuttlebay into which they'd transported and down a crowded corridor, Commander Deanna Troi looked around with interest. The outpost was obviously in its infancy; packing crates lined every wall, with exposed power conduits peeking around the untidy stacks. It was easy to forget how luxurious life aboard the *Enterprise* was, she thought. Spacious private quarters for the senior crew, replicators programmed with an endless variety of food . . . Here, she was reminded that people were still willing to give up creature comforts in the name of frontier science.

Maher showed the away team—Deanna, Captain Picard, Will, and Chief Engineer La Forge—into a makeshift conference room with a large brown table surrounded by eight mismatched chairs. A viewscreen had been mounted carelessly on the bare metal wall at the far end of the room.

"Please sit down," Maher said. "Doctor Aaron will be here in a moment. Would anyone care for something to drink?"

As he passed around cups of coffee, Maher thanked Picard for transporting over to the outpost. "As you can see, Captain, our supplies are a bit tight at this stage. We don't have transporters yet, and I think our shuttle is counting the days until retirement. Ah, Doctor Aaron," he said, as a tall man walked in. "This is the party from the *Enterprise*."

The newcomer had thick, untidy black hair and dark brown eyes, and wore a wrinkled lab coat. He sat near the head of the table, nodding at each of the visitors as Maher named them but never quite meeting their eyes. Deanna sensed both shyness and impatience; this man was ready to get down to business.

Picard seemed to come to the same conclusion. "Doctor Aaron," he said. "We've been looking forward to hearing about your work here."

"It's really quite extraordinary, Captain," said Aaron. For the first time, Deanna felt the man's enthusiasm. "Almost everything we need for this outpost can be found in Heaven's rings: water for life support and fuel; raw building materials that can be fabricated into shelter. Ennis is one of Heaven's more stable moons, in terms of orbit and geologic activity, so this is an ideal base from which to study Heaven's rings. This outpost will be very basic for quite a while, but in a few years I hope we'll have a first-class research station."

Maher leaned forward. "Not to mention a larger settlement to accommodate the scientists' families," he put in. "We haven't been in this solar system for very long—the colony on Chandra is only eight years old—but we're eager to expand our presence."

"I take it you plan to shepherd ring fragments here to provide raw materials," Picard said.

"Not fragments, Captain," Aaron said. "*A* fragment. A moonlet, in fact. We're going after Bell-B."

Aaron tapped the padd he'd brought with him, activating the viewscreen on the wall. A graphic representation of a section of the rings appeared, as viewed from above. On the left side was a curved, orange section of Heaven, with concentric ring segments radiating outward to the right.

"You can see that the rings are labeled A through H, with A the innermost ring. Heaven's rings are similar to Saturn's: bright, lots of water ice, and very well defined, especially the inner rings. The outer rings, F, G, and H, are broader and more nebulous; in fact, it's difficult to see H with the naked eye, because the particles are dark and widely dispersed, but it's very much there."

"Where in the rings does—you called it 'Bell-B,' is that right?—come from?" Deanna asked.

Aaron tapped the padd again and the screen zoomed in on Ring D, which was thin and sharp. "These two moons are called the Bell Twins, or Bell-A and Bell-B," he said. "Actually, we tend to just call them Alpha and Beta when we're feeling lazy. They lie on either side of Ring D, so they're not quite embedded moonlets, as opposed to Ares, which falls right in the middle of Ring C. But the Bell Twins are interesting because they're compositionally similar to each other, at least on the surface: rocky with a great deal of water ice. And they're obvious shepherd moons—you can see the well-defined gaps on either side of the ring, here and here. The Bells don't usually sit at the same point in their orbits like this, of course. Alpha is closer to Heaven than Beta by almost fourteen thousand kilometers, so its orbital period is more than two hours shorter."

"But why are you going after such a large moonlet?" asked Geordi.

"Wouldn't it be easier to shepherd smaller fragments in batches rather than move something so large?"

Doctor Aaron smiled. "Yes. But it's not just the raw materials we're after. There's still a lot we don't know about planetary rings. On cosmological time scales, rings aren't stable, so they have to be replenished. New material can come from moons that are geologically active, or from meteoritic bombardment that creates new ring particles through impacts, and so on."

His eyes shone. "By removing Beta from the equation entirely, we'll have an unprecedented opportunity to observe how a well-developed ring system responds to a major upheaval. Once Beta is out of the picture, we'll observe how the ring material redistributes itself and see how Beta's absence affects the ring's edge definition. It's even possible that a 'replacement Bell' will gradually accrete, if the system decides it really needs a shepherd in that location."

"You almost make it sound as though the rings have a mind of their own," Picard remarked. "I didn't realize that changes could take place quickly enough to observe in a short time frame."

"A new accretion would take a long time," Aaron conceded. "But over the next few years we should see enough signs to be able to predict what will happen. You'd be surprised, Captain. Back when Earth's early probes observed Saturn, they recorded significant changes in the rings between the *Voyager* flybys and the *Cassini* observations, and they were only about twenty years apart. And those changes happened without any external interference."

"Hadn't you already started the shepherding process?" Picard asked. "What happened?"

Aaron switched the viewscreen to an animated diagram. "The plan was to land several dozen remote thruster units on Beta to propel it up and away from the ring plane in a perpendicular direction, disturbing the surrounding ring fragments as little as possible," he said, pointing. "Once it was clear, we began a slow thrust to move Beta toward Ennis and planned to reverse the thrusters to decelerate Beta on this end. But even though our sensors say the probes were working, Beta has veered off the expected trajectory several times. We've tried to correct by reprogramming the thrusters remotely, but Beta is still acting up and we're losing valuable time. We don't know if the thrusters are at fault, or if there are gravitational factors in this system that we haven't accounted for."

"We really should have replaced the thruster units, just in case," Maher said in apology. "But this is a bare-bones operation in terms of resources. Some of the colonists on Chandra feel that we shouldn't have tackled this project before the settlement was more fully established."

Riker spoke up for the first time. "What can we do to help?"

"I'd like to start over with our gravimetric mapping of Beta and then work outward to the rest of Heaven's ring-moon system if necessary," said Aaron. "From what I understand, your sensors are more sensitive than ours. Then we can adjust our propulsion strategy based on the results."

Maher broke in again. "Also, Captain, if it's not too much of an imposition, I wonder if you might be able to smooth things over with the colony administrators. Would you consider making a side trip to Chandra? And maybe mention just how important you consider this pursuit of scientific knowledge to be."

Picard smiled at Maher in understanding, then turned to Riker, who seemed to read his thoughts.

"What about using a runabout for the survey?" Riker said. "It could get a lot closer to Beta than the *Enterprise* could. We could send a small team with Doctor Aaron on the *Colorado* and take the *Enterprise* to Chandra."

"It's a nice little settlement," Maher put in, his tone hopeful. "Some of your crew might enjoy a short visit, Captain. And on your way back, perhaps you could bring some supplies from the colony that have been delayed."

"A short shore leave certainly sounds tempting," said Picard. "Why don't we take Doctor Aaron back to the *Enterprise* with us this afternoon? He and Mister La Forge can look over the sensor equipment on the runabout and make any necessary modifications. Doctor, you're welcome to stay onboard as our guest tonight. That will let you get an early start first thing in the morning.

"Commander Troi," Picard continued casually, "you'll lead the away team on the *Colorado*. Choose a science officer to work with Doctor Aaron, and a pilot, preferably one with engineering experience."

Deanna's eyes widened slightly, but she did not otherwise let her surprise show. "Yes, Captain," she said.

"Thank you, Captain." Aaron beamed. "I just need about twenty minutes to get my equipment together. If you'll excuse me, I'll meet you back in the shuttlebay." He rushed out of the room.

"Yes, Captain, thank you," said Maher. "This outpost has had a bit of a rocky start—no pun intended—and we're very grateful for your help. If you'll excuse me as well, I'm going to consult with my operations officer so she can start working up a requisitions list for the colony administrators."

When Maher had exited, Picard turned to Deanna. "I hope you'll enjoy this assignment, Commander," he said. "It should be fairly routine, but it's a good chance to stretch your wings. Any thoughts on your crew?"

"Can you spare Data, Captain?" asked Deanna.

"Excellent choice," said Picard. "With Data as science officer, I would even suggest you choose one of our younger officers as pilot—this kind of survey is just the thing for eager young ensigns. And with Mister Data aboard, you'll have plenty of backup piloting experience."

After the group had rematerialized aboard the *Enterprise,* Deanna arranged to meet Doctor Aaron, Geordi, and Data for a working dinner at nineteen hundred hours. She turned to leave, with the intention of reviewing crew files and brushing up on away mission protocols, but as she exited the transporter room she found Will waiting for her just outside. He checked to make sure she was alone, then bowed deeply, sketching an exaggerated sweep with his arm and trying to hide a pleased grin all the while.

"Well, well. Your first away mission command," he teased.

Deanna couldn't help but smile back. "Let's hope it goes more smoothly than yours did."

Will groaned and pretended to stagger, hands clutched over his heart. "Ouch! Don't remind me."

Deanna laughed as they turned to walk down the corridor. "Well, it would take a lot to top that one, wouldn't it?"

"Commander Troi," called a voice behind them, cutting off whatever reply Will was about to make. They turned to see Geordi jogging toward them. "Sorry, I wanted to catch you before you left. Data is showing Doctor Aaron to his quarters now. I wondered if you would mind a suggestion for that pilot assignment?"

"Whom did you have in mind?" asked Deanna.

"Ensign Taurik," Geordi said.

"I'll look at his record," said Deanna. "Any special reason for recommending him?"

Even if Deanna weren't an empath, she could have sensed Geordi's sheepishness. "Well, it's just . . . he's kind of driving us crazy in engineering right now. He's been volunteering for *everything* and we're running out of 'extra credit' assignments for him."

"Looks like the after effects of those crew evaluations still haven't worn off," commented Riker. "I've seen the same thing with some of the junior bridge crew."

"You're not kidding," Geordi said, shaking his head. "It's been a month and a half, and all the junior engineers are still looking over their shoulders like they expect to see me with a clipboard and a whistle. I never thought I'd apply the term 'eager beaver' to a Vulcan, but—"

"I think there's a little more to it in his case," said Deanna. "Taurik and Sam Lavelle and Alyssa Ogawa were particularly close to Ensign Sito, and they're still dealing with her death. For Taurik in particular, throwing himself into his work isn't just practical, it's almost the only socially acceptable way for Vulcans to react to grief—which they're not supposed to be feeling, of course."

"You may be right, Counselor," said Geordi. "But that aside, I wouldn't recommend Taurik just to get him out of my hair. He's an excellent pilot and a damn good engineer. I think he'd be a good member of your team."

"Thanks, Geordi," said Deanna. "I'll talk to Taurik and let you know what I decide."

"My pleasure. I'm gonna meet Doctor Aaron in engineering in a little while. Guess I'll see you at dinner."

Geordi turned off at the next juncture, and Will looked down at Deanna, impressed. "Maybe you've been right all along," he teased. "Maybe command officers *do* need more counselor training. I have a feeling it's going to be a real asset in your case, Deanna."

"I hope so," she said. "I'll go talk to Taurik now—that is," she said, turning to Will, "if you'll take a rain check on that hot chocolate you were going to ply me with to calm my nerves."

"Hey, I never said—"

"It doesn't take an empath, Will," she reminded him impishly.

* * *

By the end of dinner, Deanna's head was swimming with more new terminology than she'd learned in an entire semester of astrophysics at the academy. No matter how many times she reminded herself that a commanding officer couldn't be an expert in every field, she couldn't help wondering if Doctor Aaron, or even Taurik, doubted her ability to lead this mission. The young Vulcan had apparently used the few hours after Deanna approached him to brush up on recent papers on planetary rings, and he had asked Doctor Aaron several intelligent questions, while Deanna's own contributions to the discussion had been few and far between.

Outside the conference room, she pulled Geordi aside and quietly asked him to meet her an hour before her team's departure the next morning to go over the equipment they'd installed in the runabout that afternoon.

The group broke up, and Deanna and Data walked to the senior crew quarters together. At the door to his quarters, Data invited her in for some hot chocolate, and she accepted, although she wondered if *everyone* on board thought she needed to be soothed. She sat down next to Data, whom she noticed had replicated a cup for himself, no doubt in an effort to be companionable.

She took a tentative sip, but the sweet beverage was still too hot. She blew on it, and over the rim of the cup her eyes wandered to the corner by the door, where an easel held an unfinished painting of a red-orange planet circled by yellow and gold rings.

"Data, I didn't know you were painting again!" Deanna said. "I thought you'd given up. What made you change your mind?"

"I recently discovered an obscure aphorism regarding Pablo Picasso, which states, 'If Picasso could, then I can.' It is unclear to what the original speaker may have been referring, but it did cause me to reconsider. If Picasso could find ways to express himself within his inherent limitations, then perhaps I can learn to better express myself within mine. Human artists do not have perfect motor control, yet many of them can produce photorealistic art. If I keep trying, perhaps I can learn to produce art that is not merely a comingling of other artists' styles."

"I'm proud of you, Data," said Deanna. "It's not easy to keep at something you find frustrating."

"Technically I am not frustrated, Counselor," Data said. "But I understand what you mean."

A small furry form demanded Deanna's attention by rubbing against her legs. "And hello to you, Spot," she greeted the android's cat. "Data, may I ask you something?"

"Please, Counselor," he said.

"I was wondering about your first command," she said, absently stroking the fur between Spot's alert ears.

"I see," said Data. "As you may recall, my first command of a starship occurred on Stardate 45020.4, when we enacted the blockade to prevent the Romulans from supporting the Duras family in their attempt to overthrow the Klingon government. However, if you are referring to my first away team command, that occurred—"

"Data," she said. "I'm sorry to interrupt, but actually I meant the *experience* of your first command. Not the physical details, but what it was like for you personally. Did you find the crew resistant to the idea of you as a commander?"

"Not particularly on my first away team command. My crew members were accustomed to my position among the senior bridge staff and were comfortable with my ability to command. However, my experience aboard the *Sutherland* was more challenging. I experienced a great deal of resistance from Lieutenant Commander Hobson, who was assigned as my first officer. He questioned several of my orders and delayed their implementation, but ultimately he obeyed and we were able to reveal the Romulan presence."

"How did you get him to obey your orders?" asked Deanna.

"I am afraid I had to resort to a rather . . . emotional tactic."

"What do you mean?"

"I raised my voice."

Deanna laughed. "Data! You mean you yelled at him?"

"It *was* effective, Counselor. Mister Hobson seemed to believe that I was merely an automaton, offering dispassionate advice that he could choose to follow or not. When I raised my voice, however, he seemed to understand that I expected to be obeyed and that there would be consequences if he did not comply. After the crisis was over, he apologized for his behavior."

"You made a good decision, Data. You showed good judgment of human nature."

"Thank you, Counselor. If I may inquire, did you ask because you are apprehensive about leading tomorrow's away mission?"

"A little, Data, although I would appreciate it if you would keep that between us."

"Ah," he said. "Counselor-patient confidentiality. Only this time, I am the counselor."

She smiled again. "Exactly."

"If it is any comfort, Counselor, I have full confidence in your ability to command."

"Thank you, Data. That means a lot to me."

Unable to move, Data could do nothing but examine the disconnected thoughts that seemed to flit in and out of his consciousness of their own accord. Images appeared in his mind's eye, superimposed on the unchanging scene before him.

His head felt heavier than it should, an anomaly in the low gravity. He gradually became aware that he was wearing a helmet, but it was not supplying oxygen. Though he did not need to breathe, his respiratory system served to regulate his body temperature.

Perhaps he was also wearing a space suit. But no—his head had fallen forward when he was being dragged, and he had seen no space suit encasing his own body.

He wondered what would happen to him in a vacuum. He thought perhaps he had been in one before, but he could not recall specifics, so he did not know what to expect. Freezing or overheating, hot or cold—the contingencies were too much to process.

He thought again of the face. He felt certain that the mouth had formed words, and he replayed the image over and over, striving to understand what she had said.

"Have you ever been this close to a ring system, Commander Troi?" asked Doctor Aaron. He had come up to look through the forward viewport as they approached the moonlet. Currently Beta was about halfway between its original position and that of Ennis.

"Not quite," she said, smiling. Even from this distance, the rings were incredible.

"Why don't we go to Beta's original position and retrace her tracks from there?" suggested Aaron. "We might find something on the sensors that will give us an idea of what went wrong. And I think you'll enjoy the view."

"That sounds wonderful," Deanna said. It wasn't entirely necessary, but the mapping would take only a day, and the *Enterprise*
would be gone for the better part of two. "Ensign, lay in a course at
half impulse, keeping us at this altitude above the ring plane."

"Aye, Commander," said Taurik. "I recommend activating the
navigational deflector array. It's not required at low impulse speeds,
but it may be prudent since we'll be encountering relatively dense
concentrations of microparticles."

Deanna fought off a flash of annoyance and told Taurik to proceed. She always felt particular pressure not to show irritation, as
though her position as ship's counselor should preclude her from
that emotion. Besides, she was more annoyed at herself than at
Taurik. She should have thought of the deflector array.

Fortunately, the vista opening up in front of the runabout soon
distracted her. Ring E, the outermost of the well-defined rings,
spread in a tawny plain in front of and slightly below them. Smooth
at first, it quickly began to display topography that made Deanna
think of small hills and valleys.

"This is my favorite part, Commander," Aaron said. "When you
fly toward a ring, there's a moment that I've always wanted to
catch—the moment when it stops being solid and becomes a neck-
lace. One second it's whole and the next it's in pieces, and it happens while you blink. I'm not sure which is more beautiful."

Deanna glanced at the scientist's profile and could see his rapt
expression even from that angle. She turned back to the viewport
and gasped with delight. It was true—the ring had transitioned,
instantly it seemed, from a continuous plane to a lovely jumble.
For a moment she was disoriented—she was flying not over a planetary structure but rather into a microscopic fractal that rushed to
meet her. The distant but direct sunlight, coupled with that reflected
from Heaven's atmosphere, made itself apparent in the form of a
billion pinpricks of light, seemingly caught by and then released
from every single ice crystal inhabiting the rings.

Doctor Aaron radiated joy. "It's incredible, isn't it?" he said.
Deanna could only nod, her eyes still feasting on the panorama
before her. Then he turned to her and grinned. "And now we get to
do it all over again with Ring D."

After another visual feast, this one with hues of orange and rust-
streaked amber, Deanna reluctantly focused her attention on the

work ahead of them. "Doctor Aaron, how would you like to proceed?" she said.

"I'd like to duplicate the path that Beta took, including the deviations, and measure the gravitational overlaps of the planet, the rings, and all of Heaven's moons, even the most distant ones that we assume have no significant gravitational impact on the rings. Shall we say one-quarter impulse? It will be slow, but we have the time and we can take multiple readings as we go."

Deanna nodded to Taurik, who turned to lay in the course. A moment later, the *Colorado* pulled slowly away from its position over the gap that Beta had left.

A little under two hours later, Taurik "parked" the runabout above Beta and addressed Doctor Aaron. "Sir, what do you consider the ideal altitude for the gravimetric scans?"

"I'd like to get as close as possible," Aaron replied. "Beta's shape is slightly irregular, and we don't know how uniform its internal composition is, so it's possible that small localized differences could affect its gravitational fields. *Something* has been causing problems, and I haven't seen anything yet that seems to account for it."

Data nodded. "I concur. The closer we are, the higher the sensor resolution will be. Even if we cannot determine what went wrong previously, high-resolution scans will allow us to better recalculate the thrust vectors. Doctor, will ten meters be sufficient?"

Aaron assented, and Deanna ordered Taurik to maintain that relative altitude, compensating for elevational changes in the topography.

"Course laid in, Commander," said Taurik.

"Let's begin," said Deanna. A soft, steady *ping* filled the cabin for a few seconds, until Data muted it with a keyed command. On one of the side monitors, the computer began to construct a three-dimensional representation of the surface below them.

"How long will this take, Data?" asked Deanna.

"This particular swath will take approximately two hours to complete," said the android. "We will need to map two more swaths around the long axis and then take measurements around the short axis. I estimate we will be finished in eight hours and forty-seven minutes."

"Commander," said Taurik from the pilot's seat, "Captain Picard is hailing us."

"On screen," said Deanna, and moved to the space behind the two command stations.

Picard's expectant face filled the portside comm screen. *"Commander,"* he said. *"We've just arrived at Chandra. I trust things are going smoothly so far?"*

"Yes, Captain. We just started the detailed mapping, and we plan to retrieve one of the thruster units for analysis."

"Well, don't let me keep you," said Picard. *"I'll check in with you in the morning, and we'll rendezvous back at Ennis no later than twenty-one hundred tomorrow. Call us if you have any problems."*

"Aye, sir," Deanna said.

She put her hand on Data's shoulder. "Data, what's the best way to retrieve a thruster? Can we transport one aboard without interfering with the mapping?"

"Yes, Commander," said Data. "Doctor Aaron, if you will pull up your schematic showing the thruster locations and ensure that they are turned off, I will beam the nearest unit into the isolation chamber."

Aaron nodded and tapped the aft starboard console.

"The thruster is aboard," announced Data moments later.

"Data, why don't you—" Deanna started to say, when an explosion rocked the rear of the runabout. All of them except Data cried out as they were thrown off balance. Data and Taurik were pitched forward over their consoles while Deanna and Doctor Aaron both lost their footing.

"Report!" cried Deanna, as she pulled herself up and along the bulkhead toward the forward viewport. Through it, she glimpsed stars moving in a disorienting, circular motion, then an alarming view of Beta, which was far too close.

"Commander, it appears that an explosion near aft starboard has caused us to start spinning. Attempting to stabilize," said Data, his fingers dancing over his console.

By this time Taurik was scanning his own instruments. "One of the aft thrusters is malfunctioning."

An alarm klaxon began to blare. *"Warning,"* said the dispassionate voice of the computer. *"Collision alert. Warn—"* The alarm cut out as abruptly as it had begun.

"Computer, shields," said Deanna.

"Shield generator is off-line," said the computer. *"Backup generator is operational. Shields at 80 percent."*

"Reroute power to the backup generator—" The runabout lurched sideways and Deanna staggered.

"The aft port impulse engine is firing intermittently," Data said. "It fired near the top of our spin and almost sent us into the moonlet. An impact may still occur if we cannot get the thruster under control."

"Can you cut off its fuel supply?" Deanna asked.

Another lurch.

"Negative, Commander," said Data. "The computer is unable to reestablish communications with that engine. Some of the relays must have been damaged in the explosion. I am attempting to compensate by reversing forward engines—"

He was interrupted when the collision alarm sounded again. Through the viewport, Deanna saw Beta rushing up to meet them as the runabout dove at a steep angle.

"Brace for impact," Data called over the sound of the klaxon.

Time seemed to slow as the nose of the runabout burrowed into the moonlet's surface, sending debris flying. As Deanna pitched forward into the back of Data's seat, momentum lifted the back of the runabout, throwing it into a clumsy end-over-end somersault that took it back off the surface. The runabout rotated completely, throwing her against the ceiling, before coming back down hard and skidding sideways across Beta's surface until it was stopped by a ridge that was more solid than it looked. The sudden stop slammed Deanna into the bulkhead across from the station where Doctor Aaron had been monitoring the sensor readings.

Confusion. Concern.

Deanna groaned as the emergency lighting kicked on, illuminating the runabout's interior with a red glow, and felt the back of her head. No blood, and her vision didn't seem to be blurred, so she probably didn't have a concussion.

Gingerly, she pulled herself up, using the bulkhead for support. A dazed Taurik was checking his limbs for injury, but Data, still wedged in his seat, was motionless, and Doctor Aaron lay unmoving on the floor at the back of the cabin.

"Are you hurt, Ensign?" Deanna asked Taurik.

"I do not think so, Commander," he answered, in spite of a small cut on his forehead.

"Check Data. I'll check Doctor Aaron," she said, staggering. Without the minimal protection that the pilot seats had afforded Data and Taurik, the scientist had been thrown about as much as she had. He lay on his back, one arm thrown over his face as if to protect himself. As she made her way toward him, Deanna stopped to pull an emergency medkit from the port wall.

"Doctor Aaron?" said Deanna when she reached him. She gently moved his arm away from his face in case it interfered with his breathing.

Except he wasn't. His head lolled at an alarming angle, and his sightless eyes stared at nothing. She didn't need the tricorder to tell her he was dead, but she ran it over him anyway.

"Commander," said Taurik from the front of the runabout. "Lieutenant Commander Data is injured. It's possible that a power surge disrupted his systems. His station is severely damaged as well."

Deanna took a last look at Doctor Aaron and passed her hand over his eyes to close them. With a slight limp, she pulled a blanket from a storage cabinet and laid it over the scientist, then went back up front, where Taurik was examining Data. Deanna shuddered. In spite of their unusual yellow color, the android's sightless eyes looked just like Doctor Aaron's.

Deanna pushed Data's shoulders forward and felt along his back.

"Commander?" said Taurik.

"He has an off switch. I'm going to try to restart him," Deanna said. "I expect you to keep that information confidential."

"Yes, ma'am."

Deanna's fingers found the switch and depressed it. She counted to five and pushed it again.

Nothing.

She turned Data off again. "Ensign, use the tricorder and tell me if you detect any energy readings when I flip the switch again. Ready . . . now."

Taurik studied the tricorder. "There was a definite surge in energy levels, Commander. I believe that his brain is still generating a positronic field. It's possible that the damage is keeping his brain from communicating with the rest of his body."

"Almost like a stroke," Deanna mused. "I wonder if he can hear us."

For a long moment, Deanna's mind went blank as she took in the scene around her, surreal in the emergency lighting: Data, eyes blank and scorch marks on his chest and face; the blanketed figure at the back of the cabin. Then she looked at Taurik, who was shaken but calm as he waited for her orders.

It was the expectation in Taurik's eyes that restarted her brain. "Ensign, we need to assess the damage as quickly as possible," she said in a brisk tone. "Check structural integrity to make sure we're not venting atmosphere, then look at communications, weapons, and propulsion. I'll look at sensors to see if I can figure out whether that was an accident or an attack. Either way, we need to know if the worst is over."

"What about Commander Data?" asked Taurik.

"As long as he hasn't experienced a cascade failure, almost any other damage can be repaired," she said, hoping she was right. "If we can contact the *Enterprise,* they can meet us at the outpost, or come to us here if we can't take off. Lieutenant Commander La Forge is best equipped to repair Data."

As Deanna went back to the cockpit's aft stations, she felt Taurik's unease recede into resolve as he began to work. His emotions, as quickly masked as they were, reminded her of the confusion she thought she sensed during the crash. Was that Taurik, before he'd gotten his feelings under control? Or Doctor Aaron before he'd died?

Or had she completely imagined it?

In any case, she didn't sense anything now. She turned to the console Aaron had been using and rerouted the sensor controls to that station. She was relieved to find the sensors still functioning, if a bit unevenly. She set the array for a broad sweep, instructing the computer to search for weapon and engine signatures in particular.

Nothing unusual: there were no residual traces to indicate weapons activity and no warp or impulse trails anywhere nearby. Not an attack, then. But there had also been no warning of an imminent system failure, so an actual engine explosion seemed equally improbable.

"Ensign," she said, remembering something she'd read the evening before, "Beta is full of volatiles—that's one of the main reasons the outpost is interested in mining it. Could something have triggered an explosive outgassing event?"

Taurik considered the question. "It's possible, Commander. However, Doctor Aaron had not indicated that Beta is prone to outgassing, and it is not approaching a heat source that would cause sublimation, the way a comet outgasses as it approaches a sun. But it is possible that chemical reactions inside the moonlet could build pressure to the point of outgassing."

"Could outgassing explain the deviations from Beta's planned trajectory? If there were many small events, not easily detectable from the outpost?" she asked.

"Again, it is theoretically possible, but highly unlikely," said Taurik.

Deanna frowned. "What's the status on communications, Ensign?"

"I should be able to reestablish short-range communications soon, with enough power to raise the outpost. I am still assessing the damage to the subspace relays for long-range communication."

"Concentrate on short-range for now. Director Maher can relay our messages to the *Enterprise* if necessary."

"Aye, Commander."

"I'm going to check whether the thruster unit made it on board before the explosion. That's when this all started, and there might be some information we can use."

Trying not to look at Doctor Aaron's covered form, Deanna picked her way back to the runabout's laboratory module, directly aft of the cockpit. A sizable isolation and decontamination chamber was situated along the back wall. Through its window, Deanna could see a hulking metal object that was difficult to make out in the dim illumination. She instructed the computer to reroute power to the lighting.

Better. The machine's silver surface was blackened in places, and its crevices contained a mélange of rust-colored sand and grit. She touched the chamber's control panel, which lit up in response. She input commands for two simultaneous tasks: assessing the thruster unit for mechanical failure and performing a compositional analysis on any materials that were not part of the unit itself.

After a few minutes, a list of elements began to scroll on the display. Deanna studied it without knowing what she was looking for.

"Computer, do you detect any evidence of current or former biological activity in these samples?"

"*Negative.*"

"Computer, reorder the list with the least common elements, those that generally occur less frequently in nongaseous planetary bodies, on top. Describe any noteworthy properties of those elements, beginning with the first one."

After a brief pause, the computer stated, "*There are notable quantities of several radiogenic elements, which are produced by the process of radioactive decay. In order of abundance, these elements are argon-40, nitrogen-14, and lead-207. There are also significant quantities of helium, which is common throughout the known universe but which also can form as the result of radioactive decay. There are also several complex isotopic compounds including—*"

Deanna interrupted the litany. "Are there pockets of these materials on Beta's surface?"

"*Negative. These materials do not appear in significant quantities on Beta's surface. However, minute quantities are present, scattered thinly. There is also a dissipating cloud of helium emanating from a fissure in the moonlet approximately twenty-three kilometers from our current position.*"

"Behind us?" asked Deanna.

"*Affirmative.*"

"Computer, is that where the explosion that damaged our engine occurred?"

"*Affirmative.*"

Outgassing seemed more and more likely to Deanna, in spite of Taurik's doubts. But the event had happened just as Data transported the thruster unit aboard. "Computer, was the thruster unit active when we transported it?" she asked.

"*Negative. The thruster unit was dormant.*"

"And does it show any signs of malfunction?"

"*Negative. The thruster unit is capable of operating within normal parameters.*"

It was only one thruster out of dozens, but if it and the others were working, why hadn't Beta remained on course? Taurik believed that outgassing was an unlikely explanation, and Doctor Aaron hadn't mentioned any outgassing activity on Beta at all.

"Computer, has Beta's trajectory changed since the explosion?"

"Affirmative. Beta has changed its course by two degrees."

Something Captain Picard had said back on Ennis came back to her. *You almost make it sound as though the rings have a mind of their own.* Could Beta be protesting being dragged from its home?

It was ludicrous, when the sensors detected no signs of even low-level biological activity on Beta.

"Commander," Taurik's voice came over the comm. *"Short-range communications are online, although there may be some interference."*

"Good work, Ensign," said Deanna. "I'll be right up. Raise the outpost."

She went back up front. "This is Commander Deanna Troi calling the Ennis Outpost," she said at a signal from Taurik. "We have an emergency situation. Please respond." A moment later, she repeated the message.

The screen crackled in response and a jittery picture appeared. *"Commander Troi?"* More static. *"This is Maher. We're tracking Beta from here and it seems to have shifted again. What is your status?"* The picture cleared enough for Deanna to discern Maher's worried expression.

"An explosion caused one of our engines to malfunction, and we crashed into the moonlet," Deanna said. "We're not sure what caused it, although we're working on a theory. Director Maher, I'm sorry to have to tell you this, but Doctor Aaron is dead. His neck was broken in the crash."

The pause was longer this time. Finally, Maher spoke again, his voice heavy with sorrow. *"Understood, Commander. I'm sorry to hear that. You said you don't know what happened?"*

"No," she said. "Lieutenant Commander Data has also been damaged, and we won't know the extent of his injuries until we get him back aboard the *Enterprise*. We're attempting to repair our systems now, but it may be a while."

"I can send our shuttle for you. It will be cramped but it should get you back safely. Can you rig the runabout to self-destruct?"

"What?" said Deanna, startled.

"I think we need to cut our losses," he said, running his hand over his tired face. *"This project has been a disaster from start to finish. We need to destroy Beta before it causes more harm, and*

initiating a warp core breach on the runabout would probably be the easiest way."

"Destroying the runabout is not an option I'm currently considering," Deanna said, still not believing that Maher had suggested it. "Now that the crash has happened, the damage has been done, and as far as the runabout is concerned, it doesn't seem to be irreparable. I don't believe we're in danger at the moment."

"Doctor Aaron is dead, and Beta's course has shifted yet again," Maher said, his tone sharp. *"How much danger do you have to be in before you act? Beta is still roughly on course to intersect with our orbit, and taking chances at this point would be reckless. If you don't want to destroy the runabout, can you repair it and take off? Are your weapons capable of destroying Beta?"*

"No," said Deanna. "Even at full capacity, our weapons wouldn't vaporize the entire moonlet—they would create a lot of debris, some of which could threaten the outpost as well. At the rate Beta is moving, there's plenty of time to take action if we need to, especially if we recall the *Enterprise* from Chandra. Our long-range communications are damaged, so if you contact them—"

"Commander, I'd rather not involve the colony," Maher said. *"There are certain individuals on Chandra who've been working against this outpost from the start, and this will just fuel the fires. We can take care of this ourselves without any more excitement."*

Deanna sighed with frustration and hoped the continuing static had masked the noise. "Director, please. If you'll contact the *Enterprise,* I'm sure Captain Picard can smooth things over with the colonists. He has a great deal of diplomatic experience.

"And there's something else," she went on, hoping she was about to say the right thing. "I don't know if you're aware, but I'm an empath—I'm half-Betazoid. I don't know for certain, Director, but I thought I sensed something during the accident, and I think it's possible there may be life near here, perhaps somewhere in the rings or on one of the other moons if not on Beta itself."

Maher's face was a picture of disbelief. *"Life, Commander? Are you sure?"*

"No, I'm not," she said. "It was a very brief contact, if that's what it was, and I couldn't tell where it came from."

"Commander, surely you know that indigenous life in this part of the system is extremely unlikely. There's no energy source, and

there's been no sign of biological activity anywhere. We surveyed extensively before we began building the outpost."

"I understand, Director. But since neither we nor the outpost appears to be in immediate danger, it would be irresponsible to destroy Beta if there's even a remote chance of finding life."

Maher sighed. *"Commander, with all due respect, being irresponsible is exactly what I'm worried about. You're responsible to Starfleet, and I'm responsible to the scientists who work here and the colonists who've entrusted me with this project. I disagree that there's no immediate danger. Are you sure you're not just worried about being blamed for losing your ship?"*

Deanna fought to control her anger. "Director, I assure you, that's the least of my concerns. Please contact the *Enterprise* and we'll be able to determine if there's anything to my hunch. If not, the *Enterprise* will be able to help you deal with Beta."

"I'm sorry, Commander, but the answer is no," Maher stated flatly. *"I'm not going to let you or Captain Picard jeopardize my outpost without more than a vague hunch to go on. I'm sending the shuttle to Beta, and I suggest you either find a way to lift off or prepare to come aboard the shuttle when it gets there. Maher out."*

Deanna stared at the starfield that had replaced Maher on the viewscreen, her thoughts racing. The life-form, if there was one, wasn't here on Beta—at least, she didn't think so.

She could almost hear Captain Picard's voice asking for options, so she answered him in her thoughts. If they took the runabout back to Beta's point of origin—assuming Taurik could restore propulsion—Maher might really attack the moonlet with the shuttle. His weapons would be limited, but he could probably do a fair amount of damage.

Or she and Taurik could try to restore subspace communications and contact the *Enterprise.*

"Ensign," she said, "which system is more badly damaged, long-range communications or propulsion?"

"Communications, Commander," Taurik said. "The power surge shorted more relays than we can replace. Propulsion is down one engine, but now that we're stationary, I should be able to manually disconnect it and compensate with the other engines. One of the starboard thrusters is also damaged, but I believe I can fix it."

"Warp drive?" Deanna asked, knowing it was too much to hope

for. Under warp, they could get to the rings and back before Maher could blink.

Taurik shook his head. "No, ma'am. The impact knocked the warp coils out of alignment and, well, warped them. They won't generate a stable field."

Impulse power, then. But how to keep Maher from attacking the moonlet?

If only Data were functioning properly, surely he would think of a way—

Data. She turned and looked at the back of Data's motionless head. Then she looked at the space-suit locker, and back at Data.

"Ensign, drop everything else and work on propulsion. Keep me informed of your progress." She walked back to the science station. "Computer," she said, taking a deep breath. "How long can Lieutenant Commander Data survive in a vacuum?" she asked.

"Unknown," said the computer.

"Will Data's current condition affect his ability to survive in a vacuum?"

"Unknown."

Deanna sighed. She was fairly certain she'd heard Data relate an incident in which he'd been unprotected in a vacuum, but she wasn't sure.

One last question. "Computer," she said. "What is the status of the runabout's EVA suits?" Deanna mentally held her breath.

"The EVA suits are undamaged," said the computer.

As Deanna struggled into her suit, she vowed to practice emergency procedures back on *Enterprise* at least once a week. She'd kept up with Starfleet's minimum certification hours, but clearly they weren't enough. Beside her, Taurik was already snapping his helmet into place.

"I don't think we'll be able to wrestle Data into a suit," she said, "but I want to put a helmet on him to protect his eyes. Can you create a seal at the neck? He doesn't need an oxygen supply, but I want it pressurized if possible."

"Yes, ma'am," said Taurik. He took down another helmet from the locker and moved, somewhat tentatively in the unaccustomed gear, to where Data sat. By the time Deanna had closed her own helmet and run the suit's autocheck sequences, Taurik had finished with Data.

"Ensign, activate your suit's mavlock," she said, pressing a button on the front of her own suit. "Computer, turn off artificial gravity." Instantly she felt buoyant in spite of her suit's lock on the floor, and she had to overcome a surge of nausea. Although Data was now light enough for them to move him, his mass was unchanged, and maneuvering was tricky. Together, she and Taurik pulled Data to the runabout's tiny airlock and attached tethers to their suits. Deanna tied a third tether around Data's waist but did not attach the other end to the runabout.

"Let's move him farther away," said Deanna, her voice tinny and distant through the suit's radio. With awkward movements, they pulled Data several meters and leaned him against a rocky ledge. "Ensign, you're better in a suit than I am. Can you tie his tether to this rock, just in case?"

When Taurik had finished, Deanna sent him back toward the runabout. Then she knelt down to look into Data's face. Obviously he wouldn't be able to hear her, but maybe his eyes were registering *something*. She switched off her helmet radio so Taurik wouldn't hear and then said slowly, "We're coming back for you, Data. We can do this. Remember Picasso." She forced a smile, just in case he could see her, and then she turned away.

Just before she entered the airlock, Deanna pulled a small sample container from the belt at her waist and scooped up some of the regolith that had been displaced by the runabout's skid.

Deanna spent the entire trip back to the rings second-guessing herself. There had been another tense exchange with Maher, during which she'd told him that Data was remaining on Beta "for further study." A suspicious Maher had reminded her that she'd told him that Data wasn't functioning.

"We fixed him," she'd lied, signaling Taurik to cut the connection.

Taurik, too, had doubts about her proposed course of action and had requested permission to speak freely.

"Commander," he said, "have you considered the possibility that Director Maher will contact Captain Picard, but will relay only partial information? Even if Maher will not attack Beta himself while Lieutenant Commander Data is there, he may convince the captain that Beta presents enough of a threat to warrant destruction and fail to mention Lieutenant Commander Data's presence there. I have occasionally observed that people who are normally rational sometimes invent faulty chains of 'logic' when they are affected by strong emotions, particularly grief." He stopped for a moment, then went on. "And Captain Picard will have no reason to suppose that anyone is on Beta when he detects our runabout near the rings."

"Maher is an administrator worried about his people and his facility," Deanna stated definitely. "He's trying to bully us because he thinks he's right, but he won't allow the *Enterprise* to fire on Data any more than he would do it himself."

"But Commander—"

"I understand your concerns, Ensign, and yes, it *is* a risk. But I believe it's remote. Remember, I can sense his emotions, and he's more worried than anything else—he's not a cruel man. So this is a risk we're going to take. There's a lot at stake, and Data of all people would understand why this is important. Besides, if the *Enterprise* comes back, we should be able to hail it ourselves on short-range communications. Prepare to lift off."

When Taurik did not move immediately, Deanna looked straight into his eyes. "That's an order, Ensign," she said calmly, "and I expect you to follow it."

"Aye, Commander," he said, his doubts apparently assuaged.

As Taurik eased the runabout off the moonlet, skillfully compensating for the disabled engine, Deanna thought of Data yelling at his first officer on the *Sutherland,* and smiled in spite of her anxiety. *That,* she knew, would have been exactly the wrong thing to do in Taurik's case.

This foray into the rings was unable to captivate Deanna as the first trip had done. When they reached the gap where Beta had been, Deanna instructed Taurik to hover above it as before. "Ensign, try to configure the sensors to search for the isotopic compounds similar to the ones that the computer detected on the thruster unit from Beta. Start from Beta's original position and work outward."

"Aye, ma'am," said Taurik. "There do seem to be concentrations of similar compounds on several of the larger fragments near Beta's original position."

"Is the transporter working well enough to bring a sample on board?" asked Deanna.

"There is not much power to devote to the transporter, Commander. However, if we get quite close to one of the fragments, I believe the transporter can bring a sample aboard."

"Do it," she said. "Approach one of the larger fragments very slowly, no more than one-eighth impulse. Watch for signs of outgassing and be prepared to react quickly."

"Aye, Commander."

Deanna tensed as they approached the nearest sizable fragment, but Taurik was as skilled a pilot as Geordi had claimed. He eased the runabout closer until they hovered only thirty meters above the fragment and then transported several cubic centimeters of the fragment into the isolation chamber.

A spark of *confusion,* flaring briefly and then gone. *That was from the fragment,* Deanna thought. This time she was sure. And inside the chamber, a faint . . . *satisfaction.* "Ensign," she said over the comm. "I think the material you just pulled from the fragment is reacting to the particles from Beta that are still inside the chamber. It's as if they're aware of each other on some level. And I think the fragment is confused, as if it knows there's something missing. Pull away from it, just in case it's going to react somehow."

When Taurik reached an altitude of five hundred meters above the plane, Deanna told him to hold position.

"Once more, to make sure," Deanna whispered to herself. She retrieved the sample jar she had brought on board from Beta and pushed it through a pressurized seal in the side of the isolation chamber. She then eased her hands through a slot covered by an ultrathin, flexible membrane that allowed her to manipulate the jar without actually contacting anything else inside the chamber. She unscrewed the lid and poured Beta's soil on top of the sample they'd just transported aboard.

Satisfaction. Confusion. Fulfillment.

Coming directly from the isolation chamber.

She was right. There was life here. It might not be any form of life recognizable by the sensors—yet—but it was here in the rings, and it was, not quite happy, but content, to have even this small bit of itself restored.

She went forward to share the information with Taurik, who raised his eyebrows in an expression that might have indicated pleased wonder had he not been a Vulcan.

A beep from the console redirected their attention. "Commander, the *Enterprise* has dropped out of warp only a few kilometers from Beta."

"Can you raise them?" Deanna asked.

"We should be able to contact them, but I can't get through," said Taurik. "I believe we are being jammed."

Enough is enough, thought Deanna. "Ensign, put your helmet back on. Divert *all* power except sensors and short-range communications, including life support, to propulsion. I want full impulse and then some. Is there any sign that *Enterprise* is powering weapons?"

"No, Commander."

"Engage," said Deanna. "I'll keep trying to raise them, just in case."

The trip back seemed twice as long, even though they were traveling faster. When they arrived at Beta, Taurik, without prompting, parked the runabout squarely between Beta and the shuttle, which was piloted by two rather confused technicians from the outpost. Apparently Maher had not fully explained matters to them either.

The jamming, now futile, quietly disappeared, and Deanna found herself looking at the familiar bridge of the *Enterprise.* Giddy with relief, she almost laughed when Riker, exactly as she had expected, demanded, "What the hell is going on here?"

"I'll explain," she said. "But first we need to get Data off that rock."

In sickbay, Deanna sat next to the portable anbaric chamber, a thin pane of glass separating her from the table on which Data lay.

As always, the suddenness with which Data woke and sat straight up startled her.

"Data," she said with a tired smile. "How are you feeling?"

For several seconds, Data's eyes gave the impression that he was looking inward as his diagnostic subroutine assessed his condition, then he looked back at Deanna. It was wonderful to see thoughts behind his eyes again.

"I am fine, Commander," he said. "My memories are somewhat fragmented but I am in the process of reindexing them." He looked around. "I appear to be in an anbaric chamber."

"Yes," she said. "You were in a vacuum for a little over four hours, Data. Doctor Crusher thought the chamber would help your skin repair itself more quickly. I hope you aren't uncomfortable?"

"No, Commander."

"Data . . . I'm sorry. I put you at risk, and it was one of the hardest things I've ever done, but I thought it was necessary."

"At risk?" he asked.

"Yes, Data. I left you on the moonlet, completely unprotected. Well, almost completely. Director Maher had threatened to destroy Beta and I left you there as, well, as a hostage."

"Why, Commander?"

"There's life in the rings, Data. We're not sure what kind of life yet, and the sensors couldn't detect it at all until we told them what to look for, but there's a life-form that we think has been spreading slowly across the rings, probably for thousands of years. Geordi and Taurik have been making such wild speculations that I can hardly keep up with them. They think the rings may have been seeded at some point by comets carrying organic compounds, and that radiogenic decay of some of the rings' elements provided a heat source strong enough to allow cellular reproduction. When the outpost scientists moved Beta, the life-form seemed to sense that it was being taken away, and it reacted by causing outgassing. It was trying to get back to its own kind, but it didn't know how."

"Intriguing," said Data. "Doctor Aaron must be very excited as well."

Deanna's face fell. "Doctor Aaron is dead, Data. He died during the crash."

"I am sorry, Commander."

Deanna was silent.

"I hope you do not blame yourself," Data said. "You could not have known. We could not have predicted the moonlet's reaction."

"You're right, Data," she said. "But it's difficult."

Doctor Crusher came over to the chamber. "Good morning," she said with a smile. She peered at the readout in the lower left corner of the chamber's window. "We'll bake you for another hour, Data, and then I'll let Geordi get his hands on you again. I think he's repaired you just fine, but he wants to double-check. It's good to have you back."

"It is good to be back, Doctor. I look forward to conversing with my colleagues about the recent discovery in the rings—"

"Speaking of which," Deanna broke in, "I have to go, Data. I have to file the report that will assign Prime Directive protection to Heaven's rings. There are plenty of people interested in watching what will happen here over the next thousand years."

"Congratulations, Commander," said Data. "That is quite an honor."

"I also need to talk to Doctor Aaron's family," Deanna said. Beverly threw her a sympathetic look. If anyone could understand what that would be like, it was the doctor.

"You'll do fine," she said, touching Deanna's shoulder briefly before walking away.

"Yes, Commander," said Data. "With your training, I imagine you are well suited to the task."

"I'll give it my best, Data," she said. "If Picasso could, then I can."

FRIENDS WITH
THE SPARROWS

Christopher L. Bennett

Historian's note:
This tale is set several months after the events
of the feature film Star Trek Generations.

CHRISTOPHER L. BENNETT

Christopher L. Bennett has been lucky enough to get to explore many different corners of the vast *Star Trek* universe. With this story, he becomes the only author to have stories in all four *Star Trek* anniversary anthologies, the others being ". . . Loved I Not Honor More" in *Star Trek: Deep Space Nine: Prophecy and Change*, "Brief Candle" in *Star Trek: Voyager: Distant Shores*, and "As Others See Us" in *Star Trek: Constellations*. He has also visited the original series in *Star Trek: Ex Machina* and the eBook *Star Trek: Mere Anarchy Book Four: The Darkness Drops Again*; the Corps of Engineers in *Star Trek: S.C.E. #29: Aftermath*; Riker and Troi after the *Enterprise* in *Star Trek: Titan: Orion's Hounds*; and Captain Picard before the *Enterprise* in *Star Trek: The Next Generation: The Buried Age*. He has branched out beyond *Star Trek* with *X-Men: Watchers on the Walls* and the upcoming *Spider-Man: Drowned in Thunder* (January 2008), and is working on various original fiction concepts as well. More information, original fiction, and cat pictures can be found at http://home.fuse.net/ChristopherLBennett/.

DEANNA TROI'S DESTINATION WAS NOT HARD TO IDENTIFY.
It was the only one of Starbase 264's guest quarters to have a guard
posted outside the door. "I wouldn't recommend going in there
alone," the starbase's security chief advised her.

She threw the Ktarian a look. "The commander is under confinement at his own request," she reminded him. "I'm certain he's
no danger."

"I know you served with him for eight years. But you didn't see
what his little tantrum did to that lab. Maybe he's not the person
you knew anymore."

"And were any *people* hurt in that outburst?" she said pointedly.

The security chief sighed. "We'll be right outside if you need
anything."

"Thank you," she said, reminding herself that the man was simply doing his job. And from what Geordi had told her, even he had
been afraid for his safety at the time. Clamping down on her own
momentary burst of fear, she stepped inside.

The room was dark. She spotted him brooding in the shadows
and moved closer. "I would not advise that, Counselor," he said.
"It would be safer if you kept your distance."

"Nonsense. I know you'd never hurt me."

"Not if I were in control of myself. But the way I am now . . . I would never forgive myself if anything happened to you, Deanna."

She eased herself into a seat opposite him. "The way you are now is something you can learn to manage. And I'm here to help you do that. If you'll let me." She reached over and placed her hand atop his. "I'm not running away from you, Data."

Her eyes were adjusting to the dark now, and she saw his nervous smile and blinked-away tears. "Thank you, Deanna. Your friendship means a great deal to me." He gathered himself, pulling his hand back to rest upon his lap. "Still, it is best if I avoid becoming overemotional."

She sat back. "Is it all right if I turn on the lights?" He nodded, and she gave the computer the order. She studied his face, trying to gauge the extent of his tears. It was harder with him. Although the emotion chip Data had implanted in himself several months ago allowed his brain to simulate human emotional states, it did not enable his face to simulate puffed eyelids and red eyes. And she didn't get the psionic input from him that she'd get from an organic being. Sensing Data's emotions was not unlike reading them over a viewscreen, relying mainly on a skilled reading of body language and expression plus whatever EM-frequency neural emissions she could pick up.

Still, she gave him a reassuring smile. "There, that's better. One thing you should learn about emotions is that darkness tends to promote depression."

"I am aware of that, Counselor. Yet oddly, despite the unpleasantness of depression, I find myself motivated to prolong the experience. Perhaps because I deserve the punishment."

She studied him. "Data, why don't you tell me what happened?"

He moved uneasily in his seat. "I am uncertain how to characterize the experience. It is . . . disquieting to reflect upon."

"Well, let's ease into it. Talk to me about the work you were doing. How you and Geordi came to this project."

He frowned, but it was a classic Data frown of puzzlement. "I assumed you had been briefed on the Tamarian communication project."

"Oh, I have been. I was invited to participate, but unfortunately I had other obligations." The former Enterprise-D command crew had scattered to various short-term assignments, expecting to be reassembled once the new *Enterprise* was completed. For the second time, Picard's reputation as a commander and importance as a statesman had spared him the stigma that befell most captains who lost their ships, ensuring he would remain at the vanguard of the fleet and have his pick of command crew. But for now, Deanna had been busy counseling former shipmates—many of them civilian scientists and their children—who were still suffering trauma from the *Enterprise*'s destruction at Veridian III. "But I want to hear it from your perspective."

He nodded. "Very well. It began when Captain Picard introduced me to the noted xenoanthropologist Doctor Sofia Borges, who had come to him with an intriguing request . . ."

"There's no question," Sofia Borges said, "that what you and Captain Picard achieved with the Children of Tama was a remarkable breakthrough."

"I cannot take credit," Data told the doctor, who was a human female of approximately thirty-five standard years, standing 1.72 meters in height, and showing a mix of Native American and Mediterranean in her physiognomy. He felt a desire to impress her, one he believed to be associated with his moderate physical arousal at her appearance, but this was overridden by his loyalty to Picard and his commitment to accurate presentation of the facts. "Captain Picard achieved the breakthrough independently of the more limited work that Commander Troi and I were able to perform aboard ship."

"Still," Borges replied, "the work you did in determining the nature of the Tamarian ego structure was valuable for putting the captain's achievement in context."

"I am pleased that you think so," he told her, smiling.

"Besides," Picard said, "all I did was help set the process in motion—or rather, make it possible for the late Captain Dathon to do so."

Data took a few microseconds to review the events of stardate 45047.2 to 45048.6. The *Enterprise* had traveled to El-Adrel IV to meet with the Children of Tama, an enigmatic race that had made several prior, unsuccessful attempts to open relations with the Federation. Though universal translators had been able to interpret their basic vocabulary, their grammar had remained incomprehensible, their statements appearing to be merely a hodgepodge of names and descriptions. Despairing at Picard's lack of comprehension, the Tamarian captain, Dathon, had beamed himself and Picard to the planet's surface while his ship had generated atmospheric interference to prevent rescue. On the planet, Picard had learned that the Tamarians communicated through metaphor and allusion based on their culture's mythology and literature. Dathon's plan had itself been a metaphor of sorts, reenacting the myth wherein the hunter Darmok and the warrior Jalad met on an island, battled a beast, and departed as friends. Regrettably, reality had diverged from the myth and Dathon had not survived the encounter. But his sacrifice had been recorded by the Tamarians as a new myth, and they had departed peacefully. More recently, they had sought to engage in further diplomatic discourse with the Federation.

Picard continued. "Doctor Borges and her colleagues are doing the real work of building upon that first contact and establishing a meaningful relationship with the Tamarians."

"Which is proving difficult," she said. "With all due respect to Captains Picard and Dathon, the understanding they brought us was only the first step. Yes, we know now that Tamarian is a series of allusions to myths and history, but that just raised a wealth of new questions. How do they teach the basic vocabulary to their children, or convey the full stories of those myths in the first place? How do they communicate technical information or give instructions on how to build and operate ships? And most important, how do we express ourselves in terms that are meaningful to them, without having to settle for a pidgin—"

Data had begun nodding impatiently. "Yes, I have followed your research on the matter, Doctor Borges," he assured her. "You have made impressive advances. For instance, your recognition that the spoken word is only one of multiple semantic channels within Tamarian, alongside vocal intonation and gesture."

"Thank you, Data," Borges told him, though her tone had cooled for some reason. "But there's still a long way to go. The key problem is that the Tamarian brain is simply structured differently from the humanoid norm. That's why it's so hard to get a full computer translation. You see," she explained to Picard, "the fundamental rules of grammar that underlie all human languages are innate in our brains. Different languages put those rules together differently, but they share the same building blocks."

"Transformational grammar," Data interposed. "A theory formulated by Noam Chomsky in the twentieth century on Earth, and independently by T'Soni of—"

"Yes, thank you, Data," Picard interrupted, as he had done many times in the past. Data snapped his mouth shut. Before he had installed the emotion chip, he had never realized how irritating it was to be interrupted.

Borges continued, "And since most humanoids have similar brain structures—presumably due to the shared genetic program you and Professor Galen discovered two years ago, Captain—their languages usually follow those same patterns, patterns the translator is designed to recognize and use as a Rosetta stone of sorts."

"But the Tamarian brain structure is different," Picard said, nodding.

"That's right. They don't have a strong sense of themselves as individuals. They perceive reality in terms of archetypes and see themselves as manifestations of those archetypes. Instead of Sofia Borges embroidering a dress, say, I'm Arachne at her loom. If I then go to mop the floor, I'm Herakles in the stables. Or I'm embodying him for as long as he needs me to."

"Remarkable," Picard breathed.

"I suspect," Data said, "that this is related to the Tamarians' vaguely defined sense of time. As you know, their language is based on images of successive moments rather than descriptions of change or action. Their only time referent is 'when' or 'during.' They have little sense of past and present, and thus may perceive themselves as indistinguishable from the figures of their mytho-historical past. Also—"

"That's exactly what I'm thinking," Borges said, interrupting again. "And it leads to a problem. It makes the Tamarians intensely concerned with proper ritual forms. Everything has to be done consistently with the appropriate mythic precedents, or it isn't done at all. That's why they insisted on making contact on their terms, requiring us to figure out their language, rather than making an effort to communicate in our terms. To them, a first contact has to be carried out in accordance with one of the contact tales in their cultural background, whether Rai and Jiri, Zima and Bakor, or Darmok and Jalad—which, by the way, is considered a last-ditch, desperation tactic."

"I should hope so," Picard said dryly.

"And the same goes for diplomatic relations as well. We have to negotiate within their ritual context in order for it to have meaning to them. If we don't follow the right pattern, it upsets the balance of the universe in their view, and they're likely to react badly."

Data nodded. "The Tamarians responded aggressively when we attempted to diverge from the ritual script of the Darmok scenario. Historical precedents include the death of Captain James Cook at the hands of—"

"Right. If we can't play by their rules, it could lead to the end of diplomatic relations at best, war at worst."

"And," Picard added, "it would render Captain Dathon's sacrifice meaningless. I am not willing to accept that, Data."

"I understand, sir. But what does Doctor Borges believe I can contribute to the effort?" He said it with a touch of skepticism. He could forgive Picard's quirks, but Borges's tendency to interrupt him made him doubt whether she really valued his input.

Borges gave him an impatient look, supporting his hypothesis. He was finding her much less attractive. "Like I said," she told him, "the problems arise from our different brain structures. We can scan the activity of the Tamarian brain and deduce some things about how it works, but we can't fully understand their way of thinking unless we can approach it from the inside. We need someone who can think like a Tamarian but then come back to thinking our way and report his insights in terms—"

"So you need a cerebral shape-shifter." Data chuckled, but broke off as he realized that, as usual, nobody else thought his joke was particularly amusing. He sighed.

"Sort of," Borges said. "And, uh, you've just demonstrated why you qualify."

He frowned. "Because of my emotion chip?"

"Exactly. Emotion is a cognitive process, one you didn't have before. And it isn't just something that's superimposed on your previous, unemotional thought process. It's something that affects the way you think, the way you perceive and experience the world, on a fundamental level. That chip has transformed the way your brain works. And if it did it once—"

He anticipated her meaning. "It can do it again. You propose to modify my emotion chip in order to simulate Tamarian cognitive processes in my own brain."

"Exactly. You'd be able to communicate with them on their own terms, gain insights we never could otherwise."

"It is an intriguing proposal," he said, though he kept to himself the fact that he found it intimidating as well. "However, it is clearly flawed. Once I were . . . 'reset' . . . to my normal cognitive mode, I might no longer understand those insights."

"I *have* considered that, thank you," she replied, biting off the words. "But you'd still have the direct experience, and at least that could help you formulate better analogies. When you get right down to it, we all think in analogies. We understand our experiences by comparing them to the precedents in our minds. The difference between us and the Tamarians is largely a matter of degree."

Data's unease compelled him to move, so he began pacing as he considered her proposal. In the past, he could have completed a risk-benefit analysis in milliseconds. When he had "paused to think," it had largely been an affectation to reassure his humanoid listeners that his statements were not offered in haste. These days, he found he needed time to process his emotional reactions and had more difficulty perceiving a clear course of action.

In this case, he found Borges's proposal worth contemplating but was not sure he had faith in her judgment. "My concern," he said at length, "is that we still understand relatively little about the functioning of the emotion chip. I am not sure it would be viable to modify its function and then restore it to its previous state."

"My experts have reviewed its specifications, and I'm confident it could work."

"You cannot know that for sure."

"There's never any certainty," she replied. "But the risk is minor. Captain Dathon was willing to give his life to achieve communication, you know."

"Doctor," Picard interposed, silencing her. "Data . . . as important as this project is to me, I would not ask you to place yourself at risk for it. And I'm not your commanding officer at the moment. However, I would suggest that you review Doctor Borges's proposal with Commander La Forge and assess its feasibility. Geordi knows your emotion chip and your other systems as well as any man alive."

"Aside from myself, of course." Data nodded. "Very well. I will discuss it with him." He turned to Borges. "And if I do agree to this proposal, I will request that Commander La Forge be in charge of the actual modifications."

"Of course. We'd be glad to have him on the team." She studied him. "I really believe this can work, Commander. We just have to work together to pull it off." She extended a hand.

He shook it briefly, without enthusiasm. "We shall see, Doctor."

"It sounds," Deanna said, "like there was some tension between you and Doctor Borges."

"She has repeatedly demonstrated an unreasonable hostility toward me," Data replied. "She reacts badly to my attempts to provide information, clarify issues under discussion, or correct oversights and errors in her work. It has proved an impediment to a smooth working relationship between us."

"I see. And why do you suppose that is?"

"Perhaps it is a result of the prejudice I have often encountered from organic beings. However, her attitude seems to have infected the rest of her staff as well."

"You took the assignment despite this personal difficulty."

"Of course, Counselor, or we would not be here. Geordi and I reviewed the doctor's research and found it valid. And he agreed with me that it was important to ensure that Captain Picard's breakthrough with the Tamarians did not go to waste. At the time, I assumed the doctor would be professional enough to work efficiently with us despite the minor tension I noted at our initial meeting."

Deanna tilted her head. "But the tension wasn't just on her end, was it?"

"No, it was not. I found her hostility somewhat . . . hurtful. I had done nothing to deserve it."

"Did you ask her what the source of her problem was?"

"I did. She accused me of being condescending and arrogant, of being a 'control freak' and a 'show-off.'" Data sounded confused by that.

"You don't think that was valid?" Deanna asked him.

"I behaved the same way I always have, Counselor—seeking to provide the most accurate information possible for the benefit of all parties."

"Which sometimes meant correcting her mistakes."

"Only in the interest of providing her with more accurate knowledge for the good of the project," Data insisted. It was odd to sense defensiveness in him. "I was trying to help her, and she irrationally responded to it as an attack."

"And how did that make you feel?" It was just as odd to be asking that, the most routine of a counselor's questions, in a session with Data. Deanna was still feeling her way when it came to counseling the newly emotional android. The old strategies she'd devised for him were no longer valid, but she had to guard against the assumption that he could be treated like any humanoid. There were still differences, most of all the sheer novelty of his emotions.

"Surprised. Confused. Hurt. Irritated. Frustrated."

"Angry?"

"Increasingly so, Counselor."

"Yet when you had your outburst of anger, it was directed at Geordi."

Data fidgeted. "Yes, it was."

"Tell me what happened."

"We had been working on the computations for modifying my emotion chip with Tamarian cognitive parameters. Specifically, we were debating how to modify my self-diagnostic protocols to accommodate a diminished sense of ego identity. I had just gained an insight in how to proceed and was attempting to explain it to Geordi."

"Attempting?"

He frowned. "Yes. He was slow to comprehend the ideas I was expressing. To be fair, the computations were very involved. I suppose I could have been more patient with him. But you must understand, Counselor . . . given the speed at which my mind functions, it can be frustrating to wait for others to catch up. That is something I am still learning to cope with."

"But you weren't coping with it effectively the day this happened."

"I fear not."

* * *

"No! No, Geordi, you are not listening. If you simply reverse the polarity of—"

"No, Data, *you* aren't listening! Modifying the recursive filters like that would never work. It would create a dangerous feedback loop."

"I have already explained how to compensate for that. Why are you fighting me on this, Geordi?"

Data could see Geordi struggling to rein in his anger. He had found that the VISOR over Geordi's eyes did not appreciably hamper his ability to read the man's expressions, perhaps due to their long friendship. "I'm not fighting anything, Data. I just don't like being talked down to, that's all."

That came as a surprise to Data. "You sound like Borges."

"Yeah, well, maybe she has a point, did you think of that? Frankly, ever since you got that emotion chip, you haven't been that easy to get along with. I've tried to be patient, since you're new at this, but—"

"Patient?" Data laughed. "If you had any idea how patient I have had to be to function while surrounded by people who think thousands of times more slowly than I do—"

Geordi thrust a hand in his direction. "There. You see? This is the sort of thing Sofia's talking about. You keep reminding us how much smarter than us you are."

"That is no more true now than it was before I installed the chip."

"But you were never so damn *smug* about it before."

"Why do people keep *saying* that?" Data shouted, surprised by the fierceness of his outburst. But hearing the accusation from his own best friend, the person he thought would be on his side, was the last blow he could withstand. "All I am trying to do is help people! To share the benefit of my knowledge, just as I always have! And yet every time I have tried to give that help to Borges and her teammates, I have been met with resentment and hostility for my efforts. And now you turn on me as well? *Et tu,* Geordi?"

"Well, maybe the problem is with *you,* did you ever think of that? Your positronic brain works so much faster than our lowly human ones, yet that possibility never occurred to you? The reason so many people are calling you a condescending show-off is because you *are.*"

"That is not true! How can you say that? I thought you were my *friend*!"

His voice had grown louder with each sentence as the buildup of pain, betrayal, and bitterness burst free. With the final word, he smashed his hand down on the console, crumpling it. Geordi took a step back and was holding his hands out in what he no doubt imagined to be a calming gesture. "Just take it easy, Data. Maybe we should take a break, okay?"

"Stop pretending, Geordi! You despise me! You all do! Get out! *Get out!*" The outburst was as much a warning as anything else. He could feel rage overpowering him, filling him with a need to strike out at something. And his efforts to control it were failing.

". . . As Geordi and the others fled, I gave in to the rage and directed it against the contents of the lab itself." Data gave his head a small, uncertain shake. "Afterward, I found I did not feel better. Merely . . . empty. And extremely guilty," he added, looking up at Deanna. "I could have harmed my best friend."

"But you didn't," she assured him. "Even when your anger and pain overwhelmed you, you still instinctively chose to direct your anger away from people and toward inanimate objects. And you were so concerned for the safety of others that you requested confinement to quarters before it could even be ordered. And that's why I'm convinced it isn't necessary. You wouldn't hurt any living thing out of anger. It's just not in you."

"But I did harm my friendship with Geordi. He may never trust me again."

"I'm sure you can rebuild that trust. But it will take effort on both your parts. You now know Geordi feels that you've been treating him with less respect than he deserves."

Data shook his head. "I think as highly of Geordi as I ever have. I am simply having difficulty managing my impatience. Under the circumstances, surely you can see why that impatience is understandable."

"I can," she said. "But you need to see why it's understandable that others would feel slighted by it, whether you intend it that way or not. Accommodation has to go both ways."

He sighed. "I thought that having emotions would make it easier to understand humanity. Instead, it has left me more confused than ever."

"Welcome to the humanoid condition," Deanna said with a smile. "Let me put it this way. You've always been smarter and faster than the rest of us, and you've always liked to give detailed lectures and explanations about the things you know. But when you were emotionless, it was simply a matter-of-fact presentation, and people could see that. So they didn't take it personally. Now, though, they can perceive you as an emotional being. So when you make a point of emphasizing your knowledge and intelligence, or hastening to point out their errors, it's natural for them to sense an emotional motive behind that. To suspect that you *enjoy* showing them that you know more than they do. It's easy to feel slighted by such a thing, especially when it's an ongoing pattern."

"But no slight is intended, Counselor. Simply a desire for precision. Surely if Geordi can understand that I do not mean any harm by it, then things will be all right."

Deanna took a slow breath. "I'm not sure it'll be that easy, Data. You need to ask yourself—could it be that they're sensing something real? Some emotion in yourself that you haven't recognized?"

He was surprised, hurt. "Surely you do not believe I *intend* to belittle others."

"No, of course not. But the thing about having emotions is that our conscious intentions are not always the only things that influence our actions. Sometimes we can be hurtful to others without even realizing it."

She leaned forward. "You spoke before of how it irritated you to be interrupted, and how impatient it made you when Borges lectured you on things you already knew."

"That is correct."

"So would you say your pride was hurt? That you felt you were being condescended to?"

"I believe that would be a valid interpretation."

"And you think it was justified for you to react with irritation and impatience in those cases."

"Perhaps I could have handled the emotions better, but yes, I believe I was entitled to feel them."

"Then what about when the situation is reversed? When you are the one doing the lecturing, the interrupting, the correcting? Isn't it reasonable to expect them to feel the same way?"

"I suppose so," he said after a pause.

"So if you act as though it's justified for you to react that way when they do it to you, but unreasonable for them to do so in the reverse case, doesn't that suggest a double standard? The idea that you're somehow above the restrictions they should be bound by?"

"That is not—" He broke off, frowning, and did not continue. At length, he spoke again. "So what you are saying is that . . . the emotion chip has made me obnoxious and insensitive." He seemed genuinely concerned at the possibility. "Perhaps it is malfunctioning or innately flawed. Doctor Soong was often regarded as imperious by his colleagues, so perhaps this is reflected in the chip's programming. Or it could have absorbed something from its time in Lore . . ."

"Data," she said, "I can't speak to the technical side of the matter. That's something you and Geordi will have to explore if you think it's necessary. But I want you to consider the possibility that the problem could be within yourself."

He examined her. "What specific fault do you propose? Some form of incompatibility between my positronic net and the emotion chip?"

She shook her head. "That's not what I mean. From what you've told me, it sounds as though Borges's disapproval, and particularly Geordi's, made you very hurt and angry."

"Correct."

"Often, the things that make us angriest are the things we fear the most. Arrogance and hostility are often compensation for feelings of inadequacy and insecurity." She leaned forward. "All your life, Data, you've believed that you wouldn't be complete until you achieved humanity. And since you weren't human, you've always believed you were less than you should be. Before, that was simply a detached appraisal to you, with no strong value judgment implied. Now, though, you have an emotional context for that feeling of deficiency, and it worries you. It's possible that it's manifesting as an inferiority complex."

Data frowned. "I do not understand, Counselor. How could my beliefs from the time before the emotion chip affect my emotional state now?"

"Emotions aren't separate from cognitive thought, Data. They interact with it closely, and it shapes them as much as they shape it. Your belief in your incompleteness is a lifelong habit." She paused. "Tell me: why did you feel you needed this chip?"

He was surprised at the question. "Because I wished to possess emotion."

"But isn't that a contradictory statement? Doesn't the very existence of the wish suggest that you already had emotion of a sort? True, you didn't have the same kind of passion that we humanoids have. But you obviously had preferences, affinities, dislikes, ambitions, regrets. They may not have been human emotions, they may have been subdued and understated, but that doesn't mean they couldn't have qualified as a *kind* of emotion, if you'd been willing to perceive them in that way. You could have chosen to embrace and develop your own distinctly android emotions—been satisfied with being the unique entity that is Data. But instead, you've always thought of being an android as a handicap you had to overcome."

"But it is, Counselor. I do not live among androids. I live among humans and other humanoids. Installing the emotion chip was the only way to overcome my inability to relate to my friends and colleagues in the fullest possible way."

She smiled sadly. "And has it worked the way you thought it would?" He opened his mouth to reply, then closed it, taking her point. "Maybe that's part of the problem. You saw this chip as a solution to your difficulties, but it's just created more. You haven't achieved your longed-for understanding of humanity, and that may be reinforcing your feelings of deficiency.

"Data, perhaps the hostility and arrogance others sense from you is a preemptive defense against the disapproval you expect from them. And it becomes a self-fulfilling prophecy."

He pondered her words for some time. "And . . . if this hypothesis were correct . . . what would be the treatment?"

She thought it over. "Maybe the key is to stop looking so hard for external causes and solutions. We're all ultimately responsible for our own actions and choices. Even when we're provoked by others, we still choose how we respond to that provocation. So you need to learn to manage your own emotional state regardless of whatever incitements or judgments you perceive from others.

"If the problem is with your own self-image, then the crucial thing is to make peace with it. If you do that, then nothing from outside can threaten your sense of self."

"And how would I achieve this?"

"By learning to accept yourself on your own terms. Don't worry about whether you're human enough, or emotional enough, or liked enough by others. Don't feel you have to conform to others' expectations. Just try to be the best Data you can be. I know it seems paradoxical to say that the way to be more sensitive to others is to stop worrying about what they think of you. But dwelling on external causes for our emotional states can keep us from recognizing or exercising our own ability to manage them, to calm our own anxiety and find peace. And when we're at peace with ourselves, it's easier to make peace with others."

After a while, Data shook his head. "I am sorry, Counselor, but I am not convinced by your analysis. I believe my problem is simply a matter of control and discipline, or else the result of a technological malfunction." He stood. "However, I appreciate your reassurance that I am not likely to inflict physical harm on anyone, and I will endeavor to be more sensitive to the egos of my colleagues. Thank you for your time, Counselor."

"Data, it won't be that simple. If you're thinking of returning to duty, I wouldn't advise it yet."

"Unfortunately, I am urgently needed on the Tamarian project. Captain Picard is counting on me. And I would appreciate it if you would tell the starbase commander that I am fit to return to duty."

Deanna was reluctant to accede to Data's request. As she saw it, he was in denial. She could understand his reticence to let go of a life-long priority, to admit that the pursuit of humanity that he had devoted so much effort to might have been a fatuous goal. But she felt it was blinding him.

Moreover, she felt it had been a bad idea to let him return to duty so soon after installing the emotion chip. He was still at a juvenile level of emotional maturity, and while he could learn far faster than most humanoids, he still had a way to go, as his tantrum had shown.

But the pressure to return him to work was too strong. The Federation was counting on this diplomatic breakthrough. Doctor Borges was still determined to work with Data despite their personal clashes, and she had readily accepted his apologies and his promise to be more understanding in the future. And Deanna herself shared the determination he and Geordi felt to ensure the success of the process Captain Picard had started.

So she gave her guarded approval for Data to return to duty, with the proviso that she would remain to monitor him. This also let her work directly on the project after all, and she relished the opportunity. After months counseling her former crewmates, it was refreshing to exercise her skills as a contact specialist again.

It fascinated her to study Sofia Borges's work on the Tamarian language. Deanna recalled Picard describing how he had divined the meanings of Dathon's phrases from context, tone, and body language. The Tamarians, it seemed, did the same on a much deeper level. As with Mandarin or Betelgeusian, variations of meaning and syntax were communicated through pitch. Body language and gesture conveyed other specifics much like a sign language. Borges's insight had enabled the revision of universal translator protocols to record these tonal and gestural cues—often too subtle for most humanoids to read—and gain a fuller translation as a result. She'd also recognized how integral their written language was to their communication, particularly where mathematics, science, and engineering were concerned. Though the emphasis was different, the Tamarians saw writing as an extension of their normal communication. Their language was one of symbols and images, and that had always included physical symbols, whether ritual objects or written markings, as much as verbal or gestural ones.

One of the most intriguing things was how closely their mathematical notation was tied to their musical notation. Borges had recordings of Tamarian engineers and programmers literally singing equations and instructions to one another. Even in ordinary speech, numerical information could be conveyed through the pitch of a Tamarian's vocal harmonics, though it could be hard for human ears to discern the nuances. (This answered the infamous question one linguist had posed to illustrate the apparent limitations of Tamarian as a practical language: "Mirab-his-sails-unfurled factor *what*, sir?")

While Deanna studied for the pending negotiations, Data, Geordi, and Borges's team finished up their work on reprogramming the emotion chip. The team seemed to be getting along more effectively, but Deanna could tell that Data was suppressing his frustration and unease rather than truly overcoming them. She did what she could to instruct him in anger management but considered it a palliative for the deeper problem. For what it was worth, though, Data had an advantage. For humanoids, muscular tension and fatigue played a key role in perpetuating a bad mood, but Data had no muscles per se to tense. That made it easier for him to cast off anger and anxiety, but it forced her to adapt her methods, since he couldn't use physical relaxation as a means toward emotional focus.

In time, Data and Geordi decided they were ready for a test. Deanna watched uneasily as the Tamarian cognition program was uploaded into Data's emotion chip. These were uncharted waters; there were few cases of an individual changing the very way he thought and perceived the world, except in instances of brain damage—or that of Data's own installation of Soong's chip. And he was still new at adjusting to that. But despite her concern for a patient and a friend, Deanna had to admit to great curiosity about the results and what they would mean to the science of psychology.

Once Data rebooted and opened his eyes, he looked around in confusion. "Data? You okay?" Geordi asked.

"Omicron Theta. *Tripoli.* What?" He blinked, looking around in confusion. "The crew on the bridge. When the Satarran scan occurred."

"What does that mean?" Borges asked.

"He's referring to a time when we had our memories erased," Deanna told her. "I think he's using it as an image of confusion, disorientation." She moved closer. "Data, concentrate on my words. Do you recognize me?"

"Daughter of the Fifth House."

"That's right." She had never thought she'd be glad to hear that pretentious title her mother loved to invoke. "Can you understand what I'm saying? Do you know where you are?"

"Holmes in the drawing room," he said thoughtfully. "The Dancing Men." Enlightenment dawned on his face. "Sato with the Antianna!" Deanna recognized the allusion to the famous moment when inspiration had struck the inventor of translator linguacode, while Geordi was able to identify the Dancing Men as a code broken by Sherlock Holmes. Apparently Data was deciphering regular communication sufficiently to understand it, though communicating in his own variant of Tamarian idiom.

Once they were satisfied the process had worked, Data was deactivated again and his chip reset to default parameters. To everyone's relief, he appeared to function normally once reactivated. It seemed to prove that the reprogramming technique would be a valid means for communicating with the Tamarians. After a second test confirmed the results of the first, they decided it was time to proceed.

The team traveled to the rendezvous point aboard the *U.S.S. Krishna.* As before, the Tamarians had chosen a meeting place midway between Federation territory and their own. This time, they allowed Data, Troi, and Borges to beam aboard their vessel, though a sizable contingent of armed guards met them in the transporter room. "Don't worry," Borges told Deanna sotto voce. "It's part of the ritual."

After a period of waiting, the Tamarian ambassador and her aides entered and stood before the party. Ambassador Denin touched the small metal talismans attached to her tunic in a certain sequence and spoke, the translator filling in some of the nonverbal meanings. "Menos [king] of Kyjo [City]. Menos at the [city] gates. [Guarded welcome.] His feet unmoving [determined]."

Data strode forward, making similar gestures. "Uzani [king] of Fenmir. Uzani [arriving] at the gates. His army on the plain [waiting]." He removed his phaser and laid it at Denin's feet. "Uzani. His sword [and theirs] laid down [in friendship]. His neck bare [vulnerable, trusting]."

Denin removed a small but sharp talisman from her tunic and tapped it ritually on Data's exposed neck. "Uzani risen [accepted]. Uzani [guest] at Kyjo."

As Data rose and began a ritual exchange with Denin—a UFP insignia pin for one of her talismans—Deanna sighed. *The translation may be a bit clearer now, but it was prettier before.*

The ensuing dialogue went on for hours, yet it served as little more than an introduction. Tamarian was not a compact language; it was built more for poetry than efficiency. When Data was "tuned" back to normal afterward, he confirmed that the negotiations would be lengthy. From what he had divined, the extensive enactment of tales would be a vital element. "I suspect they teach their own children in much the same way," Data told the others in *Krishna's* briefing room. "Through repetition, the young gradually learn the meanings of individual words through their overall context and usage, rather than being taught each word discretely." Deanna reflected that a similar method had probably been used for millennia on Earth and elsewhere before anyone had conceived of schools or grammar books.

Gaining mutual cultural insight, Data explained, was vital to the contact process. "The Tamarians are migratory by nature and have been traveling among the worlds of their home sector since before they even developed warp drive. Like the ancient Polynesians of Earth or the Shesshran of Daran V, their history is replete with cases of rediscovery and reconquest of colonial populations during successive waves of new migration. As such, contact incidents play an integral role in their history and culture. It is not enough for them simply to be aware of a neighbor's existence. Their history tells them that encroachment between neighbors will inevitably occur, and it is imperative to discern whether a more powerful neighbor's intentions are benevolent or rapacious. This is why they have made multiple efforts to establish contact with the Federation—in the hopes of resolving this lingering question."

"But those contacts were decades apart," Geordi said. "Doesn't seem so urgent."

"Only because our time sense is more linear than theirs," Data reminded him. "Now that we have achieved initial contact and sought a dialogue, the question has become more urgent to them. If we do not successfully demonstrate our ability to coexist harmoniously with the Children of Tama, they will see no other choice but to declare war on us. Partly out of self-defense, partly because that is simply what the mythic duality demands."

"So the stakes are even higher than we knew," Borges said. "We can't afford to fail."

After the briefing, Deanna pulled Data aside. "I must say, I'm impressed at how patient you were with the Tamarians' rather . . . inefficient way of conducting a dialogue."

"Thank you, Counselor, but my emotion chip deserves the credit. When my mind is functioning in Tamarian mode, I have little sense of the passage of time."

"Well, maybe that could help you improve your patience the rest of the time."

Data shook his head. "I doubt it. All it does is throw my problem into relief. It is taking all my control to avoid outbursts of impatience with others."

She frowned. "Data, I think there are still underlying issues you aren't allowing yourself to confront."

He closed his eyes, and she felt his attempt to rein in his irritation. "I am not surprised that you have not moved past that yet. You are a dog with a bone. A *reyfel* on the scent. Granny Ku'ula when her mind is made up. The Zerekian Oak before the flood."

Deanna stared at him. "Data?"

He broke off, pondered for a moment, and gave her a small smile. "Nothing to worry about, Counselor. A touch of metaphor spillover." He chuckled to himself. "If you will excuse me, Daughter of the Fifth House." He walked away, still giggling. Deanna watched his receding form with concern.

Deanna reported her observations to Geordi, but when he reset Data back to Tamarian mode the next day, his diagnostics gave no indication of instability. "At least, nothing outside expected parameters," he told her. "Going back and forth like he's doing . . . it's bound to confuse anyone a little. But he still passed all the perceptual tests. This is Data we're talking about, after all."

She wasn't reassured. "Does any of us know what that means anymore? Even Data?"

But she had no grounds for vetoing Data's role in the day's ritual. This involved an exchange of myths and stories to give each group insight into the other's heritage and worldview. The Tamarians had several planets' worth of myth and literature at their beck and call, and Deanna absorbed it with interest. (She was particularly curious about the lore of Shantil III, home of the Darmok myth. The *Enterprise* computer had held only fragmentary references to its mythos, courtesy of a summary in an anthropological text discovered in the ruins of Promellia. But Shantil had been one of the Tamarians' first alien contacts, apparently providing them with much of their mythic vocabulary as well as their advanced technology.)

On his part, Data regaled the Tamarians with the lore of the Federation, acting out tales ranging from the *Ramayana* and Shakespeare to Tarbolde and the Gestes of Andor. Like them, he employed a detached nonverbal mode to indicate that the tales were being told for ritual or didactic purposes rather than as earnest metaphors for his own intentions. Given the violence and venality inherent in so much of ancient literature, this was a vital distinction.

But Deanna sensed something changing as Data related Othello's murder of Desdemona—something that had been lingering beneath the surface and was now beginning to emerge. "Othello with a light. Desdemona in her bed," she heard. She had set her translator to tune out the annotations and render only the basic words, doing her best to read the subtexts on her own. "The light quenched. Prometheus with the fire. Desdemona restored?" He shook his head. "Shaka. When the walls fell."

"The rose on the vine. The rose in the hand? The rose withered. The rose's scent—Justice, her sword broken?" He shook his head. "Tears fallen from heaven.

"Desdemona awake. Desdemona pleading! The handkerchief. Cassio. His beard! Desdemona on her deathbed!" He was growing more agitated by the second. Before Deanna could call out, he cried, "Down, strumpet!" and lunged at Ambassador Denin, reaching for her throat.

Deanna was the only one who'd sensed trouble before the sudden attack, and given Data's speed and strength, she knew she had to act fast. Luckily, Tamarian ceremony demanded she carry a phaser at all times, as their officers carried ceremonial daggers. She wasn't sure its stun setting would affect Data, but she drew and fired anyway, hoping for the best. But his hands were already on Denin's throat, and her beam had little effect.

But it was enough. Distracted, he let the ambassador drop and came at her. "Not dead?" She upped the level and fired again, knocking him off his stride but only briefly. *Don't make me do this,* she thought.

Just then, Geordi moved in behind Data's back, jabbing his manual shutdown control. Data fell limp and hit the floor, and Deanna clutched her heaving chest.

But her relief was short-lived. A wave of fury poured over her from the Tamarians. "Zinda!" cried an aide who knelt over the gasping ambassador. "His face black! His eyes red!"

Borges rushed forward to try to smooth things over. "Callimas at Bahar. Callimas on bended knee."

"Chenza at court!" the aide cried, silencing her. "Shaka! When the walls fell! Shaka of Utomi! Makova. His army at Utomi! Utomi aflame! Utomi in ruins!"

The Tamarian diplomats stormed out and the guards moved in. Borges called the *Krishna* and requested an immediate beam-out. Once they rematerialized on its transporter pad, Geordi said, "Please tell me that wasn't a declaration of war."

"Not exactly," Borges said. "But it will become one if we don't fix this right away." She looked down at Data's motionless form. "And the only one who can fix it has just gone crazy."

"It's bad," Geordi reported later as he, Deanna, and Borges stood together in the *Krishna*'s engineering lab, where Data lay motionless on a diagnostic slab. "I tried tuning him back to normal again, but it's not taking. All this going back and forth between different mental states has . . . well, it's unmoored him. His neural pathways can no longer remember which state they're supposed to be in." He shook his head. "We should've known this would happen. Forcing him to shift around the way he perceives people, time, his own sense of self . . . he can't figure out how to interpret reality anymore."

"So you're saying he's schizophrenic," Deanna interpreted.

"Something like that. But more basic. His brain doesn't seem to be processing anything normally at the moment. Even simple things like his spatial awareness have gotten erratic. We had to disconnect his motor functions below the neck to keep him from slamming into the walls—or into us." But Data's face was still capable of expression. He looked lost, confused, verging on panic. Geordi studied him sadly. "I can't imagine what he must be going through in there. Maybe it's something like when I first got my VISOR, before I learned to interpret the input—but that was just one of my senses, and at least the way I *thought* was the same. I knew who I was, what I was. From what I can tell, Data's sense of even such a basic thing could be changing from moment to moment."

"Is there anything you can do to fix it?" Deanna asked. "Can you shut him down and purge the program, like when the Iconian virus infected him?"

Geordi shook his head. "It wouldn't work here. The modifications to his emotion chip aren't just a program—they change the way his neural circuits interact on a basic level. We still don't have a very good understanding of how Doctor Soong's chip even works."

He put a hand on her shoulder. "I promise you, Deanna, I won't rest until I fix this. Even if I have to rewire every positronic pathway by hand. But it could be a long time."

"Time we don't have," Borges told him. "We have to fix this before the Tamarians start shooting."

He is lost.

That thought comes to him in those moments when he is able to formulate it, before it drifts away again to be replaced by . . . He does not know what. But sometimes he does. Flashes of familiarity. A jumble of shapes and colors is briefly recognizable as a face, then is meaningless again. It does not change; he does. He loses *face* but remembers *sound,* hears: "Data, can you understand me? Do you know who I am?" For a moment, he knows. *Troi. Troy. Destroy. Was this the face that launched a thousand ships, / And burnt the topless towers of Ilium?* He is lost in the city, fires burning, a great quadrupedal animal looming overhead, but he cannot remember its name. He is Shaka, his mighty walls falling around him, his great ambition to protect his city forevermore proving his greatest failure, for the army is too weakened from building the wall to defend the city within. He hears the sound of the trumpet, and shouts with a great shout, that the wall of Jericho falls down flat. A trombone blows, rising as a bearded figure in red and black moves its slide. Red light flashes, a sliding, rising tone sounding *danger, danger,* as consoles explode around him and a vast blue-green orb looms larger before him . . . *Oh, sh—*

It is gone. He does not even remember it was there. For a time, he is not even aware there is a *he* to be aware. Ten thousand years of history on ten thousand planets unfold within him. He *is* it, is of it, without knowing himself, and yet it is there . . . until it is gone and never was. He remembers there is a universe, senses it, but is not aware of himself as distinct from it. His awareness focuses on a room. He is the room. A body—goldwhite in goldblack—lies in the center. Worried shapes/figures/friends (blueblack, goldblack, glint of metal) hover above him. He is the worriers. "His cognitive destabilization is accelerating," he says. "Isn't there anything we can do?" his other self responds. He shakes his head, metal glinting. He has no eyes. *What are eyes?* Black eyes, wide and deep, gazing down at himself. "Data," he calls to himself. "I need you to focus. Focus on the sound of my voice. Follow it."

He focuses on the sound but loses the words. It is only sound now. He is not inside it any longer, sees the face it comes from. Black eyes, wide and deep. Deep black void. Black, slick, roiling, it strikes out and Tasha dies. Agony! Pain, as he never knew it before, did not know it then. *Then? It is now. There is only now. Or there was.* Now, she lies broken on the sand, a cruel black stain on her face. Now, she lies beside him in the bed, laughing, eyes wide in discovery. Now, Ard'rian kisses him and he does not know/finally knows why. He fires the phaser at the aqueduct. He fires the disruptor at Fajo. He knows hate for the first time. Crosis shows him. *The Borg . . . assimilation . . .* He dissolves into the mass, only this time he is not becoming, he is losing himself, and he fears. *Help me,* some part of him pleads, though the rest of him does not understand it. *Talk to me. Somebody. Give me a voice to follow.*

The voice comes again, but from another place. *"Maybe the key is to stop looking so hard for external causes and solutions . . . learn to manage your own emotional state.*

"If the problem is with your own self-image, then the crucial thing is to make peace with it. If you do that, then nothing from outside can threaten your sense of self.

"Just try to be the best Data you can be."

Data. I am Data. He caught that concept, held on to it. *"Dwelling on external causes for our emotional states can keep us from exercising our own ability to manage them."* Outside was chaos—erratic, unstable. Nothing stayed the same. All he had was himself. *I am Data! Remember that!* It started to drift, but he clung to it. He stopped casting about for input and turned his attention inward. He shut out all the noise, looking deeper, until he found something that was stable, something that endured. *Data.* Who he was, in purest form, independent of anything else. Who he had always been. Who he would always be, no matter what was changed in him.

And it was whole. It was enough.

Liberated, he surrendered himself to it.

"Oh, no."

Geordi's anxiety spiked through Deanna's mind like a phaser hit. "What's wrong?"

"He's shutting down! No, no, no, don't do this to me, Data! Don't you do this, dammit!" He worked desperately at Data's peeled-open skull, trying to get a response from the positronic net within. But its status lights had stopped blinking, and nothing he did made any difference.

Finally he slumped and lay down his tools, his defeat a heavy weight upon her. She asked, "Is he . . ."

"He's in . . . I guess you'd call it a deep coma. There's power, there's a baseline of activity, but there's no response to stimuli. And I can't do anything to change it."

The more accurate term would be a vegetative state, she knew. But that hardly mattered. "Is there any hope?"

He shook his head wearily. "I don't know, Deanna. There's *something* still going on in there, but just barely. If he were human, there'd be a chance he could wake up from the coma on his own. It happens, right?" She nodded. "But with him, there's no precedent. I just don't know."

They sat silently for some moments. Finally she could be silent no more. "Geordi? Would you like to tell me what's making you feel so guilty?"

He winced. "I know you'll tell me it's not my fault. But . . . I can't get over the fact that we were fighting. We'd patched things up enough to work together, but I was still sore at him, and he knew it, and . . ." He ran a hand over his head. "What if I didn't watch him closely enough? What if being mad at him meant I didn't do enough to make sure he'd be safe?"

"I *will* tell you it wasn't your fault. You wouldn't let that happen. But I'll also tell you it's natural for you to wonder that at a time like this. Try to keep that in mind, to recognize that those thoughts are part of the process. If you can step back from them, you can cope with them more effectively."

"Or you could look behind you."

They whirled. Data lay there looking up at them, an impish smile on his face. "And while you are at it, could someone tell me why I am unable to reactivate my motor functions?"

Geordi was beaming. "Data! You're all right!"

"Mentally, yes. But about those motor functions—"

"Of course, I'll get right on it."

They pulled him to a sitting position and Geordi went to work at the back of his neck. "Data, are you yourself again?" Deanna asked.

"Hm. In the sense that my cognitive processes and emotion chip are now restored to baseline mode, the answer is yes. However . . . the definition of 'myself' is still undergoing reappraisal, I think. I am still . . . gathering Data." He smiled, and she raised him a laugh.

"So what happened?" Geordi asked. "How did you . . . reset yourself?"

He answered, but to Deanna. "I have you to thank for that, Counselor. I recalled the advice you gave me about using peace with myself as a foundation for relating peacefully with those around me. My perceptual input was chaotic, so I focused my awareness inward to my baseline cognitive parameters. I was able to use that substrate as a reference point for rebuilding my perceptual model."

Suddenly his body shuddered into mobility again. After briefly testing his range of motion, Data rose. "I seem to recall physically assaulting the Tamarian ambassador. Is this correct?"

"I'm afraid so," she replied.

"Then we must hurry if we are to defuse the situation."

"Data," Geordi said, "I'm not willing to risk retuning you to Tamarian mode again."

"I do not believe that will be necessary, Geordi. I know what to do."

It was an impressive performance. Even while in standard cognitive mode, Data was able to adapt himself to communicate in Tamarian terms—and his strategy showed he had little trouble thinking in their terms either. He reminded them of the myth of Palwin of the Fields, a well-intentioned but naïve monarch who had affronted the gods with his hubris and been stricken by madness. He had inflicted horrors on his people until he was deposed, blinded, and cast out into the fields to wander as a beggar. But without his sight to blind him and his power to fetter him, his madness had brought him sacred insight. His wisdom and humility had inspired his people, and the new faith that arose around his Delphic proclamations had tempered the harshness of the regime that had deposed him, eventually winning the new king to the cause of peace.

Through his presentation, Data redefined his actions to the Tamarians as a reenactment of this myth. Rather than an affront against the proper ritual patterns of the universe, they had simply been the intervention of a different ritual. And since that ritual/myth involved madness, it was only natural that it had intruded when least expected. Like many cultures steeped in myth and mysticism, the Tamarians had great respect for madness, seeing it as a source of divine wisdom. In their view, it would be most unwise not to heed the message that Palwin had unexpectedly sent them through the person of Data. And that message was one of peace.

Moreover, once they understood the experiment and its consequences, they gained a new respect for Data. His willingness to risk himself in the name of communication evoked—and honored—the memory of Dathon's sacrifice at El-Adrel. The parallel even helped the Tamarians identify with the Federation, in the same way that they identified with their ancestors and archetypes through metaphoric parallels. Rather than bringing war, Data's actions had supplied an even stronger foundation for peace.

"And all it took was finding the right metaphor to define it with," Borges told the others once they reconvened in the briefing room. "It's a testament to the power that symbolism has. It can change the way we perceive the world—even without a special chip to retune our brains."

"I am glad you feel that way, Doctor," Data told her. "Because in the wake of recent events, I think it would be unwise to continue the experiment with my emotion chip."

"Now, don't be so quick to say that, Data," she cautioned. "You did find a way to recover your balance all on your own, without any outside intervention. That strongly suggests you'd be able to do it again. And it would be a valuable asset to the Federation. There are other species besides the Tamarians whose alien modes of thought make communication difficult."

"I acknowledge the value of your work, Doctor Borges," he said. "I hope you can continue it. However, I must decline to participate any further." He took in Deanna with his gaze. "For some time, I have believed that my emotion chip would make me more complete. Lately I have attempted to rely on it to make me a better communicator. But when I restored myself to sanity, I did so *despite* the influence of the chip. It was still active, but it did not hold my answers. It required the intellect and discipline I already possessed to enable me to manage it.

"I still value my emotion chip for the insights it can bring me into my friends and colleagues, and for the new experiences it allows me to explore. But I recognize now that I cannot let it define me or control me. With or without an emotion chip, I am still Data. That is what defines me. And I believe my greatest value can come not through seeking to emulate others, but through appreciating my own unique nature."

Borges glared. "You mean being an android is better than being a human or a Tamarian?"

"Only if one is an android to begin with," he said with a gentle smile. "Polonius, when Laertes departed, Doctor."

She blinked. "Remind me."

> "'This above all: to thine own self be true,
> And it must follow, as the night the day,
> Thou canst not then be false to any man.'"

SUICIDE NOTE

Geoff Trowbridge

Historian's note:
This tale is set between the feature films Star Trek: First Contact
and Star Trek: Insurrection, *sometime after the events of*
the sixth-season Star Trek: Deep Space Nine *episode*
"In the Pale Moonlight."

GEOFF TROWBRIDGE

Having spent his childhood in northern Indiana captivated by the episode reruns, movies, and novels of the original *Star Trek* series, Geoff Trowbridge was initially skeptical about *The Next Generation*. In fact, he watched the first two seasons only sporadically while spending his nights playing in a big-hair rock band. But after he settled down with his lovely wife, Heidi, the third season reeled him in. Today, he continues trying to indoctrinate his three children—Trevor, Kayla, and Hannah—into fandom, with marginal success.

Geoff's first project with Pocket Books was helping to collate the Timeline data for *Voyages of Imagination*. Editor Marco Palmieri graciously agreed to consider his manuscript for "Suicide Note," despite Geoff having already submitted it to *Strange New Worlds 10*. Even Geoff's most optimistic expectations were surpassed when both editors simultaneously offered to buy it.

When he isn't writing or working as the Computer Network Manager for the Elkhart Public Library, you'll often find Geoff researching the family genealogy, managing his fantasy football league, scorekeeping at the local Little League, or engaging the local conservatives in spirited debates about politics, religion, and the Great Pumpkin. His latest antics are usually chronicled at http://troll-bridge.livejournal.com.

THE YOUNG GIRL HANDLED THE GARDEN TROWEL WITH THE same delicate artistry of a painter taking a brush to canvas. Holding the flower in place, she swept the soil around it, causing the dirt to cascade into the small divot slowly and evenly, until the bright pink blossom was firmly set into its new home. A warm breeze blew the girl's dark hair into her face, and she reached up to push it back, leaving a dirty smudge upon the tapered point of her ear.

She stood facing the raised stone flowerbeds like a lone sentry guarding a barricade. Yet despite her harsh demeanor, it was with warm gentleness that she padded the soil surrounding the new addition, just the way her father had taught her all those years ago.

Her clearest recollections of her father were of the two of them working in the garden; not this garden but the one at the old house—the home where they had once known happiness as a family. She was only three years old when he was lost to them, so she couldn't always be certain about the accuracy of her memories, but she had no doubts about her father's strong stature and his commanding presence—things that weren't always obvious in the few holo-images that they had retained.

Then one day he was gone.

"The colors of the garden are like a mirror unto our world, Tiaru," her father had told her prior to his departure. "Even our entire galaxy. And every hue must co-exist for the mosaic to be complete." Her friends never understood what he had meant, but she believed she did.

But something had gone wrong, and her father had died. And just days later, the men with their grim-looking uniforms and their cold, unfriendly stares started to come to the house. Her mother would always get upset when they showed up; fraught with anxiety, she would tell Tiaru to stay out of sight and say nothing. But they would always just ask a lot of questions, and then they would leave. Eventually she and her mother moved to their current house—to "get away," her mother had said, but the men kept visiting. And her mother remained afraid. And always sad.

Taking a step back, Tiaru looked over the garden as it sprawled out before her, evaluating the new flower's small contribution, and her dour expression softened into a smile of satisfaction. Lost within her thoughts, she was oblivious to the footsteps of the man approaching her.

"Excuse me."

Startled, Tiaru whirled to face him, instinctively brandishing the small shovel as a weapon. But upon seeing the uniformed Starfleet officer, she relaxed slightly and cocked her head, her brow furrowed with both puzzlement and curiosity. "You're a Terran, aren't you?" she asked.

"That's right," the man replied with a gentle and disarming smile, apparently not alarmed by her aggressive stance. "My name is Jean-Luc. I am a starship captain for the Federation."

Tiaru straightened her head and dropped her arms to her sides but maintained her quizzical stare. She had seen images of aliens before, but never had she met one in person. The man seemed striking in an exotic sort of way, with his smooth brow, small ears . . . and weren't Terrans supposed to have hair? "I am Tiaru," she offered. "This is where I live." She pointed along a path of finely hewn cobblestones that invitingly led the way through the colorful gardens to the front door of her home. "Why have you come to Romulus?"

For a moment the man seemed to hesitate, as if her question had caught him off guard. Or perhaps he simply wasn't used to questions from young children. But then he regained his confident air and kneeled down to look her directly in the eyes. "Well, Tiaru," he replied, "you may have heard that a power known as the Dominion has invaded both our quadrants of the galaxy. The Federation and your leaders have joined together, to help drive them back and to keep you safe. My ship was sent to bring a Starfleet admiral to Romulus today. Right now he is meeting with the admirals of your own armies."

Tiaru's eyes widened and her heart jumped with enthusiasm at the mention of the admiralty. "My father was an admiral!" she proudly exclaimed.

"Yes, I know," Jean-Luc replied. "In fact, I once met your father, and I found him to be a man of high principles." He paused, as if choosing his next words carefully. "As it so happens, he is the reason I've decided to stop by your home this morning. I don't suppose your mother is here?"

Tiaru couldn't believe what she was hearing. Not wanting to look ridiculous in front of the Starfleet captain, she struggled to keep her enthusiasm under control. "Of course," she replied as calmly as possible. "Follow me and I'll show you in."

The captain stood up and began to follow Tiaru along the walkway.

A thousand thoughts buzzed through her mind, but she hardly knew where to begin. She had heard about the war. Her classmates clearly believed it was all the Federation's fault; that they had kicked into a *tesrat*'s nest, and now the Romulans had to rush in to save the foolish aliens from being stung to death. But this man did not appear to be a fool. And he had known her father. That had to count for something.

"Have you been to Romulus before?" she called back to him as he lagged a few paces behind her.

"Yes I have," Jean-Luc replied, "but never before did I have the luxury of appreciating its beauty. In fact, your flower gardens are among the loveliest I've seen."

Tiaru's chest swelled with pride. Indeed, this Terran was no fool.

On the heels of the spirited Romulan child, Captain Jean-Luc Picard shielded his eyes from the bright Romulan sun as its rays pierced the rooftop of the house standing before him. Like many homes in the rural outskirts of the capital city, the edifice was not particularly large, the construction was traditional brick and mortar, and the colors were mostly drab shades of gray; nonetheless the architecture possessed a grandiose quality, with tall spires reaching toward the sky and ornate trim embellishing the framework.

The captain inhaled deeply, enjoying the curious fragrances of an unfamiliar world. The oxygen-rich atmosphere had actually made his brisk walk from the public transport station an invigorating experience.

Of course, the inconvenient detour was made necessary only because the local magistrates had refused to allow transport into a residential area. Despite the tenuous alliance, the Romulans' insular nature remained very much in evidence. Current allegiances notwithstanding, Picard knew these were the same people who had recently attempted to conquer Vulcan; the same people who had threatened to destroy the *Enterprise* countless times . . .

Tiaru had reached the end of the path and began to bound up the short steps at the front door of her house.

Picard stopped at the base of the steps, unexpectedly gripped by apprehension. He had faced countless touchy situations throughout his years as a Starfleet captain, but never could he recall a circumstance quite so unfamiliar, or a feeling of such awkward uncertainty.

He had precious little time to come to terms with these fears as the door suddenly slid open, and a middle-aged Romulan woman with a careworn face appeared. Tiaru finished scaling the steps and stood by the woman's side. "Mother, we have a guest!" she said excitedly.

The woman looked down upon the captain, her jaw firmly locked in place. "Yes?" she finally said.

"Ai'lara Jarok?" Picard asked. After waiting for her nod of confirmation, he continued. "Good morning to you. I am Captain Jean-Luc Picard of the United Federation of Planets."

"I know who you are," Ai'lara said. "The consulate informed me of your arrival a few moments ago." She looked down at her inquisitive child. "Tiaru, please attend to your studies in your room."

The girl opened her mouth to protest, but a stern look from the woman caused her to reconsider. Her shoulders drooped with disappointment. "Yes, Mother," she said. Obligingly, she turned and retreated into the interior of the home.

"My daughter," Ai'lara explained. "She is precocious and often far too curious for her own good."

"She is a charming little girl," Picard said with complete honesty. Nonetheless, he was grateful for Ai'lara's discretion. His errand was likely to be difficult enough on the mother, let alone its potential impact on the child.

A beat passed while the two of them regarded each other in silence, until the captain was unable to delay his mission any longer.

"Lady Ai'lara," Picard said, feeling as though each word was another cautious step through a minefield. "I was with your husband, Admiral Alidar Jarok, in the days leading up to his death eight years ago."

Ai'lara said nothing but continued to stare at him without expression. Picard felt loath to continue, believing that the woman might ask him to leave.

"Come in," Ai'lara finally spoke, turning into the house. Relieved, Picard climbed the steps and followed her through the entrance.

Almost immediately he noted a pleasant grassy aroma that seemed to emanate from a doorway at the far end of the main corridor. As they walked down the hall toward it, Picard briefly noted the adjoining rooms—a comfortable living area on the left and a practical study on the right. While both appeared clean and accommodating, they were austere and sparsely decorated, in marked contrast to the home's exterior.

Ai'lara glanced back over her shoulder. "Can I get you something? I've just made some *hvetollh*."

Picard searched his memory for names of Romulan cuisine but without success. Based upon his prior experiences, he desperately hoped that she wasn't offering him soup.

Ai'lara noted Picard's puzzlement. "Oh, my apologies. *Hvetollh* is . . . a beverage, prepared by filtering hot water through the dried leaves of an *rreinnte* tree."

Picard smiled. "That sounds wonderful," he said.

Picard sipped his Romulan tea and savored its spicy, nutty flavor, while across the small table with her own cup, Ai'lara watched him intently. The captain's gaze casually wandered about the large room that served as both a kitchen and dining area. The shelves jutting out from the pale yellow walls contained boxes of what he assumed to be typical Romulan staples as well as stacks of dishes and tableware. On the counter, most of the appliances were recognizable; food preparation was essentially the same no matter which side of the Neutral Zone you were on. But like the rest of the home, the room appeared rather modest—functional but not extravagant.

Setting down his cup, Picard decided to break the silence. "Forgive me," he began, "but I don't know if you're privy to the circumstances surrounding your husband's defection to the Federation."

"I learned enough," the woman replied with a slight hint of disgust. "The Tal Shiar made sure of that when they debriefed me afterward." She paused momentarily, as her mention of the Romulan intelligence service clearly evoked a sense of dread. "My husband was suffering under a delusion that our military was planning to start a war with your Federation. He fled Romulan space and encountered your ship, and somehow convinced you to indulge his fantasy. And after he was proved wrong, his life ended while still in your custody."

Picard exhaled deeply and hastened to clarify the events surrounding the death of the Romulan defector. "Ma'am, you must believe me. We did not hold your husband accountable for the incident at Nelvana III or seek any punitive action against him. He took his own life with a felodesine chip, and we were powerless to revive him . . ."

Ai'lara softly let out a chortle. "Don't worry, Captain," she said with a dismissive wave of her hand. "I don't hold you responsible for his death. Alidar was simply a coward. Your involvement was unfortunate happenstance—"

"Pardon me," Picard said, "but with respect, I cannot begin to imagine the sense of loss he must have felt, believing that he was forever separated from his family and his home. Under the circumstances, it wasn't an act of cowardice that he chose to end his suffering."

Ai'lara blinked at him. "You misunderstand, Captain. Ending his life was not the cowardly act. Suicide was the most honorable means of atonement for his disloyalty."

With his cup at his lips, Picard frowned, beginning to appreciate the true breadth of the cultural gulf that separated him from his host.

"Alidar's weakness was his irrational and unrealistic pursuit of pacifism," Ai'lara continued. "You know the dangers we face in this galaxy, Captain. It was only a matter of time before he ensured his own downfall." She sighed and grew more contemplative as she sipped her own tea. "It is true that I loved my husband. Not long ago he was a powerful leader, yet gentle and kind to those he held dear. But at the end, his misguided idealist philosophy was a threat to the entire Romulan Empire."

Picard shifted uncomfortably in his seat, wondering if this personal visit had not been a huge mistake. "Of course," he said, "I understand that Alidar's ideas may have seemed outlandish. But he was unfairly misled into believing that a true threat to galactic peace was at hand. And his bravery—"

"Please, Captain," Ai'lara interrupted. "You can't possibly understand what we have endured due to his 'outlandish ideas.' Simply put, we are the family of a traitor. Do you realize, Captain, that most families of dissidents tend to disappear quietly? Dozens of times we were visited by a high-ranking agent of the Tal Shiar, always so polite, always asking cloyingly pleasant questions . . . always leaving us terrified that this visit would be the last before they hauled us away as coconspirators.

"For whatever reason, they've allowed us to live, but the rest of our lives will be spent under a cloud of constant suspicion. We had no choice but to sell our home on the seafront, release our servants, and move to a district where at least my daughter no longer suffers the insults from her peers."

She stared down into her cup, looking as if the conversation were draining all the strength from her. "We left everything from our former life . . . except for some sprouts to regrow the plants that surround our front walkway. Alidar always loved those plants . . ." As her voice trailed off, for a long moment her mind appeared to be in another place, at a simpler time. Finally she looked up, her lips pressed into a tight smile. "Truly, Captain, this is a pointless discussion, so let us dispense with the pleasantries. Why are you here?"

Though humbled by the brusqueness of her question, Picard was grateful for the opportunity simply to fulfill his obligation and put this debacle behind him. He reached into his jacket and retrieved a small padd. "Your husband left a message to you and your daughter," he explained, setting it on the table between them. "Due to obvious circumstances, we were unable to deliver it properly until now."

Ai'lara regarded the small device with obvious disdain. "A suicide note?" she said with cold detachment.

"I suppose it is," Picard said.

Tiaru stepped through the doorway at the far end of the dining area. "A message from Father?" she asked, ignoring her mother's icy stare. "What does it say?"

"I don't know," Picard replied. "It seems to be biometrically encoded so that only your mother can unlock it, and he left instructions to deliver it in strict confidentiality. But even so, I never felt that it was my place to view it."

The girl approached them, her eyes focused upon the curious gadget. Slipping into the open chair at the end of the table, she reached out for it.

"Tiaru!" her mother chastised her. "You don't know how to operate it. Leave it alone."

Tiaru retracted her arms but appeared unfazed by her mother's reproach. She looked up at Picard. "Captain, sir?" she said. "Do you believe my father betrayed the empire?"

Picard froze. In his mind, he heard the voice of Admiral Jarok in the captain's ready room eight years earlier: *She will grow up believing her father was a traitor.* How was he to answer? The question was difficult enough without having to gain the understanding of a child.

Thankfully, Ai'lara intervened. "That is enough," she said sternly. "Return to your room at once."

"I'm sorry, Mother, but I cannot," the girl boldly replied. "I must hear the captain's answer."

Inwardly, Picard winced at the girl's dogged persistence. Outwardly, he folded his hands and tilted his head toward her. "Tiaru," he said, hoping not to sound patronizing. "Your father was faced with a very difficult decision. But in the end, I believe he did what he felt in his heart was the right thing."

"Wonderful," Ai'lara said, rolling her eyes. "An answer grounded in safe human moral relativism."

The hint of a scowl creased Picard's brow. "Do you believe humans are immoral?"

"The need for a stable and honorable society *dictates* morality!" Ai'lara said, raising her voice. "Your human culture promotes anarchy over security. Do you honestly believe that an empire can survive if every leader is free to follow his own fallible conscience?"

Picard tilted up his chin ever so slightly. "Perhaps it is the strength of our 'human' conscience that enables us to survive."

Ai'lara lifted her cup and rose from the table. "Well then . . . I trust Alidar was right at home aboard your ship." She walked back toward the replicator.

"On the contrary," Picard said. "His own home was nearly all he would speak of."

Ai'lara tossed the cup into the recycling unit with a loud crash and remained there, with her back turned toward her guest. "He should have thought of that before he left us."

Picard thought he could detect the faintest crack in her voice. Hoping to defuse a volatile situation, he softened his tone. "Obviously this is not just about your husband's loyalties to the empire," he said gently. "You've been abandoned—left alone to raise a daughter."

His words seemed to pierce her chest as she momentarily stiffened, then slumped forward. She glanced over at Tiaru, still seated and watching the exchange with wide-eyed fascination, and the anger in the woman's eyes dissolved into mere melancholy. "My daughter," she said. "She is the end of a tainted family line. No man will take a wife whose honor has been shattered."

"I don't need a mate," the girl stated confidently.

"One day you will wish to begin a family," her mother insisted, returning to the table to stand beside her daughter. "But we are without *mnhei'sahe*—we have no honor."

"You don't know my wishes!" the girl nearly shouted. "We don't ever talk about them. We never speak of any of this! He was my father . . . and you won't tell me anything about him."

Ai'lara opened her mouth to respond, but no sound came forth. Her face no longer conveyed any emotion but pain.

"I know about honor," Tiaru continued. "The youth institute taught us that if you remain true to yourself, no one can take your honor from you!"

"Oh, Tiaru . . . ," Ai'lara whispered. She reached out and ran her fingers through her daughter's hair.

Now distinctly uncomfortable, Picard cleared his throat. "I believe I should let myself out."

"No," Ai'lara said with sudden assertiveness. "You must tell me why."

"I beg your pardon?" Picard replied.

She reached for the padd on the table. "Why he would force us to relive his greatest failure!" Her hands shook as she picked it up, and for a moment Picard wondered if she might simply hurl it across the room.

"Lady Ai'lara," Picard spoke calmly, looking directly into her eyes. "It seems clear that the scars you've suffered have not entirely healed. Perhaps your husband knew this was the only way to bring you a sense of closure."

Ai'lara stared back at him. She said nothing but slowly regained her composure. Her breathing steadied as she absently ran her finger along the edge of the padd's display. Then, with a click of her tongue, she gently set down the device, seated herself, and keyed it to begin playback.

The small screen flickered to life and the image of Alidar Jarok appeared upon it. Picard leaned forward to catch a glimpse of the admiral's face, triggering his memory—recollections of the confrontation in the Neutral Zone, of the manner in which Jarok had been deceived, and of the last phrase Picard had heard uttered from Jarok's lips: *I did it for nothing.*

But surprisingly, within the solitude of his final moments in his cabin aboard the *Enterprise,* the admiral had apparently found cause to reconsider. On the screen was not a man in the throes of despair, bereft of any remaining purpose in life. Instead, upon Jarok's visage was the same grim determination the man had displayed while imploring the *Enterprise* crew to act upon his information, seemingly unaffected by the knowledge that his efforts had been in vain.

His message began.

"To my beloved wife and daughter,
    "I cannot know under what circumstances this message will reach you. If it is the result of formalized relations be-

tween our people and the Federation, then one of my many dreams will have been realized. In any event, I know that you will face a future filled with both trepidation and optimism, with new enemies and new allies. And as that future unfolds, my actions, for better or for worse, will be viewed through the lens of history either as the recklessness of a foolhardy romantic or as the genius of a progressive visionary. I regret that I will not survive to know which is my legacy.

"To my beautiful Tiaru . . . I still remember, like it was yesterday, holding a tiny babe in my arms, at dusk beneath the glow of Remus, and swearing to protect you from any harm. And I have kept my oath to the best of my ability. Knowing that I shall not see you again is a burden that I cannot bear. But I know that you will grow to be noble and strong. It is in your blood.

"I don't know if you will ever understand the reasons why I had to leave you, or the motives of the men whose lies drove me to do so. But if nothing else, you and your generation must understand the awesome and dangerous power of fear.

"It is fear that sows the distrust between our worlds and those of the Federation. It was fear that culminated in the bloodshed at Cheron during our war with Earth, long before you were born. It was fear that prompted our own leaders to use deception to divide my loyalties between conscience and empire. And it is fear that will destroy our people if your generation fails to overcome it.

"As fear drives our hatred and the building of our war machine, we consume the resources that could feed and clothe our people, we misuse the wisdom of our scientists and the labors of our industries, and we extinguish the light from our dreams of the future. There is no strength in fear. Strength arises from the courage to cast off fear's oppressive chains and gives you the power to build a safer, more secure galaxy using instruments of peace."

Jarok paused for a moment and raised a cup of water to his lips. Picard marveled at the stoicism of the man who was basically writing his epitaph as he prepared to end his own life. The admiral's wife and daughter sat silently staring at the screen, their faces revealing no emotion. Jarok continued.

"My dearest wife,

"You must think me a coward . . . at the very least, a deserter of our family; at worst, a traitor to our people. I am both, and yet I am neither. My loyalty to our house and to Romulus has always been unimpeachable. But my responsibility to safeguard our civilization from those who would destroy it out of senseless pride transcends any duty to an institution or to an individual. My honor is intact.

"I know the means whereby the Praetorate achieves their ends. They will manufacture further 'evidence' of enemy aggression to promote the imperialist doctrine. They will force out other men of character and fortitude who believe as I do. And in the end, they will collapse under the weight of their own deceptions and paranoia, and bring all of the empire down with them."

Again he paused and for a moment seemed unsure if he should continue. Then his voice lowered and took on a deadly serious tone.

"Rest assured that I am not alone in my endeavors. About a year ago, our intelligence teams began to collate data from our most distant listening posts, and they have determined that a race of powerful cyborg creatures in the Delta Quadrant are moving this way, destroying and assimilating everything in their path, representing the greatest single threat we have yet faced in our galaxy. Yet the Continuing Committee refuses to resolve petty differences with those who should be our allies in an ultimate battle for galactic survival.

"Therefore, a number of us who are like-minded have networked together, prepared to share information with other powers in the region, should it become necessary for survival in this or any other catastrophic scenario. My contact is a good man—a general of the Tal Shiar by the name

of Koval, and he has pledged to discreetly look after you
and Tiaru in my absence."

Ai'lara gasped, her eyes wide open with shock, suggesting that
the name was quite familiar to her.

"My love . . . Since you have received this message, I
trust that you are in contact with someone from the Federa-
tion. I am attaching data regarding encrypted frequencies
that Starfleet may use to contact Koval. I cannot offer this
to Captain Picard now—I fear that I have lost his trust and
confidence. So for the sake of our people, I implore you to
see this information safely delivered to those across the
borders who can best help us."

Observing the data on the screen, Picard committed the frequencies and decryption codes to memory as Ai'lara sat nearby, still
stunned, her mouth slightly open. "Koval," she whispered to herself. "All this time, he was protecting us . . ."
Her late husband continued:

"For my part, I've done what I can to ensure that our
safety continues to be protected. I was deceived, yes . . .
but I believe my defection may nonetheless be a first step
to a better understanding between our peoples. But it is not
my place to see it through. I am neither an emissary nor a
diplomat. I am a relic who has denied his own future, and
therefore my life must end here."

Jarok closed his eyes and took a deep breath, evincing a sense of
peace with his fate.

"My love for both of you runs deeper than the Apnex
Sea. Perhaps not this day, but one day, you will understand
the depth of my sacrifice and my resolve to secure your fu-
ture and that of our grandchildren. And perhaps then, I will
have your forgiveness. Do not forget, and do not capitulate
to those who sow fear and reap despair. The power of hope
is yours now. Good-bye."

The screen slowly faded to black, and a suffocating silence filled the room. For the first time, Picard noticed the whisper of a breeze blowing through an open window and the tick of an archaic time-keeping device on the wall. He did not wish to interrupt the still-ness, but words somehow escaped his lips. "He held strong to his convictions," he murmured, "even after losing everything he held dear. What an amazing man."

Tiaru quietly sucked in her breath and blinked rapidly, shed-ding the moisture that had welled up in the corners of her eyes. Ai'lara sat motionless, continuing to focus upon the padd's dark-ened display.

Picard sat with his head slightly bowed for what seemed like hours, until he felt sure that his presence was no longer appropri-ate. Slowly, he set down his cup, pushed his chair from the table, and stood, displaying all the poise he could muster. "I am very sorry for your loss," he said, and with that, he turned and marched resolutely toward the door.

"Captain," Ai'lara said, prompting him to stop at the doorway and turn around. "Until today, I had forgotten what I had lost. Thank you."

"*Jolan'tru*," Picard said with a nod. Then he exited the home and the door closed behind him.

He stood there on the doorstep for several minutes as the afterim-age of Jarok's resolute countenance continued to haunt him, grap-pling with the unexpected shock of receiving fortuitous and possibly invaluable information from a man long deceased, speak-ing all but from another era.

Eight years earlier, this man died aboard his ship while attempt-ing to bring information to the Federation. Now the man's last wish was known: to bring another pragmatic government official—a man already leading a duplicitous existence—under the shadowy and dangerous cloak of espionage.

But in the intervening years, fate had brought about a most improbable alliance as the two galactic powers shared the fight against a seemingly implacable enemy. And as allies, the two gov-ernments could not simply rely upon secret government opera-tives for intelligence sharing; their exposure could undermine everything they had gained, and lives could be lost for lack of trust. The captain was not about to allow additional blood to stain his hands.

He surveyed the landscape spread out before him. The sun was now higher in the sky, blanketing the landscape with comforting warmth. Along the horizon, the towers of the nearby city punctuated the skyline, and the splendor of the distant mountain ranges provided a powerful, majestic backdrop. Down the street at the end of the walkway, Picard observed the bustle of people moving about their daily tasks, oblivious to the drums of war beating in distant star systems. From somewhere nearby, he heard the joyful sounds of children playing.

As Picard meandered back down the path, flanked by the flowerbeds that teemed with exotic plantlife, his fleeting serenity was pierced by the chirp of his combadge.

"Riker to Picard."

Picard tapped the insignia on his chest. "Go ahead, Number One."

"Sir, Admiral Dougherty has reported in. He's finished his meeting at Galae Command, and he'll be beaming aboard in about ten minutes."

"Acknowledged. Any word from the admiral on the progress of the talks?"

The pause on the other end of the transmission lasted mere seconds yet spoke volumes with distressing clarity. *"Well, sir,"* Riker responded, *"he's not particularly pleased. It seems at this point the Romulans are unwilling to share enough useful intelligence to effectively coordinate our initial campaigns against the Dominion."*

The captain made no attempt to hide the disappointment in his voice. "That's unfortunate, Will. Inform the admiral that I'm on my way to the station now . . ." Feeling a slight tug on his arm, he stopped and gently removed one of the plants' long tendrils that had snagged upon the fabric of his uniform.

Picard stroked the rough filaments on the tip of the appendage as his eyes drifted over the strangely alien and radically variant species of flora he had passed along the path, all peacefully coexisting in a soothing panorama. Golden, crimson, and violet flowers burst out from a mass of tentaclelike green sprouts—some long and spindly, others bloated and bedraggled, and all seemingly reaching out to him.

Eventually his gaze had retraced his steps back to the house, where behind the large oval-shaped front window, enveloped in a translucent glare from the sun's reflected rays, stood the lone figure of Tiaru.

She had regained her composure, her greenish bloodshot eyes fixated upon him, providing a lens into a wisdom that belied her age. And within those eyes, Picard could plainly see the very hope that he himself so desperately sought.

"Anything else, Captain?"

Yes . . . His duty was clear, as was his obligation to spread the seeds that Jarok had sown. Perhaps in time, they would blossom into a peaceful future for both the Federation and the Romulan Empire. And perhaps in peace, they would one day discover the level of trust that Jarok had known.

"Number One . . . What information do we have on a Romulan government official by the name of Koval?"

"Stand by . . . Koval . . . Seems that he was just promoted to vice chairman of the Tal Shiar, the position formerly held by Senator Vreenak."

"Arrange a meeting with the admiral once we're both back aboard. I have some information he may find useful."

"Aye, Captain."

"Picard out."

A smile and a nod toward the young girl at the window sealed his unspoken covenant with her. Picard released the tendril, then turned and walked on.

FOUR LIGHTS

Keith R.A. DeCandido

Historian's note:
This tale is set between events of the feature films
Star Trek: Insurrection *and* Star Trek Nemesis,
several weeks prior to the seventh-season
Star Trek: Deep Space Nine *episode*
"Field of Fire."

KEITH R.A. DeCANDIDO

"Four Lights" is one of three contributions Keith R.A. DeCandido is making to the celebration of the twentieth anniversary of *Star Trek: The Next Generation*. The other two are the novel *Q&A*, which the author describes as the ultimate Q story, one of the novels that carries the *Enterprise*-E's story forward after the feature film *Star Trek Nemesis;* and the eBook *Enterprises of Great Pitch and Moment*, the final installment of the six-eBook miniseries *Slings and Arrows*, which chronicles the first year of the *Enterprise*-E's existence leading up to the film *Star Trek: First Contact,* due in spring 2008. Through the end of 2007, Keith has written thirteen novels, one novella, six short stories, ten eBooks, and one comic book miniseries in the *Star Trek* universe, with much more on the way, starting with the *Klingon Empire* novel *A Burning House* in early 2008. He's also written in the worlds of the TV shows *Buffy the Vampire Slayer, Doctor Who, Supernatural, Xena, Young Hercules, Farscape,* and *Gene Roddenberry's Andromeda,* the games *World of Warcraft, Resident Evil, Command and Conquer,* and *StarCraft,* and his own universe, seen in the 2004 novel *Dragon Precinct* and several short stories. Keith is also the editor in charge of the monthly *Star Trek* eBook line and has edited dozens of anthologies, among them *Star Trek: Tales of the Dominion War, Star Trek: Tales from the Captain's Table,* and the forthcoming *Doctor Who: Short Trips: The Quality of Leadership.* Find out less at Keith's Web site at www.DeCandido.net, read his inane ramblings at kradical.livejournal.com, or just e-mail him your raspberries directly at keith@decandido.net.

I WATCHED THE *GRISSOM* DIE.

I never used to anthropomorphize starships that way. I used to find the human tendency to give vessels a personality to be suspect, and possibly dangerous. I've lost two commands—the *Stargazer* at Maxia Zeta and the *Enterprise*-D at Veridian III—and I weathered those ships' losses primarily because I viewed them solely as objects.

Since the commencement of the Dominion War over a year ago, however, I'd seen so many ships destroyed, seen so many proud Starfleet vessels reduced to debris or less. You would think that multiple exposure to such would have inured me, made me view them even more as things than living creatures, but I found that I felt the loss of the ships more keenly than ever before.

Perhaps it was by way of avoiding feeling the loss of sentient life. The *Grissom*'s crew complement was one thousand two hundred and fifty. Easier to lament the loss of a single ship than over a thousand lives.

And perhaps that feeling was due to helplessness. The *Grissom* was one of ten allied ships at Ricktor Prime—six Starfleet ships, including my own *Enterprise*-E, and four Klingon Defense Force vessels—against four Jem'Hadar attack ships and two Cardassian

Galor-class cruisers. Numerically, the odds would be in our favor, but the Jem'Hadar did not require numbers to have an advantage. Both sides lost one ship each at the start of the battle: one of the *Galor*s and the *U.S.S. Winchester* destroyed each other.

We were likewise unable to save the *Grissom*, which now hung dead in space, as we were too busy coming to the aid of the *U.S.S. Christopher*. My chair vibrated beneath me as the *Enterprise* took fire from the remaining *Galor,* the *Elokar,* which was trying to send the *Christopher* to the same fate as the *Grissom*.

Will Riker, my first officer, was directing the battle. To our tactical officer, Lieutenant Daniels, he said, "Full torpedo spread to their engines on my mark."

"Aye, sir."

"Ensign Perim," he said to the conn officer, "change course to 197 mark 5, but at full impulse." After a second, "Mark!"

I nodded my approval of Will's plan. The *Enterprise* had been at one-eighth impulse, and the sudden burst of speed would catch the Cardassians off guard. It also gave Daniels only a slim window of opportunity to fire on the *Elokar.* Of the spread of six quantum torpedoes, two missed their mark. However, the other four struck, the detonations flowering across the Cardassian cruiser.

From the operations station, Data reported calmly, "The *Elokar* has suffered catastrophic engine damage. Their warp core will breach in seven minutes."

Will got up from his seat to my right and walked around to the tactical station behind him. Standing next to Daniels, he said, "Ready tractor beam—as soon as the Cardassians eject the core, lock onto it and send it right at the Jem'Hadar."

I added, "Mister Data, alert the other vessels—particularly the Klingons—of that tactic."

Data nodded and said, again calmly, "Aye, sir." Not for the first time, I envied him his ability to switch his emotions off at will.

Data continued: "*U.S.S. Vaklar* and *I.K.S. Kortir* closing in on third Jem'Hadar vessel. *I.K.S. Worvig* and *U.S.S. T'Mala* engaging second Jem'Hadar vessel. *I.K.S. Ya'Vang* taking heavy damage from fourth Jem'Hadar vessel."

"The Cardassians have ejected the core," Daniels said from behind me. "Engaging tractor beam."

"First Jem'Hadar vessel coming about," Data said. That was the one that destroyed the *Grissom*.

"Do it, Mr. Daniels," Will said.

"Aye, sir."

The blue tractor beam engulfed the *Elokar*'s critical warp core and redirected it toward the *Grissom*'s murderer.

It would seem I was indeed anthropomorphizing.

Even as the *Elokar*'s warp core destroyed one Jem'Hadar ship, two others were taking considerable damage from the four allied vessels.

But then they changed course.

I felt the blood drain from my face. I rose to my feet and said, "Data, warn them, they're about to—"

But it was too late.

The Jem'Hadar introduced themselves to the Alpha Quadrant five years ago in a suicide run against the *U.S.S. Odyssey*, a sister ship to the *Enterprise*-D. These two Dominion attack ships did likewise, taking out three of their enemy at the same time. Only the *T'Mala* recognized the tactic as I did and veered away in time, though they took on considerable hull damage from the explosion.

After a moment of quiet on the bridge, Data spoke. "The *Ya'Vang*'s impulse engines are off-line and their warp drive has engaged emergency shutdown. They are—"

My second officer cut off his report when the final Jem'Hadar ship went to warp.

"Ensign, heading?" I asked Perim.

"Their heading is 111 mark 19—back to Dominion territory."

Will came back around to the center of the bridge to stand next to me. "Do we pursue?"

I hesitated. It was tempting to hunt them down, but nothing would be gained. The Dominion's attempt to take Ricktor Prime had failed. Our enemy would gain no new intelligence from this endeavor—all the ships involved were surely already known to the Dominion, and no particularly inventive tactics were used—so we had nothing to lose by allowing one ship full of Jem'Hadar to escape.

Besides, even if we did pursue them and destroy them, the Dominion would simply make more.

Staring at the screen, I saw only death. The debris clouds of vaporized vessels, the dimmed lights of the ships that were damaged. The only real survivor was the planet below: Ricktor Prime, the Zaldan colony we were trying to protect.

Daniels said, "Incoming hail from the *T'Mala,* sir—it's Captain Dell'Orso."

I nodded and sat back down in my chair; Will did likewise next to me. "On screen, Lieutenant."

The scene of death was replaced by the haggard image of Kirsten Dell'Orso. *"Looks like we're the last ones standing, Captain Picard."*

"Indeed. Do you require any assistance?"

Batting a lock of dark hair out of her sweat-streaked face, Dell'Orso said, *"We're fine, but we're also picking up three escape pods near the debris of the* Grissom."

"Confirmed," Data said. "Reading six life signs."

"My chief engineer's having a fit as it is. I'd rather not add maneuvering in that mess to her worries."

"Of course. We'll take care of it, Captain."

To the conn, Will said, "Ensign Perim, set a course for those pods. Lieutenant Daniels, ready tractor beam."

"Speaking of tractor beams," Dell'Orso said, *"that was a nice trick you pulled with the* Elokar's *warp core."* She let out a breath, puffing her cheeks. *"I'm really glad you guys were assigned to this detail. Without you, the Zaldans'd be brushing up on the Vorta's language by now. Thanks to you, we won."*

I thought about six people who were the only survivors of a ship of twelve hundred, and five other ships that didn't have as many as six survivors, and I shook my head.

"This does not feel like victory."

The day after what was already being referred to as the Battle of Ricktor Prime, I stood outside Deanna's office, feeling a fool.

The bridge of the *Enterprise* had not felt right of late. That was due in part to two who were missing. One was Worf, now serving on Deep Space 9. Still, Padraig Daniels had been serving more than adequately at tactical since the *Enterprise*-E's earliest days.

However, it was the other person missing who concerned me at present: Counselor Deanna Troi. She still served on the *Enterprise,* of course, but she spent comparatively little time by my side on the bridge. Instead, her presence was required most often either in her office or in sickbay with Doctor Crusher, tending to those who needed her aid.

The doors parted, and Ensign Lobato, one of Commander La Forge's engineers, came out. She nodded, said, "Captain," and continued down the corridor.

Deanna was sitting in her chair, reading a padd. She didn't look up when the doors closed behind me, as she probably thought they were closing on Lobato. But then she looked up, her face brightening. "Captain! I wasn't expecting you."

I gamely attempted a smile of my own. "I would have thought you'd have sensed me coming."

She set the padd down. "Lately, I've taken to putting up mental barriers. The emotions of the crew are very strong under these circumstances, and . . ." She trailed off, but I understood.

Indicating her patients' chair, I asked, "May I?"

"Is this a session?"

I hesitated. "Perhaps an informal one. I suppose—" Another hesitation. "I suppose I have grown accustomed to having you by my side."

"You know my door is always open to you, Captain. What's troubling you?"

"Is it that obvious?"

She smirked. "Perhaps not to the crew, but I know you a bit better."

Nodding, I said, "I've been thinking back over yesterday's battle. When hostilities with the Dominion started to flare up, I was, naturally, concerned that war would be the eventual result—particularly once Cardassia joined the Dominion. I promised myself that I would never get so . . . so jaded that I would take pleasure in the taking of another life. It was easy at first—we very rarely were sent to the front lines, after all. Starfleet preferred to hold us in reserve, use us for more diplomatic assignments. But now . . ."

Deanna hardly needed me to finish the sentence. She'd been on board for all our missions, from the relatively sedate mission to Evora to the liberation of her homeworld of Betazed. "Now you find you haven't been able to fulfill that promise."

"No," I said in a whisper. "When Lieutenant Daniels used the

Cardassian warp core to destroy the Jem'Hadar ship, I was *glad*. I was almost immediately ashamed, but at the moment of impact, I felt joy at the deaths of the Jem'Hadar who destroyed the *Grissom*. I knew her captain," I added, realizing that I was anthropomorphizing again. "She was a fine officer, an excellent leader. And after I saw her ship pulverized, I wanted nothing more than the same fate meted out to those responsible."

Deanna leaned toward me. "Captain, it's nothing to be ashamed of. What matters far more than your joy is the shame you felt right afterward. It's when you *don't* feel the shame after a perfectly natural instinct that you have to worry."

As she leaned forward, I leaned back, crossing my legs in a failed attempt to get comfortable. "We're on our way now to meet with a Klingon civilian ship that allegedly has intelligence about Dominion activity—at which point, we will likely again be sent into battle." I sighed. "Remember at Evora when I asked if anyone remembered when we were explorers?"

"Yes. And we will be explorers again, Captain, I'm sure of it."

"Assuming we do win the war. Assuming we aren't all killed. We've been so very lucky, Deanna—even when we lost the *Enterprise*-D, we all survived. But now, I see the *Grissom* and the other five ships destroyed, the *Christopher* possibly needing to be scrapped as well, and I wonder when our luck will finally run out."

"Captain—"

"*Riker to Picard.*"

I pulled down my uniform jacket and tapped my combadge. "Go ahead, Number One."

"*We're picking up a distress call from a Cardassian ship. It's adrift in interstellar space. Data picked it up on long-range, and it seems to be legitimate.*"

Normally, I would recommend caution, but the urge to save a life rather than take one became almost palpable. "Have Ensign Perim change course." After a moment, I added, "And go to yellow alert. I'll be on the bridge shortly, Picard out."

Getting to my feet, I turned to the counselor. I did not need her empathic senses to determine that she was worried about me. "Captain, I think we should speak further."

"I agree, Counselor—but later, in a formal session, perhaps?"

She picked up her padd, we agreed on a time the following afternoon, and I went to the bridge.

The distress call came from an old *Akril*-class vessel. I was amazed that any were still in service, as that model was prominent when I was captain of the *Stargazer* but had become less common in recent years. As usual, Data had an explanation. "Sensors show several deviations from the known design of *Akril*-class vessels. It is likely that Dominion engineering has been used to augment this ship."

Will added, "The last squib from Starfleet Intelligence indicated that Cardassian shipyards had been converted by the Dominion to upgrade Central Command's fleet."

"Well," Daniels said, "this upgrade must not've taken. I'm reading hull damage over 40 percent of the ship, structural integrity field down to 25 percent and falling—and the distress call is now a disaster beacon."

Data added, "Ship's registry indicates it is the Central Command vessel *Pakliros*."

I tugged the front of my uniform jacket again—a comforting habit that I'd never seen any reason to break—and said, "Bring us in slowly, Ensign."

"Aye, sir," Perim said.

Disaster beacons were far more difficult to forge—though not impossible—and increased the likelihood that this was a legitimate call for help.

Will asked, "Any life signs, Data?"

"The ship's engines are putting out considerable radiation, sir, making life-sign readings difficult. However, sensors do read two Cardassian life signs in the forward cargo section."

That put them as far as possible from the irradiated engines. I tapped my combadge. "Bridge to transporter room 3. Lock onto the two life signs in the forward section of the Cardassian vessel and stand by." I moved toward the turbolift. "Mister Daniels, have a security complement meet me in the transporter room."

"Yes, sir."

"You have the bridge, Number One."

"Yes, sir," Will said. "Lieutenant, keep a weapons lock on the *Pakliros*—just in case."

Daniels's acknowledgment was swallowed by the turbolift doors closing. "Transporter room 3," I said.

Will's caution was quite sensible. A *Sovereign*-class ship would be a valuable prize for a Dominion soldier to bring home to Cardassia Prime. This still could have been a trap.

But it might not have been. If there were only two survivors, it meant the *Pakliros* was worse off than the *Grissom*. We'd saved those final six—they'd been transported to the *T'Mala*, who were tasked with towing the *Christopher* back to Starbase 522—and could we truly not do likewise for our enemies?

Once, I would have had a much easier time answering that question.

Ensigns Seo, Jeloq, and Cruzen from security were approaching the transporter room from the other direction. They all had their phasers out. There was a time when standard procedure was to leave one's weapons holstered until necessary, but those times had passed.

I entered the transporter room, the three security officers trailing behind me. As they got into a triangle formation, weapons pointed at the platform, I turned to the transporter operator, Chief T'Bonz.

The Vulcan woman said, "I have acquired a lock on the two Cardassians. Continued scans have detected no other life signs on the *Pakliros*."

I nodded. "Energize."

Two Cardassians materialized, a man and a woman. Their uniforms were torn and filthy, and both had evidence of injury. The woman had the insignia of a glinn.

However, I barely noticed her, as I found my entire focus on the man. It was a face I'd last seen in person on Cardassia Prime six years ago, but which I'd seen in my nightmares with alarming regularity ever since.

"Gul Madred."

Palming the blood from around his right eye, the Cardassian gul looked at me with as much shock as I'm sure I viewed him. "Captain Picard. What a surprise," he said flatly.

The glinn collapsed on the platform and started shaking. I turned to T'Bonz. "Beam her to sickbay." I tapped my combadge. "Picard to Crusher. Doctor, you're about to receive a wounded prisoner."

"Understood."

I looked back on the face of one of the few sentient beings for whom I had ever truly felt hatred. "Are there any other survivors?"

Slowly, Madred shook his head. "No. Glinn Driana and I are the only ones left."

"Very well." I affected a more formal tone of voice. "You are on board the *U.S.S. Enterprise*. By order of the Federation Council, I hereby declare you, Gul Madred, and Glinn Driana to be prisoners of war." I turned to Ensign Seo. "Take him to the brig. Alert sickbay—they can treat his wounds there."

Without another look at his face, I left the transporter room.

A Cardassian brings me into a large, dark room. My wrists are cuffed together in front of me. There is another Cardassian with small eyes and a gul's insignia sitting behind a large desk.

"A challenge," he says. Then he gets up and walks around the desk toward me. With a nod, he dismisses the one who brought me in, leaving us alone in the room together.

"You should prove an interesting challenge—possibly the most interesting to come through that door in many years."

I ask, "What do you want?"

"Why, you, of course," he says, as if it were blindingly obvious. "Picard. Jean—"

"—Luc?"

Beverly Crusher's voice startled me out of my reverie. It had been six years, yet I remembered my time with Madred as if it were last week. Indeed, I remembered it with greater clarity than I did the events of the previous week.

But my chief medical officer was providing a report. "Yes, Beverly—I'm sorry, you were saying?"

"My patient has received third-degree burns over several parts of her body. I can treat that, but it's secondary to the greater issue. She has radiation poisoning. Luckily for her, we were able to access the *Pakliros*'s medical database. She has a flag on her file that says she's allergic to hyronalin."

"But there are alternative treatments," I said.

She nodded, her red tresses bouncing slightly. "Yes, but they're less effective. I honestly don't know if I can save her."

I could hear the fatigue in her voice. The war had gone on for a year and a half, and wars are never easy times for physicians. I put what I hoped was a comforting hand on her shoulder. "Do what you can, Beverly."

Again, she nodded. I squeezed her shoulder and then moved toward the exit.

"Jean-Luc?"

I stopped and turned.

Her expression had modulated to one of concern. "Are *you* all right?"

Obviously she had heard who the other prisoner was. "I'm fine," I lied.

The look on her face indicated that she saw through that falsehood. "If you need to talk—"

"Of course," I said dismissively and left sickbay. Now was not the time to indulge in emotionalism. I was captain of the *Enterprise,* and I had a job to do.

Daniels and Deanna were waiting for me in the corridor.

My security chief spoke first. "Captain, we've received orders from Starfleet Command. They'll send an S.C.E. ship to tow the *Pakliros* back to Starbase 522. We're to proceed to the rendezvous with the *B'Orzoq* and interrogate the prisoners here."

Glancing back at sickbay, I said, "Glinn Driana is in no condition to be questioned."

Nodding, Daniels said, "Understood, sir. I'll proceed to the brig, then, and—"

"No. I will handle Gul Madred's interrogation."

Daniels frowned. "Sir?"

I could feel Deanna's eyes burning a hole in me as I said, "I believe my words were clear, Lieutenant."

"Er, yes, sir."

Deanna said, "Captain, are you sure—?"

"Yes," I said. "I'm fully aware of my history with the gul, Counselor, and I hardly need you to remind me of it. Nevertheless, I shall interrogate him. Return to your posts."

I turned my back on them before they could acknowledge me and tapped my combadge as I headed down the corridor toward the turbolift. "Picard to bridge."

Will replied. *"Go ahead."*

"Proceed to the rendezvous with the *B'Orzoq*, Number One. I'll be in the brig."

There was a considerable pause before Will said, *"Yes, sir."*

"Is there a problem, Commander?" I asked, even though I knew the answer already.

"Sir, perhaps it would be more appropriate if Lieutenant Daniels or Counselor Troi—"

"I've already spoken with both of them, Number One." I let out a breath. "I appreciate your concern, Will. Carry out your orders."

"Aye, aye, sir."

I entered the turbolift. "Brig."

"In this room, you do not ask questions. I ask them—you answer. If I am not satisfied with your answers, you will die."

It begins that way. It continues with drugs designed to compel the truth from me. I remember little of that, save that I answer every question I am asked. My next clear memory is of being brought back into the room, again cuffed, this time also blindfolded.

"Captain Picard."

I waste no time in asserting my legal rights. "I demand to see a neutral representative, as required by the Federation-Cardassian Peace Treaty."

Madred removes the blindfold. "We have already sent a message to Tohvun III, the nearest neutral planet. They assure us they will dispatch someone."

It is the first lie Madred speaks to me. It is not the last.

Madred's wounds were being treated by Ensign Mak, one of Beverly's medical technicians, when I entered the brig. Ensign Seo was in the brig with them, a phaser pointed directly at Madred's head should he try anything, but the Cardassian seemed uninterested in that.

That almost disappointed me. A part of me wanted him to try to escape so Seo could kill him. He would be justified in the act, especially if Mak's life was put in danger.

I found myself visualizing the phaser burning through Madred's chest, his small eyes widening at the impact.

But Madred did nothing. He merely sat on the bunk and allowed himself to be healed. Mak finished his work and nodded to Seo, who in turn nodded to Lieutenant Houarner, the officer on duty at the brig controls. Houarner lowered the force field. Seo kept his phaser on Madred as he and Mak departed the brig.

Once they were clear, Houarner raised the force field again. Only then did Seo lower his weapon.

Mak walked up to me. "He's fine, sir. Just a few scrapes and bruises."

"Thank you, Ensign."

Nodding, Mak departed.

I walked up to the edge of the force field. Seo, I noticed, did not leave but took up position next to Houarner's desk. I debated ordering them both out of the room, but standard procedure during wartime was for two security guards to be present during any interrogation, and I saw no reason to put either officer in a conundrum by ordering them to violate that procedure.

Madred looked up at me, his face having been repaired. "So, it would seem fate has thrown us together again, human."

I stepped forward. "You are on board my ship, Gul Madred, and you will address me as 'Captain.'"

Inclining his head, he said, "My apologies. I'm afraid I'm far more accustomed to my role as jailer than jailed." He gave a small smile and added, "How grateful I am that it is you who are my interrogator, Captain. So often in that room, I found myself dealing with dullards and simpletons, enemies of the state who provided no challenge whatsoever. I feared that now, with the positions reversed, I would be confronted with a boorish chief of security who would badger me with tiresome questions."

"Such as asking you what you were doing on an outdated ship so far from Cardassian space—or, rather, Dominion space?"

Again he smiled. "Yes, rather like that question. And you give the *Akril* class far too little credit. It is one of our finer designs." The smile fell. "Or rather, it was."

I had to admit that a certain smugness crept into my tone when I said, "Your Dominion masters were unable to make the upgrades work, were they?"

"They are hardly our 'masters,' Captain." Madred's tone struck me as defensive. "We are part of the Dominion now, not its slaves."

"Really?" I started to pace back and forth in front of the force field. "Your government is run by the Vorta—yes, I know, Legate Damar is nominally in charge, but he's obviously a puppet of the Founders. You can practically see the strings."

"Perhaps—but Cardassia is great once again."

"Cardassia is *nothing*! Your entire culture, your entire nation has been subsumed in order to become part of a larger totalitarian state."

Madred whispered, "And what, pray tell, was the alternative? Cardassia was in a shambles, Captain. I am the last to lament the end of the Obsidian Order—they were a collection of paranoid fools—but their destruction left the government vulnerable to civilian takeover, which in turn left us even more vulnerable to outside attack. Our people were dying in droves. We lost worlds to Klingon aggression and Maquis terrorism. By joining the Dominion, Cardassian lives were saved."

"And how many more lives were lost since the war began?"

"I would be a fool to deny that sacrifices have been made. But at least the losses are now primarily soldiers who have pledged to give their lives in service to Cardassia. When the Klingons attacked, they showed little interest in limiting themselves to military targets, and the Maquis were even more indiscriminate."

"A life is no less valuable because it has agreed to serve. *All* life is precious, Madred."

He chuckled at that. "What a charmingly naïve point of view. Allow me to refute each of your points, Captain. Life is not at all precious—if it were, it wouldn't be so easily disposed of. As for the military, its primary function is to protect the state and the people within it. Of *course* a civilian life is of more value, because the military's job is to put itself in danger to protect civilians. There is no other conclusion to be reached from that position—unless your Starfleet does *not* protect civilians."

"Of course it does."

"Then why do you continue to fight the Dominion?" Madred rose and walked toward the force field. "You must see that this war is a tremendous waste."

I raised an eyebrow. "Then why do *you* continue to fight it?"

Another smile. "That is my question to you, Captain. Why do you resist the inevitable? Why fight the Dominion?"

"What alternative do we have?"

"Join us!" Madred spoke with passion, now, more than I'd ever seen him evince. "If you join the Dominion, you can *save* lives—a position your Federation, as well as the Klingons and Romulans, would have been far better off emulating rather than fighting. If you don't believe me, you need only to glance at your collective casualty figures to see that I am right."

Now he was simply playing games. And, I realized, I was playing them as well. One of the last things Madred ever said to me before I was released from his torture chamber was, *"I would enjoy debating with you, you have a keen mind."* Now, here, we were doing that very thing.

I wasn't about to continue letting him manipulate me. "What were you doing on that ship, Madred? I can't imagine you were reduced to captaining an old wreck like that."

"I was not the *Pakliros*'s shipmaster, if that is what you are asking, Captain. But I see no reason to share my mission with the likes of you."

"If not with me, then with one of those boorish security chiefs you were lamenting earlier. It would be easier for all of us if you spoke now."

Madred turned and sat back down on the bunk. "Perhaps. I would ask a boon in return for that information, however—I demand to see Glinn Driana."

For the first time, I smiled. "In this room, you do not make demands."

With that, I turned and left the brig.

He brings his daughter Jelora into the room, telling her that humans don't love their mothers and fathers the way they do—the usual tired propaganda regarding one's enemy.

After she departs, I tell Madred the truth: "Your daughter is lovely."

"Yes, I think so. And unusually bright. It's amazing, isn't it? The way they're able to sneak into your heart. I have to admit I was completely unprepared for the power she had over me from the moment she was born."

"I am surprised that you let her come in here."

Madred seems genuinely confused. "Why?"

"To expose a child to—this. To someone who is suffering. To see that it's you who inflict that suffering."

"From the time Jelora could crawl, she's been taught about the enemies of the Cardassians and that enemies deserve their fate."

"When children learn to devalue others, they can devalue anyone—including their parents."

He rises and walks toward me. "What a blind, narrow view you have. What an arrogant man you are."

I took my place on the bridge, ignoring the look of concern from my first officer as I sat next to him.

"Report," I said.

"We're approaching the rendezvous point," Will said.

Data added, "Sensors are picking up the *B'Orzoq* at the designated coordinates."

"Slow to impulse," I told Perim.

"Aye, sir," the Trill said.

Moments later, the stars on the main viewer that had been streaking by from the warp effect settled once again into single points in space. Data put the *B'Orzoq* on the viewer. It didn't follow the avian design that the Klingon military favored, but the empire's trefoil emblem was prominent on its hull.

"Hail the *B'Orzoq*, Mister Daniels," I said.

Moments later, a squat Klingon face appeared on the viewer. *"You are Picard of the* Enterprise?"

"I am Captain Jean-Luc Picard, yes."

"I was told it would be you. My name is Grantor, of the House of Klarat, and I bear news of value to the war effort. The Dominion is constructing a large military base on the Cardassian world of Raknal V. It will include a weapons production plant, a Jem'Hadar base, and a ketracel-white facility."

Will and I exchanged glances. He seemed dubious, and I felt much the same. "How have they accomplished this in secret?" I asked.

"They've masked their movements to the planet by traveling through the Betreka Nebula."

"What is the source of your intelligence?"

"Many turns ago, Cardassians and Klingons both lived on

Raknal V, before the empire ceded the world to those spoon-headed petaQpu'. *Even after that, however, some Klingons remained on that world. One of them is a member of the House of Klarat."*

"And you trust this family member?" I asked. Normally, I would not insult a Klingon by even asking, but these were treacherous times, and besides, this was a civilian, not a warrior.

Grantor broke into a wide smile at the question. *"He owes me twelve bricks of latinum, so the* toDSaH *damn well* better *be telling me the truth."*

Definitely not a warrior, I thought.

He went on: *"I have images that he took of the construction, which I will gladly share."*

From behind me, Daniels said, "Receiving file now, sir."

I nodded briefly to the tactical officer, then said, "On behalf of the allies, Grantor, I thank you for your intelligence."

"You're welcome, Picard of the Enterprise. *In return, I ask only that you stop them. My House-mate has enough trouble living on that rock without the Dominion turning it into their playground."*

After Grantor signed off, Will said, "Lieutenant Daniels, send a secure message to Admiral Spahiu at Starbase 522."

"Aye, sir."

"Sickbay to Picard."

I looked up. "Go ahead, Doctor."

Beverly hesitated before going on. *"I'm afraid that I've lost my patient."*

He takes the bejeweled knife and slices off my clothing, leaving me naked and exposed. "From this point on, you will enjoy no privilege of rank, no privileges of person. From now on, I will refer to you only as 'human.' You have no other identity."

His men shackle me to a pole that hangs from the ceiling, leaving my arms raised. Then he touches his padd, and the pole retracts, lifting my legs from the floor.

He walks out, leaving me alone to hang like that for the entire night.

The next morning, his men take me down while he drinks in front of me, knowing how parched I am.

"Thirsty?" he asks, unnecessarily. "I would imagine so." He drinks again. "Well, it's time to move on."

My voice cracking, I say, "I've told you all that I know."

"Yes, I'm sure you have." He touches a control on his padd, and four lights behind his head blaze into existence, temporarily blinding me. I blink the spots out of my eyes as he asks, "How many lights do you see there?"

Thinking it a simple question, I say, "I see four lights."

"No. There are five. You're quite sure?"

"There are four lights."

As soon as I entered the brig, Madred said, "I wish to see Glinn Driana."

Ignoring his request, I said, "I'm afraid your remanding to a starbase will have to wait a while longer."

"Why is that?"

I tilted my head. "Does it matter?"

"If you are engaging in a mission that will endanger Cardassian lives, then it matters a great deal to me."

"What were you doing on the *Pakliros?*"

"Why does that matter to you?" Madred had been sitting on his bunk, but now he rose and walked over to the small water basin. "I must confess to being greatly disappointed in you, human. You've been given an unparalleled opportunity, and you're wasting it." He splashed some water on his face.

"To do what?" I asked. "To get some of my own back? To torture you as you did me?"

He whirled around, his face still wet. "Torture? I did no such thing."

That stunned me. I almost lost my footing. Then I recalled that the entire time I was in his office, he very rarely told the truth. In fact, I suspect that the only time he did not lie was when he spoke of his daughter—and of his own childhood.

I clung to that, the memory that had given me strength six years ago. *"Whenever I look at you now, I won't see a powerful Cardassian warrior, I will see a six-year-old boy who is powerless to protect himself."*

"What do you call what you did to me, then, Gul Madred? Interrogation? That part was over and done with a few hours after I first walked into your office. You were trying to break me to your will."

"Isn't that what we all do?" he asked, drying off his face. "Our lives in this universe are simply attempts to gain control over our surroundings. The fact that I am particularly expert at it has proved useful in my career."

"And provided you with an outlet to enact revenge on those who tormented you in your youth."

Madred sighed. "Again you revert to amateur analysis."

"Yes—only this time, you do not have your neural implant to get me to stop."

He stared at me. I stared back.

To my surprise, he looked away. "Where are we going that you cannot remand me to a starbase?"

I thought a moment and decided I had no reason not to share the information. "We are meeting a fleet of Starfleet, Klingon, and Romulan ships at the Betreka Nebula and then proceeding to Raknal V to destroy the Dominion base being constructed there."

"Really?" Madred looked at me again, this time with a surprising intensity in his eyes. Prior to this, he was engaging in his usual tired word games, but now he seemed eager. "Captain, I have intelligence that would be of use to you."

I regarded him with derision. "You expect me to believe that?"

"I am a gul in Central Command, Captain. I have the rank and position to know a great deal about the inner workings of our war effort, and I know what is happening at Raknal V."

"And you will just *give* me this information?"

He nodded. "In exchange for getting to see Glinn Driana. After I have spoken to her, I will gladly tell you everything I know about Raknal V."

"Tell me first, then I will allow you to—"

"No!" The vehemence with which he said that one syllable almost struck me like a slap. The two security guards on duty, Horowitz and Simone, both moved their hands to their sidearms.

Seeing that, Madred made a show of calming himself. "I will see Glinn Driana, or you receive no information from me."

With that, he turned and sat back on the bunk, staring straight ahead.

"You have my terms, Captain" was all he would say.

I left the brig.

* * *

"Be quiet!" he screams as he again turns on the four lights that he claims are five.

"In spite of all you've done to me, I find you a pitiable man."

"Picard, stop it," he says, raising the control for the neural implant, "or I will turn this on and leave you in agony all night."

I bark out a laugh and point at him. "You called me 'Picard'!"

"What are the Federation's defense plans for Minos Korva?"

I give him only one answer: "There are four lights!"

He activates the implant. Pain racks my body as he insists there are five lights. I try to resist, taking refuge in an old song from my childhood . . .

Ironically, it was time for the appointment I'd made with Deanna. I had forgotten that I'd even made it until I was outside her office, simply wishing to speak with her.

Once again, I entered to find her reading over a padd. "Captain," she said at my entrance. "I'm glad you could make it."

I took my seat opposite her, tugging my uniform jacket.

"How has the interrogation been going?"

I filled her in on what Madred had said—which was very little—and then told her about the trade he proposed.

Deanna put a finger to her chin. "Do you believe that his intelligence will be useful?"

"It's impossible to be sure. He's correct that he is of sufficient rank to possibly be aware of what is happening on Raknal. But he might also be lying in order to see his subordinate." I gave a half smile. "Lying is Madred's modus operandi, after all."

Leaning back in her chair, Deanna said, "What I find curious is Madred's interest in the glinn. Why does he wish to see her particularly?"

That brought me up short. I honestly hadn't given that a moment's thought. "You know—I have no idea."

"It might be worth discovering that."

I shook my head. "But it almost doesn't matter—I can't fulfill my end of the bargain either way. Glinn Driana is dead. And therein lies my dilemma."

"Which is?"

Again, I tugged on my uniform jacket. "The only way I will be able to obtain Gul Madred's intelligence is to lie to him. I must . . . I must do to him what he did to me."

"Captain," Deanna said, leaning forward and putting a reassuring hand on mine, "there is *no* danger of your doing to him what he did to you."

"He manipulated me, Counselor—he lied, he caused me pain, and in the end he broke me. If I lie to him, if I tell him that Driana is alive and well and gain intelligence from him, and then renege on my part of that bargain—how does that make me different from him?"

She removed her hand. "Captain, there *is* a war on, and—"

"I don't accept that rationalization."

Tartly, Deanna said, "It's not a rationalization, Captain."

"Isn't it? When we use war as an excuse for extreme behavior, where does it end? Madred tortured me, ostensibly to obtain information about Minos Korva. His nation was at war with mine, or at least they intended to be, so does that justify his actions, done as they were for the greater good of the Cardassian Union?"

"Of course not," Deanna said.

I gestured in a manner that was almost pleading. "Then how do I justify manipulating Madred now?"

Deanna stared at me for a moment, her face unusually opaque. "At Ricktor Prime, would you consider your actions justifiable?"

I shrugged. "The Dominion invaded Ricktor Prime. We were defending our territory."

"Exactly. But if there wasn't a state of war between the Dominion and the Federation, would your actions at Ricktor Prime have been justified?"

I hesitated.

Deanna went on. "You would have at least attempted a peaceful solution—but war has been declared. If there is to be a peaceful solution, it would not have happened at Ricktor Prime. Ethics can be situational—what you did at Ricktor Prime would have been a court-marial offense three years ago but is an act of heroism now."

"Hardly that," I said, but did not argue the point further. "Yes, all right, perhaps so, but where does it end?"

"I think the better question is, why did it start?"

Again, I was brought up short. "What do you mean?"

Now Deanna was speaking more formally, counselor to captain

rather than therapist to patient. "Captain, it is completely inappropriate for you to interrogate Gul Madred—and potentially damaging. Besides undermining Lieutenant Daniels's authority, you also are exposing yourself to psychological damage. Madred's treatment of you six years ago is a wound that his presence has ripped open. This ship cannot afford a wounded captain right now."

"Counselor, you don't understand, I needed—"

Now she was back to being a therapist. "Captain, I understand completely, more than anyone, because I know the truth. As you just said, he broke you. So why do you keep going back to see him? Why do you continue to let him hold power over you?"

Shaking my head, I said, "He doesn't have any power over me, Counselor, he's my prisoner."

"No, Captain. You're still his."

I found I had nothing to say. The notion was ridiculous.

Wasn't it?

Very quietly, Deanna said, "I've watched the recordings of your sessions with Madred. He has manipulated every conversation you two have had. As far as he's concerned, you never left his office, and he's still trying to break you."

I thought back to the conversations in the brig and realized that—as usual—Deanna was right.

"I've been a fool," I whispered.

"No," she said, "you've been a victim. That's not a crime, Captain."

"Perhaps not." I stood up, straightening my uniform. "But allowing him to continue to victimize me is."

With that, I turned and left the counselor's office.

"It's up to you. A life of ease and reflection and intellectual challenge—or this." He indicates the office where I have been for the past several days, subject to his whims and manipulations.

Barely able to speak, I ask, "What must I do?"

"Nothing, really." He looks up at the lights. "Tell me how many lights you see."

I look up. The lights blind me, but I stare directly into them. Madred has said that the Enterprise is destroyed, and I am believed to have perished with them. I have nothing left.

"How many?"

I stare at the lights.

"How many lights?" The door behind me opens. "This is your last chance. The guards are coming. Don't be a stubborn fool. How many?"

I'm about to answer, to tell him that I do in fact see five lights, when another Cardassian gul appears at my side. He's furious at Madred. "You told me he would be ready to go."

"We had some unfinished business," Madred says rather lamely.

Angrily, the other gul says, "Get him cleaned up! A ship is waiting to take him back to the Enterprise.*"*

It was another lie. Only this time, I believed it.

From my ready room, I instructed the computer to show me the feed from the brig. The station on my desk lights up and I see Lieutenant Daniels standing where I had stood previously.

Madred sat on his bunk, looking confused. *"Who are you?"*

"My name is Lieutenant Daniels, chief of security of the Enterprise. *I have a few questions for you, Gul Madred."*

"What has happened to Captain Picard?"

Daniels smiled. *"The captain is a busy man—he has better things to do than listen to the likes of you."*

And then Madred threw his head back, and he laughed.

I frowned. This was not what I was expecting.

"What's so funny?" Daniels's tone was of great annoyance.

Madred shook his head. *"From the moment I beamed onto this ship, I wondered if I would be able to learn the truth. For six years, I've been plagued with not knowing the answer. But now—oh, Lieutenant, you cannot possibly know how happy you've made me."*

"You can't imagine how little I care about your happiness, Gul."

Nodding, Madred said, *"Understandable. Still, I am, at last, satisfied. You see, I never knew if I broke him. Lemec, that tiresome fool, came in before I had my answer. I could never be sure if he remained defiant to the end, or if Lemec's entrance provided him with the hope that I had so meticulously taken away from him."*

Daniels shook his head. *"You're crazy."*

"Am I? Given the opportunity to hold my request to see Glinn Driana over my head, he instead runs away, afraid to face me as a prisoner, afraid to treat me that way. I know she is dead—she had

radiation poisoning, and she is allergic to hyronalin—but Picard could have lied to me, manipulated me, as I did him. But when we reached the endgame, he chose to retreat rather than confront."

Madred then decided to laugh some more, at which point, I almost turned the screen off, but then Daniels interrupted him. *"Captain Picard didn't use the glinn against you because he didn't need to—and we didn't need you. The intelligence we had was more than sufficient. The raid on Raknal V went off without a hitch. There's never going to be a base on that planet, Gul Madred, and you were completely helpless to prevent it."*

That got Madred to stop laughing, at least, but he was still smiling. *"It doesn't matter. I've won."*

Daniels asked a few more questions, but Madred said nothing. Disgusted, I turned off the screen and went back to the bridge.

Will and Deanna were both seated at their places on the bridge when I came out. The former said, "Captain Kartok has beamed down an occupation force to hold Raknal V. We've been ordered to deliver Gul Madred to Starbase 522."

"Grand. I'll be glad to be rid of him." I sat in my seat, my two trusted advisers at either side.

From my left, Deanna said, "You should be proud, Captain. Madred is a bully, and ultimately the only way to defeat a bully is not to engage him." She smiled at me. "You won."

I thought about how close I came to admitting to there being five lights six years ago, and how easily I let Madred once again trap me in his web of words three days ago, and I shook my head.

"This does not feel like victory."

'TIL DEATH

Bob Ingersoll & Thomas F. Zahler

Historian's note:
This tale unfolds in the weeks leading up
to the feature film Star Trek Nemesis.

BOB INGERSOLL & THOMAS F. ZAHLER

Bob Ingersoll is a practicing attorney with the Cuyahoga County Public Defender Office in Cleveland, Ohio, who hopes to get it right one of these days so he can finally stop practicing. For over twenty years he used his legal background to write the regular column "The Law Is a Ass" for *Comics Buyer's Guide,* a weekly trade newspaper for the comic-book industry.

He has written scripts for numerous comic-books, including *Star Trek, Star Trek: The Next Generation, Lost in Space, Quantum Leap,* and *Hero Alliance.* He was the co-author of the novels *Captain America: Liberty's Torch* and *Star Trek: The Case of the Colonist's Corpse.*

He has no idea what he wants to be when he grows up.

When Thomas F. Zahler's father introduced him to *Star Trek* and comic books, he probably had no idea what an impression they would make on the boy. Thom became obsessed with both, but decided it would be easier to become a cartoonist than join Starfleet.

After graduating the Joe Kubert School of Cartoon and Graphic Art, where he learned to draw funny pictures and tell stories, he began a successful career as an artist, working for clients across the country. His work has been seen everywhere from advertising campaigns to magazines and throughout the world of comics. He wrote and drew the action-adventure-spy series *Raider,* and is currently writing and drawing the critically acclaimed superhero sitcom comic book *Love and Capes.*

Zahler lives in northeast Ohio. He has not yet completely given up on a career in Starfleet. He can be found on the web at www.thomz.com.

WILL RIKER AWOKE WITH A RATTLING GURGLE IN HIS THROAT.

His lungs burned as if they couldn't fill with air fast enough. He felt colder than he thought it was possible to feel. And his chest hurt like hell.

He looked around, desperately trying to regain his sense of place, but nothing looked familiar. He was on a warm floor. A muggy, musty smell filled the air. Beverly Crusher was kneeling in front of him, unmoving. Her eyes were wide and unblinking. Her mouth agape.

As if . . .

As if she had seen a ghost . . .

With that, memories spun about him. *Tellarite . . . swamp . . . Deanna . . . the shuttlecraft . . . Deanna . . . some kind of outpost . . . Beverly . . . Deanna . . .*

Desperate to ground himself, Will tried to lock eyes with Beverly, but he couldn't catch her gaze. She was looking *at* him, but not at his face. She was looking at his chest. Riker moved his head downward, following her line of sight.

That's when he saw a large hole in his chest, a hole that a surprisingly detached part of his mind told him was too large to be anything but fatal. Protruding from that hole, sitting right in the center of a gaping chest wound, was a small, triangular piece of highly polished metal.

And Riker screamed.

". . . although these polar shifts are a natural occurrence, we are still at something of a loss to explain their cause."

Riker tried to focus on Data's droning recitation of the mission briefing but was failing miserably. Having an emotion chip may have changed the android's personality, but, unfortunately, it had no effect on his speaking style. Try as he might, Riker couldn't concentrate on this briefing. All he could think about were the two major changes that were about to take place in his life. His upcoming captaincy of the starship *Titan* and, even more important, the fact that, finally, he was getting married to ship's counselor Deanna Troi.

Deanna was more than just his friend and fiancée. She was his *imzadi*. It was a word from Deanna's homeworld, Betazed, that translated loosely meant "beloved." But like so many words transposed from one language to another, the fullest meaning would not translate well. *Imzadi* meant beloved, but it also meant so much more. Betazed was a planet of telepaths, a world of beings who knew what bonding between two people on every level truly was. A world that gave such true bonding a name all its own.

Riker fumed silently, upset that he couldn't let his full frustration show. He was *supposed* to be with Deanna right now on Holodeck 2 in a re-creation of L'Astrance, a Parisian restaurant overlooking the Eiffel Tower that was Deanna's favorite place to eat on Earth. They had reserved the holodeck time weeks ago as a getaway, promising themselves there would be no wedding plans. No discussions about the delicate seating arrangements required when the bride was a Daughter of the Fifth House or finding a menu that would satisfy a guest list that included vegetarians and devotees of live *gagh* worms. Just him and Deanna together for one night in the City of Lights. Rich food and richer company.

It was where Riker was supposed to be. Where he *wanted* to be. There. With Deanna. In Paris. Not in some boring briefing of the *Enterprise*'s department heads called just because one of the ship's damned probes came back with a "startling revelation."

Riker pictured Deanna in his mind, eating a *Soufflé au Bleu d'Auvergne* and talking about something amusing she had heard during lunch in Ten-Forward. He was trying to remember the exact taste of L'Astrance's exquisite *crème brûlée,* when Geordi La Forge put his coffee cup down on the briefing room table, just loud enough to snap Riker out of the daydream.

Riker half turned his head and looked at La Forge with mild annoyance. Then he caught a hint of smile on the chief engineer's lips that seemed to say, "Hey, if *I* have to suffer, we *all* have to suffer."

Riker glanced out of the corner of his eye over at Jean-Luc Picard to see whether the *Enterprise*'s captain had noticed his earlier lapse in concentration. But Picard was looking squarely at Data in rapt attention and, in contrast to Riker's own lack of focus, having no problems maintaining his interest.

"What would this have meant to the inhabitants?" Picard asked. "Losing their homeworld for a second time . . ." Picard let the sentence trail off.

Of course he's interested, Riker thought. *It's archaeology.*

Then Riker noticed that Picard's expression wasn't so much one of interest as one of shared sorrow. Like those Riker had seen at his mother's funeral on the faces of the people who experienced a loss of their own. Riker realized it wasn't just Picard's interest in archaeology. In a sense, for the captain it *was* personal, as he knew what it was like to lose a world, just as the Fabrini had.

The Fabrini were an ancient and advanced race that colonized other worlds some ten thousand years ago, after its home star went nova. Traces of the Fabrini had been found scattered around the galaxy, but only traces, until the discovery of an entire Fabrini colony on Yonada, a multigeneration spaceship constructed inside of a hollowed-out asteroid.

Now *Enterprise* had chanced on another Fabrini colony. This one was found when the ship had sent a probe to a small, former Class-M planet in an unexplored solar system. On the planet, the probe discovered the remains of a Fabrini colony established almost seven thousand years ago that had thrived for close to five hundred years before rapid polar shifts rendered the planet uninhabitable and the Fabrini were, again, forced to flee their home.

Beverly Crusher, chief medical officer, broke the somewhat awkward silence. "As near as we can tell from the probe, the shift rendered the planet inhospitable to life. And fairly quickly. The Fabrini colony that lived there would have had to leave in a hurry. If they were able to leave at all."

"So it seems the Fabrini," Riker started, trying to get his mind back in the game, "were smart to establish multiple colonies rather than place all their eggs in one basket again."

"How much damage would have been done to the structures after the polar shift?" Picard asked. "The Fabrini were extremely advanced in the medical sciences. Any intact relics would be a remarkable find."

"The structures themselves are mostly undamaged, sir," said Data. "As to how much of their culture survived over several thousand years of exposure to . . ."

"We'll need an expedition to find out," Beverly finished. She was clearly excited by the thought of the Fabrini's legendary medical knowledge. Moreover, Riker could tell she wanted to experience the colony and that knowledge firsthand, not talk about it in the abstract.

"Agreed," said Picard, and Riker could see that his captain's face mirrored the enthusiasm found on the doctor's face.

Riker glanced down at his padd and accessed Data's prepared presentation. He flipped ahead in Data's outline to see where all this was leading. The now-abandoned colony was on a planet that could no longer sustain humanoid life for an extended period. The polar shift had played havoc with the planet's atmosphere and continued to do so. Magnetic fields were constantly in flux. Without proper shielding, no human life could survive for more than a few days.

"We won't be able to beam down?" Riker asked, cutting off Data's lengthy description of the decay rates of Fabrini construction techniques.

"No, Commander," Data answered. "The planet is bathed in heavy magnetic interference that is thick as pea soup." Riker found himself smiling at the description, remembering a time when Data would have been incapable of using a phrase like that properly, or so easily. Riker realized at that moment how much he was going to miss serving with his friend.

Geordi leaned forward. "Because of the interference, transporters and communications will be severely limited. A thousand meters at best for the transporters, maybe a little more for the communicators."

Riker glanced down, consulting the scans of the planet's magnetic field. "Looks as though the ride through the upper atmosphere is going to be choppy as hell." Riker grinned. "You're going to need a damn good pilot."

"Are you volunteering, Number One?" Picard asked. Riker could tell that Picard was more than a little disappointed; the captain had hoped to lead the mission himself.

Riker grinned. "Captain, in less than a month, I'm going to be sitting where you are, with some full-of-himself first officer telling me that I can't leave my ship. I'd better get in on all the away missions while I can, sir."

Picard responded with a smile of his own. "I think you're just trying to avoid working on your wedding plans, Number One."

Riker's scream faded away. Beverly's own shock was gone, too, replaced with a clinical distance as her medical training took over her reactions. "What do you remember, Will?" she asked.

Riker could tell she was thinking three steps ahead of where he was, so he decided to trust her clarity and follow her lead. "You and I took a shuttle down to this planet. We started looking around, and you identified this building as a medical center. We came in and split up. You managed to turn on the lights, and then I saw . . ." Riker's voice trailed off.

Beverly put a hand on his shoulder. "Go on, Will."

". . . I saw a Tellarite. A scavenger. He looked like he had some sort of weapon, so I drew my phaser. He didn't see me at first. He . . . he couldn't have gotten a shot off before I did. My phaser must have malfunctioned. And that . . . that's the last thing I remember. What happened after that?"

"You died."

"I *what*?" Riker sat forward, some of his earlier panic returning. A sharp pain in his chest made him regret sitting up so quickly.

Beverly looked him straight in the eyes. "Will, you've got a hole the size of my fist in your chest where your heart used to be. You don't survive that."

Riker looked down at his wound again. His blood-drenched uniform had a circular hole in it, one that exactly matched the hole in his chest. The image beyond that was surreal. There was an open, perfectly smooth crater in his chest. Through the shadows, he could make out some of his organs—his spine, his lungs. He moved slightly to try to allow more light to pierce the shadows, and after illuminating more of his internal organs, decided against it.

Reflexively, he brought his hand up to probe the wound but was rebuffed by a force field. It didn't provide a warning shock, like the ones in the *Enterprise*'s brig, just enough of a repulsion to keep him from pressing further.

And in the center of everything, hovering in the void of his chest, was the triangular spike that he guessed was keeping him alive.

"I heard you cry out," Beverly said, intentionally distracting him from his self-examination, "and came here just in time to see the Tellarite run out as those doors over there"—Beverly nodded toward the two large doors that were the medical center's main entrance—"were closing."

"For a six-thousand-year-old facility, this place seems to work remarkably well."

"And you're lucky it does. When I got here, this room was already powering up. I think it's an emergency room of some sort. There were self-actuating probes coming out of the ceiling, examining you. And they attached that device to you," she said, indicating the sliver of metal Riker had noticed before.

"As near as I can tell," Beverly continued, "it's the only thing keeping you . . . well, as alive as you are."

Will started to say something but stopped, realizing she wasn't done. "Will, whatever that thing is, it's not so much keeping you alive as animating you. I scanned you, and your heart is completely *gone*. You're not pumping blood, you're not even breathing.

"The device is generating . . . something to replace your damaged or missing organs. It's stanched the bleeding. It's keeping your tissue from necrotizing. It's even providing some sort of energy to keep your brain functioning. I just don't know *how*."

"So what you're saying is I'm dead, but I'm not getting any deader."

Beverly smiled. "That's pretty much it." She got up off the floor and started to circle the room, pointing out displays or consoles. "Admiral McCoy wrote quite a few papers about the Fabrini. Their medical knowledge saved his life once. Over coffee at Starfleet Medical once, he hinted that he had been quite . . . friendly . . . with one of their descendants."

"Sounds like my kind of guy."

"He wrote that the Fabrini had a very clear protocol for medical emergencies: first assure that the patient doesn't get any worse, then try to make the patient better. Between that and their artificial intelligence capabilities, this emergency room must have been set up to implement the first part of that protocol."

Riker noticed for the first time his phaser on the floor near him. He picked it up and checked it. "My phaser's dead." Riker smiled. "Deader than me, at least. What happened to it?"

Beverly checked her own phaser for the first time and found that it, too, was not working. "I think that's my fault. When we first arrived and managed to turn on the lights, I think I activated the entire medical facility. Along with standard sterile fields, it must have some sort of weapons deactivation field."

"But the Tellarite shot me."

Beverly looked puzzled, then almost annoyed, as if she didn't like her theories being proved wrong. She knelt next to Riker and flipped open her medical tricorder. When she finished scanning him, she showed him the display. "I don't know what he used on you. There's a residual energy around the area of your wound that doesn't resemble any known weapon signature. It looks more like the aftereffects of a transporter."

"It wasn't a weapon," Riker said. He stroked his beard and remembered something Captain Picard had told him once. For the first time in a while, Riker actually felt glad for paying attention to one of Captain Picard's archaeology talks.

"It was a catalog gu . . . No, a *cargo* gun."

"A what?"

"A cargo gun. It's a kind of a short-range, portable transporter focused through a gun barrel. I've heard about them, but I've never seen one before . . . well, before now, I guess. They're used by scavengers and some less-reputable archaeologists. Say you're out picking through some ruins alone. You can't carry a heavy statue by yourself, but you can beam it into a buffer carried in a backpack and keep it there until you can rematerialize it somewhere else."

"But wouldn't keeping anything in a transporter buffer like that risk pattern degradation? The statue might not come out intact."

"Like I said: scavengers and disreputable archaeologists."

Beverly started to say something, then stopped and stared at his wound. There was an expression of concern on her face, but Riker couldn't tell if she was thinking of her patient or her friend. Eventually, she looked up and continued. "So you're saying he beamed out your heart?"

"A cargo gun needs time to scan its target. The Tellarite was surprised. He didn't have time for a full scan, so he just aimed and pulled the trigger." Riker looked at the hole in his chest. "Then ran away with a chunk of me, it seems."

"Why?" Beverly asked, looking at the doors the Tellarite used to exit the facility.

It wasn't difficult for Riker to follow Beverly's chain of thought as she looked at the door that led to the outside; she wasn't asking why did the Tellarite shoot. "He's probably alone. And scared. He just killed a Starfleet officer. He wanted to get out of here before any other Starfleet personnel that might be around found him."

Riker noticed that the pain in his chest had started to subside. He decided to test himself and slowly, unsteadily got to his feet. Beverly leaned in to restrain him, but he waved her off. The fog of shock was giving way to anger now.

Beverly shot to her feet. "Will, stop!" She waved her tricorder over his chest wound.

"What is it, Doctor?"

"There's an indicator light on the device. And it's dimming as you walk. Hold on . . ." Beverly consulted her tricorder display. "Will, that lifesaving machine has a finite amount of power in it. When you move, you're using it up faster."

"So how much power does it have?" Riker realized what he was asking. "How much time do *I* have?"

Beverly looked at Riker and tried to muster her most calming look. "I have no idea."

They held each other's gaze for a long moment. Beverly could be coolly calm and analytical. It was a skill Riker envied right now, since he needed to do *something*, even if he didn't know what.

"We have to get back to the shuttle," Riker suggested.

Beverly shook her head. "My tricorder's been picking up one intermittent life sign outside. That scavenger's still out there, waiting for us. And with a weapon he can use to finish what he started with you."

Riker looked around the room, thinking about their situation and the Tellarite with the cargo gun, all while hoping he didn't task the device's power too much.

"He thinks he's killed one Starfleet officer. He probably wants to make sure there's no one to connect him to the crime." He paused and regarded the walls of the emergency room. "Why hasn't he come back in? He's had time to check things out by now. He must think you're alone, with me out of the way. But why is he still out there instead of coming in to finish the job?"

"Fabrini medical protocols again. When this ER detected the drastic change in your condition, it was programmed to assume the worst, a contagious biohazard, and the entire facility went into a quarantine lockdown. The whole building is sealed. Blast doors. Metal coverings on the windows. Sterile fields. And a facilitywide shield that keeps everything out. Even transporter beams."

"Can you reopen it?"

"I think so. The system seems designed to open sections of the building after a humanoid operator has declared them safe. But with that Tellarite out there, it's probably better to keep the whole place sealed."

"So we're trapped."

"For now, yes. But *Enterprise* will find us. You *know* they will." She stopped short of reminding Riker of all the times the crew of the *Enterprise* had managed some last-minute rescue. Riker had, after all, engineered enough of them, himself. "In the meantime, I'm going to go through the Fabrini medical records. Most of our knowledge of the Fabrini comes from the book found on Yonada. But the Yonadi had stagnated while this branch of the Fabrini continued to progress for centuries. So I've got some catching up to do."

Will started to say, "What do you hope to find?" when it hit him. Beverly had been talking around the issue, driving the conversation away from the most logical question. "Even if we get back to the *Enterprise,* you can't fix me, can you?"

Beverly set her jaw. "No, Will, I can't. Your damage is too severe."

"If we find that Tellarite, get the cargo gun . . ."

She shook her head. "I can't just beam your heart back into your chest. Even assuming no pattern degradation, there's no way to do that kind of precise integration. The shock alone would kill you."

The enormity of his situation crashed down upon him. He managed to conceal most of it from Beverly, but she did notice that his knees weakened, just a little bit. She'd had to give this news to far too many people in her career, and she knew the signs. For just a second, he let the mantle of command drop. The slight swagger and the twinkle in his eye disappeared. It was an unvarnished, honest Riker who asked his friend, "What do I do?"

Beverly picked up Riker's tricorder, which had also slipped from his belt during his attack. "Think about what you want to say," she said and handed Riker the device.

". . . I mean, what do I say?"

Riker took a sip of his tea, Darjeeling with honey this time, and settled into his chair in Picard's ready room. He was going to miss a lot of things about the *Enterprise,* and his teatime with Picard was probably at the top of that list. Even if, in all his years aboard *Enterprise,* he hadn't managed to find a tea he'd liked.

Picard eyed him closely, then gave a smile. "I think that you're the one who should be answering that, Number One."

"Look, it's bad enough Deanna wants to have two weddings. Doubly bad that she wants the one on Betazed to be a traditional Betazed wedding, complete with nudity." Riker smiled wryly and patted his stomach. "Hell, I haven't had dessert in three months."

"But now," he said as he rubbed the bridge of his nose, "she wants us to write our own vows for the Earth ceremony."

"And what's your problem with that?"

"First off, have you actually read my log reports?"

Picard grimaced and considered his answer. "You *do* have an interesting way of attacking syntax."

"Beyond how to say it, *what* do I say? How do I distill how I feel about Deanna into a few sentences? Sentences that I then have to read in front of everyone we both know."

"I see your quandary, Will," Picard said, then looked away, giving the matter some serious contemplation. He stood up and walked behind Riker, going over to his well-read volume of the complete works of Shakespeare, the one that had survived the destruction of the previous *Enterprise* on Veridian III. Although Picard denied belief in any sort of good-luck charm, Riker noted that he treated the book like a reservoir of strength, one to be dipped into sparingly. Riker turned to see Picard heave the book off its stand. He handed it to Riker.

"Well, Number One, you can never go wrong with Shakespeare."

Will Riker sat on the low wall that surrounded a reflecting pool holding his tricorder up so that it would record his face and the pool in the background. He had wandered through several rooms in the medical center looking for just the right place. He settled on what he figured was a waiting room, because he liked the relative tranquillity of its reflecting pool. That seemed the appropriate venue to record a final message.

He wondered if the room was typical of Fabrini architecture. The materials were ornate. Marble, stones, and polished metals, all of which had the familiar triangular shape to them that the Fabrini seemed to favor. The blast door that had covered the entrance, although a functional device, was still made of an ornate, polished metal. Each surface was inlaid with Fabrini writing and more triangles. Even the pool was three sided.

He had left Beverly to her research and came here to collect his thoughts so that he could then record them. He imagined that quite a few people before him had come to this room to do the same thing: think, reflect, and wait.

Riker was lousy at waiting.

He put the tricorder down on the wall, stood up, and paced around the pool. The Lifesaver, as he and Beverly had taken to calling the alien device, seemed to provide some of his biological needs. He knew, looking at the murky, algae-covered water, that he should be thirsty, but he wasn't. That was just as well, as the water had the same swampy, unappealing look as the ponds they'd seen just outside the facility on their way in.

"Besides," he said to himself, "the water would probably just pour right out of my chest." He smiled at that. He'd always wanted to laugh in the face of death.

Recording a message for his comrades hadn't gone well. In the *Enterprise*'s first year, one of her crew, Tasha Yar, had died. Later, Tasha's friends learned that she had prerecorded a good-bye message to all of them. Riker admired her foresight. He even tried recording his own message. After his first attempt, all he came up with was "Well, at least you won't have to hear me play the sax anymore." The next year, when he considered updating it, he just deleted it instead.

He always figured there would be time enough for final messages later. Until now. Now he *had* to record his message. It was his last opportunity. But the urgency of the situation didn't make the task any easier.

He'd tried a couple times, the perfunctory "It's been an honor and a privilege to serve with you" sort of thing, but it seemed hollow. It just wasn't him. Riker had never gone in for the dramatic speeches and flourishes that Picard seemed to espouse so effortlessly. Instead, he kept things light. But there wasn't a lot of lightness to be found now.

The problem, as usual, was Deanna.

No matter how many times he tried to record one of those damnable things, he stumbled when he got to her. It wasn't that he didn't know what he wanted to say to her. In fact, he always found himself saying too much.

Years earlier, when Riker had been stationed on Deanna's homeworld of Betazed, he and Deanna had been more than friends. More than lovers. They had been *imzadi.*

But their relationship ended abruptly and not well. Riker had left without even saying good-bye.

When they met again, serving together aboard the *Enterprise,* they always said they were just friends. It was true enough. But it was also, in many ways, the worst kind of lie. What they meant to say was that they were *only* friends, and in his own heart, whether he could admit it to himself or not, Riker knew it wasn't true.

Riker had his share of relationships with women after Deanna, but he never committed to any of them. He couldn't commit knowing she was still in the universe. He may have convinced himself that their relationship was over, maybe even believed it, but there was always a part of him that hoped they might reconnect somehow.

But he'd acted as if they were just friends. Nothing more. When Deanna revealed her betrothal to Wyatt Miller, Riker could do little more than watch and take out his frustrations on a hapless holodeck.

But it was the firebreak he needed to bury those feelings for her.

Even so, when Deanna began her relationship with Worf years later, it strained his friendship with both of them. He wasn't sure what would have happened if the Klingon hadn't transferred to Deep Space 9.

But recently, on Ba'ku, they had rekindled their romance. Riker realized he had to let Deanna know that he still thought of her the same way he had so many years ago, that they were far more than just friends. Since telling her, he now wondered what the hell had taken him so long.

Riker returned to his tricorder, positioned it so that the pool was behind him, and thumbed its recording tab. "Deanna," he said into the tricorder, "I'm sorry. I'm sorry I didn't come back, and I'm sorry that I waited so long to tell you how I felt. And I'm sorry that . . . this is such a lousy message."

Riker swore in disgust and hit the tricorder's Stop and Delete contacts in one fluid motion. He'd had enough practice with the maneuver; this was his fifth aborted farewell. But one more false start hardly mattered. He simply *couldn't* let his last words to Deanna be a litany of "I'm sorrys."

He buried his head in his hands. It just wasn't fair to get so close and then have it all taken away. He didn't want this. He didn't want to die.

He wasn't ashamed to admit it. Worf and he had discussed death on occasion, and the Klingon seemed unaffected by the concept. It was just part of being a warrior to Worf, and as long as it was a good death, an honorable death, he would welcome it.

Riker's death may have been honorable, but it was far from good. Despite what Worf would say, one month before your wedding was a *terrible* day to die.

He had faced death early when his mother died and secretly thought that if she'd fought harder, if she'd *wanted* it more, she'd still be alive. And just as secretly, he hated himself every time he thought it.

Riker railed against the grim reaper every chance he got. In his time on the *Enterprise*, he'd avoided certain death any number of times. Maybe he had gotten used to it. Maybe he had become so comfortable with the concept of avoiding his own death that he just couldn't believe it could happen to him anymore.

"Speak for yourself, sir," he'd once told Picard. "I plan to live forever." Picard had smiled at the joke, but in Riker's mind, it wasn't meant to be humorous. Even though he knew it wasn't possible, he meant every word.

The fact that death might finally best him, *that* bothered him. Hell, it infuriated him.

Death wasn't something to be accepted, it was something to be *fought*.

Riker had fought a few losing battles before and found himself thinking back to the *Kobayashi Maru* from Starfleet Academy. "Everyone loses," his instructor told him afterward. "But I've never had a cadet order an EVA suit be brought to him so he could fight an enemy ship by hand."

There was nothing wrong with losing, Riker figured, as long as you didn't give up.

With that, Riker opened his tricorder and made sure his face would be squarely in the center of the recording field but that the reflecting pool would not be seen. This was about just him and Deanna, nothing else. He knew what he had to do. Both for Deanna and himself.

And then he smiled.

"Don't smirk at me, Will Riker."

Deanna Troi threw a pillow at her fiancé, which he allowed to hit him. He then picked it up from the floor and rushed headlong at her, pushing them both onto the bed. He leaned over her, pinning her to the mattress. "Is this what our marriage is going to be like? You throwing things at me, and me dodging them?"

"You didn't dodge that one."

"I let it hit me."

"Of course you did."

Riker stared into her brown eyes. He could have easily got lost in them, but just as he was losing his focus, Deanna's eyes narrowed. "You're *serious* about this?" he asked more in dismay than seeking information.

"Absolutely. I want us to write our own vows."

Riker got off of her and sat on the edge of the bed. "What's wrong with the traditional ones? I like tradition."

"Typical military man."

"I'd like to think I'm anything but typical."

Deanna draped herself over Will's shoulders, breathing into his neck. "That's certainly true. But my mother once shared her memories of her wedding ceremony with me, and my parents wrote their own vows. I always thought it was romantic."

Will sighed. "But Deanna, you, better than most women in the universe, know exactly how I feel about you."

"You're right, I do. I feel how much you love me every time I see you. It just pours out of you." Since they had gotten back together, they had reestablished the slight mental connection they had once shared. They were again truly *imzadi*. On rare occasions they could even pick up a stray thought or two. But the emotional bond, that was strong as could be. And it had become so effortless that they no longer knew how much of it was intuition and how much was their empathic connection. "But our wedding, it's when we stand in front of our friends, our family, and the entire universe and declare our love for each other. Declare. We can't just say"—she lowered her voice, dropping her jaw into her chest, to do her best impression of her husband-to-be—"'Hey, you know how I feel.'"

Riker cocked his head and smirked. "Was that supposed to be me?"

"Do I need more facial hair?"

"I don't think I'd ever say that."

"Will, when you live among a race of telepaths, the things you choose to say are as important as . . . no, *more* important than the things you think."

"I'm not really a man of words, Deanna, I'm more a man of action."

She leaned over him and kissed him. "Fine, then show me."

Riker closed the tricorder, saving his message. He strode into the main chamber, where Beverly was standing at a podium computer, buried in the displays in front of her. "How's it going?" he asked, trying to sound casual.

She shook her head. "Not well. Several hundred years separate these Fabrini from the ones on Yonada. Their language evolved a bit over that time. The universal translator and I can make out a lot of words but not *all* of them. Maybe if I were aboard the *Enter-*

prise . . . It's got a larger database of linguistic algorithms. And I'm having particular issues with certain nouns."

"Such as?"

"There are words like 'cavity' and 'vein' that translate fairly easily because of context. But there are other words, like 'ventricle' and 'hypothalamus,' that are more just designations. *We* use centuries-old Latin to name a lot of these things, so there's no telling what the Fabrini used." Beverly looked at Riker, trying to gauge what effect her words were having on him. "I'd hate to be someone a couple of thousand years in our future trying to translate our medical databases."

Riker stared at his tricorder, remembering the problems he had just had trying to record a final message, then placed it on the table. "Words are nothing but trouble. I'm *done* with them."

"I wish I had something more for you to do, Will, but working on this database is fairly arcane at this point. I don't know how much you could really help me."

"I'm not looking for something to do, Beverly. I *have* something to do." Will started looking around the chamber, obviously not finding what he was searching for. "Where are our phasers?"

Beverly pulled them out of her medical bag. "They won't work, Will."

"Not in here, sure . . ."

"Actually, not anywhere. I had to pull out the power cells to energize this console."

Will stood in front of Beverly and placed his hands on the podium. "What?"

"The facility uses geothermal power to fuel itself. That's why most of the systems are still working. But the power conduit from this console to the main source was decayed. I couldn't reconnect it, so I replaced it." Beverly paused for a moment. "Why did you want the phasers?"

"Because I'm going out there."

"Will, you can't. It's too risky. The *Enterprise* will find us . . ."

"Beverly, I know they will, but we don't know *when*. There's so much interference that we don't know when they'll be able to locate us. And *they* don't know that they'll be walking into an environment with a hostile Tellarite who's already shown no compunctions about killing Starfleet officers."

A wave of realization hit Beverly. "You have a plan."

Will smiled a confident smile. "You bet I do."

"Is it a good plan?"

"I can't say that. Let me show you something." Will led Beverly out of the chamber and into the waiting room. He pointed at the pool. "Anything look familiar?"

"The architecture?"

"The pool." Riker sat on the edge of the pool and scooped up a handful of water. "I thought it was a simple reflecting pool, until I recognized this. It's the same ratty, algae-encrusted muck that we saw in the ponds outside. But there's no vegetation in here. So I scanned the pool. It's not a reflecting pool, Beverly, it's a moon pool. It connects to that pond outside of here. There's a pipe goes on for about a kilometer. Too long for me to hold my breath . . ."

". . . if you still had to breathe," Crusher finished.

"Exactly," Riker said while pressing the keypad on his tricorder.

Beverly looked at the indicator light on Riker's Lifesaver. Riker didn't need to look to know it was blinking noticeably faster; he could feel the pulses the Lifesaver sent through his body. He also knew Beverly feared that the alien device's power supply would never be able to withstand whatever he had planned. He figured she'd look for a way to talk him out of his plan, and he was preparing his counter.

"But the blast doors," Beverly said in protest. "Surely, there's a door in the pipe, and I doubt I can isolate just that one . . ."

Riker cut her off. "You won't have to. It's been underwater for six thousand years with nobody to repair or replace it. Look." Riker held up the tricorder so that Beverly could see the screen. "The mechanism rusted through. When the shutdown occurred, the blast doors in that pipe couldn't even close."

"Even if you can get out, Will, then what?"

"I figure I'm dead enough that our Tellarite friend won't be able to scan me, no matter what kind of instruments he's got. So maybe I can get the drop on him. Even if I can't, I *can* make enough of a distraction for you to open the doors of the facility and make a break for the shuttle."

Beverly couldn't hold herself back any longer. She pointed to the flickering light on the Lifesaver. "Will, stop. We don't know how much power that thing still has. As your doctor, I can't . . ."

Riker waved her off. "I may be your patient, Doctor, but I'm also a superior officer." Riker straightened to his full six-foot-four-inch height and put all the authoritarian air he could muster into his next statement. "Consider it an order, Commander." Then he gently put his hands on her shoulders and added, "Beverly, if I'm going out, I'm going out the same way I came in."

"I can't talk you out of this?"

"Good-bye, Beverly." And with that, he plunged into the pool.

Riker slowly poked his head out of the water, letting just his eyes surface over the waterline. His tricorder indicated that the Tellarite was near the front entrance of the medical facility, but given all the interference, Riker wasn't taking anything for granted. He'd chosen to walk rather than swim the length of the pipe so as to disturb the surface of the pond as little as possible. The walk itself through the drainpipe and into the pond had gone remarkably well. The hardest part was fighting the urge to breathe. It was like breaking a habit.

Slowly, Riker began to pull himself out of the pond. He moved carefully to keep the water from dripping off of him and back into the pond. He wanted no noise to alert the Tellarite. He pushed himself onto the muck-encrusted ground. Even though the blinking device in his chest reminded him how short his time was, he forced himself to creep forward with disciplined motions. After freeing his back foot from the last of the sticky morass, he surveyed the area more carefully and decided that this area had probably been a tropical paradise before the polar shift. Now it was a swamp, and a particularly unpleasant one at that. Some of the hardier vegetation had managed to survive, and even thrive, overrunning the area surrounding the facility.

Riker kept low, crouching to stay behind the unkempt bushes that ringed the facility. He moved closer to the vegetation, using it for cover but careful not to rustle it too much. Between that and the florid trees, he was able to work his way to the edge of the building. Along the way, he managed to find a decent-sized branch that he might be able to use as a weapon.

He took a quick glance around the corner of the building, taking in as much information as he could of what lay in front of the facility. He could see the Tellarite fifty meters away. He was overweight, even for a Tellarite, but for a being whose girth indicated inactivity, this Tellarite was anything but sedentary.

He was pacing near the main entrance of the medical center, waiting for whoever was inside finally to emerge so that he could attack. He moved back and forth with quick, agitated steps that caused the wire connecting his cargo gun to the backpack to bounce up and down. Occasionally, he would strike the blast door with his fists or probe it with the barrel of the cargo gun, looking for a weak spot. When his blows proved ineffective and his probing accomplished nothing, he returned to his pacing, more frantic than before. The waiting seemed to be killing this Tellarite. *Good,* Riker thought grimly. *Turnabout is fair play.*

The Tellarite still held the cargo gun at the ready, poised for action. But the backpack that held the gun's transporter buffer was large and unwieldy, and Riker figured it would make the Tellarite relatively awkward. It was his only advantage and he intended to press it. He definitely didn't want to get shot with that device again.

The quarantine shield and blast doors held firm, frustrating the scavenger's every attempt to use his gun to burrow through the wall. Clearly, the Tellarite was intent upon finishing the job of covering his crime by waiting out the witnesses left inside and eliminating them when they came out.

Riker adjusted his combadge to silence the normal chirp activation sound and contacted Beverly. "Doctor," he whispered, "I want you to disengage the quarantine protocols and open that door on my mark. Stay out of sight as best you can until I've engaged him." Riker took one last look at the Tellarite, the distance he needed to cover, and the sealed facility. On a good day, he could cover the distance pretty quickly, but this wasn't a good day. The bushes he'd used for cover ended at the edge of the facility and would provide him with no more protection. Still, he resolved himself to his plan and gripped the branch tighter. He tried to find the Tellarite's pacing rhythm, to have Beverly open the door when the scavenger was looking away. "Mark."

The quarantine doors opened with a grinding screech and the Tellarite turned to see what had happened. While the alien was looking at the opening doorway, Riker broke into a dead run. When he was ten meters from the Tellarite, Riker began his diversionary tactics by shouting his favorite curse at the piglike scavenger. *Let's see your universal translator handle that!*

The Tellarite turned and started to point his gun at the onrushing human, but Riker was already upon him. Riker swung the branch at his enemy's head, but the Tellarite moved quickly and brought up his cargo gun to block the branch's path. Still, the force of Riker's blow knocked the cargo gun out of the alien's hands and drove him backward. Gravity and the Tellarite's backpack did the rest, and he fell onto the ground.

Riker charged, cocking his arms back by his head so that he could swing the branch full force. The Tellarite kicked upward with his left leg, aiming his blow at the large hole in Riker's chest. Riker twisted his body, moving his wound away from the kick, but the Tellarite's hooflike foot caught Riker on the right arm. He cried out in pain and dropped the branch. He could see the alien trying to retrieve his cargo gun by pulling on the wire that connected it to the backpack, and Riker knew he had to act quickly. Almost by instinct, he dived on top of the Tellarite, letting every iota of frustration pour out of him and into his fists.

Fueled by his own anger, Riker pummeled the scavenger over and over. He wasn't sure how much his murderer's natural padding was protecting him, so he kept pounding away. Riker lost himself in the moment. He continued to punch, kick, and elbow the Tellarite with all of his heart . . . if he had still had one. The Tellarite blocked several of Riker's blows, even landed a few of his own, but the human didn't let up. The scavenger still wore his cargo gun and Riker had to keep the Tellarite's attention directed at him and away from Beverly as she ran to the shuttlecraft.

This is for taking me from Deanna! Riker thought and rained more blows on the scavenger. *You're not going to beat me! You're not going to win!*

And just then, as if sensing Riker's hubris, the indicator light on the Fabrini Lifesaver went dark.

Searing hot pain exploded in Riker's chest. He gasped in agony and the Tellarite took advantage of the moment to kick Riker off of him.

The scavenger got to his feet. Riker was expecting him to say something, some sort of confident boast or explanation of how he couldn't allow Riker to compromise his salvage operation. The Tellarite, though, much like Riker, was a creature of few words. He said nothing. Instead, he merely reclaimed the cargo gun that dangled from his backpack and pointed it at Riker once again.

A rumble filled Riker's ears. His world was starting to go dark. The Tellarite smiled a snaggletoothed grin when Riker noticed, just over the gunman's shoulder, a flash of blue and red. It was Beverly. She hadn't gone to the shuttle. She was right behind the Tellarite.

Riker's last thought was, *Dammit, Beverly, I told you to run!*

Then all was black.

Riker opened his eyes and saw the ceiling of the *Enterprise*'s sickbay. He'd seen it a number of times before, and it was comfortably familiar. He squinted at the light and counted the ceiling tiles in an effort to guess which diagnostic bed he was in. *Number three,* he thought.

Then he realized that he was thirsty.

Riker felt a pressure on his hand, and he looked at it to find another hand squeezing it. Riker knew whose hand it would be.

Tears were rolling down Deanna Troi's cheek. Riker looked up at his *imzadi*'s face and thought, *Either I'm not dead or heaven is going to be a pretty good place.*

"Sorry," Riker rasped, returning her squeeze. The warmth of Deanna's hand in his own told him he was, indeed, alive. "You're going to have to go through with the wedding anyway."

Deanna started to sob harder and kissed him. Her tears fell upon his face.

"What happened?" he asked, noticing that his voice was husky and his throat hurt as much as it had when his tonsils were removed.

Beverly walked into Riker's field of vision. He was pretty sure she had always been there but had stayed back to give Deanna her moment. "How are you feeling, Will?"

"Like hell."

"Believe it or not, that's a good sign."

"Don't take this as a complaint, but why aren't I dead?"

"Because I am a very good doctor and a very quick study."

Beverly told Riker how she had used his distraction to sneak up on the Tellarite and inject him with a neuroparalyzer from her hypospray. She got them all onto the shuttle and flew it back into open space. Once she was clear of the planet's interference, she contacted the *Enterprise* and had them beamed directly into sickbay.

The Lifesaver was almost out of power so had gone into an energy-saver mode. It kept Riker preserved but not animated. Data and Geordi figured out how to keep it powered and even stabilized the cargo gun's transporter buffer while Crusher and her medical staff attacked the Fabrini database. After two days' research, they managed to reimplant his heart and missing tissue, and stabilize him.

"Two days?" Riker thought aloud. "And the Tellarite?"

"We had to give Worf *something* to do." Beverly smiled. "You know, you're quite the hero. Our scavenger's name is Sakal and he's wanted all over the quadrant. Starfleet already has extradition petitions from seven different systems. But until the JAG corps sorts it all out, he's in our brig." Then Beverly's smile broadened until her face could barely contain it. "Recovering."

"So I'm going to be okay?"

"Given a little time, a little Regen, and a lot of rest, yes. I've put Deanna in charge of supervising your recovery." Deanna looked at Crusher for a moment. "I think I'll leave you two alone now."

Once Crusher had left sickbay, Deanna turned to Riker. "Don't you ever do that to me again."

"I'll try my best."

Deanna composed herself. She let go of his hand, straightened, and stood almost formally at his side. Her smile disappeared and Riker felt a wave of confusion and anger from the connection they shared. Deanna pulled a tricorder off her belt. Riker's tricorder. "Now, would you tell me what this is?" She flipped open the device to display the recording Riker had made, a solid minute of Riker, smiling and silent. "*This* was your last message to me?"

"Pretty much."

Deanna furrowed her brow.

"Deanna . . . *imzadi*. . . . I tried over and over to record you a message. Something weighty . . . important. Hell, something worthy of you. It was going to be the last thing I'd ever say to you and I wanted it to be memorable, but memorable in the right way." With an effort, Riker reached out and placed his hand atop Deanna's, closing the tricorder's display.

"I couldn't do it. I tried and tried. But nothing sounded right.

Then I realized why. Those last messages, they're for people who've held back." Riker's throat was getting drier, the pain more severe, but he continued. "I spent years denying how I felt. When we finally got back together, I stopped holding back. There hasn't been a day since then when I haven't given you, told you, and shown you exactly how much I love you."

Riker held Deanna's gaze. "You know I love you, right?"

"Yes."

"And you know that I won't let any force in the universe get between us again? Not without one hell of a fight."

"Yes."

"Then what was there left to say?"

Deanna leaned in and kissed him tenderly. She hugged him as much as she could without disturbing his recovering chest and whispered, "Well, you'd better think of something. You *still* have to write your vows."

ON THE SPOT

David A. McIntee

Historian's note:
This tale is set during the epilogue of the feature film
Star Trek Nemesis, during the weeks the Enterprise
was under repair in orbit of Earth.

DAVID McINTEE

David A. McIntee has written a dozen novels based on the British TV series *Doctor Who*, as well as ones based on *Space: 1999* and *Final Destination*. He has also written various audio scripts, several nonfiction books on subjects such as the *Aliens* and *Predator* franchises, and *Quatermass*. He has also written for the *Star Trek Communicator*, *SFX*, *Dreamwatch*, and the UK's official *Star Trek Magazine*. His most recent tie-in work has been writing *Jason and the Argonauts: The Kingdom of Hades*, the official sequel to Ray Harryhausen's movie, for Blue Water comics.

When not writing books, he studies martial arts, explores historical sites, builds models, researches Fortean subjects, teaches stagefighting workshops, and collects SF weaponry.

Dave is married to Ambassador Mollari and lives in Yorkshire with B'Elanna, Seven of Nine, Cannonball, and a Stripey Git.

Captain's log, Stardate 56934.1

Repairs to the Enterprise *continue as we prepare for our next assignment, but the crew, I fear, will never completely heal from the damage inflicted by Shinzon and his* Scimitar. *Commander Data, and so many others, will be greatly missed. As indeed will Commander—correction, Captain Riker and Counselor Troi, and also Doctor Crusher. So far the crew rotation is going smoothly, both in the departure of those leaving for other posts and the new arrivals.*

IT HAD BEEN CONSTRAINED FOR TOO LONG. IT DIDN'T MIND losing track of time while it had been cooped up and not knowing whether it had been imprisoned for hours or for days. Nor did it mind the darkness. It hated the physical sensations of the walls hemming it in.

Frustration built up like charge in a battery. It tried to calm down and put its concerns aside. It reminded itself that there were others, somewhere, in just the same situation. It knew that it was not alone, and that helped a great deal.

Best of all, it knew it would soon be free.

Lieutenant Commander Worf stood in the control booth overlooking the *Enterprise*'s shuttlebay and watched an angular cargo shuttle settle into place on the deck. He checked a padd that he held; this would be the delivery of new transporter phase coils. Phase coils could not easily be transported themselves without risking their delicate balance, and in any case the *Enterprise*'s one working transporter room was being prioritized for personnel movement rather than cargo.

A few uniformed figures emerged and began to unload crates from the shuttle. Things seemed to be going efficiently enough, but Worf still felt uneasy. The sleek form of the *Sovereign*-class *U.S.S. Enterprise* had been built for speed and grace, but now, in the embrace of an orbiting drydock, she felt weary and vulnerable. Once the ship and her crew were free of this mechanical nursemaid's influence, Worf would know he was back where he belonged. He would feel better then.

As Worf made his way toward the bridge, he passed several technicians working on the innards of the power distribution systems. Having to pause or step aside irritated him, but he said nothing. It was just another symptom of the strangeness of being tethered to a drydock. There was something ironic in so many more corridors than usual being obstructed, when the crew complement on board was a shade over half the normal strength.

He took a turbolift to the bridge and triggered the chime at the ready room door. *"Come,"* the captain's voice answered almost immediately.

Captain Jean-Luc Picard looked up from a screen as Worf entered. Picard looked a little tired but was fully alert. His professionalism was the best Worf had ever seen in a human; he bore difficult times with equanimity, as a warrior should. There was no doubt that times had been difficult lately. The triumph over the Reman pretender, Shinzon, and his warship *Scimitar* had been soured by the loss of many comrades, including Lieutenant Commander Data. Having the *Enterprise* towed home like a barge had been the final insult.

ON THE SPOT

Picard bore the shame well, but Worf could see that he felt it. He could see it in Picard because it was an attitude they both shared.

"Captain," Worf began, proffering the padd, "the final supply delivery from Station McKinley has arrived on schedule. All new and replacement hardware has either been installed or is on board ready to be installed."

Picard nodded. "Good. What about structural repairs?"

"All structural repairs are progressing ahead of schedule. Engineering reports we will be ready to conduct maneuvering tests later today."

"That is good news, Mister Worf." Picard gave a very genuine smile. "It feels good to be standing aboard a functioning *Enterprise* again, doesn't it?"

Worf allowed himself a smaller, answering, smile. "It does, sir."

"I believe you're off duty now, is that correct?"

"It is." Worf paused, then decided that he had to bring up an issue that he had known would come. "Sir . . ."

"Yes?"

"About Commander Data's effects . . ."

"I am not a cat person," Worf had insisted.

"It looks like you are now," Geordi La Forge had told him. Worf and La Forge had taken care of the inventory of Data's quarters after his death. La Forge had been the android's best friend, and Worf had felt that assisting was the best way to honor his fallen shipmate.

Some items had been bequeathed to Data's comrades, while others would be returned to Starfleet. Still others, including the prototype android designated B-4, had been sent to Bruce Maddox of Starfleet's artificial intelligence division, since Data's android nature was of interest to them. Pieces of equipment that weren't personal possessions were reassigned to where they might be needed. In their sorting through Data's effects, the pair had unexpectedly come across something that didn't fit into any of those categories.

More accurately, it had leaped into Worf's arms and begun to purr. La Forge had immediately expressed guilt that he had forgotten all about the cat. Worf just wanted to drop it to the floor before it made him sneeze. He had resisted the urge; the animal was an inconvenience but had earned no harm from him.

Now that he had a moment, Worf decided it was time to bring the matter up. Spot was as much a part of Data's belongings as anything else and ought to be dealt with as appropriately. "Has a new home been found for Data's cat?" Worf asked Picard.

Picard tilted an eyebrow. "I'm afraid not. With the crew at half strength, there are fewer options available." He frowned. "Where is the cat now?"

"In a carrier in my quarters. I would like it to be moved to a more appropriate location as soon as possible. Perhaps—"

"Mister Worf, it would not be my ideal first choice to put you on the—" Picard hesitated, then bowed to the inevitable with a faint ironic smile. "On the spot like this." Worf said nothing; he had long since become used to human speech patterns making these ironic connections, whether consciously or otherwise. "I'm afraid that, for the moment, you're rather stuck with the cat."

Worf shifted uncomfortably. "Captain, I am not a cat person. And my duties are increasing as the repairs progress."

"I see. . . . Do you feel . . . burdened by your duties?"

"No," Worf snapped immediately. "The increase in workload is . . . challenging."

"I think the phrase anyone else would use is 'thankless hard work,'" Picard said. He rose, straightening his uniform. "It would appear to me that looking after Spot is a minor addition to your duties. Neither thankless nor, I should think, hard work."

"Yes, sir," Worf said reluctantly. "But it is not a task that appeals."

"And what exactly do good Klingons—and good Starfleet officers—do when they receive an . . . unappealing duty?"

"The honorable thing."

Picard nodded, and Worf could see he was amused. Worf didn't mind; Picard had earned the right, many times over. "Then it would appear that the honorable thing to do would be to go down to sickbay and get inoculated against feline allergens."

After Worf had left the ready room, Picard closed his eyes for a moment and allowed himself a small smile. There was always something new in commanding a starship—some unknown or forgotten fact, usually a small one. The devil was in the details, his father used to say. A captain could have planned out all kinds of strategies and missions, he might know all about navigation and the mechanics of warp travel, but there would always be those tiny details which came as a surprise. Such as having to find a home for a cat.

Worf would find this out as he went along. With no XO currently aboard, Worf was doing an admirable job holding together all those small details. Someday, Picard thought, Worf would make an excellent first officer, just as Will Riker would make an excellent captain for the *U.S.S. Titan,* when he and Deanna returned from their honeymoon.

He returned to his screen, running an eye over new personnel files. With repairs nearing completion, new crew members were arriving all the time and others leaving.

Sickbay wasn't busy. The amount of work that had been taking place on the ship over the past few weeks had afforded the opportunity for a wide variety of industrial accidents, but there were far larger and better-equipped hospitals on the planet below, so the *Enterprise*'s sickbay wasn't being used for more than routine shipboard physicals and minor ailments.

Worf had hoped he would see Beverley Crusher and wish her success in her new career at Starfleet Medical. She would be a good leader for any medical team or organization, he thought. When he arrived at sickbay, he found only Doctor Tropp and a human nurse tending some growth cultures in some kind of incubator.

"What can I do for you, Worf?" Tropp asked cheerily. He was a Denobulan, and Worf found his enthusiasm somewhat wearing.

"Captain Picard has"—he wanted to say "ordered," but that wouldn't be right—"required me to seek an inoculation for a task."

Tropp brandished a hypospray. "A shot, eh? What sort of inoculation? Rigelian fever? Varnak's disease? Orion plague?"

"Allergens," Worf said reluctantly.

"Allergens? I thought that indomitable Klingon physique was resistant to most types of allergy."

"Most," Worf agreed.

"Well, there's no catchall inoculation, so what type of allergen—"

"Feline."

Tropp looked at Worf as if he thought the Klingon was joking. "Feline? You mean cats? Earth cats."

"Yes." Worf could read Tropp's curiosity in his expression and was not in a mood to explain in great detail. "Commander Data's cat will require a home. Until one is found, the captain has given me responsibility for care of the animal." Worf grimaced. "I have looked after Spot before."

"And that's when you found out you were allergic?"

Worf nodded. "I was sneezing on her."

Tropp nodded slowly. "Well, I'll get that sorted out for you." He busied himself at a chemical synthesizer. "It's actually quite unusual to find feline allergies in this day and age. And even for people who are allergic, only about two-thirds of cats are allergenic."

"Spot is one of them," Worf assured him, as Tropp gave him his shot.

"Well, it shouldn't be too much of a problem now. That should keep you hale and hearty."

"It had better," Worf muttered.

Worf entered his quarters and stopped. The carrier containing Spot was right next to the door, ready to be handed over to, or taken to, Spot's eventual new home. Worf hadn't anticipated that he would even have to open the carrier himself.

A plaintive mewling was coming from inside the cat carrier. Spot had clearly not been enjoying her imprisonment. That was a thing Worf understood. He bent down and opened the container. "You may come out now," he said. Nothing happened. He waited a moment, then bent to see if the creature was all right. Perhaps the mewling sound was a noise of pain or illness? There was a breeze of motion, and Worf almost sneezed. The inoculation seemed to be working, however.

As Worf straightened, Spot moved quietly forward. She looked around, sniffing the air. Without warning, she dashed for the bed, a fluid orange blur, and leaped up onto it. Worf did not want to share his bed with cat hairs. He lifted her back onto the floor and received a withering look in return.

Worf glared at the creature. It was repulsively . . . fluffy, too much like an accursed tribble, in the same way that swimming was too much like bathing. Spot jumped back up on the bed and began to wash herself. Worf gritted his teeth; at least tribbles were not so athletic. This creature was undisciplined and did not know its place. These were both things it would have to learn if it was not to get in the way. "Computer," Worf said, "restrict door exit privileges to these quarters. Door sensors should not respond to"—he glanced at the signage on Spot's carrier, which gave Spot's transponder code—"feline one-four." All pets on board a starship were chipped with a subcutaneous transponder so that the computer could track them.

"Confirmed. Door exit protocols have been modified to exclude activation by feline one-four."

Now, Worf realized, the cat was essentially locked in with him. Some duties were definitely more onerous than others.

Freedom! It stretched itself, working out muscle cramps it had developed from its time in confinement, and tried to determine where the others might be. It got no sense of their locations but could tell they were somewhere in the vicinity.

A curve of plain carpet led away from the container that had been its home for the past several days. There was no sign of any other beings around, which was good. It should have complete freedom of movement now, to find the others. They would be doing the same.

Wasting no more time, it set off.

Spot cautiously watched the large Klingon . The last time she had spent any length of time in his presence, he had sneezed on her several times. She didn't want to give him the opportunity to repeat the offense.

The bed, though clean, still held an odor of him. It was strong and distinctive, reassuring in a way that his appearance and manner were not.

Ejected from the bed, Spot prowled round her new territory. The distinctive scent of the one she would be sharing her quarters with, Worf, adhered comfortingly to the furnishings and to the strange objects that adorned the walls. It was a much stronger scent than that of Data, who used to share Spot's other quarters, but it was good. Spot liked it. She wondered whether the scent or the pose was the truest sign of the real being. She kept her distance for the moment but began to have hope that he wasn't going to sneeze in her face this time.

She peered around the corners of the bed and the storage areas. There was nothing in the tiny gaps between the furniture and the walls. Gentle breezes wafted in from vents near the floor, and she followed them to their sources, wondering whether there were any openings through which she could fit. She had approached the door, of course, and it had not opened for her. She didn't mind; she was only curious as to whether it would work for her or not. This was a territory she could be comfortable with.

There were several blades supported on the walls. One was large and curved, like a huge double claw. The scent of old blood clung to it, and to a pair of smaller angular blades. They had all been cleaned and smelled of disinfectant as well as the blood, but that tang of victory couldn't quite be erased. Spot considered this. Worf must be from a worthy lineage. Cats value lineage, though they believe that each generation should go off and make its own way in the world—or galaxy.

Spot missed the golden-skinned companion who had shared so many years of her life. He had fed her well and responded well to her needs and wants. She had no doubt that this new companion was going to be very different.

Worf sat, preparing to enjoy the *rokeg* blood pie that his adoptive mother had had transported up to the ship for him. She always sent him some home-cooked food when the *Enterprise* was in Earth orbit. The replicators on board synthesized a reasonable approximation of the Klingon dish, which was nutritious enough, but they did not use the true ingredients. The replicator could not properly create live *gagh* or blood that had oxygenated a living creature. To put it simply, it could not replicate good home cooking.

Just as he was about to eat, Spot jumped up onto the table.

The dish smelled interesting. It smelled like fresh prey. She looked at Worf, who glared back. This was interesting; Data the Golden had never brought forth the spoils of a hunt. This one liked his food raw and fresh caught; that was much more understandable. And the smell . . . Much stronger and richer than Data or any of the humans. A scent of vibrance and full of life, yes. Like all cats, Spot preferred scents that were strong and clear.

Spot didn't mind the glare, or the tone of voice, or any other aspect of the Klingon's demeanor. He was not the doting kind, she recognized, so he wouldn't interfere with much-needed sleep to make baby talk. He seemed able to keep himself to himself, and he understood the value of just sitting quietly, but if the smell of the fresh kill was anything to go by, he too was a killer, ready to spring at any moment. He might not like her, but he should understand her. He probably wouldn't challenge her with rude stares. As he was trying to ignore her, he would not be smothering, and that was good, in Spot's opinion.

Worf let out a low rumble in the back of his throat and put Spot back on the floor. He moved to the replicator and said, "Feline supplement number . . ." How many of these cat food recipes had Data programmed? He recalled Data once mentioning number twenty-five being Spot's favorite, so there must be at least that many. "Twenty-five," Worf finished. A glass dish with the requested food materialized in the slot, and Worf put it down for Spot.

Spot was nearby, watching, but made no immediate move toward the food. Worf ignored the cat's behavior. It would either eat the food now or not. It was the cat's choice to make, and if she wanted to go hungry, or save it for later, then so be it.

Picard had long since got into the habit of making walking tours of his ship when he had the time, and not just when there was an important event in the offing. Originally he had conducted inspections, but he and his crew had now been working together for so long that keeping tabs on them wasn't necessary. However, he took pleasure in seeing his crew—many of them his friends—working at their best. In turn, they were reassured by his interest.

Leaving the bridge, he had taken a turbolift down to Deck 16 and walked into main engineering. Geordi La Forge was standing near the dilithium chamber, overseeing the sealing of its articulation frames. "Captain," he said, alerting others in engineering to Picard's visit. Nobody sprang to attention or began working harder; they were all doing their jobs to the best of their ability, and they knew that was all that Picard asked.

"Mister La Forge. How is the engineering refit going?"

"It's going pretty well, Captain, if I do say so myself." He squinted one last time at the dilithium chamber and ticked off something on a padd. "The final engine upgrades have been installed and all systems reset."

"Good," Picard said with a nod. "I'll want to begin engine tests as soon as possible. Run her in, so to speak."

Geordi nodded in agreement. "We still have some simulations to run, and it'll take a while for the warp core to reach optimal settings, but we can begin impulse testing anytime."

"We'll start with maneuvering systems while we're within the moon's orbit," Picard said. "It's a straightforward engineering test in friendly space, ideal for a skeleton crew and new recruits."

"Before going out on a real mission?"

"Just so." Picard took a last look around and smiled. "Carry on, Mister La Forge."

Worf could feel Spot's eyes on him throughout his meal, but she had either the sense or the decorum to not try to steal any of it. Afterward, it was time to check the progress of the crew rotation. Picard had asked to be notified when the last of the week's new arrivals had boarded. According to the data downloaded into his padd, this had now happened.

Leaving his quarters, Worf headed toward the nearest turbolift. He had made only one turn when he had to stop. A trunk was sitting in the middle of the corridor. Worf stood over the trunk and looked both ways along the corridor, seeing no sign of its owner. It was a standard piece of Starfleet-issue luggage; he had at least one in storage himself.

For a moment, Worf wondered if the trunk might contain a bomb, or be booby-trapped in some way. He discounted the possibility immediately. If it was a terrorist bomb, it would have been placed out of the way, where it would not likely be discovered, rather than left to trip anyone walking down the corridor. Crouching beside it, Worf saw that the lid was slightly open. He briefly returned to his quarters and collected a tricorder. The scan showed no signs of explosives or active devices. Satisfied, he opened the lid. The trunk contained nothing but clothing. There was a Starfleet code on the lid, which the data on his padd said was assigned to a Lieutenant Gregory of stellar cartography. "Computer, where are Lieutenant Gregory's quarters?"

"Deck 8, section 4-alpha," the computer responded promptly.

"And where is Lieutenant Gregory now?"

"Lieutenant Gregory is in his quarters."

Setting his teeth, Worf carried the trunk to the nearest turbolift and instructed it, "Deck 8." In moments, he was carrying the trunk along a curving corridor, his eyes scanning the tiny signage on the doors. When he found the right door, he thumbed the chime and folded his arms.

A blond human of less than thirty years of age appeared in the doorway, his uniform crumpled and open at the throat. Behind him, padds, books, and other bric-a-brac were scattered untidily around the floor between open bags and boxes.

"Lieutenant Gregory," Worf said without preamble. He dumped the trunk into Gregory's arms. "Is this your trunk?"

Gregory nodded eagerly. "Why, yes, it is, uh, Commander." His eagerness stalled a little when he realized the rank of the big Klingon. He smiled uncertainly. "Thank you, sir. I thought I'd never see it again."

"Then perhaps you should not have left it in the corridor."

"But, sir, I didn't." Gregory waved his hands vaguely, a human propensity that always set Worf's teeth on edge. "The last I saw that trunk was at Space Station McKinley. It didn't make it over to the *Enterprise* with me, and I thought it had been lost in transit."

"Did you report this transporter malfunction?"

"I called back to McKinley to ask why they didn't send it with me. I'm still waiting to hear back from them."

"Open it," Worf ordered bluntly, "and confirm its contents. Is anything missing, or has anything been added to it?"

Gregory retreated into the cabin and put the trunk on a chair. "Uh, please, Commander, come in." The invitation was unnecessary, as Worf was already watching over his shoulder. Gregory shuffled through the clothes and boots in the trunk. "Everything's just as it should be, Commander."

"Nothing is missing?"

"Not that I can tell. And there's definitely nothing extra in here . . ." His voice trailed off in a way that suggested there was something he wasn't sure whether to mention.

"If you have any more to say, do so now."

"It's probably nothing. I just thought there was a bit of a . . . a funny smell there for a minute. I thought I'd had all these things cleaned before I packed them, but maybe I missed something." Worf refrained from commenting, but he could tell from the lieutenant's expression that his own expression said all that needed to be said.

Picard had settled into his new seat on the bridge. It felt physically as comfortable as his old one, but he couldn't help thinking that it didn't. "Maneuvering thrusters," he ordered, "three-quarters forward. Take us out." The ensign at the helm was already executing the maneuver, as she acknowledged with, "Three-quarters, aye, sir."

Tiny flares of heated gas flickered, shoving the great starship into forward motion. Effortlessly, like a brig whose sails have caught the wind at the harbor mouth, the *Enterprise* slid out from the grip of the orbital dock.

Although Earth orbit was always busy with traffic approaching or departing, Starfleet had made sure there was a wide corridor for the *Enterprise.* Their newly restored thoroughbred would be in no danger of running down smaller travelers in her path.

It had been reunited with its fellows. The reunion was a great joy and a great relief. It was good to be normal once more and with all the emotions and intelligence that it knew and deserved.

The reunion was also short, for there was much work to be done, and none of the fellow travelers were work shy. It had made its way to a storage area where there was a viewport. No parts of the dry-dock now obscured the view of Earth below. The ship was in free flight.

That meant it was time.

Worf had tried to put the trunk out of his mind, but he couldn't. He wasn't sure why, but somehow he could imagine Captain Riker following up on it. Or perhaps Data, in one of his Sherlock Holmes holodeck fantasies. What would either of them do, in his position?

Data would probably know the answer already, but Riker would keep at it like an animal feeding on its kill.

Perhaps it was an indication of a transporter malfunction? If so, it would be important. With only one transporter room operational, it could leave the ship reliant entirely on shuttles. Feeling vaguely and uncomfortably like an XO, Worf sought out Geordi. He was sitting at his master display panel in engineering. "Commander La Forge."

"What can I do for you, Worf?"

"Have there been any reports of transporter malfunctions lately?"

Geordi looked surprised at the question. "No, none at all. The phase transition coils are all brand-new anyway, and all the crew rotation transports have been boosted from Station McKinley's transporters."

"Could their transporters be malfunctioning?"

"Well, McKinley's been in service for decades, but it's Earth's main transit point for orbital transfers. Its engineering team is one of the biggest in Starfleet and would be pretty quick to pick up on any malfunction." Geordi shook his head. "Why do you ask? Is there some problem?"

"I found a piece of luggage in a corridor. The crew member it belonged to says he lost it in transit."

"You mean it materialized in a corridor instead of on the pad?" Geordi sounded as concerned as he was curious. He turned his chair around and pulled up a schematic. "Did he call in a report?"

"Not yet. He says he believed that the trunk simply was not sent from McKinley, even though it was on the pad next to him."

"Well, it's always possible they could have selected one pad to activate and not another, but there would have to have been a reason to split up a set of transports that are all going to the same place."

"Such as?"

"I dunno . . . Maybe there was a malfunction warning on one pad, and the transporter operator decided to shut it down. Or maybe there was something the operator thought was dangerous and decided to hold in transit. But that would happen only if, say, someone was firing a weapon as they were picked up in the beam."

"And could one object be separated in the pattern buffer and rematerialized in a different location from the rest of the pattern?"

"It could be done, but it'd be tricky and probably not worth the effort. Or the risk. But I'll have it checked out."

Worf considered all of this. None of it sounded likely to have happened, but this meant another possibility. "Then perhaps we have a thief on board, who was disturbed before he could steal from the trunk and had to drop it."

"Or maybe a grudge," suggested Geordi. "Some kind of prank aimed at Gregory."

"That is also possible," Worf admitted. "Thank you. I have much to think about before the next security briefing."

Spot had eaten well. The Klingon had known her favorite food and given her it. She had, of course, waited until he had left before she ate it. It wouldn't do for her companion to consider her too predictable.

Satisfied, she strolled through the quarters again. There were gaps between walls and furniture, and the occasional openable closet or drawer. These would all be good places in which to hide when she wanted to have fun watching her companion's reactions, or when she wanted a nap that wouldn't be disturbed. She was about to settle down for a doze when a breath of air ruffled her fur. Curious, she turned her head around until the breeze was in her face.

There was a vent high up in the wall above a strange chair made of dense black globes. A mesh grille covered the vent. Spot leaped up onto the chair and onto the highest of the black globes. Another jump took her onto a thin ledge right next to the vent. There was a strange scent coming from it, something she had never smelled before.

Spot rubbed the side of her head against the corner of the grille, and it moved slightly, coming away from the wall. The tip of her tail writhed from side to side with excitement. She wondered if she could get inside. One paw could get between the grille and the edge of the vent, and then her narrow nose and snout could follow.

In moments, Spot had wedged her head and one front paw into the gap and was trying to get the rest of her shoulders in. For several long, horrible moments, she thought she was stuck. Her heart raced faster and faster with the terror of ending up hanging from the wall in such a position, her neck twisted and dragged sideways more and more painfully until it snapped.

Then the grille buckled, and Spot was so surprised that she almost fell back out of the gap. Recovering, she pushed her way through. There was a horrible moment when she thought she might get stuck, but she stretched herself out and felt her ribs bend uncomfortably, and then she was through. She straightened and stretched and flexed her tail, then examined her surroundings.

She was in a crawl space that was much like any other. Blinking indicator lights here and there cast very faint colors onto the conduits and pipes that filled the space. A hint of a breeze wafted through the crawl space, bringing with it the scents of the materials the environment was made of. Those scents, she was already familiar with. It was that other scent that she wanted to know about, the one that had passed by the vent so recently.

La Forge found Worf hunched over a prune juice in the crew's lounge, which Captain Riker had dubbed "The Happy Bottom Riding Club" just prior to his departure. The fact that Worf detested the name and refused to use it had become no small source of amusement to the engineer.

Geordi picked up a drink from the bar and sat opposite Worf. "I checked out the transporters," Geordi began. "Level-three diagnostics and a trawl through the transporter logs show no malfunctions or anomalous transports. However Gregory's trunk got into the corridor on Deck 6, it wasn't beamed there."

"That suggests a thief." Worf almost spat the word.

"Maybe."

"I will begin checking, beginning with the new arrivals."

"It's your department, not mine. I wish—" Geordi fell silent. "Never mind."

"What?"

"I was just going to say I wish Data were here. He could think faster than any of us."

"I must agree." Worf's fist tightened around his glass. "His death has robbed us of a fine officer." He paused. "As well as a friend."

"It's . . . 'Ironic' would be the wrong word, I guess, but . . ."

"But?"

"Data always wanted to be human. Be . . . alive. And in the end, like all human life . . ." Geordi didn't finish his sentence but just spread his hands. "I guess none of us were expecting it."

Worf thought about it. What La Forge said was true. Data had always sought to be human. In the struggle against the Praetor Shinzon he had died. "Death is the inevitable conclusion of life."

"He always thought there was a possibility that he could eventually cease functioning, but I know I always expected him to outlive all of us."

"As did I," Worf admitted. He sipped at his prune juice, and both men fell silent. "He sacrificed his life to defeat an enemy," Worf rumbled at last. "Data sought to share the life of a human, but—" He smiled, showing teeth. "He died like a Klingon." Worf gazed into his juice. "I do not know if Data would have thought about the possibility, but I am sure there is a place for him in Sto-Vo-Kor."

Geordi pursed his lips. "I never thought of it that way, but I guess there's not much that would surprise me anymore." He cheered up, with a little visible effort. "Which reminds me, Worf, how are you and Spot getting along?"

This was the last subject Worf wanted to discuss right now. "She is . . . under control." Geordi laughed. "She is as soft as a tribble and does not understand her place! But she will adapt."

"And so will you, once she gets you trained." Worf only glared in reply. "Hey, you've already switched from calling her 'it' to 'she.'"

"At least I could always tell the creature was female," Worf said pointedly.

Geordi laughed again. "Yeah, that you could. I've never been than much of a cat person either." He turned as someone approached, and Worf did likewise. It was one of Geordi's engineering crew. "Commander, do you have a moment?" Worf considered simply saying no but realized the woman was speaking to Geordi. "We're getting reports of door malfunctions on Decks 8 and 9."

Malfunctioning doors didn't sound like a threat to Worf, but it was unusual. The unusual was more often a threat. "What kind of malfunctions?" Geordi asked.

"Jamming open, mainly." Now Worf's interest was piqued. Doors were made to close for many reasons—privacy, convenience, safety—but aboard any kind of spacegoing vessel, they were vital to maintaining atmosphere if there was a hull breach. For a moment, Worf thought about leaving it to engineering, but Geordi's team would be taxed to the limit as it was, with testing all the new and newly repaired engine systems. Besides, he wanted to know first whether this really was an engineering problem. A thief would find jammed doors quite useful.

Ordinarily this sort of variation from the norm would be an XO matter, in Worf's opinion. With no XO on board, most of the duties of the post had ended up in Worf's lap, and he would not shirk any duties. If looking after Spot was a duty he had accepted, this was another one he should accept. "Show me these doors," he said.

Spot had been enjoying herself in the crawl spaces. Some tunnels came out into Jefferies tubes, giving her access to different decks. She had free run of the ship now, and there were a lot more easily accessed gaps opening out of the crawl spaces than there had been allowing her in.

There were places to run, places to slink, and places to climb up or down. And there were so many places to hide, more than she had ever imagined.

The strange new scent was closer now, and there were sounds ahead too. There were always sounds in crawl spaces, of course: beeps and chirps and all sorts of very artificial sounds. This was an organic sound. There was something in here with her, ahead. It wasn't one of the other cats on board, as she knew them all by sight and scent. It wasn't a prey animal, either, or any other creature Spot had encountered before. This was entirely new and gave Spot pause.

Spot had met new creatures before, of course. There was a first time for every creature she had met, and she had always reacted the same way. She would sniff, and watch, and think. Then she would repeat those stages as often as she needed before approaching. If nothing else, she needed to know whether the creature was prey or a threat. If it was neither, then she could look at her other options. Suddenly, it came out of a side passage, a few body lengths in front of her. She stopped silently, not wanting to alert it if it hadn't already noticed her.

It was leathery in patches, with short coarse hair and stubby protrusions of leather and bone. It seemed to be balanced on several protrusions and flexed them to move. Spot couldn't see any ears or eyes, or any other sense organs, on the creature. It was dark in the crawl space, so Spot thought maybe she just wasn't noticing them. Or perhaps it had something she wouldn't recognize. There were several types of animal she had encountered in her travels who did not have normal eyes or ears.

It didn't seem to be a threat. It wasn't desirable.

It was prey, then.

Spot leaped, digging her claws into the creature. It thrashed around under her, and she belatedly realized that she didn't know how to kill it. A rodent, or even another cat, she might kill with a neck bite that would crush the windpipe, but this thing didn't seem to have a neck, let alone a windpipe. Spot dug in her claws and bit where she could. Belatedly, the creature extruded claws made of bone, but it was too little, too late.

Its struggles became weaker and weaker. Eventually it was still.

Spot hissed at the unfamiliar taste. It wasn't unpleasant, exactly, but she didn't fancy eating the whole thing. Perhaps, she thought, it would make a good exchange for the favorite food the big Klingon companion had given her.

Deck 8, in a different quarter from Gregory's cabin. Worf carefully eyed the edges of the sixth pair of doors, seeing no scuff marks or scratches that would suggest they had been jammed by manual force. He ran a quick diagnostic on the access panel, and that too seemed to be normal. Finally, he scanned the mechanism with a tricorder; there was definitely nothing wrong with that, either.

It had been exactly the same on the other doors. No sign of forced entry, and none of the occupants—all new arrivals—had reported anything missing. Worf arranged interviews for all of them with his security team and then retired to his quarters to review what he had found so far. Perhaps studying the data he had acquired would offer a clue.

"Commanders Worf and La Forge," the captain's voice came over the ship's communications net, *"please report to my ready room."*

"On my way," Worf responded.

Captain Picard had read the reports filed by all his department heads and was not pleased. "We're now flying freely," Picard began, taking a cup of tea from the replicator, "and I should very much like to give the ship's repairs a good shakedown as soon as possible. Yet I find we're experiencing a spate of minor malfunctions, most recently the problem with the doors on Deck 8. I also have some reports of replicator and holodeck malfunctions."

Geordi grimaced. "These malfunctions are small, but they're proving pretty tricky to track down."

"Tricky?"

Geordi spread his hands but didn't look too concerned. "Well, it's taking up a lot of man-hours, but it's nothing too difficult. And, to be honest, it's pretty much what I expected after the repairs and upgrades anyway."

Picard sipped his tea and nodded understandingly. "Teething troubles. Version conflicts."

"Version conflicts," Geordi agreed with a sigh. There was a lot of feeling in his voice. He shook his head. "The bane of Starfleet engineering."

"You're certain that's the cause."

"Personally? Sure. But as chief engineer, no. We're following up on every avenue."

Picard nodded approvingly. "I must confess that some of the circumstance does remind me of the effects of Wesley's 'evolved' nanites."

Geordi grinned. "Would you believe that was the second or third thing I thought of? But there are definitely no nanites on the loose this time, sir."

"And you, Mister Worf, have another theory that may account for some of these events?"

"It is possible there may be a thief on board." Worf couldn't get the distaste out of his voice. Not only did he believe the old Earth saying about "honor among thieves" to be nonsensical, he couldn't even imagine how a thief could have any honor. "Security is conducting interviews and background checks on all the newly arrived crew members."

"Good. I want to test out maneuvering control with translunar orbital insertion exercises on the next watch, and I would prefer there to be no more malfunctions."

"We'll do our best, Captain," Geordi promised. He left, and Worf moved after him.

"Mister Worf, a moment," Picard said. Worf paused at attention, hands behind his back. "Worf, you may find that there isn't always a need to be too much of a micromanager about small things like door malfunctions. But if ever it comes to it, you're showing signs of learning to be a good XO."

"Thank you, sir, but it is not an ambition that I have."

Geordi had returned to engineering and was making good progress with starting up the new dilithium chamber and the warp simulations. He was almost convinced that he could relax, when there was a sudden, distant, scream. "What was—" Before Geordi could finish the question, an alarm began warbling. Geordi glanced at a screen. "Uh-oh, we've lost an EPS junction." He turned to the nearest ensign. "Shut down everything that goes through junction four-oh-one-four-kappa and reroute to a backup."

"Aye, sir," the ensign replied, already getting on with it as he spoke.

Geordi jogged out through a wide corridor toward the Jefferies tube where junction 4014 kappa was located. The source of the scream was immediately obvious.

He had been a human in his early thirties, in the yellow trim of an engineering uniform. Now he lay sprawled at the opening of a Jefferies tube. One of his half-closed hands was badly burned, smoke still curling from his sleeve. There was another burn on his face, and the hair on the right side of his head had been shriveled almost down to the skin.

Geordi slapped his combadge. "Medical emergency in engineering!" He tapped it again. "Engineering to Worf."

"Worf here."

"We need you down here on Deck Sixteen. There's been a death."

"On my way."

Worf walked into engineering a bare fifteen seconds later, next to Doctor Tropp. "Where is the body?"

"This way," Geordi said, leading them toward the Jefferies tube.

Any death aboard ship had to be handled in a certain way, regardless of whether it was due to accident, enemy action, crime, or natural causes. Security and the ship's executive officer both had to be notified. With Worf temporarily acting in both capacities, it fell to him alone to make sure that all the proper reports were filed and the captain kept up to date with what had happened.

Worf was used to seeing death, and it didn't trouble him the way it troubled his human crewmates. He felt a slight regret on the technician's behalf that he hadn't fallen in battle against a worthy opponent, but he reflected that the man had at least died doing his duty.

"Plasma burns," the Denobulan said immediately, before he even activated a scanner. "Quite distinctive, I'm sorry to say."

Geordi nodded and peered into the Jefferies tube. A blackened and shattered EPS junction unit reeked of burned plastic. "And there's the source of the plasma. Looks like it blew when Davis was working on it, and the discharge killed him."

Tropp nodded, but Worf preferred to be thorough. "There will have to be an autopsy to be sure."

"I'll get on it right away," Tropp confirmed.

Picard settled into his chair and watched Luna grow visibly larger on the main viewer.

The *Enterprise* was following the same course that the very first manned interplanetary missions had taken. Back then it took three days to go from Earth to the moon, but the *Enterprise,* even under maneuvering thrusters, would be there in thirty minutes. Most people, Picard knew, were so used to modern forms of transport that they would never think about how astonishing that difference was.

"We're approaching the Lagrange 1 point," the conn officer noted.

"Launch target drones," Picard ordered. The lieutenant at ops did so, and Picard glanced at the current tactical officer. "Select targets and fire at will."

The officer nodded and started blowing away target drones with the ship's phasers. "All weapons systems fully functional. Targeting fully functional."

"Very well. Helm, give me a slingshot around the moon and bring us back into Earth orbit at half impulse."

"Aye, sir."

* * *

Worf returned to his quarters two hours later than he had expected. As the doors slid open, he instinctively looked around for anything unusual. Everything was as it should be, so he switched his attention to Spot. The creature was not in the same place that he had last seen her. As if the day hadn't been embarrassing enough already, Worf called out, "Computer, where is the feline creature called Spot?"

The reply took a couple of seconds, as if the computer was taken by surprise and had to adjust. *"Feline one-four, Spot, is in Commander Data's quarters."*

"Did the door open for the cat?"

"Negative."

"Then how did it get out of these quarters?"

"Unknown."

Worf suppressed a snarl as he stalked down the corridor to Data's old quarters. The cat was indeed there, in the middle of the lightless room's floor. She was making a strange and, Worf thought, extremely irritating wailing sound. For a moment, he wondered if the animal was dying and almost called the computer to ask if the ship's veterinarian had reported for duty yet. The cat stopped making the noise and looked intently at Worf. Then it wailed some more.

The cat bounded ahead of him and stood over something that most definitely did not belong in Data's quarters.

It was a leathery organic creature of some kind, a little bigger than Spot herself. It was mostly covered in stiff, wiry hair. Stubby digits—they were too stubby to be called limbs—were half curled and lifeless. Sticky brown fluid had dried around the edges of several cuts and bites. Worf snapped a piece of metal from a shelf and crouched beside the dead thing. He didn't recognize the species.

He had no fear of such a toothless creature, living or dead, but had been trained to follow Starfleet protocol in case of biological hazards that might carry disease or contamination. So he used the metal to turn the body over. It was definitely dead. He rose and fetched a box, hoping that Doctor Tropp was still on duty.

Spot was still looking up at him, and he realized the sounds had been a victory call, the signal of having made a kill. He approved.

"You are," he said, "a good cat." He called up to the captain. "Captain, Worf here. I am in Commander Data's quarters. There is . . . a creature here."

"An intruder?"

Worf shook his head. "No, sir. It is some kind of animal, vermin."

"How did you find this creature?"

"It was already dead."

"Dead?"

"Data's ca— Spot," he corrected himself, "killed the creature. I do not know where she found it."

"It's reasonable to suspect that if one . . . rodent, if that word applies, has found its way aboard, then perhaps others have too. Have environmental look into it."

"Yes, sir."

"Captain," the conn officer said suddenly, "we're drifting off course. Half a degree. No, a full degree . . . The moon's gravity well is affecting us more than it should."

Picard glanced at the main viewer, where the pitted and sterile lunar surface was passing by. "Compensate."

The ensign calmly made an adjustment, then paled. "Captain!" An alarm began to blare, and Picard knew the malfunctions were back in force. "Maneuvering thrusters off-line!"

"Go to impulse."

"Impulse power off-line!"

"What's our degree of drift? It seems clear it isn't enough to draw us onto the lunar surface."

"No, sir, but it has altered our slingshot course." The ensign was definitely paler than before. "Earth-orbital insertion won't be possible. We are now on a collision course with Earth. I estimate we'll impact off the coast of Madagascar in a little over an hour."

Picard could feel the blood try to drain from his face. He pressed a button on the arm of his chair. "Mister La Forge, is our warp drive active yet?"

"No, sir. Simulations will be finished in a couple of hours, and the core temperature should reach optimal about an hour after that."

"I'd appreciate if you could hurry that process along, Geordi.

– 369 –

We've lost maneuvering thrusters and impulse power, and are on a collision course with Earth."

La Forge's voice was crisp when it came back. *"I'm on it, sir."*

"Contact Starfleet. Have—" Picard's voice tensed. He knew that everyone would know how much he hated saying anything like this. "Have a ship tractor us out of danger. Request they stand by with transporters in case of need."

Tropp was pulling a sheet over a recumbent form as Worf entered. "Is this Ensign Davis?"

"It certainly is," Tropp agreed. "Or was, I should say. I was just finishing the autopsy."

"Have you determined the cause of death?" The creature Spot had killed could wait, as far as Worf was concerned.

"It was the power surge from the ruptured EPS conduit, just as Mister La Forge and yourself suggested. No mystery about it." He looked at the pet carrier Worf was holding. "Which is more than I can say for that."

Worf put the carrier on a biobed and opened it. "Spot brought this as a trophy."

Tropp peered at the creature with interest. "A most interesting specimen, Commander," he said. "Most interesting."

An *Akira*-class ship had dropped into formation with the *Enterprise* a few minutes earlier. The conn officer looked up. "The *Korolev* is ready for tractoring, sir."

Picard gave a curt nod. "Make it so." He let out a short breath through his nose, and Worf understood completely. They both shared a sense of loss of face at having to have his ship towed to safety from such a short trip.

"Well," said Tropp, after Worf had returned to sickbay, "I have managed to conduct an analysis on the dead . . . creature."

"What species is it?" Worf demanded impatiently.

"Oh, I haven't the faintest idea." Worf gritted his teeth. "None of its DNA is on record in any medical database that I've been able to access."

"Then we are no closer to knowing what it was doing and how it got on board."

"Perhaps not, but I can tell you some interesting things about it. Two things, anyway. First, I can tell you what type of species it is, and it isn't a rodent or anything analogous." Tropp brought up an image on a desk screen and turned it to face Worf. The screen showed the creature, its fur and flesh almost totally transparent so that networks of nerves and muscular structures were clearly delineated. "It's not, technically, a creature."

"It is inorganic?"

"No, no, it's organic, but it would be more truthful to call it part of a creature. Look at the layout of the muscle structure and you'll see quite obviously that it is intended to work in concert with other structures that are not present. Look at the terminations of several of these nerve plexus points." He indicated spots on the screen. "At first I thought they were part of its reproductive system, but then I saw that this thing has no discrete reproductive system and that some of these nerve highways actually go from one opening in the body to another, without connecting to any part of its central system. That can mean only that this creature is merely part of the actual creature."

Worf nodded slowly. "A gestalt." Many subcreatures forming one main being. True gestalts, as compared to parasitic or symbiotic relationships like the Trill, were rare but not unheard of. "But you do not know of which species . . ."

"There are only five true gestalt species in Starfleet Medical's records, and none of them fit this specimen." Tropp looked admiringly at the corpse. "It's quite fascinating: a sixth gestalt species to be added to the database. Beverly will be kicking herself that she didn't stay aboard a few days longer."

Worf nodded curtly. He was glad that Tropp had something to interest him. "And what is the second thing you've discovered?"

"I can tell you where it has been." Tropp tapped the screen, and an image of a molecule replaced the previous view. Chemical and medical notations flowed underneath. Worf didn't recognize more than a couple of words. "Some of these were still attached to hair follicles. They're molecules of particulate matter formed from chemical compounds in an atmosphere." Tropp smiled with the unmistakable satisfaction of a job well done, the sort of pleasure Worf understood well. "In this case, specifically the atmosphere of Karenzaa."

"I have never heard of that world."

"It's in the Delta Quadrant. Perhaps Admiral Janeway can shed some light on the matter."

Geordi's investigations had also gone well, Worf soon discovered, when both commanders met with the captain again. "There's good news and bad news," Geordi said. "The good news is that Davis was killed by an EPS failure; it was just bad luck that he happened to be there when it went out."

"And the bad news?" Picard asked.

"The bad news is the EPS junction failure was no accident. A refractive feedback loop had been programmed into it. That pretty much turned it into a randomly timed bomb. When enough charge had built up over a period of use . . . bang."

"Deliberate sabotage?" Picard was alert immediately. "To what purpose?"

"It's not a vital system . . . Maybe to test the saboteur's ability to do the job without detection. And he succeeded."

"Which means he will have been confident that he can sabotage more vital areas."

"Such as helm control," Worf said.

"Exactly."

Picard's lips thinned. "This is no accident. The loss of maneuverability and helm control was designed to crash us into Earth, but . . ." He shook his head sharply. "Whoever is responsible must have known we could be tractored out of the collision course."

"Perhaps he didn't think of it?" Geordi asked.

Worf shook his head. "Our opponent has great skill and intelligence. This plan is one of subtlety. He, or they, will have anticipated our actions." He looked at Geordi. "If you were trying to destroy a ship that was being tractored, what would you do?"

Geordi sat deep in thought for a moment, then his eyes widened. "Siphon off kinetic energy from the tractor beams and feed it into the intermix chamber while the start-up process was ongoing. That could set up an unstable feedback loop and cause a misfire. Blow the intermix chamber to pieces; the antimatter would escape and take the rest of the ship with it. Thankfully there have been no malfunctions in that area, and engineering has been too busy. Nobody could have done any harm in there without being noticed."

"How long would the process take, once started?" Picard asked.

"Ten, maybe fifteen minutes from siphoning the power to the engines exploding."

Worf looked at the main display of the *Enterprise*'s systems on the wall. "Then perhaps they have not yet struck."

"They won't waste much more time."

Worf pointed to Deck 6. "I found the trunk here." Deck 8. "The door malfunctions were here." He pointed out the locations of a couple of other malfunctions, and then EPS junction 4014. "The events started in scattered areas throughout the ship, but their locations converged and have been following a line."

"Yes!" Geordi exclaimed. "And if you wanted to siphon tractor power from farther along that line, you'd do it from"—he stabbed a finger at the layout—"there!"

Picard nodded and looked at Worf. "Assemble your security team, Commander."

Worf grinned.

The room was almost pitch-black but for the soft pastel lights of power indicators. Worf closed his eyes, listening for movement and trying to feel any shift in the air. Three more security officers were in the room with him, and he could barely hear them. He hoped the intruder wouldn't notice them either, until it was too late.

He watched the door, which was invisible in the dark. The instant it was opened, he and his team would pounce. He was vaguely surprised that nothing had happened yet. Another few minutes and the tractor beams would be disengaged; the saboteur would have missed his chance.

He listened. Nothing.

He sniffed the air. Nothing.

He felt—

There was a skittering sound, and another, and another. They didn't sound like footsteps, and they seemed to be coming from all around. Then came the strangest sound Worf had ever heard. It was like the sound of large hermit crabs being prized apart from the angry kittens they had been superglued to. Then something passed between him and the lights on the control panels, and Worf shouted, "Lights!"

The computer responded immediately, filling the room with light. Worf and his team raised their phasers, pointing them at an intruder. Worf wondered how it had gotten in, as the door had not opened and there had been no transporter beam.

The intruder turned, and Worf had a quick impression of a large and bulky figure, taller than himself, with six bloated and segmented limbs. It gave a rasping hiss and raised itself up, spreading its two arms wide. The creature leaped at Worf, who instinctively adopted a blocking stance and prepared to counter its move. No blow came. Instead, the creature exploded around him.

For an instant Worf thought someone had hit it with a phaser on a high setting, but then there was skittering all around him. Creatures like the one Spot had killed were leaping through the air and diving for small vents around the floor. A phaser beam caught one, and it flopped to the ground. Worf batted another out of the air with the back of his hand, and another security guard stood on one. Those two were delayed for only a moment, then disappeared into the vents.

"Computer," Worf shouted, running out the door. His team were already following. "Erect a level-three force field around Bussard control." He paused at a turbolift and turned to one of his men. "Go to sickbay and have Doctor Tropp use the dead gestalt creature to tune some tricorders. We should be able to detect the others now that we have their cellular pattern." He stepped into the turbolift. "Deck 6." He knew just the help the team needed.

Spot prowled the crawl spaces in Deck 16. The scent of the creature it had killed earlier was everywhere. This surprised Spot. Individual creatures, in Spot's experience, all had individual scents, even if they were of the same species. Here it was scenting multiple tracks of the same scent.

Spot hissed at the very thought. How many times would she have to kill the same prey? As if called by her thoughts, the creature she had already killed ran out of the darkness at her. Spot darted forward, claws digging in and fangs tasting it. This time the creature fought harder than before, and Spot narrowly avoided its bony claws.

The lower ceiling here favored the creature, as Spot couldn't jump, but she could twist around almost within her own skin.

Together they rolled around the crawl space, Spot hissing a warning, and the creature eerily silent.

On the deck above, Worf saw the tricorder display change. "This creature is dead." Several others showed as being nearby, and he wished he could find a way to direct Spot to each.

The muted shriek of a phaser beam came from nearby, and he turned to see one of his men approach another motionless creature. "Is it dead?" Worf asked.

The security guard scanned it. "I don't think so, but it's definitely out of action." Worf nodded. So far Spot had killed two, and two more had been phase red. He wondered how many parts the creature was actually composed of.

Spot reappeared out of a duct. She did not carry a prize this time, but Worf's tricorder had shown him all he needed to know. He picked up the cat and carried it to a duct closer to engineering. His tricorder showed another creature within three meters of the vent. Sure enough, he heard hissing and snarling almost immediately.

Suddenly, one of the creatures burst out of a vent. Then another and another. Worf phasered one on heavy stun, his men doing likewise. He checked the tricorder again. No more creatures were showing.

He allowed himself to relax and lowered his phaser. "Spot. You may come out now." The cat did not return. He considered sticking a hand in the vent to try to grab Spot but then straightened. Spot was an effective predator, and she did have a tactical mind of sorts. She was a calculating hunter and an efficient killer who lived by her own code. He knew where that code would be taking her.

A force field shimmered in the air not just across the entrance to the brig's holding cell but against the walls and ceiling too. The creature that stood in the cell was much like the one Worf had seen in Bussard control, except it was now quite short. Shorter than the average human, certainly. At least two of its component creatures were dead.

"Who are you?" Picard asked. He stood with Worf. Tropp was nearby.

"We are Feledrin," it answered. "We were. We are less now."

"Who were you working for?"

"We don't remember."

Picard's expression showed what he thought of that, but Tropp cleared his throat. "Actually, that's probably true, Captain. The gestalt creature's intelligence center is spread throughout its component creatures, and several are dead now. It's almost certainly suffering from the equivalent of brain damage."

Clearly frustrated, Picard nodded. Worf said, "The Feledrin had smuggled itself aboard by stowing away in several different packages and items of luggage belonging to the new crew members. It was attempting to make it look like a series of minor bugs caused by the repairs would lead to the destruction of the *Enterprise*. Ensign Davis was killed when he saw it, or part of it."

"And we don't even know whom to repatriate it to." Picard sighed. "Very well, Mister Worf. It looks as though you—and Spot—have earned a shift off."

Worf retired to his quarters for the night. As he walked in, Spot approached cautiously and rubbed her neck and shoulders against his legs. Worf resisted the urge to shove her aside with his foot. Her attempts to show some alien kind of affection by trying to trip him were more irritating than he had expected.

When he sat in his chair made of black globes, Spot settled into his lap and purred while he scratched behind her ears—two warriors who had shared a victorious battle, now enjoying the silence.

TRUST YOURSELF WHEN ALL MEN DOUBT YOU

Michael Schuster & Steve Mollmann

Historian's note:
This tale is set in late 2379 (Old Calendar), during the
epilogue of the feature film Star Trek Nemesis.

JEAN-LUC PICARD STARED AT THE PADD AND, SIGHING, finally checked it off. There. Virtually all his crew was gone now. He leaned back in his chair, turning to look out the window of his ready room.

The *Enterprise* had been ensconced in one of the San Francisco Fleet Yards' orbital drydocks for a week now. It was a homecoming of sorts; almost nine years ago, the first components of the starship had been assembled here. The journey home had been a slow one, but not unexpectedly so. One didn't relinquish all control over the ship's forward motion to a small *Nova*-class starship like the *Foundation* without experiencing what Will had likened to being dragged across the beach by a tired tortoise. After the battle with Shinzon that had ended with Jean-Luc's decision to ram the enemy ship, the *Enterprise* had lost her warp capability and was in need of being towed home. The *Foundation* was equipped to provide such a service, and her captain was glad to help out.

Yes, he'd been glad to help the captain and the crew he credited with "saving Earth yet again," but that had just made Picard feel guilty. *He* had been totally inactive after he had slain Shinzon on the control deck of the *Scimitar*—it had taken Data to save the day by sending Picard to safety and detonating the *Scimitar*'s thalaron matrix before it could release the deadly radiation within. The *Enterprise* had lost many crew members on that day, and Jean-Luc felt each loss deeply, but Data's was the deepest of all. For fifteen years he'd been able to look forward across the bridge and see the android's head, covered in its slicked-back hair, there in front of the viewscreen—and now that was gone, all because Jean-Luc had just stood there, holding the corpse of Shinzon in his arms.

Since their return to Sector 001, some minimal repairs had been carried out—Beverly had compared it to "stabilizing" a patient—but the real bulk of the work had yet to get under way. There were a lot of parts to be requisitioned, a lot of labor to arrive, and a lot of design work to be done. Until then, there wasn't much for anyone to do on the damaged hulk that was the *Enterprise,* and so Picard had elected to allow leave for anyone who had requested it—which seemed to be basically everyone. Between leave and transfers, the entire senior staff was gone: Will and Deanna were on their honeymoon on Pacifica (though they wouldn't be returning in any case, as they would be heading to the *Titan*), Beverly was transferring to Starfleet Medical again, Geordi had requested some time on Earth to visit an old friend, Christine also was moving over to the *Titan,* and Worf was visiting his parents in Minsk. Most of the rest of the crew had requested and been granted leave as well.

But Jean-Luc stayed with his ship. He had things to do. There were reports to fill out on what had happened on Romulus and in the Bassen Rift, there was a major structural repair to organize, there were personnel assignments to sort and approve, there were . . .

There were a lot of things. But most of all, he just wanted some time alone. To think about what had happened. *I wrecked my ship,* he thought to himself. *Purposefully rammed it straight into Shinzon's battle cruiser because I couldn't think of anything else to do.*

Unfortunately, when he *did* think recently, they weren't the best of thoughts. The idea of organizing this repair, rebuilding the *Enterprise,* assembling another crew for her, taking her out on a new mission . . . somehow it held very little appeal for him. Not after what had happened. Maybe it was time to return to Labarre, to settle down, to put an end to a part of his life that he had previously thought integral to his happiness. He just wanted to *stop* for a while.

He'd thought these thoughts before, of course. When he'd been forced to abandon the *Stargazer* at Maxia Zeta, he'd deemed himself unfit for command before he'd even been summoned before the Starfleet court-martial. And when the *Enterprise*-D had crash-landed on Veridian III, he'd spent almost a year contemplating alternatives before finally committing to her successor. With the help of his friends, he had pulled through the self-doubt that had plagued him.

But now, he stood alone on a desolated and deserted *Enterprise*-E, with nothing to do but think.

Well, there was one thing he could do. *Should* do.

The open file sat before him, two words blazed in yellow. *Dear Will.* The cursor blinked at him, patiently awaiting further input, as it had been for fifteen minutes now, while Jean-Luc sat in his quarters, contemplatively sipping from a cup of hot tea.

It was a Starfleet tradition for captains whose executive officers had just been given captaincies of their own to send them a letter, offering congratulations and maybe a nugget or two of wisdom, and Jean-Luc had no intention of breaking that tradition now. He wanted to send the letter soon, so that it would be waiting for Will when he set foot on the *Titan*. But what could he say to him? What sort of "wisdom" could he impart that he hadn't already over the many years they had served together?

The sad truth was that no one had ever written Jean-Luc such a letter. The circumstances under which he had become captain of the *Stargazer* had been both abrupt and unconventional, to say the least. No one had imparted to him any sort of great knowledge at the time that he could now pass on to Will. He didn't really know what kind of content normally went into these things, having never read one himself. He had just sort of heard of them, was familiar with the concept.

He was not feeling particularly wise at the moment, anyway.

But he needed to do this. If he didn't, he would be letting Will down. He felt that he had left enough people down recently. But what could he write? Tentatively, he began typing out the next few words: *I am writing to offer my congratulations on your achieving command of one of Starfleet's best and newest vessels.*

No. That sounded stiff and formal—this was not a letter to a man he had known for fifteen years. He needed something deeper, something personal. Something like . . .

With a start, Jean-Luc stood up from his desk and hurried over to one of the storage cabinets. He opened up the bottom drawer, revealing a number of personal items he had acquired over the years, many of them objects that had survived the crash of the *Enterprise*-D, including the Picard family's photo album and—beneath it, at the bottom of the drawer—a very battered and old padd.

Of course, he hadn't needed to save the padd. The file on it could have been transferred to any other computer, but it was one of those things he had never gotten around to doing. So he had held on to the device all these years, and eventually it had reached the point where he didn't *want* to transfer its contents to somewhere else—an entire padd being devoted to just one file made that file special, in its own way.

Jean-Luc returned to his desk chair and tapped the padd on, reading what was displayed on its screen.

> *Dear Jean-Luc Picard,*
>
> *I am fully aware that in an organization as large as Starfleet it is impossible for all the officers of a rank to know each other, much less all those that are above and below them. Nevertheless, I feel that there is a certain bond between us, and it is that bond that made me sit down tonight and write this letter to you, a man I know only as a name on a personnel file.*

It was a letter from Thomas Halloway, the man who had commanded the *Enterprise*-D for that brief span of time before Jean-Luc had taken over—not to mention, the man who had *built* her.

Jean-Luc had found the letter waiting for him when he had come aboard the *Enterprise*-D just before its first mission, the trip out to Farpoint Station on Deneb IV. In the assorted business of assuming command, and then the excitement brought on by Q and the duplicitous Bandi, Jean-Luc hadn't had time to read the letter right off the bat. He'd finally gotten around to doing so once the *Enterprise* had taken her first steps on her mission of exploration into the Denebian galactic mass.

The letter explained why Halloway hadn't taken command of

the *Enterprise*-D, as had been offered to him by Admiral Satie.
Jean-Luc skimmed through the long document until he found the
part that had stuck with him.

> *You are chosen to take over the ship, by Admiral Satie's*
> *expressed wish. Far be it from me to object; after all, it was*
> *I who let her down. I could have taken the ship out there,*
> *beyond the fringes of known space, and yet I know, deep*
> *down inside me, that I wouldn't have enjoyed it even half*
> *as much as you are bound to do. As I have said before, I am*
> *an engineer at heart, always have been, and the prospect*
> *of leaving my work at the yards behind for years, perhaps*
> *even decades, of exploration in deep space left me cold,*
> *I'm sorry to say. It's an important job and a great one, I*
> *am sure, but it is not my job. It's an honor to have been*
> *considered as the captain of the* Enterprise, *but I know*
> *that it's an honor reserved for someone like you. If there is*
> *anything being an engineer has taught me, it's that there is*
> *always a best tool for any job—and that for any tool there is*
> *always a perfect job. I know what my perfect job is. It is not*
> *command.*
>
> *The other part of the reason I chose to disappoint Admi-*
> *ral Satie that way was my desire to be with my family. From*
> *the beginning, my wife made it very clear that she would*
> *not go into space with me, no matter how long I was gone.*
> *The* Enterprise *would've been big enough for the crew's*
> *families to accompany them on their first mission, but that*
> *wasn't enough of an incentive for my wife, Solveig. She is*
> *a public works manager, and there is little call for such a*
> *person on a starship in the depths of space. As important*
> *as my work in Starfleet has been to me, my wife and my*
> *children are more important, they are my everything, so I*
> *said good-bye to the* Enterprise *and all the people on board,*
> *knowing full well that I stood a very good chance of never*
> *seeing either of them again in my life.*

When he had first read the letter, some fifteen years ago, Jean-
Luc had had great difficulty believing it. At the time, Jean-Luc had
wondered if the man was merely a coward. He'd heard of the acci-

dent with the torpedo launcher that had killed twelve engineers during construction. Had the man lost his nerve for space travel? Did the unknown frighten him so much? Back then, Jean-Luc had almost considered him a failure as a Starfleet officer.

And to be so tied to family! Jean-Luc had basically destroyed his relationship with his father for the sake of Starfleet and outer space, and his relationship with his brother Robert had not fared much better. When he'd first met Will, he'd told him, "I'm not a family man," and that had most certainly been true. For most of his life, Jean-Luc had maintained a careful distance from family ties. Viewed through that lens fifteen years ago, Halloway's stated reasons had seemed flimsy at best.

He had reread the letter only once since that first time, and as on that occasion, he was struck by the foolishness of his younger self—this time, even more so. Estranged from his family, *of course* he'd thought he could do without it. But time had proved the thoughts of that younger, more arrogant man untrue. There had been the encounter with the Ressikan probe, where Jean-Luc had lived the life of a man named Kamin for thirty-five years in less than half an hour. There he had married and had two children—not to mention one grandchild—and though he had been glad to return to his own life, the part of the experience that had always stayed with him was the joy he had felt at seeing "his" two children grow from infanthood to maturity, together with the sadness that he had never been able to experience all that firsthand.

Not to mention that without his brother, he doubted he could have ever pulled through the ordeal the Borg collective had put him through, when they had assimilated him and turned him into Locutus. Robert had watched over him afterward, helping him regain his confidence in himself and his abilities.

And then . . . there had been the fire. After his reconciliation with Robert, he'd vowed to spend more time with his family, but sadly the duties of the *Enterprise* had meant it never came to pass. Robert and his son René had both perished before their time, and Jean-Luc had never been so aware of what they had brought to his life until then.

Now, fifteen years after he had first read the letter, Jean-Luc could understand why Halloway had attached so much importance to his family. It was an opinion Jean-Luc himself had come to in the end.

The man had hardly been a coward or a failure.

Actually, do I have any way of knowing that? Beyond that letter, Jean-Luc had no idea what had happened to Thomas Halloway. His early, casual dismissal of the man had meant that he had never again given him much thought. He couldn't even recall seeing his name in a Fleet bulletin over the years, or on one of the promotions lists—or, heaven forbid, casualty lists. But then, there were a lot of names on those lists.

He had had one encounter with his predecessor, though, in a way. Once, Q had shown Jean-Luc another world—possibly another time-line—where he'd never ascended to the captaincy. He'd still been stationed on the *Enterprise*-D, but as a lowly lieutenant j.g. in the sciences division. At the time, he had focused on his own problems, but one detail of that other world had stuck with him: the captain of the *Enterprise* had been Thomas Halloway. That, sadly enough, had been the closest he'd ever come to meeting him: being on the same ship in an alternate reality. That experience had caused him to reread Halloway's letter for the first time, but even then, it had never occurred to Picard to find out what Halloway was *really* up to.

"Computer," he ordered, "access Starfleet personnel records. Halloway, Thomas Bhupender."

The computer chimed in compliance, and Halloway's service file replaced Jean-Luc's barely started letter on the display screen. After completing construction of the *Enterprise*-D, Halloway had continued to work on a number of projects at the Utopia Planitia Fleet Yards. First, he had worked with the Advanced Starship Design Bureau on the design of the new *Andromeda*-class explorers, applying the lessons learned with the *Galaxy* class.

Then he'd gone on to supervise the construction of the *Melbourne,* the first of a new breed of *Nebula*-class starships incorporating some radical design changes. The *Melbourne* had still been under construction when the call had gone out for all available Starfleet vessels to convene at Wolf 359—the Borg were coming for Earth.

Though the *Melbourne* was merely five weeks from flight, awaiting only a few tweaks and a shakedown cruise, she hadn't yet had a commanding officer assigned. In fact, as Jean-Luc knew, Will had been offered the command and turned it down, causing a delay as Starfleet looked elsewhere.

With no one else to assume command and answer the signal, Halloway had given the order to prepare the *Melbourne* for launch. Assembling a skeleton crew out of dockworkers and engineers, he had run the ship through its launch preparations as quickly as was humanly possible and taken her out into space, speeding toward Wolf 359 . . . and certain death.

For as everyone had known at the time, no ship returned unscathed from a confrontation with the Borg. Everything in their path fell before them, no exceptions. And that included thirty-nine of the forty ships Admiral Hanson managed to assemble at Wolf 359.

Like many of those vessels, the *Melbourne* had been lost with all hands. Destroyed before her ragtag crew had even had a chance to make it to the escape pods, because the Borg had had the knowledge of Jean-Luc Picard on their side.

In a way, he had killed Thomas Halloway.

It was a guilt he had felt many times since that terrible experience. It was technically not his fault, but as Locutus, he had caused the Borg to destroy so many innocent lives. It was a guilt he had come to terms with—as much as *that* was possible—but coming into contact with the deaths that had happened that day always caused those pangs to return, however irrationally.

Attached to the report on Wolf 359 was a note from one of the workers at Utopia Planitia on that day, a young civilian technician named Isaakerr:

> *I was working on the bridge that day, connecting the main*
> *viewscreen up to the ship's systems. Captain Halloway*
> *was in the first officer's chair—he always refused to use*
> *the captain's chair, saying it was reserved for the man who*
> *would really be captain—going over some status reports.*
> *Then the call came in.*
>
> *Halloway went into the ready room, a somber look*
> *on his face. When he came back out five minutes later, it*
> *looked as though he might've been crying—but I was the*
> *only one who could see it. When he turned to face the rest*
> *of the bridge crew, it was with a look of grim determina-*
> *tion and nothing else. He immediately gave the orders*
> *necessary to get the ship ready for launch, cutting corners I*
> *didn't think it was possible to cut. The* Melbourne *had been*

armed, at least, and she could still be used as a weapon against the Borg.

He gave all the Starfleet personnel the option to stay on board or remain in the dockyard—most stayed, of course—but he ordered all the civilians off the ship immediately. I told him I wanted to finish connecting the viewscreen first. If he was going into battle, he'd need to be able to see what he was doing. He smiled and nodded, telling me to get a move on. He had a battle to fight.

I finished in what was probably record time, and as I was stepping into the turbolift, he came up from behind and grabbed my arm. "I want you to do one thing for me," he said. "If I don't come home today, find my wife and children and say good-bye to them for me. I'm doing this to keep them safe, and I won't let anyone hurt them. Tell them I love them."

I nodded my assent, and he released my arm. I stumbled into the turbolift, and as the doors shut behind me, tears began to well up in my eyes. I'd always considered Captain Halloway pretty likable and a good boss, but on that day he had been extraordinary. There had been an authority in his voice I had never heard before: he had a job to do, and by God he was going to do it, even if it wasn't the job he had expected.

He did his job that day. And in tribute to him, so did I.

No coward, then. Jean-Luc found it hard to believe he'd ever felt as poorly of the man as he had. By his own admission, Halloway had been ill suited to command, yet when the time had come to do it, he had done it, and done it well by all accounts.

Jean-Luc was not surprised he hadn't noticed the other captain's name on the casualty lists from Wolf 359. There had been so many dead at that battle—eleven thousand—that he had never been able to truly read them all. Once again, he had come *so close* to meeting Thomas Halloway, and yet he had failed.

But they had certainly left their marks on each other's lives.

Picard's eyes were once again drawn to the letter on the padd he held in his lap—the last wisdom of a dead man, evidently. Halloway had refused command of the *Enterprise* because he did not consider himself an explorer, did not want to spend what could quite feasibly be twenty years of his life exploring the vastness of space.

But he wouldn't have. Despite her original charter to explore the unknown galactic mass beyond Deneb IV, the *Enterprise*-D had been forced to turn back only a couple of weeks into her journey, to answer a distress call from one of the science vessels assigned to tail the *Enterprise* and follow up her discoveries in-depth. The ensuing crisis was taken care of, but the backtracking had put the *Enterprise* in a position to be the closest ship to Ligon II when Starfleet found itself in need of a vital vaccine from that planet.

From then on, the *Enterprise* had somehow never managed to make it back out to the Denebian galactic mass, being sent from mission to mission within explored space or at least very near it. Starfleet Command had promised to get the ship's mission back on track, but they had come to view the ship as too useful to send away for any length of time. Jean-Luc had protested, of course, and the ship had had its moments "out there," but that hypothetical twenty-year mission with no starbases in sight had never happened, much to his disappointment.

If Halloway had taken command of the *Enterprise*, he wouldn't ever have been too far from his family. The Halloways had just bought a house on Earth's moon when he'd written the letter—and during the *Enterprise*'s seven years in space, Jean-Luc could immediately recall at least four times she had ended up returning to Earth!

And if Halloway had taken command of the *Enterprise*, he wouldn't have died at Wolf 359, as evidenced by that other timeline Q had shown him. With no Jean-Luc Picard to assume command in his stead, Halloway would have been forced to continue in command and so wouldn't have died on the *Melbourne*. Jean-Luc wondered if that Halloway had experienced what he had in his time as commander of the *Enterprise*. Had he been assimilated by the Borg and forced to lead the destruction of his own people? Had he been rescued by the best crew—the best friends—a man had ever had? Jean-Luc would never know.

But he would have lived.

Yet now, in this reality, in this world, Thomas Halloway was dead, and Jean-Luc Picard would never be able to meet the man, much to his regret; it now appeared that he had made a mistake in his early dismissal of the man. He would've liked to talk to his family—Starfleet records showed that his wife and children were all still alive, still residing within transporter distance on Earth's moon. But experience had taught him how those who had lost family at Wolf 359 tended to react to the man who had once been Locutus of Borg.

Halloway hadn't been a coward of any sort—just a man who had done what he believed was right, despite the pressures that had been acting upon him. Jean-Luc had come to that realization too late, unfortunately. But perhaps there was something he could still take away from his strange not-quite-a-relationship with the other man.

Halloway had done what needed to be done up until the day he died, and so could Jean-Luc. Perhaps he had messed up at the Bassen Rift, perhaps the battle with Shinzon had taken too large a toll, perhaps he had frozen in place. But that was no reason to *stay* stopped, to give up now. It would be a grave disrespect to the memories of Data and all the others who had passed away over the years to do that. Halloway had kept on going no matter what, and so should he.

His eyes flicked over the closing paragraphs of the letter one last time.

> My brief perusal of your file tells me that you have yet to form a family of your own—an unfortunate decision, if you pardon me for saying so. I don't claim to know the reasons why you chose to stay alone; indeed, I don't even know if it was your choice at all. Nevertheless, what I want to say is that a man alone is in bad company, as the saying goes. My favorite writer once wrote that "the strength of the Pack is the Wolf, and the strength of the Wolf is the Pack." It applies not only to animals but also to everybody else. Only in the company of others do we have the chance to fully realize our potential.
>
> Maybe you know these things, maybe you do not. I hope I'm not coming across as patronizing. But as the time for the launch of the Enterprise, with me as her captain, grew closer and closer, I came to realize them for myself. We must all do what it is we are called to do, regardless of what

outside factors may be pushing us in other directions. For me, this is engineering—designing and constructing the craft that take us into the void. For you, this is apparently the command of over a thousand men and women, the discovery of new life, the exploration of deep space.

Do not waver on your true path. Follow it, no matter what doubts may plague you. But try not to walk that path alone.

Jean-Luc had had occasion to regret over the years that he had never formed a family. But perhaps he had *forged* one—Data, Will, Deanna, Beverly, Geordi, Worf. If there was anything he had learned in the past harrowing year aboard the *Enterprise,* from the first problems at Rashanar to the last battle in the Bassen Rift, it was that he *did* have a family. They had stood by him when the rest of Starfleet had seemingly deserted him, when the *Enterprise* had undergone some of her toughest trials, as long as Jean-Luc had served aboard her or her predecessor. And as Halloway had told him, he had drawn his strength from them. And, he hoped, he had provided a source of strength to them.

They might be scattering across the galaxy, but they were still his family.

And there are certain obligations one has to family. Jean-Luc closed the window containing the service record of Thomas Hallo-way, bringing that impossible letter back on the screen. He cleared what was there and readied himself to start over.

Yet first there was one other thing he could do to honor the memory of his fellow captain. Halloway had not assumed cap-taincy of the *Enterprise* because he believed himself unsuited to exploring the universe. But unfortunately, the starship had done precious little of that over the past fifteen years. It was high time that he rectified that.

"Computer, begin recording a message." The computer chirped its acknowledgment. "Admiral Janeway, this is Captain Picard. I'd like to set up an appointment to discuss the *Enterprise*'s next assignment with you sometime soon. Personally, I believe it's time for the *Enterprise* to get back to the purpose for which she was designed—exploration. You told me I'd had too many of the 'easy' assignments recently; well, I'd like to get back to the hard ones."

Maybe that would serve to get the *Enterprise* back "out there." He could only hope. But that was a matter for another time. He ordered the computer to transmit the message to Starfleet Command, and then turned back to his letter.

Dear Will,

It is an old tradition in Starfleet that captains whose executive officers are promoted to captaincies of their own pass on some of their own collected wisdom, usually in the form of a letter. I'm not sure, however, how much "wisdom" I am qualified to pass on, but I can do my best. No one ever wrote me such a letter, but that does not mean that I can't perform the service for you. I must honestly admit that there were days I thought this time would never come, and I am glad that you now feel ready to move on to the next step in your career.

As pleased as I am that you have finally accepted captaincy—especially of such a fine ship as the Titan*—I'm even more pleased on the occasion of your recent marriage. One of my greatest regrets is that I have spent much of my life alone. We all need someone to share our lives with—in the time I spent living the life of Kamin, one of his greatest joys was that everything that happened to him, from the birth of his children to the end of the world, there was someone to share with. In Deanna, you definitely have such a person.*

But we all have family in other places as well, myself included. Something I've come to realize is that you, Will, are my family. And so is Deanna, and Worf, and Geordi, and Beverly . . . and Data. No matter what may happen to us, as we now spread out to walk our own paths, we will always have one another. I consider you one of my best friends—we've certainly come a long way from that first awkward encounter in my ready room where I spent most of the time complaining about children! Even as you and Deanna depart on the Titan *for the distant reaches of the Gum Nebula, I hope you remember that. Whatever you need, I will be here for you. And I am sure you feel the same way in return.*

Another thing to remember, Will: follow the path that is yours. Do not let the doubts of others—or yourself—get in the way of that. Like myself, you've always been an explorer at heart, and you're embracing that by assuming command of the Titan, *a ship designed for long-term missions of exploration, much like our old* Enterprise *was. It's a path we've strayed from over the years, and I am glad that you'll be returning to it—it's my hope to return to it soon myself.*

It's an easy thing to say, of course, not always an easy thing to do. Remember Data and the ridicule he experienced over the years in his quest to become human? The indignities he sometimes suffered at the hands of those who did not understand? And yet, he always continued forward, never doubting what he was meant to do. Over the past year he especially suffered, given the removal of his emotion chip, which we saw as a major setback. But Data was never deterred—he simply absorbed the new circumstance and moved forward. In the end, he gave his life for what he believed in, embracing one of the most human characteristics of all, our capacity for self-sacrifice. It is an honor I'm not certain I was worthy of, but I will respect what he did for me by doing my best to live up to it.

There is another man whose life encompassed these values. He always did what he thought was right, like Data, from birth right up to the end of life. I'd like to tell you about him. Heaven knows it's a story that cannot be told enough.

Let me tell you about the life of Thomas Bhupender Halloway . . .